THE
CROWN *of*
VALENCIA

Applause for *The Spanish Pearl*

"Friend tackles both science fiction and romance in this adventurous tale. Is it really cheating if you have an affair nine hundred years before your partner is born, or does love and commitment span centuries and confound the linear nature of time? A most entertaining read, with a sequel already in the works. Hot, hot, hot!" — *Minnesota Literature*

"1085 AD is a perfect backdrop for this wild romp. The observations Kate Vincent, our plucky heroine, makes about eleventh century Spain through her contemporary eyes are priceless. This is a rollicking good tale, full of adventure, humor, romance, and high stakes suspense, for Kate's friends and foes are not always who or what they seem....The author does a terrific job with characterization, lush setting, action scenes, and droll commentary. This is one of those well-paced, exciting books that you just can't quite put down." — *Midwest Book Review*

"A fresh new author...has penned an exciting story... Exciting, thoughtful, and told with the right amount of humor and romance. Friend has done a wonderful job...*The Spanish Pearl* is a hit." — *Lambda Book Review*

Visit us at www.boldstrokesbooks.com

THE
CROWN *of*
VALENCIA

by

Catherine Friend

2007

ISBN10: 1-933110-96-1
ISBN13: 978-1-933110-96-7

THIS TRADE PAPERBACK IS PUBLISHED BY
BOLD STROKES BOOKS, INC.
NEW YORK, USA

FIRST EDITION, NOVEMBER 2007

CREDITS
EDITORS: CINDY CRESAP AND J. B. GREYSTONE
PRODUCTION DESIGN: J. B. GREYSTONE
COVER GRAPHIC: SHERI (graphicartist2020@hotmail.com)

By the Author

The Spanish Pearl

Acknowledgments

Without the skilled people behind a book—publisher, editor, copyeditor, proofreader, cover designer—most of us writers would be sunk. I'm grateful the talented crew at Bold Strokes make my books look so good. To Cindy Cresap, my editor, and Julie Greystone, my copyeditor—thanks for always catching the stuff I miss, and I promise to get a grip on the whole lay-lie thing one of these days.

Many thanks to my dear friends in the KTM, Rainy Lake, and Hayward groups, who've listened to my work (and my rants) for fifteen years. Your support, laughter, and encouragement have kept me going.

Thanks to Pat Schmatz and Lori Lake for reading the most recent drafts, even though I hear you were taunting people because you knew what happened next!

And finally, my heartiest thanks goes to all the readers of *The Spanish Pearl* who took the time to let me know you loved it—you made my day, over and over again. You stayed up until 4 a.m. reading it; you missed your subway stops; you got so swept up in the story you couldn't stop thinking about Kate and Elena even while at work. Knowing that others find Kate and Elena's story riveting is more important to me than sales figures or published reviews. Satisfying you is like a drug—now that I've had a taste, I want more, more, more... my new motivation for writing.

DEDICATION

Melissa, my love,
you amaze me.
With every book I write,
you cheerfully climb on board and take
the emotional rollercoaster ride with me.
The ups and downs
and hairpin turns and sudden drops
aren't so frightening when you're
holding my hand.

CHAPTER ONE

I was flunking the eleventh century. In Spinning Yarn I gave myself a D-. Weaving was definitely an F, since it was hard to weave without yarn. Making Butter, C-. Cooking Over an Open Fire, C+. I earned the 'plus' because last week I did *not* scorch the stew.

But in my own defense, I'd been born nine centuries in the future, so my survival skills were meant for an entirely different era. I could zip my car through rush-hour traffic on I-95 and let the obscene gestures roll off me like water off a duck. I knew all the Thai take-outs in Chicago and half the surrounding burbs, so I was never more than six blocks from a plate of life-sustaining chicken satay. My idea of roughing it had once been to go two whole days without a tall double almond cappuccino, no foam.

Yet here I was, living in a rough wooden building with no running water and a chamber pot for a toilet, celebrating the nine-month anniversary of the day I'd met Elena Navarro. To live with Elena, I had left behind in the twenty-first century, my now ex-partner Anna and young Arturo, the child Anna and I were to have adopted.

Stretching my aching muscles after painting all morning, and feeling the beginnings of hunger in the pit of my stomach, I headed outside the barn, wondering where Elena might be. I inhaled deeply to take in the flowering tree outside my studio, grateful that spring had finally come to our corner of Spain, which was the high, dry plateaus of eastern Castile.

Elena was probably working somewhere since leisure made her nervous. While farming and serving as Duañez's don wasn't fighting, at least it was work. Tall, strong as a man, with black hair clipped close to her head, Elena's androgynous features hid the truth from almost everyone. At first, I'd been afraid that I might call the "man" people knew as Luis Navarro by her real name, so I always called her Luis. But after a few months, late at night when we were huddled under our woolen blankets finding innovative ways to keep warm, I had begun calling her Elena. At first it had sounded odd to both of us, but soon she'd whisper in my ear every night, "Say my name again. I love it when you say my name." I no longer feared I would call her Elena in front of everyone else.

Our rough wooden house, which the Duañez locals called a castle, capped a gentle hill surrounded by sloping sheep meadows so bright green it looked as if a child had gone wild with a crayon. The rugged sand bluffs stretched north beyond the meadows, and rich, fertile flatlands reached to the south, soon to be planted with wheat and oats. After King Alfonso lifted Rodrigo's exile last fall, Rodrigo gave Luis the small holding at Duañez and temporarily dispersed his army as political tensions chilled with winter.

I squinted into the sun, but saw nothing of Elena. Farmers yelled to the sullen white oxen dragging single plows through the soil, and metal rang as the blacksmith worked in the shed nearby. Duañez pulsed with life, except for the small acreage on the next hill. I gazed up toward the neat rows of white, wooden crosses, and felt my jaw tighten.

In the dead of winter, influenza had swept through Duañez's close-knit community. Old Señora Perez was the first to die. We took the ill into our castle, where Elena kept a vigorous fire blazing in the main hearth day and night. Marta and the others tended the children, and I did what I could. I wiped the Chavez girl's perspiring brow, told stories to a fitful Manuel, and watched as, one by one, three more adults and seven children succumbed to some sort of virus that could have been cured in the twenty-first century with a handful of pills. Thank goddess I hadn't returned to the twenty-first century and brought Arturo back with me. Life here was too uncertain, too on the edge. Over nine hundred and twenty years in the future, Arturo was splashing through neighborhood puddles and would be almost through with the first grade. Most importantly, he was safe.

I wiped my hands on my now-grungy apron, which reminded me I had a pile of laundry the size of Mt. Rainier waiting for me back at the castle. Soap making, D-. Laundry, B-. I discovered by watching the other women that I could freshen our dingy undergarments by laying them out on the rocks behind the house, where they whitened in the sun. But when it came to washing the outer clothes, I still hadn't found a system that worked. When I'd told Marta I wanted to wash Luis's shirts and my skirts, you'd think I'd just said I wanted to stick something sharp in my ear and pull it out through my nose. Personal cleanliness had yet to become fashionable among Christians.

"Doña Kate!"

I squeaked at the sudden arrival of little Miguelito, one of Marta's dark-eyed boys who seemed to be perpetually running from place to place. He looked so much like Arturo that whenever I saw him, a sharp pang of regret pierced me, not regret that I wasn't a parent, for I didn't feel the same yearnings other women did, but regret that I wasn't Arturo's parent. He was a neat kid, and I hoped Anna appreciated her life with him. I would have made a rotten parent—I wouldn't have known how to do anything, mostly because my parents hadn't known either. No use perpetuating the Vincent Method of Bad Parenting. No, young Arturo was better off with Anna as his sole parent. That's what I told Elena and what I told myself; but now and then I'd wake up before the sun and the roosters, my face drenched in sweat, my vision filled with Arturo's face, and I would wonder what I'd given up.

Miguelito waved his brown arms, hopping from one foot to the other. "Doña Kate! Come quickly. The oven is vomiting. It is vomiting!"

"What?" My Spanish had improved greatly these last nine months, but surely I heard him wrong. "Vomiting?"

The frantic boy grabbed my hand and pulled, so I followed him around the barn and down the grassy slope toward one of the common ovens the women from the twenty-five households in the valley used to bake bread. Miguelito stopped and pointed. "Shit," I breathed. Huge billowing clouds of rising bread dough spilled out the front and dripped down the brick onto the dusty ground. The sharp smell of yeast gone wild filled the air. I grabbed my head and grunted in anger.

"My bread, oh no." I sank to my knees, watching as the oven continued to vomit the overheated dough. Marta had said to leave it in the cold oven only an hour, then punch it down, but I'd been painting for most of the morning. How many times would I have to screw this up before I figured it out? If not for Marta, Elena and I would have starved over the winter. Baking Bread, F.

Miguelito had grown quiet at my elbow, eyes wide to see the doña moaning on her knees. For his sake I stopped, heaving a sigh. "Miguelito, in the shed outside the east castle door is an empty bucket and a shovel. I will need them both." Pebbles clattered as Marta's helpful son scampered away. Cursing myself, I stood and searched through a patch of weeds for a stick then approached the mess. This was going to take hours to clean up. Beyond the oven, Marta and a woman I did not know stood by the well pulling up wash water; from where they stood they couldn't see the mouth of the oven. That must be Marta's sister, back from a winter working as a servant at Burgos.

The expanding dough made an awful sucking sound as it overflowed the oven lip, then landed with a wet plop on the growing pile on the ground. What a waste. What a stupid, stupid waste. This village had few resources as it was, and I just wasted half a bag of flour and all that yeast and Marta's eggs, not to mention the generous dollop of honey I'd added, hoping to surprise Elena.

I had no business trying to bake bread. I gripped the stick and began smacking it against the oven's domed clay top. "Stupid, stupid, stupid," I yelled. When I stepped in the doughy mess and dragged my skirt hem through it, I began stamping my feet and flapping my skirt.

When Miguelito returned quickly with the bucket and shovel, I began shoveling the dough out of the oven. After just a few scoops we both heard footsteps on the rocky path behind us. Miguelito looked up, giggled, and ran off.

"So, is this how you bake bread in your century?" Elena whispered in my ear. My body quickly responded by flushing warm and going all fluttery in my belly. That Elena could affect me like this irritated me quite a bit, actually. I'd always been a practical woman, not one who went all weak in the knees, and right now I was in no mood to be needled.

I whirled and stomped my foot so hard a glob of dough splattered against her dusty boot. She stepped back, all legs and leather and wide smile. "Very funny," I snapped. "You know very well it's not." I pushed back a lock of my hair and felt wet dough streak across my cheek. Damn it. I slid into English. "No, in my century we have ovens and electricity. And microwaves! I used to live a civilized life." I waved the stick around, flinging bits of dough everywhere. Elena took another step back, her crystal blue eyes narrowed with mirth, which only fed my frenzy. "With frozen pizzas better than delivery, with ready-made tortellini and pesto, with take-out egg rolls. With a dozen choices of bread at the Happy Baker." I flung the stick to the ground and switched back to Spanish. "Damn it, Luis, if you want bread so badly, you can just bake it yourself." Why did I have to love this blasted woman so?

Marta had reached the oven by this time, her wide face brimming with concern and the same barely-contained laughter that danced across Elena's face. "Oh dear," Marta said as she reached for Elena's arm. "Don Luis, perhaps you had better come back later after we've helped Doña Kate clean up this mess."

Elena, at once breathtakingly beautiful and damned handsome, winked at Marta. "An excellent idea, Marta. It must be that time of the month for my lovely wife."

That time of the month? I scooped up a glob of warm dough and aimed it at her retreating back, but she sidestepped just in time. She bled once a month just as I did, which had been a great relief, actually, in the month after Gudesto had raped her. The only two other people who knew the truth about Elena were our friend, Nuño Súarez, and the cruel Gudesto Gonzalez. Nuño had discovered Luis's true sex years ago but had stayed silent out of love and loyalty, and since I'd stabbed Gudesto to death last fall, he no longer counted. Killing him had left me oddly satisfied, and I didn't like the feeling.

As she moved away from me, Elena's long green shirt and leather vest did nothing to hide her broad shoulders, but they did camouflage the narrow waist and woman's hips below, as did her loose-fitting pants. She moved with an easy grace, to me so obviously female that it still took my breath away that no one else could see the truth. Instead, her men saw a slightly built but fierce Luis Navarro, El Picador, a man they did not want to cross, a man they trusted to lead them into battle and out the other side, still alive.

I growled rudely as Elena strode down the hill toward town. At that, Marta threw back her head, her black braid sliding over her shoulder, and laughed. Broad-shouldered, tan, and dressed in a brown homespun skirt, she would have been called a peasant by history books, but she knew more about life than I ever would. "Pay him no mind, doña. Men think bread can be created out of thin air. Come, my sister Juliana and I will help you." I nodded to the other young woman, slighter and lighter than Marta, yet built with her same sturdiness.

Encouraged by their smiles, I sent one last glare at Elena's back and turned to face my mess. Juliana moved in and held the bucket higher for me. "Have we met before, Doña Kate?" I shook my head, struggling to balance a glob of dough on the shovel. "Well, perhaps not. There is just something familiar about you." I was grateful for Juliana's chatter, as I had little breath for speaking myself while I scraped. "I did much of the bread-baking for the court at Burgos this winter, and this tragedy happened at least twice to me."

I doubted her words, but appreciated her efforts to comfort me. Soon dough caked all our arms up to our elbows, splattered down our skirt fronts, and stuck in our hair. As we worked, Juliana amused us with stories of King Alfonso and his court.

When the oven was finally clean, we washed ourselves off at the well as best we could. "Thank you very much," I said as we rested in the shade of a spreading live oak. "I may never bake bread again."

Juliana tipped her head as she listened to me speak. "I just figured it out. You talk differently than most, and I've been trying to bring up in my mind who talks like you, and I think I know now." When I had first arrived in the past, I spoke modern Spanish, so it had been a struggle to be understood. After nine months, I thought I'd altered my language and accent enough to blend in better, but I must still be using some modern phrases that sounded as foreign as Swahili to these people. "You sound like King Alfonso's new mistress. She uses some of the same strange words that you do."

"From what I've heard," Marta muttered, "that woman has too much control over Alfonso."

Juliana nodded. "It's true. She has stolen Alfonso from Queen Constance's bed, so all the queen's ladies are furious with her." She frowned. "More troubling, however, are her abilities as a seer. When I served the court, I overheard much, and some noblemen are worried about her influence." Juliana stopped and crossed herself. "The woman isn't normal. She's been right in every prediction she's made. She knows who will win what battle, and what the Moors will do and when."

Curious, I leaned closer, pulling another glob of dough from my hair. "Where's she from?"

Juliana shook her head. "I don't know."

Curiosity was one of my downfalls. A woman who talked like me and seemed to know the future? Could there be more time-travelers besides myself and my friend Grimaldi, who lived in Zaragoza with his wife Liana?

After thanking Marta and Juliana once again, I headed for the house to change out of my now-filthy skirt. There I grabbed a pile of clothes and headed for the stream, my very own Maytag. After my bread disaster, I needed a success. Besides, if I didn't conquer the challenges of living in this century, how could I possibly stay?

CHAPTER TWO

Early the next morning I lay in bed, watching Elena sleep. She'd apologized last night for making fun of me and my bread, and we'd found the perfect way to help me forget my baking disaster. Lover, A+.

I began tracing Elena's eyebrows, her cheekbones, her jaw, but when I reached her lips I froze at an odd crunching sound coming from behind Elena. Adrenaline flooded my body. Ever since the lovely Moorish princess Walladah had tried to have me killed months ago in the Aljafería harem, I'd been a bit jumpy. A jumpy lesbian was not a pretty sight.

I looked over my shoulder across the room. Our door stood partially open. Crap—I'd forgotten to latch it last night. Holding my breath, I slowly sat up and peered over Elena's shoulder.

"Oh!" I shrieked.

"Wha—" Elena shot up, cursed the open door, and yanked the blanket up over her naked chest. A white ewe with charcoal freckles stood beside the bed, mouth full of the tulips and crocuses I'd picked yesterday and put in a crockery vase. Two speckled lambs, eyes black and huge, nibbled at the stems still in their mother's mouth.

"Sheep. Elena, there are three sheep in our room."

Groaning, Elena dropped back onto her pillow. "Is that all?"

I stared at the ewe. "Shoo. Go away. Bad sheep." Gold eyes with horizontal pupils stared back, then small, brown pellets dropped from her backside and rolled across the floor.

I yelped and leapt from the bed, scattering the startled sheep. "That's it. Elena, get up. These blasted sheep are using our room as a toilet." I threw on my long skirt and tunic, yanked on my soft leather boots, then tried to herd the ewe out the door. She ran around the room, lambs glued to her hips like a set of training wheels. She overturned the room's one chair, and a lamb nearly upset the chamber pot.

Elena lay in bed, dissolved in laughter, even when Destructo-Ewe and her evil offspring leapt onto and over the bed. "Help me," I shrieked. "These sheep are so stupid."

"Close the door first," Elena said, wiping her eyes. When I did, she rose, lithe and smooth and naked. As I watched, Elena bound her small perfect breasts with a fresh white linen strip, then dressed in leggings, long green shirt and a leather tunic. "Sheep aren't stupid," she said in her husky voice. "Why should a sheep understand the human concept of 'door?'" I tried to stay stern, but her broad grin broke me down, and we exchanged that look new lovers give each other, the one full of amazement and delight they could be together every day.

"Now open the door and stand off to the side." Gently clucking, Elena herded the now-frantic sheep along the wall until they had to choose between me or the door. They chose the door, hard hooves slipping on the flagstone as they fled down the hallway. Shepherdess, D.

Before we followed, Elena pulled me to her. "Good morning, my pearl." Our deep kiss warmed me like strong alcohol, a welcome warmth since we lived in a house with nothing but wooden shutters over the windows. While I'd been happy for months to have been Elena's pearl, Luis Navarro's wife, I wondered if, at some point, it would not be enough. One of these days I'd get the hang of bread, and then what would I do with my time?

As Elena and I herded the sheep toward the back door, the ewe bleated. She and her lambs fled the wide open door, then leaping and kicking with relief, they dashed down the slope and joined the flock Juan tended. I waved at the young shepherd, who bobbed his dark head respectfully. "You know sheep," I said to Elena. "Maybe you should be a shepherd instead of a soldier."

She folded her arms and squared her stance, always a bad sign. "Why would I want to stop being a soldier?"

We'd had this identical conversation five times already, so I didn't answer. Mercenary soldiers in this century didn't grow old. They fought until one day their shield or their sword or their strength or their luck failed them. The thought of losing Elena forced the oxygen from my lungs.

"You are holding your breath again."

"Am not."

"You are." Elena kissed my ear and slipped an arm around me, our disagreement already dried into dust by the early morning sun. We turned back toward our home. Because it was the largest residence and sat on the highest hill, its inhabitants—that would be us—were Don and Doña to the villagers clustered nearby. I loved the worn cedar siding, which turned a warm copper after a hard rain, streaks of silver flashing through the wood grain when the sun finally came out. Two kids chased a third out the front door. We'd made it clear the 'castle' was open to all, so it had become a community center of sorts. As long as Elena and I could bar our bedroom door at night, we had all the privacy we needed.

Inside, someone had left four loaves of fresh bread on the table. "Food!" Elena cried and fell upon the nearest loaf, gnawing on the golden crust.

"Oh, for heaven's sake," I scolded, hands on my hips. "You get plenty to eat." I approached the cold hearth to start a fire.

Elena wiped the crumbs off her face and reached for me. "You are right. I am still full from last night." Right in the middle of one of those kisses that turned my kneecaps to melted honey, a grinning soldier burst into the room. I pulled away. Alvar Fáñez.

"I see I'm just in time," he cried. "I'll take the next kiss." With his black eye patch and ready grin, the soldier striding across the room was a happy-go-lucky pirate, the kind who would steal your money, then steal a kiss, or more. He was also the man history claimed to be Rodrigo Díaz's first lieutenant, not Luis Navarro, a fact I'd remembered reading in one of Anna's history books. Not a day went by that I didn't look into Elena's eyes and feel the cold hand of history brush through me. Something was going to happen to Elena, and I had no idea what.

Alvar and Elena clasped arms as she threatened him with castration if he came near me, then he smoothly moved his sword aside, knelt on the dusty floor, and pressed his lips against my hand. "Oh, Kate. Your beauty outshines the sun, the moon, and the jewels of a thousand kings."

I shook my head and leaned over the ridiculous knight. Alvar Fáñez was a man I wanted to dislike but just couldn't. "And where did you hear that pile of bull manure?" I asked.

Alvar winked his good eye, which was the color of green glass pounded soft by the ocean, and leapt to his feet. "I heard a minstrel sing it last week. I was sure it would charm you right into my arms." He chuckled as Elena cuffed him across the back of the head. Hard to believe Alvar had ever considered killing Elena. He, Nuño, Gudesto, and Elena had been the last of a band of fanatical Moor-haters called the Caballeros de Valvanera. Gudesto had convinced Alvar to kill Elena, which he'd almost done on the battlefield, but at the last minute, Alvar realized which friend deserved his loyalty, and turned his sword aside. Somehow Elena and Alvar recovered their trust in each other. I'm not sure I could have been so generous.

"Enough, children. Sit down and I'll make some eggs." I reached for a bowl.

"Are you sure?" Elena said. "I saw Marta down by her garden. She could make—" Elena's brows pulled together.

"Relax." While I wasn't Martha Stewart of the eleventh century, I could handle an easy breakfast. Cooking Eggs, A.

Alvar dropped down onto the bench and leaned against the wall. "I bring news from Burgos. Rodrigo says it is time to muster the army again and wants us all back within the week. King Alfonso plans to take Cordoba from the Almoravides and will pay us handsomely to accompany him."

Elena whooped and banged her fist against the table, rattling the plates I set out. "Finally." She didn't look at me, but her flushed face told me she'd been chafing under the winter's inactivity. "I am not cut out to be a land baron." It unnerved me to see her brighten at a fight. While I cooked, trying not to think about Elena being sliced to ribbons in battle, the two old friends caught up.

Later, Alvar bent over his plate, smacking appreciatively. "Before we take Cordoba, Alfonso considers moving his court to Toledo to better position himself. The Queen disagrees, but Alfonso's mistress suggested it. They say that woman keeps the king hard all night." Alvar winked at Elena. "We should be so lucky, eh?" I bit off a smile as Elena nearly choked on her bread. Good, served her right.

"Some say the woman is a seer," Alvar continued. "They say Paloma de Palma uses pagan signs and cards to foretell the future."

"Paloma de Palma?" I squeaked. "That's her name?" I'd heard that name last fall when negotiating with King Alfonso for Luis's release, noticing it matched the pen name Anna had planned to use if she ever wrote a lesbian romance novel. A woman who talked as strangely as I did, who appeared to know the future, and used Anna's beloved pen name?

Alvar nodded. "Yes. Alfonso does not make a move now without consulting her."

Elena leaned back in her chair, the wooden legs protesting. "King Alfonso is a man of faith. How could he put so much store in astrology?" I turned my back so Elena couldn't see my face. Anna was an expert in medieval Spanish history and would know the outcome of every battle King Alfonso had ever fought. As they finished eating, I struggled for calm. No, it couldn't be her.

After a few minutes, Alvar pushed away from the table and belched. Elena did the same, sneaking a guilty glance at me through those thick lashes. Table manners had yet to be invented, and Elena resisted my gentle suggestion to at least close her mouth.

"How long will the campaign be?" Elena asked. "Does Rodrigo consider a siege? I should be in Burgos planning this. Rodrigo cannot make a plan to save his life. And what about Valencia?"

Alvar snorted. "At this point who knows? Whoever controls the crown of Valencia controls a great jewel. I wouldn't be surprised if one day Rodrigo himself went after Valencia."

I nearly dropped the precious pottery plate I was drying because I remembered enough history to know Rodrigo would do just that. He would take Valencia for himself, not for Alfonso, and when he did, history would twist events around and credit him with beginning the reconquest of Spain, the four-hundred year process of driving the educated, skilled, and civilized Moors from the peninsula. After the Moors invaded the peninsula in 711, the Moors had shaped Spain—its art, its language, its culture. Yet after 1492 Spain would kill or drive out both the Moors and the Jews, the best minds of their country. Anna had convinced herself this had been Spain's downfall, and that the Moors should have remained in Spain and ruled the entire country. So if Anna had really come back to the eleventh century, it made more sense that she'd be living with the Moors, not in Christian Spain with King Alfonso. I took a deep breath, trying to relax the knot forming in my belly. Paloma de Palma just could *not* be Anna.

"Don Luis." A stocky man from the village knocked on the doorframe. "Many pardons for the intrusion, but Menendez and Barela fight again. They are outside the mill and mean to kill each other."

Elena groaned, rose, strapped on her sword belt, and made sure her dagger rested in its thigh scabbard. She hadn't used either since we'd arrived at Duañez because El Picador's reputation—good with a sword but devastating with a dagger—had preceded us. "Alvar, can you be trusted with my wife for a short time?"

"Of course not."

Shaking her head, Elena followed the villager from the room. I turned toward Alvar, licking my dry lips. "This Paloma de Palma, have you seen her?"

"No, but she must be beautiful to lure King Alfonso from Queen Constance's bed." He broke off a hunk of bread and spread it with honey. "They say she's charming and can talk people into doing her bidding, whatever that might be." My jaw clenched. Alvar had just described my ex-lover Anna.

I lurched to my feet, fussing with the folds of my skirts so Alvar would not see my hands, which trembled not in fear, but in fury, then excused myself. If, by some horrible twist of fate, Paloma were Anna, that meant she brought a six-year-old boy back over nine hundred and twenty years to a time when a simple scratch could develop into a fatal infection.

My footsteps echoed against the stone walls as I ran down the hall and into our room. With stiff fingers I unzipped my leather fanny pack, the only thing I'd had with me the day I accidentally fell back in time. I yanked everything out: the Lion King keychain, the purple flashlight, the empty bubble pack of Benadryl. I fingered the photo of Arturo, praying he was happy in Chicago, that he loved my dog Max, that he liked his new home.

I unfolded the half-finished family drawing he'd given Anna and me the day we'd met him in the orphanage. Anna, Max, and Arturo were all complete and connected hand-to-hand-to-paw. My figure lacked a head, foreshadowing that I wouldn't be part of their family.

I didn't need to open the last item because I knew the yellow note by heart. The morning before I'd visited the cave and been flung back in time, Anna and I had finally connected after months of distance. I found the note after I'd showered. *Dear Kate, Have gone downstairs for breakfast. Join me when you're up. Love, Paloma de Palma.* I closed my eyes. Of all that I'd worried about this last winter, not once had I considered the possibility that Anna might have figured out the secret of the Mirabueno Cave and come looking for me.

❖

When I woke up the next morning, in the hazy blue between night and dawn, Elena lay on her side, her blue eyes black in the dark. This time her finger did the tracing as she slid down my nose, my jawline, across my lips. "I still cannot believe we found each other."

I nibbled her finger and was rewarded with a melting kiss that sent me throbbing. "I want to go to Burgos with you."

She raised up on one elbow, teeth white as she laughed. "You would follow the army as a camp woman? Holy Bullocks. I guess I do not know you as well as I thought." An army on the march had a dozen or more wagons trailing behind it filled with women—for cooking, laundry, tending wounds, and for pleasure.

"No." I pulled her down into my arms, praying she didn't hear how fast my heart beat. "Just to Burgos. I need to deliver the painting to Alfonso." As part of my bargaining with Alfonso for information on Elena's whereabouts last fall, the king had requested a large painting of himself victorious over the Moors.

Elena shifted in my arms. "You said last week you still had work to do on it."

"Minor touch-ups. I can finish them tomorrow. This is my best opportunity to get the painting to him."

Elena rolled over on her back, staring at the heavy beamed ceiling, pulling away almost more than if she'd physically left the room. "Does this have anything to do with...with that de Palma woman?" I said nothing. "I saw your face as we talked of her."

I swallowed. I trusted Elena with my life—that wasn't a problem. But I'd already put her through so much last fall—running away, insisting on returning to my century, then changing my mind. She'd been strapped into the seat right next to me on the rollercoaster of my life, and I couldn't bear to drag her on another ride unless I absolutely had to. Besides, speaking my fears would make them real. No use both of us feeling unbalanced. "I need to go to Burgos. You're going there. Doesn't it make sense to go together? Or would you rather I travel alone, unarmed and vulnerable?"

That brought the reluctant smile I knew it would. "I would hardly call you vulnerable," she said as I snuggled into her. She melted against me, saying nothing more.

Questions rattled through me, but I pushed them away, deciding to pull a Scarlett O'Hara and think about that tomorrow. To avoid exploding, all I could do was take this one step at a time.

CHAPTER THREE

Ex-girlfriends. You couldn't live with them and you couldn't get away from them, not even if you traveled back in time over nine hundred and twenty years. Somehow, some way, they manage to wreck your new relationship and totally screw with your head.

At least that's what I feared as I bounced along on the rock-hard seat of that damned wagon, sitting beside old José, whose crippled leg prevented him from farming, but allowed him to drive the wagon. Men rode on horseback around us, kicking up enough dust to coat my hair, face, and the inside of my lungs. We were heading for Burgos, and I could barely sit still.

José chattered endlessly. He wore his greasy, thin hair slicked back behind enormous ears, and the rough topography of his face and neck were the likely result of too much sun and too many brawls. "I'm pleased as a saint's mama to be riding wi' you, Señora. We got us two whole days to chat, we do." José clicked loudly to the two brown mules pulling the wagon. "My woman says not to talk your ear off, she did. But I'm thinking we'll have a grand time, you and me."

I smiled weakly. Up ahead and flanked by her men Enzo and Fadri, Elena rode the sleek Matamoros. During the long winter I'd come to appreciate Enzo's gruff concern, Fadri's enthusiasm, and their total devotion to Luis Navarro.

Behind us came three hundred of Elena's men, some on horseback, others driving wagons of supplies, others on foot. The procession filled the warm day with male voices raised in bawdy song, creaking wagon wheels, the almost syncopated rhythm of hundreds of horses, and the occasional high sparkle of women laughing in the wagons. Alvar was driving one of the wagons, flirting outrageously.

Bored, I twisted around on the hard bench to make sure the painting wasn't shifting during the rough ride. The busy, narrow road had rutted badly in the spring rains, but José took no notice, reins loose in palms so callused I thought at first he wore gloves. A lanky man passed us on horseback, nodding politely.

José clucked under his breath. "Beats his wife, that one does. My cousin from Ona says he has more ale in his head than good sense. Oh, look-ee there. Paco! How is the family?" José leaned toward me. "Pays more attention to his sheep than he does his wife, that one. Now I'm not one to criticize, but it ain't his wife's fault she was born with no toes. Saints above, it is true. Saw the stumps myself. Argghh—that wagon ahead? Poor family's lost three children this winter. My cousin from Calahora says they brung it on themselves, they did. Why, they never attend mass. Can you believe it? Satan's minions, that family. I can remember..."

God, why hadn't I ridden my own horse? Every hour Elena rode back halfway between us, waited a second, then returned to the front, as if that act could tug us along more quickly. Finally she pranced Matamoros all the way back to the wagon.

"Now my wife's cousin in Calahora, the one who's not married to Marta's third cousin, she was to marry this wheelwright, but would you believe a hussy from Toledo snatched him away right before the wedding? Yes, she did. The poor señorita, she says—"

"José!" Elena's face was dark with frustration. "Can you not get these blasted mules to move faster? Alfonso will conquer Cordoba before we even reach Burgos."

"Oh, Don Luis, these are sensitive mules, they are. Best not to be cursing 'em"

"Luis, dear," I said with my best smile, "would you like to ride in the wagon for a while?"

Her broad grin infuriated me. "Oh, Kate, my love. You look so comfortable there. I wouldn't dream of displacing you." With a laugh at my narrowed eyes, she galloped back to Enzo and Fadri.

When I growled low in my throat, José somehow mistook it for gratitude, too in love with mules to know much about humans. "Don Luis, what a gentleman he be, always thinking of your comfort. Reminds me of mules, it does. Why, mules are the most dependable, bravest creatures on this God's earth, they are. I remember my beloved Loca, oh, now there was a blessed mule, that one."

I closed my eyes and gripped the thick wooden seat. At least José's constant patter occasionally interrupted the obsessive loop playing over and over inside my head, the one which worried the whole Anna question as a tongue worries a broken tooth.

What would happen if Anna and Elena actually met? Elena's tongue could be as razor sharp as her sword, but Anna's marble haughtiness was hard to dent, sort of like bashing your head against a massive pedestal. She put herself up there, and she'd be damned if she'd let anyone knock her off.

Except for a brief stop for cheese and ale, we pressed on. While I'd grown to appreciate the rugged strength of Castile's square farmhouses with their brown thatched roofs, the broad plateaus flat as a table, the green pastures dotted with gnarled trees and blooming wildflowers, I missed the sheer lushness of Moorish Zaragoza, the gentle patter of fountains, the moisture that plumped up the eucalyptus trees and flushed the grapevines a deep green, the cool water that ran efficiently through the city. All that day in Castile we passed dry fields that could have produced ten times as much with Moorish irrigation systems.

My mind reeled with José's gossip, so I was extremely grateful when, toward dusk, Elena reined in Matamoros and raised her arm. Time to make camp for the night. Since it was a clear, dry evening, everyone left the tents bundled up and spread out bedrolls in the clearing, along the road, and into the woods.

Soon small campfires glowed, groups of men talked quietly, some snored from scattered bedrolls, and the women washed pans and laughed.

Finally Elena sat on a log across from me. We munched on the dried rabbit left over from last week and split a small loaf of bread.

"You're doing it again," I said.

"What?"

"Undressing me with your eyes."

Her wicked grin was her only answer. When we'd finished, she picked up a chunk of charred wood, cool to the touch, and grabbed my hand. "It's time," she said.

Ugh, not again. She led me to the edge of the clearing, found a tree with a wide trunk, and drew a black X with the blackened wood.

"I'm never going to learn this," I said, handing my dagger to Elena.

She paced off twenty feet, held the dagger lightly by its tip, inhaled slowly, then the blade was suddenly gone, now embedded in the middle of the X. "Your turn," Elena said as she retrieved my dagger.

"Wait," came a gruff call. Enzo and Fadri approached, faces serious. Enzo wrapped a saddle blanket around Elena's waist, tying it on with a scabbard belt. Fadri jammed a leather helmet on Elena's head and handed her a massive shield. They each gave Elena a solemn embrace, as if they may never see their beloved leader again, then headed back for their fire, Fadri tossing me a wink as he passed.

"I'm rolling on the ground laughing, boys," I said. "And I only hit Luis once, so it's not like I do it every time."

The blade was cool between my fingers. I stared at the X and bit my lip. Maybe I should have brought a gun back into the past for protection and been done with it. I took a deep breath and let the blade fly.

We both stared at the empty tree.

"Where'd it go?" Elena asked.

"Great mother of mules! We're under attack!" José shot up from the nearby wagon bed, eyes as wild as his sleep-mussed hair.

Enzo trotted over and calmed José down before he could start a camp-wide panic. He then pulled my dagger from the wagon's sideboard and gave it back to Elena, saying, "Please, Luis. One day someone will get hurt." Both his words and his parting scowl were meant for me, not Elena.

Sighing, I accepted the dagger and jammed it back into its scabbard. "Enzo is right, you know. I should just give up." I moved closer so I could whisper. "I have no skills."

"But you can drive high breed cars and order cap...cap..." I'd taught Elena a little English.

"Hybrid cars and cappuccino."

She snorted the eleventh-century version of "whatever," and pulled me close. "You, my love, are not entirely without skills," she whispered into my neck.

"What—you mean this?" One flick of my tongue against her earlobe and Elena's knees buckled against mine. I loved doing that.

"Jesus, woman, yes, I mean that."

Dusk had deepened into a black, moonless sky, lit only by the campfires flickering in the distance through the trees. For the rest of the evening we sat next to ours, talking quietly, holding hands, warm with happiness, as if we were the only two people in the world lucky enough to have found one another.

The next day in the wagon, I had to listen to José's never-ending theories about someone trying to kill him, but I didn't have the heart to confess. I was also too busy obsessing about how I might have changed since Anna had seen me last, a bad idea that brought on an attack of the frumpies. Instead of Levi's, Doc Martens, and Eddie Bauer, I now wore a dark muslin skirt that brushed the toes of my squared-off brown boots and totally covered my two dingy petticoats. I wore a thin undershirt and over it a loose, long-sleeved brown tunic cinched at the waist with a strip of leather Elena had tooled for me. I longed for the freedom to wear pants, but this was 1086, and I was a woman. One cross-dresser in the family was enough, especially since this culture tended to stone women who dressed as men.

The closer we rode to Burgos, the more travelers we met about whom José knew some bit of gossip. Soon it was impossible to shut out all the dirt José so thoughtfully shared with me. Thankfully, just before dusk, and just as I began to consider pulling out my dagger and threatening José into silence, we topped a gentle rise and the plateau of Burgos spread out before us, the old Roman walls rising up from the greening fields around the city. The buildings of Burgos spilled out beyond the walls, all the way to an array of dirty white, tan, and yellow tents scattered at the city outskirts. White smoke from hundreds of cooking fires snaked up into the dense clouds hovering over Burgos.

Elena urged Matamoros ahead and reached the army camp first, where the men gathered there swallowed her in a crush of welcome.

Ten minutes later, José and I rumbled to a stop near the tent city, inhaling sweat and roasting meat and sun-baked leather and rustic latrines. Elena was still greeting comrades, clasping arms and dispensing bear hugs as men swarmed around her, hungry for a word of greeting, of encouragement. A handful of mercenaries who'd been with Luis in Zaragoza saw me, Luis's wife, and hooted wildly, setting off an avalanche of leers, suggestive comments, and lewd tongue waggling. God, have men *always* been pigs?

Elena pushed toward our wagon, her fierce blush only fueling the men's wild ribbing. Christ, what would they do if they ever learned the bulge at Luis Navarro's crotch was nothing more than stitched leather filled with sugar?

Elena grabbed the nearest wheel of our wagon, stood on a spoke, and pulled herself up to grasp the wooden seat on which I sat. "You and José ride into the city. The Crazy Mule Tavern should have lodging." José squeaked with pleasure at the word 'mule.' "I will join you later." She leaned closer so José could not hear. "I am sorry about the men. It has been a long winter...and you are beautiful. The men cannot help themselves."

The hooting crowd gathered around the wagon, and I hated to disappoint. "Neither can I," I said. When I pulled her to me, giving her one of those wet, passionate kisses she loved, the men roared. Laughing, I pushed a wide-eyed Elena off the wheel into the outstretched arms of her men.

"El Picador!" they chanted as they bore her away. A few pretended to swoon at my feet, so I laughed and waved them off. Elena's men were rude, lewd, crude, and violent, but they adored her, or rather, they adored Luis.

I didn't like Burgos. After the neat cobbled streets of Moorish Zaragoza, this city's packed dirt roads felt coarse and temporary. Even a light rain made life in the city a mud-sucking hell. The people, with their open faces and loud voices, were friendly enough, but too many memories floated about this city, thin ghosts waiting to swoop down and steal my breath at every familiar corner. Last fall Elena's best friend Nuño and I had spent days here, searching madly for Elena, knowing no more at each day's end than we had at its beginning. I'd finally forced an audience with King Alfonso, only to learn the twisted soldier Gudesto Gonzalez held my love. No wonder the dreary, smelly city tightened my throat and cramped my gut.

That night, as the moon and stars hid behind fast-moving clouds, Elena and I snuggled together in a flea-ridden bed above the tavern and listened to rowdy songs drifting up through the rough floorboards. Now that I was so near the castle and possibly the mysterious Paloma de Palma, a heavy weight had settled on my heart.

Elena slept nestled against my shoulder and I watched the clouds drift over the half moon hanging outside our window. What would I do if Paloma de Palma really was Anna? Would she take my rejection gracefully?

What would Elena do? She wasn't the most tolerant of women, which I chalked up both to the century in which we lived and her tendency toward violence. When a man from our village had grabbed my ass one day by the well, she'd nearly decapitated him, stopping only when I'd begged her.

The lesbians I knew had always bent over backward to stay friends with their ex-lovers, sort of a "Why can't we all just get along?" approach. Not me. Not Anna. Certainly not Elena. If Paloma de Palma really was Anna, things would get ugly in a big hurry.

CHAPTER FOUR

After a quick breakfast of thick porridge at the inn, Elena left to find Rodrigo, leaving me to deal with the painting on my own, as I'd hoped. I straightened our room, threw on my wool cape, then stomped down the rickety stairs and out into the narrow street, moving aside just before someone dumped a chamber pot out a second story window. And people in the twenty-first century thought *they* lived dangerously. I collared two filthy boys loitering outside the stables and hired them to help me break down the protective frame and carry the wrapped canvas to the castle. Unlike Zaragoza, Burgos provided no formal education for its children, so they ran wild in the streets. Zaragoza held school for both boys and girls.

We left the stables with the two boys each gripping a side of the wrapped painting. "Hold it higher, out of the mud," I scolded, but by the time we'd gone less than half way, my skirt, the boys, and the rags around the 6' x 8' painting were splattered with mud. I yearned for the paved streets of Zaragoza.

I stopped the boys at the castle gates. The dark heavy walls towered above us, sturdy stone architecture able to protect the king and his court but lacking the grace and mystery of a Moorish palace. Some days I wished Elena's boss, El Cid, would alienate the king again and be sent back into exile so we could return to Zaragoza.

Shaking off the fantasy, I led the gawking boys inside and toward the main staircase. Last fall, when I'd been trying to rescue Elena from Gudesto's clutches, I'd been all over this castle, so I knew right where to go.

At the top of the stairs a palace guard moved to block our path. "Señora, you cannot pass." I stopped, letting a haughty smile escape, one of those irritatingly superior smiles Anna sometimes used. The young guard's swarthy face drained to the white of the stone behind him. "Oh! It is you...it is you."

I smiled at the poor man's panic. "Marcos, isn't it?" He hadn't forgotten that I'd held a knife to his precious manhood six months earlier in my desperate attempt to speak to King Alfonso. "I bring a gift to the King, one he requested last year. Take me to him."

The guard stepped back a pace, eyes darting to my hands. "The king is in council with Rodrigo Díaz and the other mercenary commanders. He cannot be disturbed. But I can take the gift—"

"No, I will take it to his throne room, where others will install it later." Snapping my fingers at the boys, I pushed past the guard and down the hall. Alfonso's empty throne room, lit only by two torches, danced with deep, heavy shadows. The far wall was still bare, waiting for my painting. Our footsteps echoed against the stone walls.

"Lean it against that wall." I paid the boys, sent them on their way, then carefully unwrapped the painting. Thank god the large canvas held its own in the throne room. I stepped back, critical of a few areas that could have used more work, but decided Alfonso wouldn't notice or he wouldn't care.

In the painting, King Alfonso, looking taller and more handsome than in truth, stood before his army, red cape flowing in the wind. The vanquished Moorish commander, his saffron robes muddied and torn, knelt before Alfonso. Clasped in the Moor's blood-stained hand was the key to his city, which he extended toward Alfonso in surrender.

I studied the painting. It was good, very good. The colors were subdued, thanks to the primitive paint I'd made using egg, oil, and crushed and boiled minerals or plants for color. The deep red of crushed madder roots dominated the painting, with saffron highlights and charcoal-tinted sky as background. Lapis lazuli was too expensive, so I'd given up on blue.

While the painting was mine, the idea wasn't. I'd stolen shamelessly from Diego Velasquez's *Surrender at Breda*, a seventeenth-century painting of a Dutch general handing over the keys to the city to a Spanish general, both with their men behind them and a burning city in the background.

Of course, because I couldn't use perspective, all the men were much the same size and looked like soldiers stacked on one another's shoulders, sort of like vertical bowling pins. Perspective wouldn't begin appearing in paintings until the fourteenth century, three hundred years in the future, which I had learned the hard way. Nine months ago, in 1085, while locked in a Moorish harem in Zaragoza, I'd innocently painted one of the emir's wives using perspective and had nearly lost my head for it. The emir had accused me of stealing his wife's soul because the painting had depth and roundness and looked more vivid than the woman herself.

My gaze drifted to the edges of this painting. I had used another element from Velasquez's work, one that had given me shivers when I'd seen it in Madrid's Museo del Prado. Every soldier focused on the two leaders at the canvas's center, except three men who stared out straight toward me, the viewer, as if to say, "Who are you and why are you watching us?" The men in my painting did the same, although their silent accusation was, "You don't belong in this century." I sighed. Some days I couldn't shut out the voice in my head that said they were right.

Even with the strong smell of paint from the canvas, the room reeked of wet, moldy walls. As I stood there, I felt, rather than heard, slow steady breathing from one shadowy corner, so I froze, then turned toward the corner. The hem of a woman's dress brushed the tile floor, the rest of her in shadow.

"I'm sorry," I said. "I thought the room was empty." She must be part of the court, or a servant taking a quiet break.

The woman stood and approached me, the gold braid trim of her brown linen shimmering in the torchlight as she moved from the shadows. She wore her chestnut hair swept off her elegant neck and held by a delicate webbing of golden strands. With her slender hands clasped at her waist, she stopped beside me and stared at my artwork. "Do not concern yourself. I spend too much time alone these days as it is." Her wistful smile, her warm brown eyes saddened by some inner pain, touched me so much I nearly reached for her hand. Instead I waited while she gazed at the painting. "You must be Señora Navarro."

I nodded, hiding my surprise.

"What city has been conquered in this painting?"

I shrugged. "Toledo, Cordoba, Valencia—whichever King Alfonso fancies."

She barely nodded, a wounded deer mesmerized by my painting. "Valencia, then. Toledo he has won and lost so many times the city has lost its luster. Cordoba is too close to Africa and the Almoravides. But Valencia..." Tiny sparks flared in her eyes. "Even I dream of Valencia."

She flicked a slender finger toward the painting. "He is not this handsome."

In my best conspiratorial voice, I confessed. "I thought I should appeal to his vanity."

Two small lines formed between the woman's fine arched brows. "Very effective. Vanity is Alfonso's greatest weakness."

As if I were the Wicked Witch of the East, the truth slammed down on me as suddenly as a house. What noblewoman would have the nerve to criticize the king before a stranger such as myself? Only his wife, Queen Constance, the woman who had recently lost the attentions of her husband to the mysterious Paloma de Palma. I now understood the aura of pain she projected. I stepped back, curtseying so awkwardly I nearly tipped over. "Your majesty, I did not know who you were. Please excuse my intrusion."

She held up a hand. "I understand this is a Moor giving the keys of the city to my husband, but what of these three men who look outward, directly at us?"

I paused. While I could easily argue with King Alfonso, I found myself tongue-tied around her, unsure how to speak to a queen. "Your highness, art is about emotion. How do those three faces make you feel?"

Without hesitation, she said, "As if they are looking deep into my very soul, as if they can see my sins and are judging me for them." She suddenly laughed. "Señora Navarro, this is a perfect painting for Alfonso. I shall pray it invokes the same emotions in him. May he be forced to confront his sins every time he gazes on this work of art. God knows he has enough sins to repent."

I bit my lip and inhaled sharply. Standing beside me was a woman who knew Paloma de Palma, knew where she slept, knew her movements, and likely hated her. Voices murmured in a nearby room, but otherwise we were alone. Fate usually didn't drop such gifts in my lap; could it be this easy? I cleared my throat. "Your highness, may I impose upon your kindness?"

Her face cleared as she pushed aside her pain, her generosity touching me even as my nervousness grew.

"I seek a woman who has been in your court these last several months. She...has wronged my family terribly."

The queen clucked sympathetically and nodded toward a carved marble bench. "Sit and tell me more, child."

I sat. "My cousin...from Calahora was betrothed to marry Marta Vasquez's third cousin on her mother's side. But the night before the wedding, this woman I seek lured away my cousin's intended, then disappeared. I have been looking for her on behalf of my cousin." *Thank you, José.*

The queen's jaw tightened and the glint I'd hoped for appeared in her eyes. "Does this woman have a name?"

"Paloma de Palma. I have heard there is a woman by this name... advising the king."

"Yes, advising," the queen replied, lips tight.

"I need to see if she's the same one."

"And if she is?"

"I will bring her back to Calahora and make her answer for my cousin's shame."

The queen licked her dry lips. "And how would she answer?"

"Public humiliation. She would be revealed as nothing more than a woman of loose morals and questionable character."

"I see." I waited, my stomach tight. Tiny lines ran out from the queen's eyes, and her brow was a map of permanent horizontal lines. "Señora Navarro, would you recognize your Señora de Palma if you saw her?"

"Absolutely."

The queen's face flushed with excitement, and she absentmindedly smoothed out her skirt. Then she stood and held out her arm for mine. "Good. Then I will take you to her."

Heart pounding, I struggled to slow my steps to match the queen's regal pace. If my good luck held, the court's de Palma would *not* be Anna.

Servants and noblemen bowed as we passed from room to room, a twenty-first century lesbian locking arms with an eleventh century queen, both hopeful but for different reasons.

I'd never been this deep inside the castle before, and I tried not to gape at the heavy red and green tapestries hanging in every room, the sideboards loaded with silver service, the elaborate candelabras, the ornate carved wooden crosses. After passing through a number of small rooms, we approached yet another open doorway. "Señora de Palma," the queen called gaily. "You have a visitor."

When the queen and I stepped inside, the ladies-in-waiting jumped to their feet, knocking over baskets of yarn, and dropped into curtsies. A blond woman in an ivory and green gown fled out a far doorway before I had the chance to see her face.

"The guilty flee," Queen Constance murmured.

"Stop!" I shouted, then grabbed up my skirts and ran through the cluster of women, reaching the doorway just as a flash of ivory disappeared from the next room. My boots slipped as I raced across the stone floor, but I kept my footing and clattered down the dark staircase. This was ridiculous. Why would Anna run from me if it were her? She had nothing to hide from me.

"Stop!" I cried, but the woman shoved through a cluster of arguing noblemen and bolted up the far staircase, her hair now half-undone and swinging wildly.

Not stopping to apologize to the portly nobleman I knocked over, I snatched up my skirts and took the stairs two at a time. At the end of a short hallway a wooden door slammed shut. Heart pounding, gasping to relieve my aching lungs, I marched up to the closed door and rapped my knuckles against the smooth wood. No answer, so I inhaled once for courage, then pushed down the heavy iron latch and flung open the door.

The small room held three benches, two tables, and one woman. She stood against the far wall, back to me, looking out the window as her fluttering fingers pinned up her fallen hair.

"Anna?" I asked. My blood bashed against my ear drums as I waited, praying when the woman turned around I'd see close-set eyes or the wrong-shaped face or a flat nose or a moustache—anything to show me I'd been paranoid. I wiped my mouth. False alarm. Please.

The woman's head dropped, then, gown rustling on the grimy floor, she turned.

"Oh, my god," I breathed. Same green eyes. Same little bump on the nose. Same firm chin. I stared stupidly at her, too numb to think.

"Kate." My former lover held out her hands as a confusion of emotions raced across her face. "I ran because I didn't know it was you." She crossed the room, expensive gown and cape flowing behind her, then before I could say anything she flung her arms around my neck. "Oh Kate, I finally found you. Now we can be together again."

Shit.

Instinctively my arms went around her, probably because I couldn't think of anything else to do with them, and because my brain flailed around like a caged animal. Holding her had once been the most natural thing in the world, but now I could scarcely breathe. She smelled of fish and a sickly sweet rose perfume. Slowly, gently, I unlatched her arms, stepping back to stare into the face I thought I'd never see again. She was clearly doing the same, and though it had only been nine months, it felt more like nine hundred years.

"Anna," I finally croaked. "You came back in time."

"Of course, my love. To look for you...and to just *be* here." A tentative smile flickered across her flushed face, then faded when I lowered myself onto the nearest wooden bench, worn smooth by decades of Burgosian bottoms, my knees feeling weird.

"But how...how did you find out where I'd gone?" I asked.

She dropped down beside me and clutched at my hand. How could she afford such expensive clothes, the smooth green silk, the gold embroidered trim, a bodice beaded with pearls? "Kate, I was sick with worry. For days I badgered the Zaragozan police, but they had no leads. Can you imagine how I felt? You left for the cave, then never came back. You were gone, you'd vanished."

"It was an accident." I dug my nails into a soft groove in the bench.

"No kidding. That weird dentist couple—"

"—the Whipples."

"Yeah. They insisted you'd dropped behind in the cave tour and they never saw you again. The vendors outside the cave never saw you leave. I was wild with fear that you might have fallen into a crack or pool or quicksand or something. I asked Carlos for help. You remember, the guide at the Aljafería?"

I nodded, feeling as if I were stuck in one of those horrible nightmares you know is a dream but that you can't escape.

"He and I tracked down Roberto at the orphanage, and that horrid little man finally confessed what he knew about the ledge in the cave." Roberto, the janitor at Arturo's orphanage, had told Anna and me to stay away from the cave. If I'd listened, I never would have met Elena.

"Anna, where is Arturo?"

She threw up hands so bejeweled they sparkled even in this dull room. "At first I didn't believe Roberto, but he had artifacts he'd brought back. And after a few weeks passed and you were still missing, I decided it was possible. God, I missed you so much." She leaned forward and kissed me, her lips warm and soft.

Slowly, as politely as I could, I drew back. She studied me with cool eyes, then made a noise of disgust. "So that's why you didn't return to the future." Her jaw tightened and my guilt reported for duty.

"I tried. God, I tried. But something always went wrong."

"And then you found someone else. Who is she? On the other hand, this century isn't exactly crawling with lesbians, so perhaps you've turned to men."

"Maybe that's why you're screwing the king," I said tightly, watching her flush as if I'd slapped her. I stood and paced, suddenly as restless as a kid in church, then stopped before the open window, the noisy city sprawled out below. She hadn't come back in time to look for me. "I didn't mean for it to happen, but this person needed me more than—"

"More than I did?"

I puffed out my cheeks, exhaling slowly. "Yes, more than you did. I'm sorry. I couldn't be in two centuries at once. I knew Arturo would be fine with you." I stopped, unsure how much honesty our sudden encounter could bear. "As for us, well...you have to admit we weren't the best together. I knew you'd find someone who fit better."

She shook her head. "I can't believe you gave up on us so easily."

Ouch. Did she truly feel sad or just want to heap on the guilt? "Anna, where is Arturo? Did you leave him with your parents? Did you bring him back with you?"

Anna stood, calmly shaking out her gown, then joined me at the window. Shade cooled this north side of the castle, and though the damp stones made me shiver, that chill was nothing compared to the icy finger of fear that shot through me when Anna cleared her throat. "Kate, I don't know where Arturo is."

The words hung in the air as I shut my eyes, unwilling to hear them. The only surprise was that I was not surprised. I turned and gripped her shoulders. "Why?"

She thrust her chin out defiantly. "I never *had* him. After I figured out you'd gone back in time, I decided to follow. I called Señora Cavelos and explained you'd disappeared and that I didn't want to be a single parent."

My photo of Arturo showed a five-year-old boy afraid to hope, and when Anna's words sank in, I understood why. We'd both failed him. Miserably. I slumped against the wall, struggling to form the words. "He's still at the orphanage?"

She shrugged. "Probably. I don't know."

"You don't know?" Rage at her betrayal—no, at *ours*—thrashed to the surface. "Anna, we promised. Señora Cavelos told him we'd take him home."

"If he was so important, why didn't you come back? The sex was too good to give up?"

"Stop it! I told you I tried. But then I finally realized how little I knew about raising kids. I've nearly drowned three or four of them. I decided you'd make a much better mother than I would. Besides, you were the one who wanted kids."

She grunted, a startling sound from a woman dressed in Burgos's finest silks and jewelry. "You're right. And if you'd died in an accident or something, I probably would have gone ahead with our plans. But, look." She steered me toward the window, her hands clammy enough to penetrate my tunic. "Pinch yourself. You're awake. Inhale. This is 1086, for god's sake. It's real. I don't understand how it's possible, but we exist over nine hundred years before we should."

I yanked my arms free and crossed them over my chest, unnerved and a bit sickened by her touch. "I've been attacked, kidnapped, and tortured, so you don't have to convince me it's real. The wonder wore off months ago."

Arturo was still in the orphanage. I could barely track Anna's words as I remembered being ten, sitting in the bay window in the dark with yet another babysitter watching TV in the other room and waiting for my parents to come home after yet another meeting or workout session. I'd felt unlovable and unworthy because my parents' calendars were just too full to spend time with me.

"Kate, we're living history as it happens. My god, King Alfonso. And El Cid. Think of what we can do, Kate. We can make things happen."

But politics was ridiculously unimportant compared to the realization that Arturo lived in the orphanage still, his wide brown eyes, eager smile, and anxious body poised by the window, wondering when we would come. No, by now he would have stopped wondering 'when,' and had probably even given up on 'if.' Suddenly weak with sadness, I returned to the bench. "Anna, don't be stupid. You've seen enough science fiction to know we could really screw things up."

Her harsh laugh grated on my nerves. "That's fantasy, love." She swept an arm out the open window. "This is reality, Kate, and being here, in Spain, at this time, is more important than any child."

I don't know what made me gasp out loud, her radiant smile or her words, since both bit deeper than if I'd been mauled by a pack of rabid wolves. Yet even as concern for Arturo settled in my heart, something about Anna's story made me worry the inside of my cheek. Then I remembered. "You loved the Moors. If you really want to influence events, aren't you in the wrong city? Why not Cordoba? Granada? Zaragoza?"

She glared at me, mouth now clamped shut. "I doubt Arturo has been adopted. He's probably still in the orphanage." Her ploy to distract me was so transparent I nearly laughed, but it did such damage I blinked furiously, wondering if I'd ever known the hard woman standing before me. As I considered my options, a flaming ache ignited deep inside me, one that I knew would consume me for the rest of my life. Elena loved me. I loved her. But I could not leave Arturo in that orphanage to grow up without a family, and I would not bring him back to live in such a dangerous time.

CHAPTER FIVE

Still at the window, tense with excitement as she drank in the eleventh century tableau, Anna radiated pleasure, as if the ox carts rumbling through the streets and soldiers teasing passing servant women were an aphrodisiac.

"I must go," I said, unsure who angered me more—Anna or myself, since we'd both left Arturo at the orphanage, unlovable, unworthy, left to grow up on his own.

"I'll walk with you," she said. In silence, we left the room and descended the nearest staircase. A knot of men gathered near the entrance. Rodrigo's booming voice carried to us and I stopped, steadying myself with a hand against the cold stone wall. As the crowd began moving toward the door, Elena turned and saw me at the base of the stairs. She waved, her lopsided grin nearly breaking my heart as she jogged toward us. I didn't understand why, but I knew Anna must never know Elena's true sex.

By the time Elena reached me, her grin had faded and her eyes clouded with concern. Without even glancing at Anna, she cupped my cheek with a callused hand. "Kate, you are white as snow, and your hands just as cold. Are you ill?"

I tried to smile, but the hard realization of what may lay ahead so paralyzed me all I could do was shake my head. I knew what I had to do, but I wasn't sure if I'd actually be able to do it.

Anna cleared her throat coyly. "Kate, perhaps you could introduce me to this fine soldier."

Elena's gaze flickered briefly toward Anna, then returned to me, frowning. I took a deep breath. "This is...my husband, Luis Navarro of Duañez ."

"Your husband?" Anna's voice tightened with shock.

"Yes, he fights with Rodrigo Díaz of Vivar."

Recovering quickly, Anna's face shone and she practically batted her eyelashes at Elena. "How wonderful."

"Luis! Let's go!" Enzo waved impatiently from the main door.

Anna extended her hand. "And I am a dear, old friend of Kate's. We go back many years. Señora Paloma de Palma."

Elena went through the motions, but her face had gone as pale as mine. She turned a troubled gaze on me, but I closed my eyes so she couldn't read them. Not now. Not here. I'd told Elena months ago all about Anna, and while I had probably never mentioned the name Paloma de Palma, it wasn't necessary. How many 'old' friends did I have in the eleventh century?

"An old friend?" Elena said thickly.

"Luis, you mule!" Enzo stopped pacing and headed toward us. "Rodrigo waits!"

With a last desperate glance at me, Elena jogged toward Enzo, and they disappeared into the sunshine flooding the castle entrance.

"Married? That didn't take you long. How long did you wait after you fell back in time? A few weeks, a month?"

"Stop it."

She linked her arm with mine, squeezing tightly when I tried to move away. "Well, he's a beautiful man, and hopelessly in love with you. I can't blame you, even though I'm surprised. I never imagined you were bisexual." Knots of court followers chatting in the huge vestibule stared at us as we passed.

I stepped into the sunny area but felt no warming of my bones, no loosening of my muscles, no relief from the pain in my belly. "I'm surprised at you as well, Anna. Stay away from the king. Fidelity used to be important to you."

"And to you."

I wrenched her warm, plump wrist back until she had to let go of my arm with a sharp cry. "Listen, I was struggling to survive. I didn't mean for it to happen. But how can you cause Queen Constance such pain and still get up in the morning?"

Anna shook her head, topaz drop earrings scattering prism sparkles over both of us. "My reasons are the same as yours. I must do whatever it takes to survive, and if that includes charming and controlling the most powerful man in all of Castile, León, and Asturias, so be it."

"Listen to yourself. You can't control a king."

Her sly smile chilled me. "You can if you slip a little blue pill into his ale, and he credits you with long nights of unbelievable passion."

My mouth dropped. "You brought back Viagra?" She grinned like a child who'd kept a secret too long. "Viagra can harm a man who doesn't need it."

She brushed me off. "He's fine. Exhausted, but fine."

"Christ. What else did you bring back?" I held up both hands. "No, don't tell me."

Troubled, I strode from the castle, elbowed my way across the packed square, and headed for the inn. Everything in my life was going to change, and I didn't know if it was Anna's fault, or my own.

❖

Back in our room at the Crazy Mule, I paced, moaned, stared out the window, then started pacing again. It took me two hours to accept what I had known I must do the instant Anna told me the truth about Arturo.

Somehow the rest of the day passed. By early evening I had nothing to do but wait for Elena to return, so I pulled the bench over to the window, unlatched and threw open the wooden shutters, then rested my chin on my hands, watching Burgos pass by.

Despite my words to Anna, I had lost none of my wonder at the miracle, or curse, that had slid me backward through time. What amazed me most were the people. I'd imagined people in the distant past somehow looked different, awkward, flat, as they'd been portrayed in art. But the people who passed below me looked exactly like twenty-first century residents, clothing excepted, of course. Large, jutting ears. Narrow, pinched noses. Tight, controlled walks, wild saunters, and open, confident gaits. One man could have easily gotten his pot belly drinking beer and surfing the ESPN channels. Another woman's grim, angry face reminded me of Mrs. Nelson, my piano teacher. A group of laughing boys tossed around a ball of rags. Put them in baggy sweats and Nikes, give them a basketball, and they'd blend into any school playground.

People struggled with health, money, war, jealousy, loss, and love.

Just because they didn't have computers or space stations or microwaves didn't mean they were less intelligent, a myth I had worked hard to release.

When I saw Elena's broad shoulders weaving through the crowd toward the inn, I let out a shuddering sigh. My joy at seeing that short black hair collided with the bile rising in my mouth as my stomach roiled. I closed the shutters, lit the two lamps, then paced.

My wait was short. Without looking at me, Elena entered, removed her cloak and scabbard, and dropped them both onto the floor.

"There is still bread and cheese left from yesterday," I said quietly.

Elena broke off a hunk of bread, but just stood there. Finally she took a deep breath. "Paloma de Palma."

"Yes."

"If she is truly an old friend, she must be Anna."

I exhaled loudly, not surprised. "Yes."

She lay the bread on the table, then folded her arms. "Do you wish to...resume your...attachment to Anna?"

If an even harder discussion didn't await us, I would have smiled at her barely concealed jealousy. "Elena, you have shown me more love in the last six months than Anna showed me in five years."

"I will not let you go without a fight. I swear on my family's grave Anna will face my sword if she—"

"Elena, you are not listening. I love *you*."

She turned, face tight, those wonderful lips pressed painfully together. "Anna will not come between us?"

"No, but—"

"Holy Bullocks." She dropped onto the bench. "I have been unable to think all day. Rodrigo almost cuffed me once when I mixed up his orders." Her relieved smile brought a lump to my throat. "I feared I must hurt Anna so she would not take you from me."

I couldn't speak, my mouth opening but no words coming forth.

"Kate?" Elena crossed the room and held my hands.

I closed my eyes, squeezing her hands for strength, inhaling her scent of soap and sweat and leather, then opened my eyes. "Anna will not take me from you. But...Arturo will."

She frowned, confused, so I repeated my words. Elena's eyes suddenly widened. "What?"

I don't know where I found the strength, but I knew I had no choice but to push on. "Anna never adopted Arturo. She left him in the orphanage. Alone. Elena, he has no one to raise him, no family."

My lover swallowed furiously, now the one unable to speak.

"I must return to the future. I can no longer put my own happiness first." Elena had lost her entire family to a Moorish raid, so I prayed she understood how much a child needed a family.

Horror transformed her face, her body, her voice as reality forced itself on her, violating the future we'd planned together. I swayed, nearly overcome by the pain we both felt. In Elena pain always ignited anger and action, so I wasn't surprised when she suddenly grabbed my shoulders, fingers digging deep. "You leave me for a child?" she whispered.

I nodded weakly.

"How can I fight a child?" she roared.

"I don't—"

"What about us? How can you leave?" She shook me roughly.

"This is the hardest—"

"Do you *realize* what we have?" she cried. "Most people spend their whole lives without someone to share their soul with." Her angry voice dropped to a low growl. "That we are both women and still found each other shows all the more we are meant to be together."

My vision blurred as my eyes filled. "I know. God, I know. But, Elena, I've seen his smile. Anna and I made a commitment to him, and while I was able to deal with not being his parent when I thought Anna was, now I can't. I must go back."

"No!" She shook me again, but my resolve had become an army of thousands she couldn't fight. She was outnumbered. With a half cry, half sob, she released me, snatched up her cape and sword, and stomped out. She slammed the door so hard dust from the ceiling timbers fell like snow.

Numb, I blew out the lamps and lay down on the gritty bed, curling up into a tight ball. Damp cold crept into the drafty room, but I couldn't move to find a blanket. I couldn't sleep. I couldn't think. Months ago I'd struggled to believe I'd landed nine hundred years in the past. Now I could barely comprehend that I was leaving.

I must have slept, for when the opening door woke me a few hours later, the street below was quiet as Burgos slept. I felt more than saw a flickering candle enter the room, then heard a scabbard drop with a soft thud to the floor, followed by two boots. Elena placed the candle near the bed, then lay down beside me, throwing a blanket over us.

"Kate." She pulled my cramped body from its fetal position until we were face to face, chest to chest. I opened my eyes.

We hesitated only a second, then slid our arms around each other, clinging as the parting lovers we were, trembling, our words muffled against each other's necks. With daylight we would find the courage to do what must be done, but tonight we ripped ourselves wide open and pressed our exposed hearts so tightly together they beat as one.

Chapter Six

When I awoke, Elena's strong fingers were entwined in mine, and her eyes, dark with an emotion I couldn't name, bore into me. "I will take you to Santillana. All the way this time." Six months ago, with Nuño along, we had traveled from Zaragoza toward the northern fishing village of Santillana del Mar, where I'd intended to enter the Altamira cave, find the right ledge, and return to the twenty-first century. Two days before we were to arrive, Elena left me in Nuño's care, unable to drag out our parting. But when she left suddenly, I'd been so hurt and stunned I finally accepted the truth I'd fought for weeks—that I yearned to remain with her in the eleventh century and relinquish my life with Anna and Arturo.

"Doesn't your army march for Cordoba soon?"

She raised up on one elbow. "There is time if we leave right away. In three hard days we will be there. If the army leaves before I return, I will just catch up with them."

"You won't change your mind?"

"Will you?" She read the answer in my face and swallowed.

"What will we do without each other?" I whispered.

Elena kissed me. "You will have Arturo. And from what you have told me about the future, you will be very occupied just trying to survive." She hopped from the bed, a forced lightness to her voice. "And I shall have Enzo and Fadri to nag me endlessly all day. I shall kiss Matamoros when I miss you. And during the long winters José will sit by my fire and tell me the same stories until I will be forced to cut his throat."

"You will kiss a horse."

"Yes."

"Instead of me."

She pulled on her shirt. "If I close my eyes, there should be little difference."

I yelped and threw my pillow at her, but no more was said of what lay ahead of us. We spoke only of the journey and what we would need, not of the journey's end.

While Elena prepared the horses and food for travel, I headed for Alfonso's castle. Anna was already up, and a stout girl had just finished tucking my ex-lover's hair under a gauzy head scarf that reached below her shoulders. While I waited, Anna dismissed her servant then scooped up a small white dog with fine, floppy hair.

"Do you know much about the caves?" I asked. "Did Roberto know if the time between the centuries is fixed?" I waited while she stroked the fussy dog.

"He apparently went back and forth quite a few times. It's a fixed number of years. So if you've been gone for nine months, then you'll return nine months after you left." She nuzzled the dog's head. "How will you get to the cave? Won't you get lost?"

"Luis takes me."

Amazement arched her eyebrows. "He understands that you're leaving for good?" I nodded. "Does he know you're from the future?"

"Yes, he does."

"I have often wondered how someone from this century could understand...*if* they could understand."

I shrugged, then uncovered the fanny pack hidden under the shawl wrapped around my waist. "When I showed him this, it was pretty hard for him to grasp at first. But he trusts me. He believes me."

Anna stared at the pack. "Stay here, Kate. You'll miss everything. The Catholic Church will go through major reformations in a few years. King Alfonso will continue to gain a foothold in Moorish territory. In eight years, Rodrigo Díaz will capture the crown of Valencia and start the reconquest of Spain. How can you not want to be a witness to all that and more?"

"Just a witness? Yesterday you said you wanted to make things happen."

She waved a slender hand. "I didn't make much sense yesterday, probably from the shock of seeing you. One person can't alter history, so don't worry. But one person can watch and marvel. So can two people."

When I shook my head, Anna stepped back, an odd flicker of

satisfaction crossing her face. "Luis knows of the time travel, so he and I will share a secret."

My stomach flipped. "Stay away from Luis."

"Why does he take you to the cave so soon? Is he in a hurry to be rid of you?" She kissed the ridiculous little dog.

My nostrils flared. "Luis Navarro rides out to meet pain, challenging it, facing it directly. Neither of us intends to drag this out. Now I must go."

"Kate, please." She hurried across the room, useless dog now flopping in her arms. "Please don't leave in anger. We'll never see each other again. We've made different choices, and I can't stand that we'll be separated both by time and by angry words."

I nodded, then hugged her slight frame so tightly the dog squeaked. Anna stroked my back twice before I was able to pull away. "Enjoy your life with Arturo, Kate. I will watch over your husband."

I started to protest, but once I found the ledge in the Altamira cave at Santillana and sat down, what happened in 1086 would be, well, history. Taking care of Arturo would be much more important than wondering if Anna had flirted with Elena. I attempted a half-smile. "Once again lesbian ex-lovers go out of their way to remain friends."

She touched a cool hand to my cheek, then I left, heart surprisingly heavy with this first farewell.

❖

I knew Elena waited by the stables, but I had one more destination, one more farewell. Dashing past stubborn oxen teams, noisy vendors, and two stinking manure wagons, I left the city gates for the army's tent city. At first the men just stared as I walked among them. "Have you seen Nuño Súarez ? He is with Rodrigo Díaz." Rude grunts and the shaking of unkempt heads were the only responses. Oh, I wished Christian men would bathe, but at least roasting meat covered some of the stench. Two men, however, decided I was a camp woman advertising my wares and followed me. Christ, I was covered in fabric from my neck to my wrists and ankles. How could that be alluring?

"Hey, beautiful, don't walk so fast," one of them called.

"She teases us," the other said.

Just when I thought I might have to lift my skirt and pull my dagger from its sheath, Fadri appeared from behind a tent and cursed the two so harshly they left without another word. "You should not be here alone," he scolded as he jammed both thumbs under his sword belt.

"I need to talk to Nuño right away."

Within minutes Nuño swallowed me in one of his crushing bear hugs. Men in the eleventh century were not so reticent about displaying emotions as modern men.

"I miss you," I whispered.

"And I you. But why are you here? I thought you had a room in the city with Luis."

I looked pointedly at Fadri and the others, so Nuño waved them off. I explained my decision to leave, but instead of time travel I made up some other story that would take me away forever. "Before the army leaves for Cordoba, Luis takes me to Santillana."

"Not Santillana again."

"Nuño, Luis needs you. With me gone, she will have no one close, and I can't leave unless I know you will be there for her."

The large man frowned at his hands, then rubbed them together. "I'm so afraid I will give him away." Ever since he and I had rescued Elena from Gudesto Gonzalez, Nuño had made himself scarce for months, never once visiting us at Duañez.

I put my hands over his. "You won't, Nuño. I know it. Will you stop avoiding her?" He pulled back, scratched his beard, tugged on his curly bangs, then yanked on his ear lobes. "Decide before you stretch yourself all out of shape," I said.

He smiled, heaved a Nuño-sized sigh, then stood. "I will do as you ask."

I flung my arms around his neck. "Luis Navarro needs you." I paused, then whispered, "and so does Elena Navarro."

"Elena," he breathed, hearing Luis's real name for the first time. I trusted only one person with that information—the rough-edged but devoted Nuño Súarez. "Be safe, Kate," he murmured, and I decided I hated farewells.

❖

For the next three days, pain was a tall, menacing shadow that rode beside Elena and me, shared our simple meals, and rested on the bedroll between us. We talked about nothing and about everything. We held hands as we rode, our horses shoulder to shoulder. The farther north we traveled, the darker the sky, the fewer wildflowers in bloom.

I felt almost drugged, as if I had no control over my actions. I didn't dare think about what I was doing, but instead pushed forward, like a salmon instinctively swimming back to where it had hatched.

Just when I thought I should have come alone to spare Elena the same crushing ache consuming me, we reached Santillana del Mar, a tiny town on the northern coast. We stood on a cliff, inhaling the salty dampness as the surf crashed below us, a scattering of homes and shops clinging to the hillside sloping toward the pounding waves.

Elena asked the older residents if they knew of a cave with many paintings of bison on its ceiling. I vaguely remembered that Altamira was discovered in the late nineteenth century, but I just could not believe earlier residents didn't know it existed.

"Up that hill, past the broken tree, and you'll see it somewhere around there," said a wizened old man, teeth nearly gone but eyes clear and sharp from years of watching his watery horizon. People knew of the cave, but were remarkably casual, I suppose because they had no way of knowing its age.

After two more vague directions, Elena rolled her eyes at me and produced a shiny dirhem from Zaragoza, the modern equivalent of flashing a twenty-dollar bill. Two adolescent boys in heavy wool pants and frayed shirts, giggling and punching each other, agreed to show us the cave. "We also need torches," Elena said. The boys disappeared and soon returned with fish-oil-soaked rags wrapped around two sticks.

The smell of the burning torches clung to our clothes as we followed the boys. On any other day we would have stopped to eat and watch the waves, but we were both caught up in the powerful need to keep moving. The climb wasn't bad, and the trees sparse enough for our horses to pass.

The boys suddenly stopped before a clump of bushes, pushing the branches aside. "In here," one said.

"We never would have found this on our own," I muttered as we dismounted. Elena lit both torches then paid the boys. Faces flushed with their sudden wealth, the boys crashed away down the hill while I tied our horses to the nearest tree.

We exchanged as brave a look as we could muster, then entered the cool darkness of the Altamira cave. The ceiling nearly brushed my head, but there was enough room to stand, and the flaming torchlight danced over scratchy limestone walls.

"Look for a ledge, someplace easy to reach from this path. There might be natural light shining above it from an overhead crack." Our hollow voices and footsteps echoed ahead of us. Either the cave's dry air or my own dread had dried up my saliva. The path snaked into a curve, and we entered a room, about twenty feet by ten feet that smelled of silence and mystery.

Elena raised her torch. "Look."

Goosebumps raced across my arms at the sight above us. "Jesus," I whispered. Powerful bison thundered overhead, joined by thick horses and massive wild boars. Still brilliant after all these years, the ochre, red, and black leapt off the ceiling.

"How long ago?" Elena whispered.

"Thousands and thousands of years," I murmured, unsure of the paintings' actual origins. We stood silently, awed to imagine an artist standing right where we were, bringing his era to life with a paintbrush. Now *that* was something to do with your life, something more than baking bread or fighting wars.

"Kate." Elena's raw voice made me jump. She touched my arm and nodded off to the left. Up a short climb of five feet was a small alcove, lit by faint sunlight.

"Oh, my god," I whispered, my heart now pounding so fast I could barely breathe.

Without hesitation, Elena strode across the room, scrambled up the rocks, and sat down on the ledge, determination and fear struggling on her strong face.

Thrilled, I ran to join her. "Oh, Elena, would you really come with me?" I hadn't dared ask. What, after all, could an eleventh century soldier do in the twenty-first century?

"Let's see if time will have me," Elena said, squeezing my hand.

But my initial joy leaked away as I stood there. Two minutes passed. Then three. My torch burned out, leaving only Elena's, which sputtered. "How quickly did it happen to you?" she finally asked.

I grimaced. "Almost instantly."

Elena slumped over in a ball of despair. She'd come this far living on the hope that she could come with me into the twenty-first century, but time would not take her.

I touched her leg. "Time must put markers on people," I babbled. "Maybe you can't go forward unless you've already gone backward." Elena slid off the ledge. Light-headed, heart now lodged in my throat, I wrapped my arms around her firm body, running my hands over her leather tunic, through her thick hair. How could I leave this woman? I knew I had a good reason, but at that moment nothing was as important. Speaking was useless as we held each other, inhaling, touching, memorizing heartbeats. My eyes began to blur. Then Elena pulled back and reached into her tunic, drawing out a small black bag.

With trembling fingers I opened it and discovered a smooth, luminous pearl. Now I truly could not speak as she kissed my tears.

I swallowed a fierce lump of pain. "Find someone to grow old with," I said. She pressed her lips together but did not say out loud what I read in her troubled eyes, that she already *had* found someone, and now I was leaving. I wiped away one of her tears. "Forget me, Elena."

She captured my hand and kissed my palm, her breath liquid gold against my skin. "When I cease to breathe, then I will forget you." She tightened her grip. "No," she whispered, "not even then."

Laughing voices reached us from the entrance, which likely meant the boys had returned with friends to meet the rich strangers. "I have nothing for you," I choked out.

"The Lion King," she said, managing a sad grin. I scrabbled through my fanny pack and pulled out the plastic key chain, the code word we'd jokingly decided to use whenever we needed each other. I pressed it into her hands. "Please be careful at Cordoba, at Toledo, at Zaragoza, at Valencia. Wherever you fight."

Despair darkened her eyes as she nodded. "Of course. I have never lost a battle..." Her jaw tightened. "Until now."

The rowdy voices grew nearer. Our kiss was slow, gentle, and spoke all we had not yet said. Then, with a strangled moan, Elena grabbed my waist and hoisted me onto the ledge. I tucked the bag with the pearl into my boot and lay back, wincing at the hard rock.

"I love you," we said together, touching hands, then a bright light exploded above me.

I cried out as I started to spin. I thought I heard Elena's answering cry, but time roaring inside my head shut out all else. I shut my eyes against the blinding white and tried to stop my spinning fall, but there was no ledge beneath me, no rocks above. Time sucked me down, down, and the world went black.

❖

When I awoke my head throbbed with a monster migraine, and my stomach had twisted into a knot. I pressed the heels of my hands against my burning eyes, inhaling dry, almost antiseptic air.

"And this, gentlemen, is the main hall of the cave. These days only select scientists such as yourselves are allowed in here, as the carbon monoxide from our breath can damage the paintings." English, spoken with a thick French accent.

I broke out in a cold sweat, then tried to open my eyes, but they refused. The world wouldn't be real if I couldn't see it.

"Of course tourists can view an exact replica of this hall in Altamira II, located right down the street."

I rolled off the ledge, crying out as my hands and knees dug into rough limestone then gagged as bile rose up in my throat.

"Hey! Who are you? You can't be in here!"

Dry heaves shook my body, but I was empty, barren, unable to vomit away my nausea.

"I say, she seems to be ill." Clipped British voice approaching.

Tremors started coursing through me, violent, teeth-clenching convulsions, and I sank into the ground, my belly flat against the cold.

"Careful, Dr. Pritchard, she might have one of those African viruses. Ebola's fatal, you know." Thick Texas accent.

I was back. My tremors came not from illness, but from a deep, bone-aching knowledge. Over nine hundred years had passed in a matter of seconds. The woman I loved had died, been buried, and ground to dust by the centuries between us.

CHAPTER SEVEN

I couldn't see time, but my face recorded its passing with little crow's feet in the corners of my eyes. "Character lines," my best friend Laura called them. I couldn't smell time, but noticed its passing if I didn't clean out the refrigerator often enough. I couldn't hold time in my hands, yet it could still slip through my fingers. Some articulate person once said the only thing that never ended was the present, because time was a never-ending loop that kept us in its grasp, second after second, always keeping us in the present, I tried to forget there was a ledge in a cave in Spain where I had once slipped the bonds of the present.

Work helped. Today computers crashed, two shipments were late, one was lost, and I fired two packers for consistently screwing up in Order Fulfillment even after three warnings. I hated Mondays, but every moment spent focusing on work, or Arturo, was one less moment I was tempted to slip into impossible daydreams about a woman long dead. I didn't know how other people dealt with loss, but I didn't seem to be able to move forward. At least I'd finally gotten the promotion I'd been angling for—more headaches, more staff, but also more money for the college fund I'd started. Managing a small distribution center wasn't my first career choice, but painting wouldn't feed a kid or put him through college some day.

I raced down Washington Avenue then whipped onto Markland, imagining my Prius banking up on two wheels. I checked my watch. Damn, twenty minutes late. Arturo would be spitting nails by now, and since my cell had died, I couldn't even let him know I was almost there.

He stood by the curb, arms crossed, fiercely glaring at every car passing on Markland, daring each one to be me. He saw me, narrowed his eyes, then scooped up his black gym bag, every muscle accusing me of incompetence. I had to bite my lip to cut off my smile—no use pissing him off any more.

Arturo tossed his bag into the back, then folded his lanky body into the passenger seat and slammed the door. "I can't believe you're late. Today of *all* days."

"Seat belt."

Grumbling, he fastened the belt and I pulled into the street. "Don't worry," I said. "We'll get there in time."

"Mom, Master Kim *hates* it when people are late. It's disrespectful. The ceremony starts at five sharp." He crossed his arms again, practically huffing as he glared out his window to punish me.

I don't know why I found his furious indignation so cute today. Usually, this latest stage, that of a fourteen-year-old stubborn know-it-all, drove me crazy. I prayed he'd grow through it, just as he had all the others. Eight years. Amazing how many changes a boy could go through in eight years. At the stop sign I reached into the back seat and produced a flat, cardboard box, which I set on his lap. "Pepperoni, sausage, green olives, double cheese."

His brown eyes came alive. "God, I am starving." He hesitated, peeking at me through his lashes, then flung open the box to release the smell of spicy oils and cheese. The sure detour around my son's anger was through his stomach.

"Didn't you eat lunch?" I finally asked after two pieces disappeared in about thirty seconds. Some days my love for this rangy, bullheaded teenager squeezed the air from my lungs.

"Hamburger, and they only let me buy two extras. That's like giving Max three little kibbles for a meal." Our geriatric lab thought he was starving if he didn't get three *bowls* a day.

"You nervous?" I asked.

He shook his head. "I get two gold bars on my belt if I pull this off today."

"Don't talk with your mouth full," I said with a wink, then I ran my fingers through my unruly hair, which I had cut short eight years ago. I could not bear to have it brush my naked shoulders. I would turn around, expecting her to be there, but Elena never was, and never would be.

Without me asking, Arturo fished out a handful of fast-food

napkins from the glove compartment, lay them across my thigh, and gave me two squares of pizza.

"Got the promotion," I said.

"Cool, Mom." He raised his hand for me to slap. "Can we use the extra money to buy me a car?"

"No. College."

"A fifty-inch high def TV?"

"No. College."

"Hey," he finally said, his mouth full of pizza. "Let's use the money to send me to college."

We ate in happy silence. I entered the interstate and headed for the Kim Tae Kwon Do Institute, but I refused to speed with my impressionable son in the car, no matter how late we were. Driving while eating pizza was bad enough. I washed down my last bite with a swig of Squirt then concentrated on weaving through the rush hour traffic.

"Mom, you're doing it again." Arturo turned toward me, slender face concerned, voice surprisingly gentle.

"What?"

"Your necklace, Mom. You're playing with it again."

With a start, I dropped the round pearl, letting it fall back onto my breastbone. This was another phase he'd entered, a sudden burst of sensitivity. He bobbed his head, then made a face. "Every time you touch that pearl, you look so sad it brings everyone down. People are going to start jumping off bridges."

"Ha. Very funny."

"Well, it's true. Mark says your face goes all funny when you touch the pearl."

"Come on. You and your friends talk about this?"

He blushed, a lovely deep peach coloring his already ruddy cheeks. "Me and the guys have been talking about girls. You know, trying to figure them out."

"Good luck."

"No kidding, but one of the things we don't get is why you keep touching it even though it makes you sad. Ten minutes, Mom, and we're gonna be late."

I took the Vargly exit. Ever since the jeweler set the pearl and strung it on a 14k gold chain, the pearl had never left my throat. Whenever I touched it, aching waves from my past washed over me. The pain faded in fifteen minutes or so; after that I could usually force myself to move on. Now and then, however, I could not stop myself, and when the pain had subsided, I would touch the pearl again, and again, and again.

I had never told Arturo about Elena, and certainly not about the time travel. As we sped along the freeway, skyscrapers piercing the horizon, even I found time travel hard to believe. The pearl made it all real, as did the Moorish dagger Elena had given me.

After I brought Arturo home eight years ago and found a job and got Arturo settled in school and dealt with the shock and anger from Laura and my other friends who'd given me up for dead, I did some research to find out what King Alfonso and his army, which included Elena, had been up to. The history books were succinct: "The Christians and the Almoravides from Morocco met at Sagrajas during late spring of 1086. There, Alfonso VI, the conqueror of Toledo, was resoundingly defeated. Twenty thousand men died in the vicious battle."

History only recorded the deaths of significant political players, so I had no way to check, but since Elena Navarro always rode at the head of her army, she would have been in the middle of that violent mess.

When I pulled up to the low yellow brick building, Arturo heaved a sigh of relief and hopped out. He dashed into the building, purple nylon pants flapping in the breeze. When had his legs gotten so long?

By the time I parked and found a spot on one of the benches lining the room, Arturo had changed into his white *do-bok*. He already wore a black belt with his name stitched in yellow. Today, however, he was testing out for the next level of black, something few fourteen-year-olds reached. He padded over in bare feet, nearly bouncing with excitement. "It's about to start. C'mon, I'll introduce you to Vanessa."

"Vanessa?" A short brunette dressed like Arturo approached.

"The new girl on my soccer team. I told you about her, Mom. She's really nice."

I tried not to feel all panicky that my little boy seemed to be picking up girlfriends right and left. I shook the girl's hand and settled back onto my seat along the wall.

Vanessa and Arturo jogged to their spots in the formation. The lower belts were tested and awarded first, so I leaned against the wall as

Arturo and the others waited respectfully as the younger children went through their forms, complete with Korean commands.

It was fine that Arturo kept falling in love. I'd had a few dates myself the last eight years, so it's not like I was jealous or anything. But those first few years with Arturo had been too draining for much else, as I learned to be a mother, and he learned to be an American. Not only did he work hard to read, write, and speak English, but I taught him to read and write in Spanish as well, determined he wouldn't lose his native language.

This worked until he turned eight and decided Spanish was stupid and refused to speak it. For months we locked horns. I'd speak in Spanish, he'd reply in English. He'd ask a question in English, I'd reply in Spanish. His teachers grew very confused when they heard us together, thinking I was the immigrant.

Finally when he was nine, someone brought a book to school on bullfighting, complete with wonderfully explicit color photographs, but written in Spanish. When Arturo was able to read and translate all the gory details for the class, he became the hero of every other nine-year-old boy, and suddenly being bilingual was cool. We now slipped so easily between the two languages we could hold entire conversations and later be unable to say which language we'd used.

When Arturo finally moved to the open space before Master Kim and bowed, I snapped to attention. He was the picture of strength, control, and grace as he executed the memorized forms, complicated kicks that I hadn't learned in my short Tae Kwon Do experience. At Arturo's first Tae Kwon Do six years ago, I'd started out sitting on the benches to wait. But when he begged me to spar with him at home, I decided I needed to know what I was doing, so I worked my way up to a blue belt with red stripe before dropping out last year. Arturo had friends he could practice with now, so instead I spent my waiting time reading novels of chivalry from the Middle Ages. Arturo's friends thought it cool I was so into knights and swords.

I let out my breath when he finished his forms, then leaned forward as he shrugged on his padded vest for the sparring portion of his test. This was Arturo's favorite part because he loved the challenge of an opponent. A young man about Arturo's size donned a matching vest, then they went at it. Arturo wasted no time in faking a block, which so unbalanced his opponent the man failed to block Arturo's jumping front kick. My son's bare foot smacked squarely into the round red target over the man's padded solar plexus. Arturo scored point after point with his lightning speed and powerful kicks.

Arturo's face and neck shone with his efforts, but he didn't falter once. When Master Kim called the spar, and Arturo bowed to his opponent, applause erupted, unusual for a testing spar. I blinked back happy tears. After eight years, that knobby-kneed, frightened six-year-old I'd brought home to Chicago had grown into a bright, funny, athletic, and stubborn fourteen-year-old with a bottomless appetite.

Arturo stood solemnly as Master Kim spoke of devotion and hard work and respect, then wrapped a new black belt with two gold bars around Arturo's waist. My throat tightened as I stood and clapped. Arturo winked at me, and I didn't touch my necklace once.

When the ceremony ended, Arturo headed straight for me, even letting me pull him into a hug. "Gracias, Mama," he whispered, and I knew he thanked me for much more than chauffeuring him to Tae Kwon Do every week. I squeezed him hard, unable to speak. For every moment I missed Elena, I had two moments of joy with Arturo. Somehow my crazy life had reached a balance I could live with.

❖

"What's his problem?" Laura asked the next day, nodding toward Arturo, who'd ridden on ahead of us. "I thought he got the lead part in that new play." Next to Tae Kwon Do, acting was Arturo's favorite passion.

I reined in my chestnut mare, exhaling deeply, enjoying these once-a-month Sunday rides because they kept me comfortable in a saddle. "He did. But he hung out with friends yesterday afternoon and came home with this huge cloud hanging over his head. He won't tell me what happened." Impatient to follow Arturo on the lead horse, our horses plodded forward again. Laura's partner Deb had a weekend poetry workshop to teach, so it was just the three of us. "I also think he's desperate about sex," I added.

"I hate that. He's fourteen. It's only been a year since he stopped hiding behind your sofa and scaring us with his fart pillow."

"He's an adolescent. He's obsessed."

"I miss my little Turito." She shook her head, running a strong hand through her thick, cropped hair, my own son responsible for a few of the rich gray highlights. Laura and Deb had been there for me, as surrogate parents when I needed a break, as loving aunts and solid friends. They had helped me find a house and get back on my feet. For the first few weeks after my return Laura had blasted me pretty good, yelling and crying that she thought I was dead, but she finally forgave me. When anyone asked where Anna was I said I didn't know.

I shifted in my saddle. "I never thought I'd be this kind of mother, but I vacuumed his room last week and found a *Playboy* under his bed."

"No! A *Playboy*?" She looked straight ahead, voice low. "So, did you look at the pictures?"

"No, just read the articles." Sputtering with laughter, we nearly unseated ourselves. Wiping my eyes, I finally regained my composure.

"I wish you were paying as much attention to sex as Arturo is."

"Don't be stupid," I said.

"I'm serious, Kate. It's been eight years, but you haven't moved on, you haven't let go of Elena." While that first year I hadn't told Laura and Deb *where* or *how* I'd met Elena, I had to share my loss with someone because I'd suddenly start crying for no reason. A few times the words, "When I traveled nine centuries back in time," had stood poised on the tip of my tongue, ready to set my secret free, but when I'd look into Laura's square, concerned face, I couldn't. She would think I'd lost my mind. Time travel was fantasy, pure and simple.

Arturo had stopped, waiting for us. "I'm bored. Can we go home?"

Laura and I exchanged glances. "Arturo, what's the matter?"

He just pressed his lips together and shook his head. Damn. I hated the adolescent walls that had suddenly appeared these last few months. Some friends assured me the walls would come down as he matured, but others said that sometimes, with boys, the walls never came down. I didn't know if I could bear that.

"It's letdown," Laura offered to Arturo. "You've been pushing for that new black belt for months. Now that it's over, you're crashing."

Arturo shrugged, body caved in with defeat. I preferred an angry son to a melancholy one and knew just the trick. "Well," I said, reaching into the pack around my waist, sifting through granola bars and gum.

"I have some entertainment." I pulled out the sheathed dagger Elena had given me at the Aljafería, its Moorish beauty undiminished by nine hundred years.

"Mom, no," Arturo groaned.

"Okay, how about that dead oak tree over there? It's what—twenty feet away?" The three -foot-wide trunk would make a great target, so I unsheathed the small dagger, running my fingers over the design etched in the blade, pearls spilling from an oyster shell.

"Mom, weapons are so violent. Didn't you listen to anything Master Kim said?"

"That knot about six feet up looks like a good target." I pointed my horse in the right direction.

"One dollar says you miss," Laura said.

"Miss the knot?"

"No, miss the tree."

Arturo boiled in his saddle, furious he couldn't control my knife-throwing hobby. He'd pleaded with me to put up a privacy fence around our small backyard so the neighbors couldn't see. "Tae Kwon Do is all the weapon you need. You have more control and more power if you use your own body, your own strength."

I pinched the cool blade between my fingers and raised myself slightly out of the saddle. "You're right. Tae Kwon Do is a great tool. But what if you aren't close enough to your adversary to use it?"

"You close the gap and then use it," came his practiced reply.

"With this dagger, I can defend myself from twenty feet away." I took aim. The dagger spun furiously, arched perfectly, and crashed somewhere in the bushes next to the tree.

"You owe me a buck," Laura cried, booming laugh echoing through the trees.

Grumbling, I slid off my horse and searched through the brambles, surprised at my rising panic. "Where did it land? Over here?" I ignored the sharp thorns tearing at my sleeves. "Where is it?"

"Mom, calm down." Arturo reached my side, eyes wide at my hysteria. "We'll find it." We kicked aside rustling dead leaves, threw aside fallen branches as I grew more frantic.

"I can't lose that dagger. I can't."

Arturo scooped something out of the leaves. "Here it is, Mom. I found it." Furious at my trembling, I accepted the dagger gratefully and brushed it off on my jeans. "Mom, you're gonna scalp some poor squirrel with that thing some day and the SPCA's gonna get you."

I smiled weakly, appreciating his efforts to distract me, then reached through his 'wall' for a quick hug. When I let him go, I caught Laura's glare over his head. She was right. It was time to let go of Elena. Arturo needed a mom fully engaged in the world, not one who clung desperately to the only two reminders she had of a lost love—a necklace and a Moorish dagger.

❖

Our Duañez hearth was still crowded with laughing men and women even though we'd eaten hours ago and the ale was nearly gone. As I shared a private laugh with Marta over her husband's latest dysfunction, I felt Elena's gaze, looked across the room, and nearly dropped my mug. A flush spread through me, warming my ankles, my thighs, my belly, even the insides of my wrists, to feel such naked desire directed right at me. Others saw Luis ogling his wife, so one by one, chuckling, with amorous ideas of their own, the couples left until we were alone.

She moved slowly, shooting me that hungry look the whole time, straightening the shelves, adjusting a chair, sweeping crumbs from the table, so by the time she approached I could scarcely breathe. "We should go to bed," I murmured.

"No time," she whispered hoarsely. "We would never make it." Within seconds my clothing was heaped off to one side, and Elena laid me back on the sheepskin before the hearth. I gasped at the silky softness of the brushed fleece caressing the backs of my knees, my thighs, the small of my back.

The honey pot still sat warming by the fire. Elena pulled it closer and removed the lid. "What are you doing?" I asked. "Elena? Oh, my god."

My eyes flew open. Teak bedroom set. Copy of El Greco's painting of Toledo. Photos of Arturo. I was still here. In the present. With a groan, I rubbed my eyes. No wonder I'd not found anyone else—Elena kept reaching for me from the past.

I stared at the El Greco. Turbulent ebony-blue clouds roiled over the walled city, darker art than I usually preferred, but something about the print had reached out to me. I assumed it was because it represented the turbulence of Spain. I relaxed my focus, almost crossing my eyes, and saw another possible explanation. The valleys around Toledo came together in a dark, mysterious Y, and the hills were rounded thighs pressed together.

I shook my head, so lonely I could eroticize anything, then checked the clock. Eleven p.m. I must have fallen asleep the instant I lay down; my bed light still burned, and the unopened book still lay across my chest. I picked up the slim red volume, wishing I was reading an easy mystery or some other mind candy, but for my Advanced Latin class in Medieval Texts, I was reading *Poema de Mio Cid* in Latin, *Poem of My Lord*. Written about one hundred years after Rodrigo's death, the poem was so historically inaccurate we studied it as literature, not as history. I'd finished the first section, "Poem of the Exile," and was ready to move on to "Poem of the Marriage."

But when I opened the book, I cried out and sat up. I recognized nothing. "What the—?" Arabic letters danced across the pages, lovely, but not a written language I knew. I checked the cover, also in Arabic. I searched my bedside table, but found no *Poema*, so I marched down to Arturo's room. Light shone under his door, and I was almost too angry to knock, but I did.

"Where is it?"

My brooding son looked up from his Stephen King novel. "What are you talking about?"

I waved the slender book at him. "You took *Poema de Mio Cid* and replaced it with some Arabic thing I can't read. Very funny."

"Mom, have you been drinking?" He rubbed his tousled hair.

"Of course not." I stood over his bed, hands on my hips. "No more jokes. Where is it?"

He frowned, shadows from his reading lamp flickering over his pale face. "I have *no* idea what you're talking about. Honest."

I was about to erupt, then remembered Arturo took the Tae Kwon Do principle of honesty very seriously. "You don't know anything about this?"

He shook his head, stifling a yawn.

"Turn out your light," I scolded, but kissed him on his forehead.

"Mom, I'm too old to kiss."

"Hush." Back in my own room I examined the book more closely. Inside the back cover was an old manila pocket for the library's checkout card, the system before computers. Yesterday I'd stuck a grocery list in an identical pocket of the *Poema*. Sure enough, I pulled the list from the pocket of the Arabic text.

"Very weird." The woven cover was torn in two places, same as the *Poema*. I checked my watch. Probably too late, but I called Yassir from my art class anyway.

"I never sleep before midnight," came the thick, Arabic accent. "What do you need, O Talented One?"

"If I sent you a photo of some Arabic writing right now, could you translate it and call me back?"

"I live to serve. Must it be an accurate translation, or might I have some fun?"

"Cute. Call me when you have something." I hung up and snapped a few photos with my phone, then zipped them off to Yassir.

It didn't take him long.

"Very odd, what you've sent me. The title is *Islam's Crown of Valencia*. Is this a novel?" Yassir asked.

"I don't know."

"This material is not history, but fiction. It speaks of a young calif named al-Rashid who took permanent control of Valencia in 1094, and how the worldwide Muslim domination of the world began at that moment."

"That never happened. Rodrigo Díaz captured Valencia in 1094."

"Precisely."

I thanked Yassir and returned to bed. Maybe it would make sense in the morning, but right now, exhausted and lonely, I didn't know what to think, so I pulled the covers up to my chin and finished my dream.

CHAPTER EIGHT

Tuesday morning Arturo still glowered over his Cheerios.
"Honey, what's wrong?"
"Nothing."
I sat down beside him, touching his arm. "Who am I?"
"The amnesia's back, huh?"
I growled softly. "I'm your mother."
"Nice to meet you." His scowl faded as he chuckled at his own
wit.
"As your mother, don't you think I've learned to recognize when
something is really upsetting you?" He had shared everything in his life
with me, but the stubbornness and silence had set in when he turned
thirteen.
He studied his empty bowl. "I suppose."
"Something's been upsetting you since Saturday afternoon when
you were over at Mark's, and I want to know what it is."
"Can Vanessa and I go on a date by ourselves to the spring dance?"
"We've discussed this. No dates until you're fifteen."
"That's barbaric, Mom. Medieval."
"I know. I want to keep you a child as long as I can." Nothing like
the direct approach. "Why don't you want to go with the others?"
He looked up, opened his mouth, then shut it with relief as the
rumbling school bus headed down our block. "Gotta go." He grabbed
his pack and was gone.
Frustrated, I put the dishes away and headed for work. But between
Arturo and my strange Arabic book, I couldn't concentrate. Both my
assistants could handle emergencies, so at noon I pleaded a headache
and took the afternoon off, feeling just a touch guilty.
I headed for the university and the part of the library where I'd
prowled the stacks during my medieval history classes, then climbed
the last flight of stairs and found my favorite section. The first few

years after I'd left Elena, I'd been a walking wounded, but taking those classes, sitting on the library floor soaking up details about the tenth through the twelfth centuries somehow reassured me I hadn't dreamt it all. Rodrigo Díaz, King Alfonso, al-Mu'tamin, and al-Musta'in had all been real. Even though I never found any mention of Luis or Elena Navarro, reading about the others made her feel real as well.

I grabbed an armful of Spanish history texts and settled into a quiet alcove. None of the indexes listed the *Poema de Mio Cid*, yet I had seen it listed before. King Alfonso VI was barely mentioned. The largest book had something under *The Great Caliph of Valencia*, but that section was in Arabic. I skimmed through the whole book, confused to find random paragraphs and whole pages in the cursive, flowing Arabic, others in English. After struggling through books for a few hours, my head hurt and I looked at my watch, thinking Professor Kalleberg, my patient history teacher, might still be in his office. I replaced the books, then hurried across campus, grateful for the green foliage brightening the campus. I waited outside Kalleberg's open office door while he talked with a student; then after the student left, I knocked on the door jam.

"Kate Vincent! My eleventh century fanatic. Come in!" Professor Kalleberg, a towering man with bony knuckles and long arms, clasped my hand and led me to a chair. He seemed tired, as if weighed down by too much history, too many details. The deep creases in his pale cheeks had always reminded me of Lincoln, but now they were deeper than ever.

I explained about the strange Arabic book and the texts in the library. Face grim, Professor Kalleberg rose and shut his door, then collapsed in his chair, swiveling nervously. "You're not the first to notice. The academic community is in an uproar because this is happening everywhere, to everything. Someone, or some group, is messing with thousands of books, literally changing history." He pulled two books off a cluttered, dusty shelf behind him. "Look, the history of Ireland is half in English, half in Arabic. The facts before 1100 are all correct, but after that, the facts have been altered." He flipped open the other book. "Instead of the Crusades, when Christian knights fought to spread Christianity into Muslim lands and take Jerusalem, this ancient text, written about 1105, speaks of a great battle in what is today Germany that the Muslims won. It's almost as if we're reading an *alternate* history, one in which Islam predominates, not Christianity."

Suspicion flowered in the pit of my belly.

No. Impossible.

But within minutes that suspicion made a speedy transition from tiny seed, to struggling stalk, to a tree heavy with certainty. "How could that be?" I asked.

"No one knows. Some suspect a radical Islamic group, trying to inflate the glory of Islam, but it makes no sense. Why mess with our books? And how *can* they?" He stopped, then leaned forward, knuckles white as he squeezed lean fingers together. "Kate, they have access to everything. In my files I have photocopies of medieval texts. Some of those texts are now in Arabic. I can't even *read* them. Salaam al-Houlaki and the rest of the Arabic Department are going mad from all the translation requests."

"Why hasn't the press picked up on this?"

He smoothed back his pale, thinning hair. "It's too crazy. What are they going to say, that someone is magically changing thousands of texts all over the world? It's impossible." He spread his hands toward the texts he'd shown me. "But it's happening."

I let my head drop forward. Even as I'd admonished Anna years ago not to mess with history, I hadn't actually believed one person could make that much difference. But she'd done something. I reached into my memory for the day Anna had argued with Carlos at the Aljafería, the day before I fell back in time almost nine years ago. She'd insisted Spain would have been a greater country if the Moors had not been driven out but had remained in power. What if that had been her purpose all along in going back in time—to do something, anything, that would tip the balance of power toward the Moors? But what could one woman do? What did *she* do?

Professor Kalleberg reached for another book. "And look at this map drawn about 1250. Clearly Arabic rulers control most of Africa, most of Europe, and half of Asia. In reality, they should only be in North Africa, the Middle East, around the Mediterranean to Turkey, and over here in Spain. In fact, by 1250 the Spanish Christians had taken back most of Andalusia, leaving only Granada for the Moors."

I sat on my hands so the agitated professor wouldn't notice their trembling. The past unfolded before me—Anna had come back in time and taken up with King Alfonso, making me think she was on his side, on *history's* side. She'd even reassured me she had no intention of changing history, but only wanted to watch it unfold. Yeah, right. I suddenly understood her look of satisfaction eight years ago when I'd insisted on returning to the future. She didn't want me to hang around and get in her way.

Professor Kalleberg and I sat in silence, each caught in our own web of horror. At one point I looked up, considered the professor's lean face, kind gray eyes, and opened my mouth. I shut it again. What on earth could I say? That time travel is possible and my ex-lover is back in the eleventh century messing around with history?

"So," I finally croaked out. "What are people doing about this?"

His sagging shoulders drew my own down. "Watching, Kate, just watching. The nightmare has started to affect late twelfth century texts. We can't fight an enemy we can't see."

I cursed my cowardice. All I had to do was explain the whole thing. He knew me to be a serious student. He'd believe me. What would Arturo think if he knew I was such a coward? What would Elena think?

I buried my face in my hands, breathing deeply. The fear gripping my chest was worse than the terror I felt the night I had come out to my parents. But like then, I knew if I could just get the first word out, the rest would follow. He had to believe me.

I opened my mouth again. "Professor, I don't understand how this is happening, but I have an idea. It's going to sound, well, crazy."

His eyes widened behind his small wire frames, his expression endearingly hopeful. "Any ideas you have would help. Tomorrow about one hundred academics are holding an Internet roundtable as we try to work this mess out. I have no light to shed on this nightmare."

"You say the original texts you've looked at all change around the end of the eleventh century?"

"More or less."

"And you're seeing an expansion of Muslim influence."

"Far-reaching. It's a fantasy, yet it's not."

"Professor, remember that reading you assigned, the one about how Spain might have been better off if the Moors hadn't been driven from Spain?"

He nodded, rubbing his chin. "Historians no longer make those subjective value judgments, but I wanted the class to see how earlier historians thought."

I inhaled deeply, then let my breath out in a slow, shuddering exhale. "I believe someone has gone back in time to change history, to make sure the Moors dominate Spain."

He blinked once. "Gone back in time."

"Yes, I've done it myself. There's a cave outside Zaragoza, Spain, that throws you back over nine hundred years. The Altamira cave at Santillana del Mar brings you forward the same amount of years." Strangely calm now, I barreled forward, explaining what had happened to me, amazed at the giddy relief washing through me. Now I wasn't the only one who knew.

He stopped swiveling in his chair, his face frozen in a mask I couldn't read. Confusion? Concern? Disbelief?

I rushed on, explaining about Anna and her obsession. "I don't know what she's done, but it must have worked. I think something she did is actually changing history, and it's showing up in all the original texts. She brought back a shitload of money with which to influence people, and Viagra, and god knows what else. It's been eight years, Professor. I never would have believed it, but maybe one person can do more damage than I thought."

A subtle redness started at the base of his throat and worked its way up his neck and onto his face. After I told him about Arturo and why I had returned to the present, I finally ran out of words. We sat in silence for a few minutes.

His hand trembled as he reached for his water bottle, gulped the last of the water, and tossed the plastic bottle into the trash can beside me with a hollow thump. "Ms. Vincent." His tremulous voice started a roaring in my ears. "I have *never* been so insulted, so enraged, as I am at this very moment." I clutched at my necklace as he struggled for control. "I am discussing the most devious, most serious challenge the academic world has ever faced, and you have the gall, the insensitivity, the *presumption* to entertain me with some fantastical story." He rose, leaning forward on rigid fingers splayed across his desk. "Time travel is not possible. It has never been possible. It will never *be* possible. This is not some *Star Wars* episode."

"*Star Trek,*" I said. "*Star Wars* doesn't deal with time travel." Oh, shut up, Kate. Could I possibly make this any worse? I stood, palms pressing against my belly in some frantic attempt to protect myself. "Professor, I—"

"It's time for you to leave."

"But it really—"

"Now!" he thundered. I hesitated, stiff with frustration and my own fury. How could I make him believe? The truth squeezed my throat tight. I couldn't. It was just too unbelievable. Without another word, I left, slamming the door behind me so hard the door's aged, frosted glass nearly popped from its frame.

❖

For the next few days I carried my slim red book with me, pulling it from my briefcase, obsessively checking every hour, but it remained an Arabic book. I don't know what I expected. Sci-fi shows rattled on about temporal fluxes; maybe I hoped things would pop back into place and the problem would go away. My days became almost surreal, as if I were living inside a fantasy novel. I would stare at the red book, finger its thin pages, and know it was real. But how or why it had switched over from a Latin text to an Arabic one was unreal. Things like this just did *not* happen.

Every time I replayed the scene with Professor Kalleberg, my chest ached and my head began to pound. What a stupid thing I'd done.

Arturo looked like I felt. Finally Friday morning before school I sat him down. "You aren't leaving this house until you tell me what's wrong."

"You first."

"What?"

He snorted, then grabbed both my hands. "You've been biting your nails."

"Very observant."

He shrugged. "You raised me to be an observant, sensitive guy. That's why the girls are crazy about me."

"Too bad I forgot about humility and modesty." I chewed the inside of my cheek, then played with the toast crumbs on my plate. "Okay. It's complicated, but I'm having trouble with the texts from my Latin class. That's all. Now you."

He shook his head. "Mom, if I moped around like that every time school was hard I'd never get up in the morning."

"It's more complicated than that. C'mon, your turn."

Arturo clutched the thick brown bangs that fell into his eyes and probably drove the girls mad. "Sometimes I wish I lived a hundred years ago. Life was simpler. I shouldn't have to deal with this crap." I waited. "First, I think I know what I have to do. So don't go all parental on me, okay?" I nodded. "Last weekend the guys made a plan for the spring dance tonight. I said it was stupid but they wouldn't listen, and I couldn't talk them out of it. They're going to spike the girls' sodas with vodka, get them too drunk to care, and then—"

"I get the picture," I said, my jaw tight. "I thought your friends were better people than that." Christ, what a world. Thank god Arturo hated the idea of altering his mind with drugs or alcohol. He even harassed me about my caffeine habit.

"Me too. I've been worrying all week about what to do. I didn't want to squeal and have my friends hate me, but I can't let them do it. I keep thinking about what you've hammered into my head since I was six, all that stuff about taking responsibility, about getting involved when it's really important."

"I said that?"

"Yeah. You said that if my actions could help someone, I should do what's necessary, even if it's not easy or popular."

My heart swelled. I had no idea he'd been listening. I jumped as he slammed his palms against the table. "So, I've decided. I'm going to call Vanessa right now. Tell her about tonight. She'll tell the others not to drink anything. And if the guys find out and hate me, I'll just have to live with that."

"Good plan," I said softly.

Suddenly energized by his decision, Arturo whipped out his cell phone, dialed, then left the kitchen. After I cleaned up, I dug out my fanny pack from the back of my underwear drawer. The items in the pack were all modern, but for some reason they felt so connected to the past, the *distant* past, that I couldn't bear to have them visible. I'd somehow lost the photo of Arturo in Burgos eight years ago, but otherwise, everything was just as it'd been the day I'd fallen back in time.

I slowly unzipped the pack, smiling. That night in 1085 when I'd finally told Elena Navarro the truth about me, she had sat on the ground by the fire, slowly zipping and unzipping this very pack, fascinated by the magic of the 'teeth.' I stroked the black leather, marveling that

Elena had once touched this pack.

I heard Arturo laughing on the phone. He had thought about the problem, come up with a solution, and taken action. I seemed to be stuck in the first phase. Telling Kalleberg had gotten me nowhere. What else could I do? Even if I were to leave Arturo and go back in time, how could I possibly figure out what Anna had done *and* undo it?

❖

Four days later I was in my bedroom on the phone with Laura when Arturo barged in, gnawing on a bagel. "Some guy's downstairs. Says he needs to talk to you. Won't tell me what it's about." With a quick good-bye to Laura, I followed Arturo downstairs.

The last person I expected to see standing in my entryway was Professor Kalleberg, his hands gripped together. We said nothing, so Arturo looked from the professor's face to mine, then back to Kalleberg, ghostly pale under a few days' stubble.

The professor's eyes were bloodshot. "Kate, we must talk."

"Arturo, let Max in, then please go upstairs and close your door. Professor Kalleberg and I need to speak privately."

"What's so secret? I'm old enough to understand stuff."

"Go. Professor, would you like some tea?" With a nod, he followed me into the kitchen, where I made two cups of tea, my insides churning. Once we moved into the living room, the loose-limbed Kalleberg perched himself on the edge of the sofa. The first time I'd seen the professor walk across campus, I'd worried the poor man's joints would come unhinged from such violent swinging and that his arms and legs would go flying. The professor cleared his throat. "First, I must apologize for my outburst in my office. You—"

I held up my hand. "It was a perfectly normal response. What I told you was probably the strangest thing you'd ever heard."

He blew out a long breath. "True, none of my other students have told me they traveled nine hundred years back in time." He gazed into his tea. "The web conference on Friday solved nothing, produced no reasonable explanation for this mess. We did compare notes and determined that anything written after 1200 has been altered, drastically, almost as if history fractured. The Arabic language shows up almost everywhere, and Islam is the dominant religion."

Suddenly exhausted, I wanted to curl up into a ball. I didn't want to understand. I didn't want to have anything to do with any of this.

"After I eliminate all the possible explanations I have no choice but to consider the impossible." Our eyes met. "You told me you fell back in time to Moorish Spain. You told me your partner Anna—"

"Ex-partner."

"Ex-partner Anna followed you back, determined to bring Spain greater glory by keeping the Moors in power. What you told me is impossible, yet it's all I have."

My heart fluttered so irregularly I pressed one palm against my chest. "You believe me."

"My brain does. The rest of me will follow eventually. Tell me more about your experience. Did you get close to anyone? Is Anna the only other person who knows about this cave?"

Max scratched at the back door, still outside. "Excuse me, professor." I raised my voice. "Arturo, you forgot to let Max in." I settled back in my chair, facing Kalleberg. I told him about the two other travelers from our century. Grimaldi was a pilgrim who'd turned out to be Walter Williams from Arizona, and who'd been injured trying to help me. The other traveler was Roberto, the janitor from the orphanage who'd issued that ominous "No go cave" warning. Also, Anna said that Carlos Sanchez, the tour guide from the Aljafería, the Moorish palace in Zaragoza, knew about the cave, but I didn't know if he'd ever used it.

"So this Roberto or Carlos could have gone back in time as well. They or Grimaldi could have affected the timeline."

I shrugged, but none of them had seemed as interested in politics as Anna.

"Anyone else?"

I touched the pearl, once again around my neck, then took a deep breath. "The first few months, in 1085, I really struggled to get back to the future, sort of like Dorothy trying to get home to Kansas. I was locked in a harem, kidnapped twice, almost raped twice, tortured, nearly murdered three times." I smiled weakly. "I was pretty clueless. The only reason I'm still alive was Luis Navarro, El Cid's First Lieutenant. He rescued me more times than I could count and kept me sane. I did some stupid things and got into trouble. He had his own difficulties, and suddenly marriage was the only way out for both of us."

I stopped, examining my hands, remembering the feel of Elena's muscles, her scars, her smooth breasts. "I soon discovered Luis was really Elena Navarro, a woman who'd disguised herself as a man to avenge her family, killed by Moors."

"Yet she lived in Moorish Zaragoza?"

"Long story. As I struggled to get back I began to see how incompatible Anna and I really were, and I doubted my ability to be a good parent to Arturo. I didn't mean to, but...but within two months I'd fallen in love with Elena." Kalleberg's face softened. He put down his tea. "Once I realized Anna would make the best parent, I decided to remain in the past with Elena. After I helped Elena recover from some pretty nasty mind games Gudesto Gonzalez played on her, we had seven months together. But then..." The end of the story didn't come easily so I stopped.

"Then you found out Anna had come back into the past."

I wiped my mouth, relieved to be finally telling someone my story. "I couldn't let go of the image of Arturo, abandoned now by both his prospective parents. I had to come back." My throat tightened. "Elena brought me to the Altamira cave at Santillana and gave me this pearl. We said good-bye." I stopped, since saying these things out loud brought back her cocky grin, the feel of her arching against me, the sound of her voice.

Kalleberg nodded, his oval-lidded eyes kind. "Kate, I have a theory that's pure conjecture at this point. May I explain? If Anna was able to bring about a major change in events, it could have affected everything that happened from that point forward."

I shifted in my chair. I blinked twice. Outside Ford Expeditions and Subaru Outbacks zoomed by. Email and voices flew over phone lines. Astronauts worked overhead in the International Space Station. How, in the middle of all this reality, could the professor and I be discussing fluctuations in the past as if they were as real as Shea Stadium or billboards or Lake Michigan?

"Everything is changing." The professor stood and began pacing. "Some material is just switching from Latin to Arabic, or being altered slightly. Other documents are totally disappearing." He waved his hands as his agitation increased. "The changes are moving forward. A colleague just called this morning. She found altered material from the early thirteenth century. Kate, it's coming *toward* us."

I shook my head. "I don't understand."

He pulled up the ottoman and sat down, reaching for me. Both our hands were cold and clammy. "If time travel is possible, if Anna changed history, those changes have begot other changes. References to events, to cities, to people, are disappearing because, under the new timeline, those events, those cities, those people no longer *exist*."

I shut my eyes. Why couldn't I just fall asleep right here, right now? When I woke up, the professor would be gone and life would be normal again.

Kalleberg worried his upper lip, then sighed. "Think of it as a wave moving through history, disrupting and rearranging the world as it advances year by year."

"What does it mean?"

He asked for a piece of paper. When I found one buried under the magazines on the coffee table, he drew a family tree, going back ten generations to the marriage of one couple. "Let's say your ancestors here are Clara and Hans. We are each a product of unions that extend back for centuries, even if we don't know everyone's names. Every child had parents who came from parents, who came from parents. If the changes moving through history affect Clara's ancestors, she might never be born. And if she's never born..." He scratched out the entire family tree, including me.

An odd coldness settled in my neck and shoulders. "Jesus," I said.

"You must go back."

"What?"

"You must go back and undo whatever Anna has done."

I leapt to my feet. "Don't be crazy. She's had eight years to mess things up. One person can't undo that. And besides, I'm not leaving Arturo again...ever."

He led me to the sofa. "I stayed up all last night with Salaam, translating documents from medieval Spain. We narrowed it down to one major event in Spain's history that never happened, but should have."

I lay back against the couch but could not speak, so I draped an arm over my eyes.

"In 1094 Rodrigo Díaz, El Cid, lays siege to Valencia and captures it in order to rub his growing power in King Alfonso's face. History distorts this, turning it into hero worship, crediting El Cid with beginning the four-hundred-year drive to expel the Moors." He touched my knee and I opened my eyes. "In the fractured history, El Cid does not capture Valencia. He does begin a siege, but then just goes away, and a young caliph named al-Rashid, still a teenager, suddenly shoots to power and captures the crown of Valencia. From there, he unites all the Moorish taifas and Islam quickly overwhelms Spain, then all of Europe, and eventually Asia as well."

I moaned softly. "And you think I can just waltz back nine centuries and put El Cid on the throne instead of al-Rashid."

He winced. "I know. Sounds crazy. But what else do we have? We certainly don't have time on our side, no pun intended. But here's what we do know: in the correct timeline, eight years after you left the past, Rodrigo marched into Valencia on June 15, 1094. This event must take place. So if you returned to the Mirabueno cave and sat back down on that ledge, where in time would you appear? I'm guessing, from what you've said, that time in either century moves at the same pace, like two movies playing at the same time. You left your life in the past in 1086, eight years ago. So if you traveled back to the eleventh century next week, you'd find yourself somewhere in mid-May, 1094. That would give you lots of time, almost a month, in which to fix this problem."

"Less than four weeks? Are you insane?" Confusion and loneliness and responsibility and pain boiled over. I stood again. "You think it's such a great idea? *You* go back. I—"

"You're the best person to do this. You know your way around the eleventh century—"

"Right. That's why I nearly died so many times."

"You have connections you can use. And one person is best because if too many people go back, they could really mess things up. We need—"

"Professor Kalleberg, Arturo is my son. I'm not leaving him again. Nothing is more important to me. I think it's time *you* leave." I stomped to the front door, waiting, until he had no choice but to follow me.

"You could see Elena again. She—"

"She could be dead. She could be with someone else. I made the right choice to raise Arturo, and I'm making the right choice to stay here."

We glared at each other. "Kate, I *believe* you now about the time travel. Why won't you believe me when I tell you how important this is?" Kalleberg towered over me, impossibly tall, but I would not be intimidated.

I opened the front door, but he stopped at the threshold. "When that wave gets closer, I don't know what will happen. You, me, Arturo—we could all blink out of existence, just like the books are doing. We won't exist in the new timeline."

I grabbed his elbow and steered him through the doorway, closing and locking the door behind him. As I leaned against the door, Max barked out back. "Arturo?" No reply. Sick with confusion, I stormed through the house and let Max in. Then I returned to the living room and watched the professor drive away. What was I supposed to do? If I returned to the past, I could get killed, leaving Arturo an orphan once again. I clenched my jaw.

Behind me Max woofed happily. I turned and my heart leapt into my throat. Max's head and shoulders were behind the sofa, his back-end squirming with pleasure. "No!" I grabbed the sofa's base and yanked it away from the wall. Arturo lay pressed against the wall, stiff and cramped.

"Oh my god," I whispered. "How much did you—?" I stopped at the wild mix of horror and confusion racing across my son's face.

Pale, his upper lip beaded with sudden perspiration, Arturo staggered to his feet. "Everything, Mom. I heard everything."

CHAPTER NINE

I waited outside the closed door until the dry retching stopped, resisting the urge to burst in and hold a cool hand to Arturo's hot forehead, much as I'd done when he was young. But instead I paced, my arms squeezing my ribcage like a vise. Finally, only silence reached my ear when I pressed it against the door.

"Honey? Arturo, may I come in?"

"No."

I leaned against the wall, my muscles limp with exhaustion with the intense horror that must be gripping Arturo. "I suppose you think your mother's crazy," I said to the oak door as I sank to the floor. No answer. "I know what you heard is too bizarre to believe. That's why I never told you. It really did happen, but if that idea upsets you too much, let's just pretend—"

"Mom." I jumped as Arturo yanked the door open. He came out into the narrow hallway wiping his face with a towel. Leaning against the opposite wall, he joined me on the pale green carpeting. He cleared his throat. "Let's don't pretend, Mom."

"But—"

"You've never been the kind of mom that makes up stupid stories to hide the truth, like Mark's parents did when his dad ran over Boomer, or Cheri's parents did when her mom was sleeping with the volleyball coach."

My eyes widened. "You knew about that?"

Arturo rolled his eyes. "God, Mom, we're fourteen, not stupid." He rubbed his face again, brown eyes dark with emotion, then reached out with his boot to touch my own sneaker. "I believe you, Mom."

Something broke loose from the wall of my chest and thudded into the pit of my belly. I clutched at my knees, half-relieved, half-horrified even to be having this conversation. We stared across the dim hallway at one another. "Thank you," I said softly.

"It's just that—" Arturo's Adam's apple began bobbing up and down furiously as he struggled with what I thought was fear.

"Honey, please don't worry. I'm not going back there. I'm staying—"

He held up his sturdy hand, shaking his head. "That's not it," he whispered, squeezing his eyes shut.

"What's wrong then?"

"You—you left her, for *me*." Sudden anguish twisted his mouth and he wiped his nose on a sleeve. "You've been lonely all these years because of *me*." He slammed his head back against the wall, rigid with fury. "I thought there was something wrong with you because you didn't have anyone. Damn it, I feel so *stupid*. You had someone and you gave her up." He stopped, unable to speak, frowning in fierce concentration as he struggled for control.

I knelt on the carpet and took Arturo's face in my hands, forcing him to look at me. "I do miss Elena, every day. I won't deny that. But every time I get up in the morning, I'm so happy because I have *you*. I don't regret for one instant my choice to be your parent. Do you understand?"

"All these years I've been happy, and you've been miserable."

I shook him gently. "Stop that. I haven't been miserable. Being your mother is the most incredible thing that's ever happened to me... *ever*."

He blinked, his lashes stuck together with unshed tears. "More incredible than time travel?" He touched my necklace, rolling the pearl between his fingers.

I nodded. "More incredible than time travel." I kissed both his cheeks.

"Aww, Mom." His complaint lacked his usual disgust, and his whole face relaxed, warming me completely. We rested in silence for a minute, then he squeezed my hand, rose, and pulled us both to our feet. I threw my arm around his shoulder, and we returned to the living room, where we collapsed on the sofa, and Max rested his head on Arturo's knee. "You have to go back," Arturo said.

"Don't *you* start."

The afternoon sun filtered across our laps, a blanket of warmth. "What was Elena like?" he asked suddenly. "Do you think I'd like her?"

I smiled. "She taught me to throw a dagger, so I'm not sure how she would have felt about Tae Kwon Do." I lay my head back against the sofa, marveling at the lightness lifting my spirits. To talk about Elena was to acknowledge her, honor her, celebrate her. "She made me laugh. She was brave and fair and devoted. She loved to lead men into battle. She thought I was a terrible cook."

"You are. But when we go back, I can cook for her. I make a mean burger."

"When we go back?" I ran my hands over the nubby sofa, too exhausted to move it back against the wall.

"Yeah. We'll ride horses, and I can hunt and maybe I can teach Elena some Tae Kwon Do. We can find this El Cid guy and—"

"We?"

"We'll make him take Valencia, and maybe we'll even bump off this Rashid guy to make sure."

"We?" I felt like a skipping CD.

Arturo leapt to his feet, face flushed. "Okay, maybe we'll just lock Rashid up so he can't run things. But you know El Cid. He'd listen to you. He'd listen to Elena."

"Not if he ever found out Luis was a woman." I stopped. Clever boy to draw me in like that. I held up both hands. "No way. You have no idea what it's like back there."

He stopped. "Then tell me."

"If a cut gets infected, you could die. If you're exposed to influenza or other plagues, you could die. The Moors and Christians are constantly raiding each other's territory. The Almoravides come up from Africa now and then to kick everyone's butt. You could be captured and killed or enslaved."

He looked out the window, then back at me. "I could get hit by a bus tomorrow. A gang could waste me in some random drive-by. My plane could crash. I could eat some E. coli spinach and die. How is that any different?"

Unable to think of a suitable retort, I closed my mouth, but Arturo dropped to his knees and grabbed my hands. "Mom, we go back together. We find Elena. She can help us. We fix things so Rodrigo does what he's supposed to do."

"Then what?" I squeaked.

"Then we come home."

"No."

"It'd be a great history lesson," he said, turning on his most convincing voice. "An experience no other fourteen-year-old guy could have."

"No."

"Then you go back by yourself. Someone has to fix—"

"No."

"Then I come along."

I leaned forward, patting his hands. "Turito." He flushed at the baby nickname. "It will be a cold day in hell before I expose my son to the eleventh century."

He bit his lip, then met my stubborn look with one of his own. We weren't genetically related; was stubbornness a learned trait? "Mom, I'd rather live in hell than not live at all. If that professor is right, some day soon this world is going to disappear, and us with it. I don't think you have much choice." He stood.

"Where are you going?"

"To pack," he said, then marched from the room.

❖

I didn't know what was in Arturo's gym bag, but he put it outside his room when he left for school the next morning, as if its mere presence would convince me to pack my own bag. Work passed in a daze, the entire day spent in meetings discussing my new responsibilities. I'm sure the company president questioned his choice several times when I had to drag my mind back to the present and apologize. Manager of Operations was the highest position I'd ever held, but it paled against the possibility that only I could stop some supposed wave of history rolling toward us, fracturing and reconstructing life as it undulated through time.

Arturo and I arrived home at the same time. "Change your mind yet?" he asked, unlocking the door.

"Nope." I picked up a plastic bag of books someone had left on the front step.

"You will," he said, closing the door behind us. "You always do the right thing." With that ridiculous, guilt-charged bomb, he headed upstairs.

Inside the bag was a stack of worn textbooks with a note on top from Professor Kalleberg that simply said "read these." I dumped the books in my room, stuck a roast in the oven, then opened my laptop and Googled 'Is time travel possible,' groaning when 99,900,000 hits appeared. I tried "theory of time travel" and narrowed it down to 38 million. I began slogging through them.

I read for an hour, struggling to wrap my non-physics brain around quantum physics' theoretical discussion of time travel, so I was grateful when Arturo popped into my office. "Mom, what's time travel like?"

"You feel nauseous, pass out, come to, throw up, and feel like you've been dragged behind a semi for ten miles down a dirt road."

"Oh." He disappeared.

After another hour, I gave up. To the physicists, time travel was still theoretically impossible.

❖

After dinner Arturo marched into my room and stood, arms folded like an army sergeant satisfied with his troops' progress. "The responsible thing for you to do is go back in time and fix things. And because the task is too big for one person, you must take me with you. I have a black belt. Together we are invincible, unyielding, unconquerable."

I chuckled, shaking my head. "We aren't superheroes, Arturo."

He grinned but didn't relax his stance. "How do you know?"

I swore I'd never say this to my son, but it slipped out. "Because I'm the mom. Now hit the sack and think about the future, or the present. Anything but the past."

Once in bed myself, I flipped through the musty books Kalleberg had left. A second note explained that the fractures had moved into the thirteenth century now, leaving behind a firmly established, but different, history of the twelfth century. Kalleberg had marked a page in the last book, luckily all in English, so I flipped to it and began reading. While the language was English, the perspective was Moorish.

In the late eleventh century young caliph Rashid survived numerous assassination attempts, then eventually conquered all of the Iberian Peninsula and crossed the Pyrenees into France. But before the great al-Rashid assumed the crown of Valencia on June 15, 1094, Christian mercenary Rodrigo Díaz, a divisive force in the region up to

*that point, laid siege briefly to Valencia. Rodrigo Díaz abandoned his
bid for power, Allah be praised, and faded into obscurity, but not before
murdering his trusted general, Luis Navarro.*

Jesus Christ. Elena. I shot up in bed, my mouth suddenly dry. She
had survived Sagrajas. She had lived eight years without me, as I had
lived eight years without her. Then Rodrigo, the man she'd devoted her
life to, murdered her.

Rodrigo Díaz. The leader of thousands. A gruff, cruel man who
would find me as threatening as a fly. A greedy, power-hungry man who
must survive and take the crown of Valencia to restore the timeline,
even though he murdered the woman I had loved.

Still loved. Could I save her?

It was late, but I punched in the phone number and waited.

Professor Kalleberg answered on the second ring. "Kate!"

"I'll do it, Professor. I'll do it."

CHAPTER TEN

W here's Arturo?" Professor Kalleberg asked. We sat on my living room floor, books and notes strewn all around, as if an academic tornado had touched down.

"He and my credit card are in the den. He's furious at me, but knows he's the whiz when it comes to finding cheap tickets to Spain. He does so much online shopping for me he probably has my credit card memorized."

"Any clever kid would," Kalleberg said, chuckling. "Where's the book on Muslim France?" The professor already had an open book balanced on each knee and one in his lap.

I reached under my thigh, tossed him the thick green volume, then tried to wade through the essay on my lap. This was like cramming a semester's work into two days.

Arturo stomped into the room, Max loping along behind him. My son dropped onto the sofa, glaring at me.

"Get the tickets?"

"Done." He pounded two fists on two knees. "You have to take me with you."

I stopped reading, rubbed my weary neck, trying to loosen the tightness creeping into my shoulders. "Arturo, I've decided. You'll stay with Aunt Laura and Aunt Deb until I return."

"What if you need help?" he asked.

"I have friends back there. They'll help me."

"What if you don't come back?"

I looked up. Arturo looked six again, an orphan without a home, without anyone to love him. What was I doing? My heart sank all the way to the ends of my toes. I couldn't leave him behind. I couldn't bring him along. "No," I said, more forcefully than I felt.

Arturo flung himself back, the sofa creaking in protest, his face red with fury.

Professor Kalleberg consulted his notes. "Okay, according to this, by now Rodrigo has broken with Alfonso for good. They'd tried to work things out, but in 1091 they had a huge fight over a tent."

Arturo sat up. "A tent?"

Nodding, Kalleberg found a page and read: "'A quarrel broke out over where Díaz pitched his tent during the Granada campaign. He placed his at the same level as the king, not on a lower slope, thereby claiming he was an equal of the king, not one of his subjects.'"

This sounded like the El Cid I knew. "I'll bet things go downhill from there."

"Yes, they do. History loses sight of Rodrigo for a few years except for raids he carried out to increase his wealth. Then in late 1093 he reappears and conquers city after city on his march toward Valencia." He removed his glasses and rubbed bleary eyes; he'd gotten as much sleep as I had. He bent over the book again. "1093 was a hard year for Valencia. The emir Ibn Jehaf runs the city while Rodrigo and his army take over town after town on their approach to Valencia. Rodrigo wasn't a very nice guy. Listen to this: 'Now that the harvest was ready, Díaz gathered it in and no longer spared the peasants who had cultivated it. All their homes, and all the boats and mills on the river Guadalquivir were burned. All the rich country around Valencia was turned into a desert, and many of the outlying houses and towers of the city were pulled down.'"

I sighed. "Then what?"

"Rodrigo demanded an annual tribute of 120,000 gold pieces from Valencia. But this self-proclaimed new caliph al-Rashid moved in, challenged Ibn Jehaf, and closed the gates into Valencia."

"Not a bright move," Arturo muttered.

"No. Pissed Rodrigo off royally. He broke down bridges and flooded the plain around the city and began the siege. Al-Rashid and Ibn Jehaf duked it out inside Valencia while the people starved."

"So what's happening in June, when Rodrigo supposedly attacks Luis Navarro?" I tried to ignore my son, who glared out the window, smooth jaw set as stubbornly as I'd ever seen it.

"I don't know. Rodrigo wants Valencia, but s*omething* changes his mind. He leaves, and al-Rashid kicks Ibn Jehaf out and takes over for good. Rashid's just a kid, fourteen, maybe fifteen."

"I could get close to this Rashid guy," Arturo said. "Maybe lure him into a trap or something."

"Arturo." Now we glared openly at each other.

To break the tension, Kalleberg tossed Arturo a small textbook. "You should understand where your mother's going. This is a good place to start."

Arturo scowled but took the book. I smiled when he turned straight to the footnotes at the end. When researching a paper on the Alamo for school last month, he'd complained about the endless footnotes, but I knew he'd read them because every fifteen minutes he'd raced into my room with some new fact. He was hooked, and I overheard him counseling a friend. "The real story's in the footnotes. You wouldn't believe all the great stuff they hide back there."

The professor continued. "Rodrigo had the city surrounded. When starving Valencians lowered themselves down the city walls by ropes, Rodrigo's men sold them as slaves."

"That's horrible." I struggled to imagine Elena part of this.

"Gets worse. Whenever Rodrigo himself found the Valencians on the ropes, he burned them alive in full view of the city, or tore them apart with pincers."

"Jesus." When I looked over at Arturo to see if he was enjoying all the gore, he suddenly gave a strangled cry and shot straight up, his eyes wide with fear. "No," he whispered, still staring at his book.

"Honey, what's wrong?" He shot me a look so shocked that my breath caught in my throat. "What is it?"

He leapt to his feet, book gripped to his chest, and fled the room. When I followed and knocked on his door, he refused to let me in. He'd locked the door.

Shaking my head, I returned to the living room. "Clearly something in the book upset him, but he won't talk to me." I tried to focus, but half of me was still outside Arturo's door, trying both to read his mind and calm his fears. "Professor, can you tell what the world is like under Islam? Is it any better than the history we know? Any worse? The Moors were more tolerant and educated than Christians."

"I knew you'd ask that. Why should you restore history if things improve, even if it means we no longer exist? I've been wondering the same thing, so I've been reading up on that. Things go well for a few centuries, but then, as is true with most religions, factions develop. A radical one comes to power in Asia, and life gets ugly everywhere, just as it did under Christian domination."

I tugged at my hair. "Enough. I can't absorb any more. All I need to remember is to get Rodrigo on the throne on June 15, and to make sure he doesn't murder Elena."

"You read the passage from the book I gave you?" His voice was gentle.

I nodded. "But how can I protect her from Rodrigo? He's a warrior. I'm an inventory manager."

"Find her. Stay with her night and day." I liked the night part, but Elena was too independent to tolerate me as her shadow. I leaned back against the sofa, working out a cramp in my calf. "I don't know how one person can do this."

"Who back there can help you?"

I closed my eyes. "Grimaldi, Liana, Nuño Súarez, Enzo Montoya, Fadri Colón, Marta from Duañez, and Elena. I know that sounds like enough people, but without Elena I'll never be able to pull this off."

"Kate, if you don't at least try, I believe we're all doomed. The wave has reached the early fourteenth century."

I scribbled on the nearest folder. "The wave's advancing almost a century a week. When will it get close enough to start affecting us?" Helpless, we stared at my figures. "What if I cease to exist before I get the job done?"

He dropped his hands in his lap, shaking his head. "I'm an educated, analytical historian. That I'm discussing time travel as casually as I discuss air travel still panics me. That I believe history is fracturing would make me a laughing stock in my circles. I have no real answers for any of this."

Arturo chose that moment to march into the room. He dropped the book at my feet. Saying nothing about his reddened eyes, I picked up the book and flipped through the footnotes. One page had been ripped out.

"Arturo! This is the professor's book. You—"

"I am tired of being treated like a child." Unsmiling, my half-child-half-man left the room without another word.

❖

The next three days were hellish. I gave Laura power of attorney to pay my bills and take care of things. My will already named Laura and Deb as Arturo's legal guardians should I die. The hardest part had been explaining to Laura where I was going. "Spain? Now?"

"It's Elena. She's still alive."

"Wow."

"She needs help, so I must go to Spain."

"She called you? After all this time she just says 'Hey, I need help'?"

I hated lying to my best friend. "Not directly. It's complicated."

"Your life always is." In the end she'd accepted my reasoning, hugged me, and told me to stay safe and hurry home.

I packed, then Kalleberg picked up Arturo and me and drove us to Laura and Deb's, where Arturo would spend the next few weeks. Kalleberg would come with me to Spain, but not follow me back in time. Instead, he'd wait in the cave for his history books to change, then he'd send me a sign, somehow, perhaps by putting a note on the ledge and hoping it came back to me. Then I'd know if I had succeeded or not.

For three days Arturo had been Mr. Ice Cube, tearing my heart apart every time he looked at me. But now, four hours before our flight, when my throat tightened at what lay ahead, he stood by Laura and Deb's front door, zipping up my jacket. "You have the boarding pass I printed out?" he asked, straightening my collar, looking me in the eye. My son was now as tall as I was.

"Yes, 'Mom,'" I said.

"And from Madrid, how will you get to Zaragoza? Hitchhike?"

"Rent a car or take the train."

"And at Zaragoza, will you sleep on the streets?"

I smiled. "Hyatt Regency."

"And how will you get to the cave?"

"Bus 27 from the Plaza."

"And will the nice bus driver tell you which stop you need?" Arturo asked.

"Yes, but if not, I'll see the sign that says 'cueva.'" I grabbed his hands as he nervously plucked lint from my sleeves. "I've done this before, kiddo. I'll be fine."

Our eyes met and we were both suddenly out of words, so I held him tightly, surprised he squeezed just as hard, as if we both ached to imprint the other's body onto our own. Finally he pulled back, his eyes dry. "Go save the world, Mom."

I swallowed, dragging a sleeve across my face. "Okay."

As Kalleberg backed down the driveway, I kept my eye on Arturo standing on the front step, flanked by protective Laura and sturdy Deb, until we turned the corner and Arturo disappeared.

❖

Everything went just as I'd laid out for Arturo. Once at Zaragoza, Professor Kalleberg and I visited the Aljafería to nose around for more information we could use. Kalleberg's jaw dropped at the massive walls, the soaring arches, the impressive towers. "How can this be so old and still be standing?"

I asked the woman at the information booth about the guide, Carlos Sanchez, but she shrugged bony shoulders and pointed toward the Administration offices. The palace housed the Aragonese government offices, so I stopped there.

An older man with smudged glasses and yellow teeth peered at me. "Carlos? He quit." The man resumed his filing.

"Do you know when?"

He stopped, exhaling with irritation. "Five or six years ago."

"Do you have his home address?"

The clerk rolled his eyes, as if I'd just asked him to re-file a thousand folders by date instead of name. "He just left. Oh, wait." Suddenly interested, he straightened. "Carlos. His daughter came in shortly after he quit. Said she couldn't find her father anywhere. He'd disappeared."

The professor and I exchanged glances. Carlos knew about the cave at Mirabueno. Had he used it?

Being near the palace brought back a flood of tastes—spicy goat meat at al-Mu'tamin's banquet, sweet honey cakes, the mango juice I shared with Elena. My feet wanted to fly straight to Mirabueno, but we'd decided to wait until morning, so once I was back in the past I'd have a full day for travel. But now that I was close, every second I waited was an irritant to be swatted aside so I could move ahead, so I could find Elena.

❖

At six a.m. I finally got up. Today was May 20. Three and one half weeks until June 15. Weariness fled as my adrenaline kicked in, and within an hour, Kalleberg and I were on the bus heading to the western edge of Zaragoza. When I asked the driver about Mirabueno, she shook her head. "Never heard of it."

I peered ahead, searching for landmarks. Not until we passed it did I see the 'cueva' sign and recognize the steep street I'd climbed with the Whipples, bumper-sticker collectors extraordinaire. We got off at the next intersection and walked back. My heavy backpack cut into my shoulders, and poor Kalleberg carried two packs. When we reached the top of the hill, I groaned. "Cerrada" signs had been pasted across the entrance. Closed. Beer bottles, cigarette butts, and used condoms littered the area.

"It would seem this is now an altogether different sort of tourist attraction," Professor Kalleberg said.

I glared at the padlocked door. "How are we going to get inside?" We hadn't come prepared to cut through a lock.

"The hinges," Kalleberg said. "If we can pop the pins out of the hinges, we can open the door that way." I stared at the scholar and enjoyed his boyish grin. "Read it in a book once." Scrounging through the long grass and weeds, we found a long, flat rock, which Kalleberg used to pound out one hinge pin, then the other. We each grabbed the edge of the door and pulled. Goosebumps spread down my arms as the protesting door squealed, but opened about eighteen inches, just wide enough to squeeze through. Thank goddess I'd lost those ten pounds two years ago. I flipped on my flashlight and slipped into the dark cave, Kalleberg right behind me.

We stood, shining our lights around the entrance room. I inhaled the moist, cool air, then sneezed, the hollow sound unnaturally loud. I reached for the light switch by the door, smiling when the dim bulbs sprang to life. "You'll have light while you wait," I said to the professor. The cave might be closed, but someone still paid the light bill. I changed into my eleventh century clothes—a long brown linen skirt, linen woven tunic and heavy black shawl.

"Very peasanty," the professor said.

I tied the shawl around my shoulders. "Just like in the twenty-first century, people don't pay much attention to poor women. I'll be able to move around without being noticed."

Heart racing now, I led him down the path and into the cave. After an easy ten minute walk, we reached the ledge. Weak sun still flickered across it like a beacon.

"That's it?" Kalleberg crowded next to my shoulder, his breath as rapid as mine. Both our antiperspirants had failed, a smell I'd have to get used to.

"Yes." We moved quickly, reaching the ledge in seconds. My heart beat faster at the memory of my last journey. "Professor, you'll be okay here? You have everything you need while you wait?"

The lanky man, just as excited as I was, set off to one side the backpack he was keeping for his stay in the cave. "I'll be fine. Whatever your actions, they will have taken place centuries ago, and the results should eventually be reflected in these books. I don't know, however, which history will reach me first, the altered, fractured history, or the one that will occur *when* you restore the timeline."

I had less than one month. How I would accomplish my task remained a fuzzy snarl in my brain, but when I found Elena, she'd be able to sort through everything and come up with a plan. I drew a deep breath, wondering if this was the stupidest thing I'd ever done, but Elena needed me, even if she didn't know it. Time had reached forward, whispered "Lion King" in my ear, and I must respond. I sent a silent promise to Arturo that I would return.

I hefted a pack up onto the ledge. "Sure you don't want to come along?"

He chuckled, then lowered his head. "I'd be dead inside a week. I'm serious."

"I know," I said, patting his hand.

He swallowed once. "But, oh, how I envy you. The things you will see—"

"You could come." Why this sudden fear to be going alone?

The man shook his craggy head and hugged me awkwardly. "My job is to stay here. I'll send a note to you when I see a change in the books."

I nodded, took a deep breath, then scrambled up onto the ledge. The professor flung his extra pack in my lap. My legs dangled off the ledge and a horrible image flashed through my head. "My legs," I cried. "What if they don't come with me?" Panicking, I pulled my legs up and curled around the packs. "I don't feel anything," I said.

A bright white flared overhead. Professor Kalleberg disappeared and the light consumed me. I clutched myself as my stomach churned, and time flooded the cave, sweeping me into its black ravine.

❖

I don't know how long I was out, but when I finally opened my eyes, I was in damp darkness broken only by the faint shred of light over the ledge. Water dripped nearby, echoing softly. Christ, my head hurt. My *bones* hurt. What did I expect? I was eight years older, and time travel had been no picnic on my younger body.

I fumbled for my flashlight, so nauseous I wished I could throw up, then shone my beam on the narrow path below. Half sliding, half rolling, I made the awkward journey from ledge to path, then tried walking, or rather, staggering. I had to stop at least three times to rest, but finally the path began sloping upward. My head still pounded as I reached the entrance room, which was awash in sunlight. I sank to my knees in the warm sand, then gulped a long drink from my leather bota. I threw up, drank some more, then crawled into a sunny patch and collapsed.

❖

The smells of eastern Castile in the spring entered my nose and swirled through my body. The flowering lavender, the myrtle heavy with pollinating bees, the tall cedar trees drawing my gaze to the azure sky. I walked through the lower cottages of Duañez, but no one was around. Everyone must be in the fields. Breathless from more than the climb, I stepped lightly up the pebble path, scanning the castle windows, shutters all flung back to let in the spring, but saw no one.

I touched my cheek. Would she notice the smile lines around my mouth? Would the 'character' lines by my eyes matter? I was thirty-eight now and even had a few gray hairs. No, she wouldn't care. I hurried toward the open front door. A rooster squawked as he scooted out of my way. She would not have changed. She would be as strong, as upright, as brave as always. I would take one look at her and be unable to breathe.

I stepped inside. "Hello?" No one sat by the hearth or stood by the wooden table. I headed down the hall, checking each room. I reached our room and stepped inside.

Her back to me, she was fastening a wide belt over her leather tunic. Her legs were still long and firm, her hair still short but curling sweetly around her ears.

"Elena."

She turned, dropped her scabbard, and stared. Fear, disbelief, loneliness, confusion crossed her face in seconds. I'd been right. I couldn't breathe.

As slowly as you'd approach a startled fawn, I moved toward her. "I'm real," I said. I stopped, seeing in her face, in the lay of her shoulders, in the tilt of her head, that she did not trust her eyes or her ears. After eight years of waiting, watching, hoping I would reappear, a person gave up, let go, and could not easily regain what had been released.

I breathed now, but just barely. Lines etched a fine path out from her eyes. A new scar ran along her jaw. My throat tightened at the dark pain around her eyes, and my need to take that pain away overcame my caution. I reached for her.

"Kate," she finally croaked, and our lips touched.

"Mom? Mom!" Arturo shook my arm. "You're muttering in your sleep, Mom. It's embarrassing."

I raised my head, wiping my mouth, and squinted at Arturo in the fading light. Laughter bubbled through me. I'd woken from one dream to find myself in another. How had I done that? "Mom, you gotta get up and shake it off. Time travel made you sick as a dog."

I pushed his hand away. "It's just a dream, honey. You're really back home. Or maybe I'm just hallucinating. Time travel's hell on my system."

"Mom." Arturo sat me up and gently shook my shoulders. "I'm here. With you. In the Mirabueno cave."

I opened my eyes, *really* opened them. Arturo knelt beside me, dressed in brown baggy pants, a woven green tunic, and a moth-eaten faded brown wool coat. I pinched myself. I pinched him.

"Ouch."

I staggered to my feet and looked around. Yes, I was in the right place, the low-ceilinged rock cavern that served as the entrance to the cave's narrow path. "God damn it, Arturo Vincent," I managed to sputter. "This had better be a dream. If it's not, you're grounded. Forever!"

"Can't do that, Mom. In the eleventh century there's no legal age of adulthood. I checked before I came back."

I rested my shaking hands on my hips, trying to think. "You are in deep shit, mister."

"I'm here, Mom. I *did* it."

"I don't understand. How—"

Arturo grinned, flushed from this horrible victory. "I bought my plane ticket when I bought yours. The night you left I snuck out of the house and took a bus to the airport. With the time difference, it worked out great. I knew once Aunt Laura found me missing the next morning, you'd already be on your way to Mirabueno. I used your credit card to pay for the train from Madrid to Zaragoza, and here I am."

I pounded my forehead. "Christ, this is a disaster. And your aunts. They'll be worried sick."

Arturo took a swig from a ratty Army canteen. "I left them a note explaining everything."

"Everything?"

"Yup. I thought they deserved to know the truth."

I struggled to accept the nightmarish fact that my son stood beside me in the eleventh century. "What about Kalleberg?"

"Sleeping like a baby. I left him a note, tiptoed past him, and climbed up to the ledge." He rolled his eyes. "Man, what a ride that was."

"We'll buy horses. We'll ride to the cave at Santillana. I'm taking you back to the twenty-first century."

"Not a good plan. Santillana is north and west from here. By the time you get there and back, assuming there are no problems, you still have to get all the way east to Valencia in time to make everything work out. There isn't time to take me to Santillana."

"You've got this all figured out, huh?"

"Yup."

I lowered myself to the ground, leaning back against the cool rock wall. "Why, Arturo?"

He knelt before me, eyes bright. "I have my reasons."

"Don't be mysterious."

"You can't do this alone. Also, if I'm here with you, you won't be torn between me and Elena. That's all I'm gonna say."

"What makes you think I'm torn?"

He shook his head. "I'm fourteen, Mom, not *blind*."

I laid my head back. "You're pretty pleased with yourself, aren't you?"

"Damn straight."

"Good grief. Where *did* you learn to swear like that?" I groaned. "This is impossible. It won't work."

"Sure it will." He reached into one of my packs, pulled out a small folding shovel and snapped the handle into place. "Now, seems to me we have some work to do." I watched him pace off five paces from the opening, four to the right, then start digging in the loose sand. I pulled six sacks of freshly minted fake coins from the packs. Kalleberg had called in a few debts, and almost overnight we had play money— Castilian coins and Moorish silver dirhems and gold dinars made to look like the few coins pictured in Kalleberg's books. I dropped two bags into the hole, then Arturo began digging another while I raked the cool sand back into the first one. We stopped once for a candy bar, but kept going until all the bags were buried and the candy wrappers burned, just in case history could change if someone in this century discovered the existence of a Butterfinger. We each tucked a bag of coins into our packs, then Arturo found a crevice back along the path and hid the shovel.

"Let's go," I said, still feeling weak, but my adrenaline had finally kicked in since I didn't have time to be sick. I had a job to do and my son to protect. Shielding our eyes, we stepped out from the cave. Through my squinting eyes, tears welled up at the sight of forests stretching up the far hillsides, the bright Ebro flowing below us, flowers and meadow grasses all around us rippling in the cool spring breeze. God, this was a beautiful century.

"Oh my god," Arturo breathed. "It's *real*." We both slid into Spanish, as we'd planned. English would be for dire emergencies, which I'd warned Arturo I would not tolerate.

"You thought I just made this all up?"

He whirled around, drinking it all in. "There's nothing here."

"Nothing but trees, a river, birds, insects, animals, meadows—"

"Okay, okay. You know what I mean. What's that?"

I squinted at the irregular speck on the eastern horizon. "That, Señor Vincent, is Zaragoza." White-washed city walls surrounded orange tile roofs and the towers of the Aljafería. The sun warmed the top of my head, my legs felt strong and lean, and my brilliant man-child stood at my side. Now that I was back in 1094, Elena's heart once again beat in unison with mine. To save her life, all I had to do was find her, and find her in time.

Arturo's face flushed as reality took hold and spun him around. "This is so *cool*. I'm here! I'm here!"

Our packs had no zippers or Velcro, just drawstrings, so we hoped they wouldn't attract too much attention. I threw mine over my shoulder. "Before we start, let's get three ground rules straight."

"I expected something like this."

"First, establish no ties to this time, establish no relationships. It will only hurt more when we say good-bye. Understand me, Arturo Vincent, when I say that after we pull this off, we're returning to our own time. You're going to college. Getting a job. Supporting me. Having a life. Got it?"

"Got it."

"Second, what I say goes, okay? I'm the pilot, you're the co-pilot. The pilot gets final say without argument from the co-pilot."

He nodded. "Okay."

"Third, you've never seen a sheep running with her lamb before, but that lamb stays right at the ewe's hip. No matter where she turns or how fast she moves, that lamb is stuck to her side like a training wheel on a bike."

Arturo grimaced. "Let me guess. You're the bike, I'm the training wheel."

"If you'd rather, I could be the mama sheep and you could be the cute, cuddly lamb."

Eyes twinkling, Arturo shouldered his own pack. "I don't care. Training wheel or lamb, I'm ready. Let's go kick some historical butt."

Laughing, we started down the hill. Maybe this would turn out okay after all. As long as Arturo remained by my side, I could laugh about anything.

CHAPTER ELEVEN

We had only taken about ten steps when the ground began to shake. Arturo stopped. "What the heck is that? A train?" My pulse quickened as déjà vu hit. "Horses, Arturo, lots of them. The last time I arrived back in time, Elena and her men were riding past. That's how I met her."

We looked at each other as the ground vibrated beneath us and the distant thundering became the sound of hooves pounding the dirt road, closer and closer. Arturo's eyes twinkled. "Maybe lightning does strike twice in the same place. C'mon!" He scooped up both our knapsacks, flung them over his shoulder, and half-ran, half-slid down the hill.

Could I be that lucky? I followed Arturo, who'd already disappeared at the bottom of the hill. By the time I reached the bottom and struggled through a stand of bushes, Arturo stood in the middle of the hard-packed road, mouth open, eyes shining, mesmerized by galloping horses headed straight for him. The Moor in the lead whooped and whipped his horse faster. They were not going to slow down even though Arturo stood right in their path.

"Arturo!" I thrashed through the underbrush lining the last stretch before the road. "Move!" But he just stood there, amazed grin on his shining face while a Moorish army bore down on him.

I struggled to the edge of the road, taking in flying cloaks, bearded faces, shields, and slashing hooves as the lead rider grinned and aimed his horse straight at my stupefied son.

Adrenaline surged through me as I raced onto the road, tackled Arturo, and rolled us both into the far ditch just as the air filled with hooves and shouts and flying stones and billowing dust. I pulled my shawl over our heads, but we still coughed and gagged for a few minutes until the earth stopped trembling and the sounds receded.

When I finally threw back the shawl, a reddish-brown haze hung over the road, but we were alone. I covered my eyes with a dusty, trembling hand, listening to the sound of Arturo's breathing returning to normal.

He coughed a few more times, then cleared his throat. "I'll bet right now you're a little sorry I'm here."

"A little?" I sat up and spat out a mouthful of dirt. "What did you think that was? A *virtual* army?" I wiped off my mouth, tried to spit again, but fear had sucked up all my saliva.

Arturo wiped his eyes, leaving two white streaks across a dust-covered face. "I'm sorry It's just so incredible. I'm actually *in* the eleventh century."

"Not for long," I snapped as I stood and shook out my skirt. I was pissed at Arturo, pissed at myself for not foreseeing he might have followed me, and pissed at Elena for not being in that pack of riders, or for pounding past without realizing it was me cowering in the ditch.

Arturo clutched my wrist. "Mom, it won't happen again. We can't go back. We have a job to do. I'll be more careful. Training wheel, that's me. I swear."

"Arturo, this isn't going to wo—"

"You folks still in one piece?" The gravely voice came from a plump Christian merchant leading a team of mules hitched to an overloaded wagon. He stopped as we scrambled up out of the ditch.

"We both swallowed a good share of the road, but we're fine, thank you."

The merchant shook his round head. "I got my team out of the way just in time. Damn that Rafael Mahfouz. He is a terror on the road. "

We exchanged introductions, and the kind merchant offered us a ride to Zaragoza. As we all three climbed onto the wagon seat, Arturo asked about Rafael Mahfouz.

"Having a Christian mama and a Moor for a papa can confuse a person something terrible. He's a mess. He lives in Zaragoza, but I hear he's hooked himself up with some young stud who thinks he's going to be the next caliph, some Moor named Rashid." The man snapped the reins and the mules leaned into their harnesses. "Mahfouz is a scoundrel, but I'd rather be run off the road by Mahfouz than meet up with that al-Saffah band."

"Al-Saffah?" Shedders of blood, if my translation was correct. I tucked my bag under my feet and shifted on the hard wooden plank.

"Almoravides. Thousands of them. So good with the damn bow

and arrow they can shoot your eye out at one hundred paces." Both Arturo and I winced. "Red-hooded black bastards been terrorizing the area the last six months."

"Terrorizing Christians?"

"Christians, Moors, even other Almoravides. Makes no difference. Them blood-thirsty buggers hate everyone. They's so cranky no one's safe."

I smirked. Sounded like me once a month.

"Say, where are you folks from? I can't quite place your accent. Never heard it before. I can't quite make out all your words."

Arturo and I exchanged a glance of panic. "We're from...Tae Kwon Do." I licked my lips. "It's a little village up in the Pyrenees. Not many have heard of us."

"Can't say that I have either. Well, you make sense enough for me. Settle back, get comfortable. We have a day ahead of us."

Yucca trees rose up from the hills above us, spindly limbs dotted with cauliflower clumps of dusty green. To the north, an abandoned Roman tower rose out of nowhere, its white stone pocked with age. We only stopped a few times to water the mules and relieve ourselves. Once I had to take Arturo by the shoulders. "I am going behind that bush now. You stay here."

"I think I should come with you." His brown eyes were deadly serious.

"Don't push it, young man." But I hid my smile as I turned away.

We stopped for the night and scooted under the wagon to sleep. Soon the merchant snored like a bear and Arturo made his soft sleeping sounds. I lay on my back, staring up at the rough boards. I was back. She was here, somewhere. Was she still alive? How could I sleep?

❖

When we passed through the west gate of Zaragoza, my heart opened like a Moor's well-tended rose. I inhaled the sharp spices, drank in the flowing robes and dark beards, soaked up the sounds of the market and music and lyrical Arabic.

"Wow," Arturo breathed into my ear. I needn't have worried about him, since the city's strangeness kept him glued to my side. I really had grown a training wheel.

We got lost a few times, thanks to the merchant's directions, but finally found the modest home. Flush with the street, the front door opened into a narrow hallway which led us into a bright, airy courtyard. "Good evening, old friends," I said softly.

Liana dropped her plate, and Grimaldi stood so quickly his stool clattered to the flagstone. "Kate!" they both cried, and suddenly I was smothered in hugs. Grimaldi finally stepped back, but Liana and I, laughing through our tears, couldn't let go of each other. Two small children tugged at her skirts.

"Saints preserve us, who is this young man?" Grimaldi no longer used the faltering Spanish, but spoke fluently.

Arturo puffed up like a satisfied rooster as I introduced him. Liana kept stroking his cheeks. "What a beautiful man."

"He's only fourteen, Liana."

Grimaldi shook his hand as Arturo glared at me. "Don't forget, Kate. Around here, fourteen is a man."

The slender girl at the table stood, long black hair tucked behind her ears. "Tayani," I murmured. The twelve-year old curtsied politely but could not take her eyes from Arturo. Liana's son Hazm, who lived in the palace as the crown prince and al-Musta'in's successor, was visiting, and he allowed me to hug him even though he barely remembered me; and I barely recognized the little boy I'd played with at the Aljafería. Hazm and Arturo hit it off right away, and they soon escaped to the roof, with moon-eyed Tayani right behind them.

"I'm looking for Luis," I said after accepting a plate of rice and bread.

Liana's forehead wrinkled in concern. "You have been gone such a long time."

Grimaldi scratched his silver head. "We have not seen him more than once or twice since our wedding six years ago. Rodrigo returns now and then to negotiate with Walladah."

"What of al-Musta'in?" The brother and sister had never gotten along.

Liana smiled. "Al-Musta'in is leader in name only because Walladah runs the province, which infuriates Rodrigo. She has begun to involve Hazm in her councils, which honors us." She lowered her kind eyes to hide intense maternal pride.

"I must find Luis. I suspect he's with Rodrigo, who should be somewhere around Valencia." I looked pointedly at Grimaldi, my fellow time traveler from the future, but could say no more while Liana sat with us.

"My birds," the pilgrim said with a snap of his fingers, and he disappeared into a side room, quickly returning with a sheet of parchment, ink, pen, and knife. "My pigeons fly to my contacts all over the peninsula—Castile, Galicia, León, Barcelona, Valencia, southern Andaluz. We will pinpoint his location."

I smiled happily as Grimaldi began cutting the parchment into narrow strips. I'd come to the right place. We chattered as we wrote notes—some in Latin, some in Hebrew, others in Arabic. Grimaldi raised an eyebrow as I easily composed the Latin notes.

"I've been busy," I said with a wink.

Finally we had forty notes, which Grimaldi gathered up into a bowl. Liana touched my arm as Grimaldi and I headed for the roof stairs. "Luis will be whole again now that you've returned." I swallowed, unable to speak. Her skin glowed with an inner peace I had only felt once in my life—those months I'd spent with Elena. "Luis looks the same, acts the same, but that fire in his eyes went out when you left. It will leap to life when he hears you are back." Liana had just described me. Nodding, I followed Grimaldi up the rickety ladder.

Hazm, Arturo, and Tayani talked at the far side of the roof. I could hear snatches of Arabic as the two young Moors began teaching Arturo their language. Grimaldi carefully attached a note to the first pigeon.

Finally alone, I told him everything—Anna's actions, the timeline, my goal to undo the damage. He attached notes and listened as I paced. Finally I ran out of words and energy, and the notes were ready to fly. Grimaldi joined me on the bench near the bird cages. "This is hard to absorb," he finally said.

"I know."

"So if the future changes, wiping out all we know, what happens to you, me, Arturo?"

"Don't know. We might cease to exist."

"Twenty-seven days from now you must make sure that Rodrigo, who has become more ruthless than ever, conquers the Moors and takes Valencia. All you know is that before he's supposed to do this, he kills Luis, wanders away and is not heard from again." I nodded, waiting. Finally Grimaldi raised his silver head. "We need Luis."

"We?" I asked.

He nodded. "All these years in this century, I have kept a low profile because I didn't want to alter history. No one has the right to do what Anna has done." I squeezed his cold hand. "But I must be very discreet." I didn't understand until he nodded toward the laughing Hazm. "I have been more of a father to him than al-Musta'in. What you propose we do is effectively weaken his world so Alfonso and the others can conquer him."

"I struggle with this as well."

"If your efforts to overthrow the current Valencian emir, Ibn Jehaf, and put Rodrigo on the throne are traced back to Hazm in any way, his life will be in great danger."

"I'm sorry. I didn't consider how awkward this might be for you." I looked toward the birds.

"Helping you find Luis is not a problem, but should Anna discover you're here, if your goals should become known, I'll only be able to help you from afar. Kate, what you propose is not only difficult, it's extremely dangerous. Know that an immense amount of wealth and power is at stake here."

Not to mention the course of the entire next millennium.

"The Valencians are tired and starving," Grimaldi said. "In al-Rashid the people see a way to reestablish power in all of al-Andaluz."

I watched Arturo, now laughing so hard he held his sides. "They're up to something."

"Of course. Aren't they always at that age?"

Nodding, I reached for my knapsack and pulled out a canvas bag. "What I'm about to show you cannot be shared with anyone, not even Liana."

Grimaldi winced. "She and I keep no secrets, except the obvious one."

I shook my head. "No, this is for you alone."

He exhaled slowly. "Okay, for me alone." I handed him the bag, which he untied and opened. He gasped, then chuckled deeply as he pulled out a *New York Times* and a one pound bag of peanut M&Ms, the two things he missed most from his own century. He slid them back in before anyone could notice, grinning broadly. "I'm not a selfish man, but these are for me alone."

A high-pitched wail drifted across the rooftop. Call to prayer. That more than anything brought memories of my time in Zaragoza flooding back, memories so vivid that my longing for Elena beat a steady pulse inside my skull. I had to find her. When I did, I could not touch her or kiss her or in any way rekindle our relationship, since my stay was only temporary. But just to look into her eyes again, to hear her voice...that was all I needed.

❖

Grimaldi released the birds the next morning, and we waited. Arturo showed Hazm a few kicks, Tayani tried to kiss Arturo in the back hallway, which I heard about from Liana, and Hazm showed Arturo a bit of Moorish swordplay, which shot my anxiety up into the red zone.

"Arturo, I think a dagger is a better weapon for you. Let's go to the bazaar."

"Mom, I was just horsing around with Hazm to be polite. I don't need a weapon," he insisted as he and Hazm trailed behind me out the house and down the narrow street. "My *body* is my weapon."

"We get separated, you're out of food. Will Tae Kwon Do kill, skin, and gut a rabbit?"

Arturo snorted as he stepped aside to avoid a pack of kids racing past the stalls. "I can't kill a rabbit and neither can you."

"I could teach you," Hazm offered. "My aim with a bow and arrow is so good I am thinking of going to fight with al-Rashid. Valencia must be defended."

"Hazm—" I stopped. Telling him he was too young would only produce teenage indignation. "Hazm, Zaragoza needs you here. Its crown prince should not risk his life." The bazaar had overflowed the square into side streets, merchants selling from wagons, hand carts, or off rush mats on the stone street.

Hazm shrugged. "Aunt Walladah says the same, but Paloma de Palma comes soon to ask for our support of al-Rashid. I could return with her to Valencia."

My heart skipped about a dozen beats. "Paloma de Palma? Here? When?"

"In two days, maybe three. That is all I know."

I tried to smile as an elderly woman seductively waved a silk tunic to tempt me toward her booth. Paloma de Palma, or Anna, must not know I had returned.

I stopped at one stall of daggers, but Hazm shook his head. "A crook," he muttered under his breath and led me to another stall with a black cloth draped across the cart bottom, a chaos of daggers piled on top. The merchant hastened to show off the jeweled handles.

"Arturo, pick one that fits your hand." I selected a medium-length dagger with a simple leather-wrapped hilt. "How about this one?"

When he didn't respond, I looked up to find he had locked eyes with a young woman, no older than seventeen, standing at the next stall. Great, first he charms Tayani, and now a total stranger. Had time travel somehow set off my son's pheromones? Because she wore a white hooded cape lined with red, only her face showed, but I could see why Arturo stared: flawless deep ebony skin, wide almond eyes with ridiculously long lashes, full lips, and a look of such confidence, such desire that I flushed as deeply as Arturo. I pulled my gaze away and poked Arturo's arm. "Enough, Romeo. Back to the knives."

But he didn't move, and the young woman, an inch taller than Arturo, glided toward us, her eyes never leaving Arturo's. The woman touched her chest, then his, then said something in an Arabic dialect I didn't understand. Hazm chuckled. "She says Arturo must go with her."

She took both his hands and pulled him with her; he followed, still drowning in those burnt sienna eyes. Because I didn't like how she put her hands all over my son, I stepped between them. "Look here," I barked in rusty Arabic. "My son will not go with you." She smelled of sweat and horses and ignored me, pulling harder.

"It's okay, Mom, she won't hurt me. She's so beautiful," Arturo finally spoke, stepping past me.

To hell with modern parenting practices. This woman wanted my child. "Training wheel," I snapped in English.

Arturo stopped, shaking his head to clear it. "You're right. Hazm, tell her I can't go with her."

The prince, still amused, translated. "She says you are the one, and she will have you despite this...I guess 'meddling woman' would be the nicest way to translate it." He smiled weakly in my direction.

"*Busaybah*," the young woman murmured, stroking Arturo's cheek.

"She called you 'Little Kiss.'" Hazm's shoulders shook with the humor of it all.

"No," I snapped. "Leave him alone."

The woman stepped closer to me, tight with a sudden fury I didn't understand. She growled something at me, jabbed my chest with a slender finger, then whirled on her booted heel and faded into the shifting crowds. I turned to Hazm, who had sobered up. "She says she'll come for her beloved while you sleep, and that she will slice you open from neck to..." He gave up, unwilling to say the rest out loud to a woman his mother's age.

"Christ," I muttered.

"Sorry, Mom. Don't worry." Arturo threw an arm around my shoulder. "Training wheel, remember?"

"We have work to do, mister, so until that's done you keep it in your pants, got it?"

"Mom!" Arturo blushed and Hazm turned away, biting his lip. I bought the dagger and scabbard, then worked my way toward the outskirts of the bazaar, followed by my training wheel and the amused prince. I was furious at both Arturo and myself. If lust had no place in this mission, then why did the flutter of every returning pigeon weaken my knees with hope and possibility?

"Kate?"

I turned toward the voice and nearly stumbled right into the tour guide from the Aljafería, a man I'd barely met over eight years ago, but who recognized me. "Carlos?"

The now elderly man clasped my hands, his grip still strong, so his health must be good. His fuzzy white hair formed a halo around his balding head. "What a miracle this is. Eight years I watch for you. I say, keep your eyes open, Carlos, and you'll see her one day." The poor man trembled with excitement, and Carlos's enthusiasm fueled my own. What were the chances we'd run into each other? Fate was surrounding me with support.

Arturo moved closer so Hazm couldn't hear. "Mom, is this guy from...you know...?" He jerked his head, I suppose to indicate the future.

"Carlos, this is my son, Arturo."

"Ahh, we meet at last." He gripped Arturo's shoulders gleefully. "I'm so happy to see you both."

At last? "Carlos, we just arrived a few days ago, and here you are. Do you live in Zaragoza? Why did you come back in time?"

He moved us out of the crowded street. "So many questions. No, I don't live in Zaragoza, but Walladah seeks a new Jewish administrator, so I'm here to meet with her. I prefer to live under Moorish rule, where the life of a Jew is much easier." He smiled warmly, then spread his arms to take in the bustling scene around us. "As for why I came back, how could I not, once I knew the cave existed? Kate, the joy of living my country's past is intoxicating. Pinch yourself. This is *real*. It's 1094. I can watch, but only watch, and marvel at the history unfolding before me."

He sounded as giddy about time travel as Anna. Personally, I found it exhausting. While Arturo and Hazm walked ahead of us, I told Carlos everything. Why we had come back. What I must do to restore the timeline. He shook his head, shocked at the news. "This is terrible. What can I do?"

"Carlos, you understand that by restoring the original timeline the Jews will eventually all be driven from Spain."

The short man nodded. "No one should disturb history. How may I help?"

For a brief second I wondered what course *I* would choose if I knew I could erase centuries of gay and lesbian oppression, but then I shook off the thought.

I asked if he had heard of Paloma de Palma. "Of course. She's a major force behind al-Rashid. But I don't run in the same circles as she. Let's go back to your lodging to talk."

Then it came to me. A brilliant idea. "Carlos, how would you like to visit Valencia?"

His eyes widened. "A city under attack by Rodrigo? A city where Jehaf and al-Rashid wrestle for political power?" He shook his head. "Sounds dangerous. Remember, I'm sixty-seven."

I turned on my persuasive charms, knowing I could never manipulate people as Anna did, and feeling relieved I couldn't. "I don't want you to do anything that would put you in danger, Carlos. I just need you to listen, to pay attention, to get a sense of what's going on."

He contemplated the toes of his scruffy boots as we walked, then straightened. "I think I know what you have in mind. I will do it. Now, where are you staying again?"

"A spy, Carlos. You could be my spy. Get to the edge of the fighting, but stay out of danger. See what you can discover. Find out what Rodrigo is up to, what Anna is up to. Arturo and I will be close behind you. Look me up at Rodrigo's camp. Ask for Nuño Súarez."

His forehead beaded with perspiration in the warm spring sun. "I am new to this spy business. Can we discuss it more?"

"No, Carlos, please leave now for Valencia. Be my eyes until I get there. Find out what's going on. And thank you."

I hugged the kind man whom I'd first met in the twenty-first century when Anna and I had toured the Aljafería. As a palace tour guide, he had spent the afternoon sharing stories about the palace inhabitants, and when I had disappeared, Anna had turned to Carlos for help. I ran to catch up with Arturo, my heart lighter. Grimaldi would help me. Carlos would help me. Maybe we could pull this off after all.

❖

The next day five more birds returned: Duañez, no. Cordoba, no. Burgos, no. Miranda, no. Toledo, not since Rodrigo's appearance there two years ago. That evening Grimaldi and I sat on the roof, contemplating the stars overhead. Hazm, Tayani, and Arturo did the same, but as far away from us as they could get without jumping onto another roof. In the last three days, Arturo had learned to drink goat's milk, eat root vegetables he'd never seen before, and, with Grimaldi, use the public bathhouse daily. I barely recognized the teenager who refused to eat asparagus or wash behind his ears. Arturo exclaimed as a shooting star streaked across the southeastern sky then faded.

Grimaldi smiled. "Muslims believe shooting stars are really missiles thrown by angels at devils who come too near to the heavens."

"That's lovely," I said.

Voices murmured from across the rooftops as couples and families enjoyed the unseasonably warm spring night. I caught snatches of Spanish, Hebrew, and Arabic. Everyone got along, more or less, but if I was successful, the Christians would, in four hundred years, drive out or murder every Moor, every Jew, in the peninsula. Mournful Arabic music, double lutes, flutes, and drums, drifted up from an impromptu concert in the street below.

"Kate, travel may be dangerous. Rodrigo's looting this last year has attracted hoodlums, thieves, and all sorts of riffraff, hungry to pick from the bones Rodrigo leaves behind."

"With my son, the Tae Kwon Do King, what do I have to fear?"

"Al-Saffah."

I sat up, brushing tiny pebbles from my back. "The merchant who brought us to Zaragoza mentioned them."

"No one has gotten close enough to engage them in battle. Their Almoravide arrows do so much damage that armies and caravans and travelers retreat."

"Why would they bother a lone woman traveling with her son?"

"Why not? They kill without reason. An arrow could hit you before you even knew they were there."

I desperately wished Professor Kalleberg were here with his dusty history books, his lanky calmness, and some clue as to what I must do next. "Will all the birds be back tomorrow?" Grimaldi nodded. "I cannot afford to wait any longer, since Anna will be here in two days." And Elena? She could be anywhere. She could be with Rodrigo outside Valencia. Actually, she might already be dead.

❖

I saw her standing by Matamoros, arms crossed, jaw set, eyes glacial. "You left," she said, voice thick with anger and pain. I ran to her, clasped her hands to my breast.

"I did, but I raised a beautiful son. And now I'm back, but only for awhile. I love you, Elena. Let's not waste our precious time together being angry." I stroked her cheek with the ball of my thumb, feeling her muscles relax.

Anger fled as she saw the truth of my words, so she opened her arms, pulling me close. Our first kiss was greedy, hard, pushing my head back against her waiting hand, my mouth an open flower seeking Elena's nectar, her flesh, her heat.

I jolted awake, stretched out on the mat in Grimaldi's home. I shifted on the hard floor, reliving my intense dream and listening to a drunken argument down the street. When Arturo and I returned to the twenty-first century, maybe I could write romance novels, really bad ones.

Arturo barely stirred when I poked him with my toe. "Hey, lazybones. Up. Hazm's coming to show you the palace."

He sat up, hair sticking out in alarming directions, rubbed his eyes, then flashed me the most satisfied smile. "I love this city. Who cares that there are no flush toilets." He yawned. "Or that everything we eat tastes like old goat."

I frowned, suddenly wary. "After I went to bed last night, you and Hazm stayed on the roof, right? You didn't go anywhere?"

Arturo lay back on his thin straw mat. "I love this city."

Before I could say more, Hazm thundered into the courtyard below and hollered up to us. When I finally got Arturo up, and we staggered downstairs for bread and cream, Arturo and Hazm exchanged sly grins. At this, Grimaldi and I shook our heads. The only thing worse than one teenaged boy was two of them together.

The morning's drizzle finally ended, but the sky remained heavy with moisture as Hazm nearly danced ahead of us, excited to show Arturo the Aljafería. The city felt freshly-scrubbed, the stone streets shone, and the trees danced in the slightly cool breeze. The bazaar slowly came to life in the puddled square, selling everything from fresh fish and sheep carcasses to glass vases and iron tools.

As we neared the palace, the boys nearly had to run to keep up with me. Once inside the palace gates, however, I stopped Hazm. "It's too complicated to explain, Hazm, but Arturo and I must not use our real names here. In a few days my...an old friend arrives, and I do not want her to hear we are in Zaragoza."

"Have you done something wrong?"

"No, but..." I worried my lower lip. "...but Arturo will be in danger if she knows we are here. That's all I can say."

Hazm shrugged, remarkably unbothered by the mystery of it all. "Do not worry. You can be my servant, and Arturo will be my personal attendant. Busaybah." He chortled and ducked when Arturo swung playfully at his head.

"Meet me here at the front entrance at late morning prayer," I said. We stepped inside, where I recognized the fountain spouting gaily in the central courtyard. The orange and almond trees were thicker around the waist than eight years ago, but then, so was I.

Servants bowed to the crown prince as they passed, but the young man barely noticed. "Come, Arturo," Hazm said. "I'll show you the throne room. The gold statues are worth thousands of dinars." With that, the two boys left me and I wandered the main floor, running my hands over cool yellow tiles, carved cedarwood arches, graceful double columns, marble benches, gold-encrusted panels. The boxwood hedges lining each courtyard had recently been trimmed; the sharp scent spoke of sun and rain and the roots running deep in the soil of Spain.

Afraid I would encounter Walladah, I kept my head down whenever anyone passed. I wasn't ready, and too many memories boiled within me. Besides, if she was to meet with Paloma de Palma, I didn't want either woman knowing I was here.

Of course, I ended up in the room Elena and I had shared, now filled with broken window grilles, extra baskets, brass pots, gardening trowels. I wove my way through the mess to the round window and watched the activity below. But because I couldn't stop thinking about Elena, I looked around the room. I could still feel her here. I could still feel *us* here. I prayed that Elena was in this time, somewhere, alive and breathing, with those eyes that could melt me in an instant, with that brash confidence that wrapped itself around me and cushioned me from the rest of the world, and often from my own stupidity.

Would our reunion be private or in front of dozens of soldiers? Would Elena, serious and strong on her horse, catch sight of me riding toward her? Would she recognize me with my short hair? She wouldn't faint, not my Elena, but she'd leap from her horse, and I from mine. Our eyes would lock, our hands would tremble, we would approach slowly, deliciously, stunned at the love pulling us together like magnets.

She would stop, a delighted smile tugging at her lips, then we'd both lean closer, each afraid the other might break apart like a dandelion puff in the breeze of the moment. Our lips would be the first to touch, soft and needy, while the world roared in my ears and the fire re-ignited in our eyes, and our knees melted and we collapsed in each other's arms.

People began to shout. A crowd had gathered outside the palace gates, but all I could see were the tips of soldiers' helmets and a blue and white standard snapping in the breeze. Someone scattered coins for the peasants, so the crowd's roar increased as the standard moved closer to the palace grounds.

The crowd parted at the gates, and a Moorish entourage rode into the palace yards. I scanned the faces for only a second before I saw her.

The woman's blond hair was swept up off her neck, and her midnight blue dress draped elegantly down one side of the black horse as she rode side-saddle. She tossed handfuls of coins to either side. Damn it. Anna was early.

CHAPTER TWELVE

Heart racing, I searched the palace yards below me, then moaned weakly as Hazm and Arturo came out the main entrance to investigate. "Arturo!" The crowds, flowing onto palace grounds with the army, chanted for more coin so loudly my words barely reached my own ears. "Arturo!"

Anna spotted Hazm and waved, so the boy nodded, hands clasped regally at his waist, now a crown prince waiting to receive his guests. Arturo stood beside him, totally unaware that it was Anna who rode straight toward him. I'd never shown him a photo of her, and he'd only seen her once, when he was five and still in the orphanage. I gripped the windowsill, terrified she would recognize Arturo. Although his face had narrowed, it was still distinctly his, with those same round brown eyes. His face glowed with the same wide innocence. My heart stopped pumping, my blood ceased to circulate. Dear Goddess, how could she *not?* All I could do, and that in almost slow motion, was to swing the window grille shut, disguising my presence with the lacy, open carving.

Anna held up her hand, and the throng eventually quieted. "Greetings, Prince Hazm. I trust your father is well." Her manners were polished and confident, her skin tanned from the long ride to Zaragoza.

"Very well, thank you. We extend to you and your party our welcome and praise Allah for the honor of your visit, Señora de Palma." Arturo froze as Hazm spoke Anna's name. "We are pleased to receive you." Hazm snapped off a command, and turbaned grooms came running from the stables. Other servants hurried to bring refreshments, leaving Arturo doing nothing, clearly not a servant.

"My lord prince, who is your friend?" Anna asked, dismounting. The whole group was so close I could have dumped a basket on Anna's head. "He looks familiar. Have I met him before?"

By now Arturo knew who he faced, but short of running back into the palace, there was nothing he could do. My stomach twisted as he felt for his back pockets, something he always did when nervous, but the breeches had none. He finally stuck them awkwardly under his arms. Please don't recognize him. Please.

Hazm hesitated, then cleared his throat. "No, I do not believe you have met. He and his mother have just come to Zaragoza."

"His mother?" Anna said. "What is your name, young man?"

Thank god Arturo said nothing, realizing that with one word Anna would recognize he spoke using modern Spanish, not an obscure accent from high in the Pyrenees. "Are you unable to speak?" She walked closer and I could see her gaze scanning Arturo's clothes; suddenly his T-shirt, visible under his tunic, screamed L.L. Bean.

"He is a simpleton," barked a soldier, and my heart sank into my toes as Rafael Mahfouz dismounted and handed the reins to a groom. "This man has no brains. He stood in the middle of the road at Mirabueno like a fool until a peasant woman threw herself at him."

Anna's spine straightened with interest. "Mirabueno? You saw this boy and a woman near the cave at Mirabueno?"

Shit. My head pounded in my ears. *Do* something. *Anything.* I whirled and ran into the hall, down the stairs, and out the back entrance. The sheep were gone, probably pastured up in the hills, but one corral was filled with horses. I raced for it, my boots skittering on the wet stones, but when I opened the rickety gate, the horses stood there, blinking those huge eyes, flaring nostrils to take in my scent. I yanked off my shawl and whipped it over my head, then whooping softly, I ran straight into the herd.

Half a dozen horses reared up, eyes white, and the others spun and jumped out of the way. Finally one smart horse noticed the open gate, and the whole herd thundered from the corral, heading in the right direction. Buildings and sloping land would take them around the east end of the palace and straight toward the palace's front entrance.

I spat out dust, wiped my stinging eyes, then scrambled over the corral fence in the opposite direction, hoping to circle around the palace's other end and get lost in the crowds by the palace gates. I held up my skirts with clammy hands as I ran, terrified for Arturo. The only way I could think of to rescue my son was to send thirty spooked horses stampeding straight toward him. Great, Kate, just great.

Surprised shouts and screams of terror rose from the front of the palace and mingled with pounding hooves and mad whinnies. Arturo's only hope was to slip away in the chaos.

People clawed their way to the gates to escape slashing hooves. The army's horses began rearing up in the mess of running humans and furious beasts. I joined the crowd easily and was swept out into the streets of Zaragoza, where I kept to the back streets until I reached Grimaldi's. Liana and her children were gone for the morning, so in the inner courtyard I splashed off my face, then paced in agony for half an hour, stopping only when a dirty and ragged Arturo staggered in through the doorway.

Without a word I held him tighter than I ever thought possible. He rested, panting, against my shoulder. Finally he pulled away. "Mom, Anna's here."

"I was at a window above you. I saw almost everything."

"Even the stampede? Man, those horses saved my ass. They—"

"—were set free by a crazy woman waving her shawl around. Were you hurt?"

"No, but you did that?"

"I couldn't think of anything else, and when Rafael opened his big mouth, I knew I had to do something. Are you sure you're okay?" His breeches and shirt were torn, his face and hands filthy, but otherwise he seemed to be in one piece.

"Yeah, but I'm sure Anna figured out who I was. She kept asking me about Mirabueno and the peasant woman Rafael mentioned. I didn't dare speak, but Hazm was starting to get embarrassed because I didn't say anything, so those horses came at just the right time." He smiled, eyes gleaming with admiration. "Cool idea, Mom. It worked."

"It bought us a few hours, nothing more. Anna will figure out quickly where we are. C'mon." I jogged for the stairs, having heard a few thumps from the roof while I'd paced. "Grimaldi!"

My friend looked up from a pigeon in his hands. "Good heavens. You both look like you've been in a fight."

"Are all the birds back?"

"Yes, but you must make a choice. My Valencia contact pleads for food because they are starving, thanks to the siege, but said he has seen a tall, black-haired man with startling blue eyes participate in negotiations between Rodrigo and Ibn Jehaf. My Calatayud contact says he knows

Luis, and saw him there, riding west toward the monastery at Valvanera two days ago. My guess is Luis is either at Valencia or Valvanera."

Great, just great. Valencia was east of Zaragoza. The Valvanera Monastery was west of Zaragoza. "Grimaldi, Anna knows we're back in this century. You can no longer help us without endangering Hazm. There can be no connection between us and the crown prince, but we need one last favor—two horses and a week's supply of food."

Grimaldi's jaw tightened. "I will do this for you."

"Where are we going?" Arturo asked, face bright, already past the stampede and ready for the next adventure.

Grimaldi sketched a rough map. "Valvanera is to the west, four days' ride. Valencia is down here, to the east, at least five days' ride."

I chewed the inside of my lip. Elena had a history with Valvanera. It was not unusual for her to visit the priests who had taken her in and trained her to fight. But why during a siege? It must be important. "Valvanera," I said. "Then Valencia. Carlos will get there before us and can be my eyes until then." When Anna had a few minutes to sort out why we were here, she'd send someone after us and we'd never have the chance to restore the timeline, or to stop Rodrigo from killing Elena.

"When do we leave?" Arturo asked. "I have some...people I need to see before we leave."

"There is no time to say good-bye to anyone. We leave now. Get your things."

"But I must—"

"*Now.*"

Grimaldi left to find horses, I sent a scowling Arturo to pack our knapsacks, and I stood, glaring at the heavy sky settling like a heavy shawl around my shoulders. Nothing about this visit to the eleventh century was going to be easy. Nothing.

CHAPTER THIRTEEN

Most of Zaragoza lay on the south shore of the Ebro River, and its massive stone walls opened to the outside world through four gates, one in each cardinal direction. We were mounted and heading for the city's north gate within fifteen minutes. Traffic was brisk, and we joined the wagons without notice. Even though our destination was west, that gate was too close to the Aljafería—and Anna—for my comfort. Our only hope was to get well on the way to Valvanera before Anna started looking beyond Zaragoza. The oppressive weather pressed me hard against my saddle, and I prayed it would break soon, since it would take us four days of hard riding to reach Valvanera.

We spoke little as we left the road and turned west, snaking our way through the dense forest that bordered the Ebro. The underbrush pulled at my skirt and thwapped against the horses' flanks until they were jumpier than I was. An hour out of Zaragoza, we found a narrow, quiet stretch of river to cross. The horses swam easily, then we joined the road heading west to Burgos, falling in behind a small caravan of donkey carts.

Only then did I stop looking over my shoulder every five minutes. Several times an odd feeling that someone was watching us snaked up my back, but if Anna's men had found us, they certainly wouldn't hang back. Once I even imagined a flash of red in the craggy rock outcroppings in the distance, but I sighed with relief when it turned out to just be deep red streaks in the exposed rock.

We soon passed the donkey carts, nodding pleasantly to the simply-dressed men driving them. Arturo barely spoke all morning and into early afternoon, and I sensed he stewed about a problem, much as he'd done back in Chicago when his friends had plotted to drug their dates. "You've been awfully quiet," I finally said. "Still shook up by this morning?" He shrugged. "Arturo, what's up?" Another stubborn shrug and I exhaled rudely. Why had the universe created teenagers?

Late afternoon when we stopped in a small clearing by the river to rest, Arturo jerked his head toward the woods. "I gotta go," he mumbled.

"Good idea," I said, then followed him behind the wide live oak tree he'd chosen, its leaves hanging around us like lace.

"Mom?"

"Go ahead."

"For Pete's sake! I don't need an audience."

"Tell me what's bugging you, and I'll give you some privacy."

Frustration fought with some other emotion. He folded his arms. "Maybe I'll just pee anyway."

I folded my own arms. "Go ahead. I never changed your diapers, but you were only six when we formed a family. I gave you hundreds of baths, so I seen you nekkid, boy."

His eyes closed, his lashes two wide feathers brushing his cheeks. "You are a cruel mother."

"Spill it, Arturo."

He scrunched up his mouth, glared at me, then sighed. "It's really nothing. I gotta pee first."

"Promise you'll tell?" He nodded, so I returned to the horses. After I unpacked some dried meat and two oranges, he joined me on a low, flat rock, which was moss-covered and cool. I bit off a piece of salty meat and chewed, waiting.

He cleared his throat, and played with the loose hem of his pants. "It's my fault Anna saw me."

"Nonsense. You didn't even know who she was until Hazm said something."

He shook his head, flinging up his hands in disgust. "I saw this incredibly rich woman ride up, surrounded by amazing horses with silver hanging all over their bridles and saddles, and those soldiers' lances and capes and turbans looked so cool. It flashed through my mind this might be Anna, but then I heard the stirrups clanging, and I just couldn't leave."

"All you had to do was step inside the palace."

'I know, I know." He tugged at his bangs. "But I didn't want to miss anything. And then everything started happening so fast."

"It usually does around here."

"Besides, I was still reeling from Hazm's apartments. Man, that guy has *the* life. He has seven rooms just for himself, and so many servants they're falling over each other."

"Hazm is the prince of a wealthy state."

"He said al-Rashid is a hundred times richer, and his clothes are made of spun gold. Hazm has heard he wears jewels on every finger. He doesn't have to do anything for himself. Al-Rashid even has a harem."

I glanced sharply at Arturo, a bit alarmed at the awe in his voice. "Don't get too carried away. We're supposed to be defeating al-Rashid, not worshiping him."

"I know, but I can't help but imagine what it'd feel like to be so filthy rich. Or have my own harem."

"I thought I raised you to be a feminist!"

He threw up his hands. "Yeah, yeah, okay. I know it's a bad scene for the women. But Mom, remember, I *am* a guy, even if I am a feminist guy."

This conversation was making me nervous. My salary kept us both comfortable, but I'd never been able to give Arturo everything he wanted—not the most expensive skateboard, not every computer game he desired, not the trendiest sneakers, and *certainly* not his own harem.

In the eleventh century, the best clue that someone was traveling in a hurry was pounding hooves, which we both heard at the same time. But before we could move, a coffee-skinned Moorish soldier, wearing a saffron cape but no turban, galloped around the last bend we'd taken in the road, curly brown hair streaming behind him. He nearly passed us before he saw us, but then reined in his horse, whirled around, and approached us, grinning broadly. Rafael Mahfouz leapt off his horse, tossed the reins to Arturo as if he were a servant, then rested gloved hands on two sword hilts, one swinging from each hip. Talk about overkill. "I have found you," he said, so pleased with himself I thought he'd pop. Perspiration beaded on his wide forehead and at the edges of his thick brown moustache; his chest rose and fell with the excitement of the chase.

"What do you want with us? I am a simple peasant woman traveling with her son."

Rafael laughed with delight. "Señora Vincent, your clothes are peasant, but your bearing is not." He squinted slightly. "In fact, you're quite beautiful." The last thing I needed was a compliment from a near-sighted fool. "But no matter. Come. Señora de Palma wishes a word with you."

I'll bet she did. Arturo and I exchanged a quick glance. He draped the reins over a nearby branch and came to stand beside me. I shook my head. "No, thanks. Tell the señora *we* do not wish to speak with *her*."

Rafael's eyebrows shot up but he recovered quickly. "You will not return to Zaragoza with me?"

"You're catching on."

He started chuckling. "This is amazing. You resist me?"

"Yes, I guess so."

This cracked up the handsome soldier again. "I am a soldier of the great caliph al-Rashid. I wear two swords. You are a woman and a boy. You will come with me." He wiped his eyes, still chuckling, and suddenly I wanted to shut him up more than I wanted to escape.

"Get lost, buffoon," I snapped. "Tell your Señora de Palma to fuck off." Arturo grunted in surprise. I rarely used the 'f' word, or in this case, in Spanish, the 'c' word.

Rafael rolled his eyes, then shook his head sadly. He stepped back, pulled each sword easily from its scabbard, then sliced the air in an impressive pattern of circles and figure eights, the massive swords humming softly. He finally stopped, the swords held at the ready. "Come with me or I'll slice your heads off."

"Kie-yap," Arturo yelled as he assumed a fighting stance.

"Arturo, no!"

In the fastest jumping front kick I've ever seen, Arturo's booted toe flew up and under Rafael's chin, snapping the man's head back like a doll's. Rafael crumbled, swords clattering on the rocks as he fell.

"Holy shit," I whispered.

"Is he dead?" Arturo had gone pale. Practicing Tae Kwon Do and sparring with a partner was one thing, but kicking a man unconscious was another.

"Turito, you just saved our butts." I felt for Rafael's pulse, which was strong, so I dragged the swords out of Rafael's reach, then unlaced his tunic and used the thin leather cord to tie his hands behind his back. I ripped part of my hem and used it to tie his feet together.

"Gag him, Mom." I ripped more hem, tied it around his mouth, then Arturo and I both stood back, panting.

"Wow," Arturo murmured.

"It's been quite a day, hasn't it?"

Arturo grinned, his face brightening despite the circles under his eyes. "I never thought I'd say this, *ever*, but I think I've had enough excitement for one day."

"That kick was fairly impressive, Señor Vincent. Master Kim would be proud." I tugged on his ear affectionately.

"Tae Kwon Do, *one*. Swords and other sharp objects, *zero*." He raised his palm for me to slap. "We make a pretty good team, Mom."

I chuckled. "With Elena we'll be unstoppable." Grunting softly, we dragged Rafael, moaning now, behind some bushes.

"Will he be okay?" Arturo checked to make sure he could breathe around the gag.

"Yeah, if no one finds him right away he'll work his way free eventually."

"I wouldn't want to be here when that happens."

I winked. "Me neither. Let's take his horse just to be safe."

We packed up, mounted our horses, then moved back onto the road, bringing Rafael's horse with us to use when ours grew tired.

In a few hours we took the side road south toward Taragona, which was nestled a few miles away against the foothills of the Moncayo Mountains. When the narrow road began climbing, we slowed the horses to a walk. Other than a few shepherds, we saw no one. Now and then a section of collapsed Roman wall rose from a field, then disintegrated at the next swale. We skirted Taragona itself to avoid advertising ourselves, then headed for the Alhama, a tributary of the Ebro that split the Moncayo mountains like a knife splits butter, providing an easier path through the blue peaks.

The air dried as we climbed away from the river. Deer and rabbit appeared now and then, and sharp-eyed Arturo pointed to a lynx sunning itself on a distant rock pile. Fertile meadows still sprinkled the foothills, but exposed rock began to dominate the higher we rode, and purple foxglove and yellow irises bloomed around us, tightening my throat at one point. I'd forgotten how deeply Spain had rooted itself in my heart. These last years, perhaps I had missed more than just Elena.

Dusk settled over the mountains, turning everything a deep violet, the mountains ahead backlit by the pink and orange sky. I stretched my neck and shoulders, then twisted in my saddle to loosen my spine. "What was that?" I said as I twisted back again.

Arturo was nearly asleep in the saddle, but jerked sideways at my voice. "Whaaa?"

I reined in my horse. "I thought I saw something move, back there against that ridge." I squinted in the fading light.

"Probably just another animal, Mom. You're making me jumpy. Relax. And please don't wake me again." He yawned. "I'm a growing adolescent and need my sleep."

"So do I," I grumbled, tired of my sore butt, my aching thighs and calves. My feet had gone to sleep an hour ago. Arturo's head was bobbing again, so I reached over and slid the reins from his hands, which gripped the saddle's front bar. This kid could sleep while parachuting from an airplane.

The next two days passed without incident, and in one small settlement we managed to trade our three horses for two fresh ones. Both our butts burned from so many hours in the saddle, but complaining about it grew boring. At dusk on the third day, the smell of the mountains and the taste of the air gave me our position. We were only an hour's ride from Valvanera, but we would arrive after dark. I was starting to feel a little insane, weak with excitement at the thought I might see her yet today.

When we arrived, all the monks had retired for the evening, save one, and the young man was able to find us some bread and cheese but was totally unsure what to do with me. Arturo and I were so tired I barely registered my surroundings, but I ended up on a hard cot in a cold, narrow room near the entrance to the Valvanera monastery, the only place the poor attending monk could think of to house an exhausted female traveler. He then escorted Arturo back into the dormitory area.

❖

Elena took me by the hand and nearly ran from room to room through the massive monastery. "Our rooms were up those stairs, off limits to women, of course." She winked slyly, then showed me the dining hall, a cavernous room filled with wide, rough-hewn tables and worn benches black with age.

We'd only been at Duañez a month when Elena insisted we brave the December winds to visit the Valvanera Monastery where she'd learned so much. The monks had greeted "Luis Navarro" with deep affection. The eldest, Father Felipe, was so overcome all he could do was smile and wipe his moist eyes.

"Now to the gardens." *I wrapped my cloak tightly around me. She led me through a small orchard, a fallow vegetable garden waiting for spring, and banks of now-dried flowers. The path led to a small stone bridge arching over an icy stream.*

"Lovely," I murmured as water gurgled beneath the bridge.

Standing behind me, Elena wrapped her arms and her cloak around me. "This is my favorite spot," *she said, nuzzling my neck.* "When I was younger I spent hours just sitting here, thinking."

"Thinking about killing Moors?"

I could feel the steady rise and fall of her bound chest against my back. "Yes."

"And now?" *I waited, pulling her arms more tightly around me.*

"And now, if I were alone and free to think, I would consider how alike we are, Moor and Christian, and how religion is a poor reason to destroy each other."

I squeezed her hand. "You're not the same woman you were when you arrived here ten years ago." *A hawk cried overhead, circling on the thermals.* "What would the monks have done if they'd discovered your sex back then?"

Elena took my hand, and we strolled across the sturdy bridge. "They would have prayed for my soul, then sent me away to a convent."

"And now?" *She stopped, a small frown marring her brow.* "If they found out now you are a woman, what would they do?"

Pain flashed across her strong face, then she smiled wryly. "To live as a man for all these years is a sin they could not forgive. They would turn their backs on me."

"Do you really believe that?"

For a second Elena's eyes matched the gray of the sky, as if she'd left and the sky had moved in. Then she pulled me to her, leaning in for a warm kiss. "I do not know, my pearl. I do not know."

I woke up, once again struggling with the line between reality and fantasy. My Elena dreams had begun to frustrate, even anger me. I was tired of memory ghosts. But as I sat up, looking around at the stone walls where Elena had spent so much of her youth, I felt in my gut that today was the day. Elena was here, or near, and we'd meet sometime before evening fell.

CHAPTER FOURTEEN

Still dressed, I rose and tried to shake out the wrinkles and road dust from my skirt. A ragged circle of red soil formed on the marble floor beneath me. I checked the calendar I'd made at Grimaldi's. May 27. Today was day eight of being back in time, and I'd done nothing but eat, sleep, and run. When I opened my door, a scowling monk directed me toward a small cold room where I waited until Arturo joined me, glowing and perky, as if he'd slept two days.

"Señorita." Father Ruiz entered, offering me his hand. "It is truly a pleasure to see you again after all these years. God's grace has kept you well." He sat in the chair opposite mine. "To what do we owe this honor?"

I stared hard at the head priest, who still moved like an athlete despite his age, and wished I could decipher his body language, his controlled smile. What did he know? "I seek my husband Luis Navarro. I thought he might be here."

Father Ruiz spread his thick hands. "We have not seen Luis for many years."

Liar. Grimaldi's contact said he saw Luis coming this way often. I took a deep breath. "I seek Elena Navarro. I thought *she* might be here."

The man's face remained as unchanged as the stone wall behind him. "I believe Elena Navarro was killed by the Moors many years ago, along with all of her family, save Luis," That had been Elena's story. Actually Luis had been murdered and Elena the only survivor. As a woman, her opportunity for revenge against the Moors was zero, so she'd donned her dead brother's clothes and cut her hair.

I pursed my lips. "Her life is in danger, Father. If you care for her at all, you must tell me where she is."

He shrugged. "I have told you what I know."

I leaned forward. "Is lying still a sin in your faith?" Arturo's eyes widened.

Father Ruiz tucked his chin, affronted. "Lying is always a sin, my child."

"Especially when done by a priest," I snapped.

"Whoa, Mom. Lighten up." Arturo winced. "If he doesn't know, he doesn't know."

Damn. She wasn't here. According to Ruiz, she had never been here, which meant we were just as far apart as if I were still back in the future. "I'm sorry, Father, that was rude. I—it's been hard. I'm sorry to have bothered you."

He patted my hand. "No harm done, my child. Will you now travel on to Duañez? I have more wheat to share with those poor souls if you plan to visit."

"Poor souls?"

Father Ruiz shook his head. "Rodrigo's army camped there this winter. Butchered every animal within leagues. Consumed every bit of stored grain, even that which was to be seed for this spring."

I snorted. "Sounds like Rodrigo." But not Elena. How could she allow Rodrigo to destroy our community? I had only lived there six months but had come to love the rough, kind farmers and their families surrounding the wooden 'castle' at Duañez, my home with Elena. Marta had tried to teach me to bake bread and spin, but all my fingers had been skilled at was painting. "How are they doing?"

"Not well. Food is scarce here, but we send them what we can. José and a few of the others have taken to begging for scraps in Burgos and bringing the food waste back to Duañez."

"Father Ruiz, I head for Valencia, not Duañez, but I have a message that must be delivered to Marta at Duañez. Could you see that she gets it along with your wheat?"

"Certainly."

"Do you know of the Mirabueno cave on the road to Zaragoza?"

"Yes, I have taken shelter there in a storm."

Since Elena had trusted him since her youth, I would too. I had no choice. I told him where Marta was to dig, and how often, and the man's eyes widened. "You are a most generous woman, señorita." He stood, taking my arm. "Come, let us feed you before you resume your journey."

While Arturo and I sat in the dining hall with a bowl of beef and mashed grain, I dropped my head back to admire the soaring arches overhead and imagined the hall filled with young, enthusiastic men, believers in the sword, and in God. Elena would have been one of them, slapping Nuño on the back, laughing at ribald jokes, listening intently to Father Ruiz's stories of fighting glory.

But the only sound now was our spoons clattering into the empty bowls. As a young monk led us toward the front entrance, we passed an open door, where the scratchy sounds of quill pens drew me closer. Even with the high windows unshuttered, the room was still so dark each desk required a flickering candle. Monks bent over the desks, carefully transcribing the brittle pages beside them.

"May I?" I asked our escort. He nodded, so I stepped inside, appreciating the scent of tempura paints and freshly powdered vellum, which were thin pages made from lamb skins. I was once again back in Duañez living with Elena, mixing my own paints, hoarding both vellum and linen canvas.

"What are they doing?" Arturo whispered as the nearest candle flickered when our entrance sent the still air swirling.

I'd studied manuscript illumination back in the future and was thrilled to be witnessing the real thing. "They are hand-copying books, making illuminated manuscripts like I made in the classes I took." I asked the nearest monk what he transcribed.

The bald man looked up from his work, then rubbed his bleary eyes. "One of our brothers has translated some of Aristotle from Arabic to Latin. I transcribe the Latin."

"Aristotle?" Arturo moved closer, fingers carefully brushing the top page. "He wrote in Arabic?"

"No," I whispered. "He wrote in Greek, but the Arabs saved the work and translated Aristotle, Plato, Hippocrates, lots of Greeks." The monk had sketched a border around the text, and my fingers itched to pick up a paint brush and add color to the page, but instead I touched Arturo's shoulder. Time to go.

Outside, a young monk waited with our horses. He held the reins while I mounted then handed them to me. "Father Ruiz says he hopes the señorita has a safe journey and that she finds what she seeks."

I nodded and the monk scurried back inside. Arturo and I headed down the narrow, winding road. "Well, that was a bust," Arturo said.

"But if Elena's not here, she must be with Rodrigo in Valencia. Let's haul ass to get down there."

"Stop swearing. And something's weird," I said. "I can't quite figure it out."

"I thought they were very polite. Calling you 'señorita' and me 'Señor Arturo.' I kind of like that."

Señorita. Wait. The word cut through the dull ache in my brain. On my last visit I'd come as Luis's wife, a señora, but now he used the unmarried term. I looked back at the towering stone and a thrill ran through me. He would only call me señorita if he knew Luis was a woman, so our marriage had not been valid. "I just figured it out. Father Ruiz knows Luis is a woman."

"How did—"

"C'mon." My heart beat faster as we turned back.

To the west several monks worked in the stables, but at the east end of the monastery, the path to the orchard and gardens was quiet, so at the first clump of trees we tied up the horses. Feeling a bit like James Bond, I slunk from tree to bush to tree with a fourteen-year-old shadow until I'd made my way around to the back of the building. We would explore the grounds first, then work on sneaking inside.

The gardens, already lush with blooms, formed a horseshoe around the orchard. A dozen monks knelt in the garden weeding, planting, and talking quietly among themselves, and the voices were all male. Two monks burned a pile of brush near the orchard.

Hunched over, we fought our way through the underbrush until we were closer to the orchard. No Elena. "She's not here," Arturo whispered, stumbling to keep up with me as I pressed on, intent on checking out the back gardens and the stone bridge. Breathing air heavy with blossoms, I reached the creek, which had swollen with the spring rains, and stopped at the most amazing sight. A young child, perhaps three or four years old, ran along the stone path among the flowers, her dark, tight curls bouncing down her back. She stopped at the bridge and I ducked behind a thick oak, pulling Arturo back with me.

"She's a cutie," he whispered.

"No, Solana, not the bridge," scolded an older monk resting nearby.

"But Father—"

"No."

Her chin lifted defiantly and I smiled, recognizing the same look on Arturo's face when I'd told the six-year-old not to flush pennies down the toilet to watch them spin.

Taking in orphans was not unusual for a monastery, but Father Ruiz and Company seemed far too stodgy for this little firecracker.

"Well, then I will climb this tree," the stubborn child announced.

"No, you—"

"Fire! Fire!" The cries came from back around the curve near the orchard, where the monks had been burning brush, and even from our spot in the trees I could see the flames licking fifteen feet into the sky.

Shouts and cries for help brought little Solana's monk to his feet. "Stay here! I shall be right back." He loped down the path and disappeared around the curve.

"Don't leave her alone," I muttered. Sure enough, the brown robe had barely flapped out of sight when Solana turned toward the bridge, face flushed with the opportunity to reach her objective. She paused, looked over her shoulder once, then dashed for the bridge, her long yellow shift billowing against sturdy brown legs.

"Uh oh," Arturo said.

With a tiny whoop and a triumphant grin, the child scampered across the bridge, then back again. Bare feet immune to the rough stone, she ran the length of the bridge over and over again, as if storing up the experience to relive when she was once again too closely guarded.

Finally she stopped in the middle of the bridge, panting, and I sensed trouble. Now that the bridge had been conquered, the next challenge would be the low stone walls lining the bridge. I moaned softly as the girl headed straight for the wall. The shouts near the fire had begun to die out as Solana, mouth clenched in concentration, dug one toe in, then the other, and flung a pudgy leg onto the wall.

"No, no," I whispered. "You're going to fall."

Talking happily to herself, Solana stood, arms outstretched, and walked along the wall, placing one foot in front of the other, short little toes gripping the uneven rock. Why did children constantly seek challenges their bodies were not yet able to handle, even in the eleventh century? I stepped out from the trees, unsure. The creek, nearly flooding its grassy banks, was only thirty feet away, and while I was downstream from the bridge and could reach it easily, I worried I would startle Solana into falling.

I inhaled sharply as the girl's arms began windmilling frantically. She was going over.

"No!" My long legs brought me to the bank just as the child splashed off the far side of the bridge with a surprised shriek. Icy water bit through my boots as I waded into the swift current, struggling for balance myself. Within seconds a sputtering Solana swept under the bridge off to my right. Weighed down by a wet skirt, I lunged and managed to close my fingers around one wrist.

"Oh! Oh!" Solana coughed and gagged as I pulled her to me. Arturo waded in and dragged us both from the frigid stream up onto the bank. "Oh! Oh!"

I knelt beside her. She gagged several times, spit, then took a shuddering breath. But instead of crying, she turned her deer-eyes up at me. "You saved me. I felled in. Father Miguel will be so vexed with me. You are *such* a pretty lady."

I bit back a smile at her quick recovery, then lifted off the wet strands of hair stuck to her face and arms as Arturo squeezed water from the hem of her cotton dress.

"And a boy! My name is Solana. Will you marry me?"

Arturo chuckled, surprisingly gentle as he pulled twigs and leaves from her hair. "You're lucky my mother caught you. We saw you start to lose your balance."

"I losted my balance. Oh!" The little girl suddenly clutched at her neck and pulled out a long chain that had been tucked into her dress. "Oh good. I didn't losted this."

Stunned at the flash of yellow, I grabbed the girl's hands. "Let me see."

"No, this is secret. I am not supposed to show it to anyone."

A lump suddenly lodged in my throat. "Please, Solana. I won't tell anyone."

Clearly torn, she frowned, then smiled so wide two dimples creased her rosy cheeks. "You did saved me, so maybe Mama won't mind." She opened her hand slowly. "This is my magic necklace. When you miss the person who gave it to you, you just hold this little lion and think about that person and then you feel better."

Hanging from a dull silver chain around the girl's neck was the Lion King keychain I'd given Elena the day we'd parted at Santillana del Mar. The paint had dulled and flaked off in places, and one leg was missing, but it was the one. There would not be another like it in the eleventh century.

"Holy shit," Arturo whispered. "Disney really is everywhere."

My heart slowed until it became a dull thud reverberating in my ears. "Honey, where did you get this lion?"

Little Solana dropped her treasure back inside the neck of her dress. "Mama gave it to me. She said if I got sad and missed her, I could hold the lion. Mama said the lion means she loves me."

"Your mama?" I could barely breath. "Does she have black hair and pretty blue eyes?"

Solana clapped her hands. "You know my mama!"

Fingers tingling, I sat down hard on the ground, my mind whirling like a dust storm, picking up debris then flinging it wildly away. Finally the truth stared back at me through the innocent eyes of curly-haired Solana. I was looking into the round, shining face of Elena Navarro's daughter.

Arturo gasped. "Mom, didn't you give this lion to...? Is this her...?" I couldn't reply but only stare at the stunning child before me.

"Solana!" Solana leapt to her feet when her missing 'nanny' returned, followed by a handful of concerned monks who must have heard me cry out when little Solana fell. The wet, dripping clothes clinging to all three of us painted a clear picture, and either from cold or fear of being scolded, Solana began to tremble.

As the stunned monks fussed over us, a strange ache spread up into my chest. "Thank you, señorita, señor, for helping our Solana," the girl's caretaker chattered. "Come, let us dry your clothes, child." The soggy Solana darted away and ran in circles around the nearest monk, eluding his grasp and giggling. I could not take my eyes off her. The eyes were brown, but as intense as Elena's could be. The nose would some day be slender, the lips full.

I finally realized my pain wasn't because Elena had turned to a man. What flamed through me was pure jealously, as green as it gets. She loved someone else. She might still love someone else. What did I expect after eight years? Of course she would move on. She knew I never intended to return. Even as I reasoned this out, a tiny voice tucked into the recesses of my neocortex screamed, "But she's mine, she loves *me*."

The monk finally snagged Solana, but she yelled and broke free, running straight to Arturo and wrapping herself around his leg. When the monk tried to pry the child off him, Solana shrieked, hugged poor Arturo even tighter, and screamed.

As she did, an angry yell rose up from somewhere far behind us, perhaps on the road, and what had to be a war horse at full gallop sent shock waves through the soil.

I met Father Ruiz's eyes, glaring my accusation, and the guilty priest simply closed his eyes briefly, all the confession I needed. My heart thundered as loudly as the horse's hooves, since I was pretty sure I knew both the horse and the rider. Torn between excitement and fear, I stepped back into the shadows of the trees along the stream, suddenly interested in seeing her through Arturo's eyes. Arturo saw me do this but had his hands full with the screaming Solana.

Solana's shrieks rose, but Arturo stopped trying to comfort her when the horse pounded around the monastery and straight toward him. When Arturo's mouth dropped open and his eyes widened in awe, I let myself smile, understanding just what a fearsome sight bore down on him.

"What harm have you done this child?" called the rider, who slid off the snorting horse and strode toward Arturo. Elena's profile came into view and suddenly my vision blurred. She had not changed—same black hair, ramrod back, fierce scowl, which my son now faced. I touched the rough bark of the tree next to me for support.

"Release the child," she bellowed. Her breeches and tunic were dirty and stained with dried blood, explained by the dead deer tied across Matamoros's wide rump.

"I…ah…" Arturo couldn't take his eyes from the 'man' yelling at him.

"Mama!" Solana finally ceased her tantrum and threw herself at Elena, removing all doubt as Elena lifted the girl into her arms. Realization flashed across Arturo's face. "You are…" I felt his confusion. This was Luis Navarro before him, but the girl had said 'Mama,' so should he say Elena? "You are…Navarro."

Elena adjusted Solana onto her hip, looking just as comfortable with her child as any other mother. I didn't know what to think. Was there a husband somewhere? A lover?

"Yes, I am. And who are you to make this child scream?" The monks tried to answer but Elena held up her hand.

My son swallowed, and I was proud of his courage. Holy crap, when had he grown up?

"I am Arturo Vincent. I am the son of a woman you once knew."

Elena froze, ignoring little Solana, who now played with Elena's earlobe. "A woman I once knew?"

That seemed to be my cue, so nearly faint with a sudden fear she wouldn't remember me, I stepped from the shadows. "That would be me," I said quietly.

Elena whirled, and although I was vaguely aware Arturo reached for Solana when Elena's grip loosened, my vision focused only on her. Our eyes met and I need not have feared she'd forgotten me. Elena opened and closed her mouth several times, but said nothing, eyes dark with shock.

My pulse raced. "It's me. I'm—I'm sorry I've been away so long." More lame words came out my mouth, but I wasn't really aware of what I said. As the air between the two of us throbbed with energy, Arturo and the monks moved away, one of them leading Matamoros, another leading Solana, who went without protest this time.

My skirts and shoes were soaking wet, so I should have been cold, but suddenly I was so warm I expected to start steaming soon.

"Is it really you?" she whispered.

I moved close enough to see a new crescent scar along one jaw, another slicing through an eyebrow. "It's me, Elena. I'm really here."

She shook her head, a sad smile dancing across her face. "No, I do not believe you are. I have imagined you appearing so many times. How do I know this is not yet another dream?"

I reached out and touched her hand.

"Mother of God!" She jerked back, breathing hard through her nose. I waited for reality to take hold. Finally, after a few minutes, she reached a trembling hand for my cheek and touched me. I swayed dangerously. How could I have gone so long without feeling this way?

"I am not seeing visions?" She rubbed a thumb across my cheek.

"No."

She touched my short curls. "Your hair."

"Long story."

"You are here, now, in this time." Her fingers lightly wandered down my shoulders, my arms, sending shivers through me.

"Yes." I dared not say more.

"Eight *years*, Kate." Only inches separated us now.

"Eight years, one month, and fifteen days." What if she loved someone else now?

"You came with Arturo." She leaned closer, drinking in every inch of my face.

I felt her breath on my lips, and I shook. "Another long story."

She narrowed those ice blue eyes, staring at me as if I were a puff of smoke likely to disappear. By now the others had reached the monastery, banging doors and scolding Solana, so we were alone. I licked my lips. All I wanted to do was fall into her arms and kiss her, but I couldn't. No ties. No rekindling a flame I couldn't keep burning.

"You have grown even more beautiful with time," she whispered.

"And you've grown even more blind."

Her lip twitched. "You have not changed."

I grinned so broadly my cheeks hurt. "So, you remember me."

She couldn't stop grinning herself. "Vaguely."

I smiled, but made no move to touch her. After eight years of imagining this moment, I was suddenly as nervous as a teenager on a first date, but then Elena slid her hand behind my neck, sending delicious shivers down my arms. "Eight years is a very long time," she said.

I moved close enough to feel the heat of her body. She'd had a child, but those eyes were sparkling like one carat diamonds, so perhaps her feelings hadn't dimmed. "Yes, it is," I said. "Much can happen in eight years." Without thinking, I lightly rested my hands on her hips, the most natural thing in the world to do, and suddenly we were in each other's arms. I buried my face in her neck and let my relief flow as she clutched me to her. She didn't hate me for leaving.

"Kate," Elena murmured against my cheek, "I have missed you beyond all reason." Then her lips found mine, and eight years slipped away as if it had only been eight hours. It was 1086 again and we lived at Duañez and held each other every night, and I felt whole again, as if a limb had been reattached, as if my heart had been restarted. As we kissed, my brain shouted that this couldn't last, that after June 15, I was taking Arturo back to the future, but I couldn't stop kissing her. I felt like a drowning woman desperate for oxygen.

When I grew so dizzy I thought I'd fall over, I finally managed to pull back. Too overwhelmed to speak, Elena led me to a bench and we sat down. I burned to ask her about Solana, to tell her about Rodrigo and ask for her help, but I wanted nothing to interfere with this moment. We sat there, grinning at each other.

"I cannot tell you how it makes me feel to have you here," Elena said. "Tell me about your life, about Arturo." Not until she took my hand in hers did I remember how well we'd fit together.

Relieved to be on safe ground for a few minutes, I shared stories about Arturo's childhood, about my mishaps as a mother. Body heat and the warm stone bench dried my skirts as Elena and I got reacquainted. Twice I wanted to kiss her again but suddenly felt shy.

Finally, as the bench fell into the shade, the sun now well below the tree line, I steered the conversation in the direction she'd avoided. "I have told you all about Arturo. You've met him. I couldn't help but notice that you, too, have had a child."

Elena grinned with pride. "Yes, I do. She is a little hellion." Her face softened. "Sometimes she reminds me of you."

"She lives here at the monastery?"

"Yes. The poor monks have all become gray-haired, thanks to Solana. Every day she is like a storm sweeping through here, yet the monks do love her." She sighed. "I live here with her in the winters, then during King Alfonso's summer campaigns all I can do is dream of her. I dare not take her from this place, because as you can see, she freely calls me Mama, which would reveal more than is safe." We locked eyes, and Elena clearly struggled with a thought. "Kate, since Solana, I...I understand now why you returned to Arturo."

I swallowed as eight years of guilt threatened to leak out my tear ducts. Determined that my waterworks wouldn't spoil our time together, I took a shaky breath. "Elena, what happened after I left?" Surely this would help lead her to telling me about the father.

She pressed her lips together, then gazed out toward the monastery. "I died," she said. A door banged open and little Solana came flying out, followed by Arturo carrying a small bundle. As the 'hellion' came careening down the path, Elena watched her daughter. "And Solana brought me back to life."

"Mama! Do you know this pretty lady?" Solana climbed into Elena's lap.

"Yes, I do, little bird." Elena kissed the toddler's rosy cheek, and

I was nearly moved to tears by Elena's tenderness. She'd never shown this side of herself to anyone but me before, and I was so pleased she was sharing it with her child.

"Mom, I brought you some dry things." As I changed my socks and shoes, Elena put Solana aside and stood.

"Arturo, I am Elena. I must apologize for my words of anger." They shook hands, Arturo grinning so broadly I knew he was thrilled.

"No problem," he breathed. "It is an honor to meet you." Arturo flashed me a wistful look, one that shocked me, but clearly said, "We could be a family, the four of us." I shook my head. No, we could not. Arturo's safety and health and college education had to come first, not my heart. The only thing that would prevent me from returning Arturo to the safety of the twenty-first century was if something unthinkable were to happen to him.

CHAPTER FIFTEEN

All evening I kept trying to find a moment alone with Elena to explain that I needed her help putting Rodrigo on the throne of Valencia, but Solana was an inexhaustible whirlwind not to be ignored. Besides, I couldn't concentrate. Every time I tried to marshal my thoughts, I imagined Elena's hands on my body. At one point I watched her hands move as she described a battle to Arturo, and my body responded as if she'd caressed me, not the air. Arturo's eyes shone as they talked, and once he even had her on her feet trying a few Tae Kwon Do moves.

After the simple meal of soup and bread and an hour of playing with Solana and Arturo in the gardens, Solana began to fuss. Elena announced she'd had enough, and the child must sleep. As we herded the little girl toward her room, Arturo gave me a hug, whispering in my ear, "It's so nice to see you really happy."

"I've been happy," I started to protest, but Arturo shook his head.

"Not like this. I've never seen you smile the way you've been smiling tonight." Before I could answer, he gave me the most irritating and inappropriate wink, then jogged down the hall toward his own bunk. With Elena leaning against the doorjamb, I told Solana "The Three Little Pigs," and "Cinderella," and "Chicken Little" until she dropped off.

By now the monks had all retired, leaving only a few oil lamps burning. As Elena and I returned to the main hall, our footsteps echoed through the dark room, and my palms began to sweat. Where did Elena sleep? What was I supposed to do next? Elena looked as distressed as I felt.

"I can't," I suddenly said. I didn't know what I meant. I can't resist you? I can't let myself fall into bed with you? I can't hurt you like I did last time?

Elena stopped walking and lightly touched my arm. "Come outside with me. I cannot be inside right now."

The warm air felt good as we stepped outside, but instead of reaching for a torch, Elena took my hand. "I know the garden well. We do not need light."

Moonlight filtered through the trees, turning the ground into patches of pale lace. God, was there anything more romantic than walking through a garden in the moonlight with the woman you loved?

I licked my lips. "It's been a long time, Elena. I know some things have changed, but—"

"Kate, do you still—" She stopped, her voice hoarse and strained.

Suddenly too hot to breathe, I loosened my shirt collar. "There has been no one, really, since..." My nervous fingers toyed with my necklace, now visible against my throat. "I know, though, that you... that you have—"

"What is around your neck?"

Nearly faint with fear, or desire, I couldn't tell which, I swallowed hard, then dropped the necklace so she could see it. "My pearl. It's my pearl."

Her soft gasp set me throbbing every place a woman can throb, then her uncertainty seemed to melt like butter in the sun, and she reached for me. Sparks flew in the dark as we met, red-hot and without control. Our lips devoured and burned as we wrapped ourselves around each other. I couldn't breathe and relished the unbearable tightness in my chest. Tears formed when Elena kissed me with a strength as desperate as my own, then without another word our fingers struggled with laces and belts.

"You came back," she whispered, roaming from my lips to my now naked shoulder. "So much has happened."

"Yes," I said, still not breathing right. "So much we haven't yet talked about—"

She covered my mouth with her own, and although I suddenly forgot what we needed to talk about, reason struggled to break through the passion. "Elena, while I've been away, I know some things have changed, but—"

"Kate, my world is not the same as the one you left." Her breath tickled my collarbone, and I grew weak under her hands. "*Everything has changed.*"

"Yes, it has." I stroked her back and slid my hand lower. "That's why it would be foolish to act on any needs we might feel."

Elena took my face in her hands. "I agree. You and I are not foolish women."

My reply, totally inappropriate, was to kiss her long and hard.

Elena finally broke away and chuckled. "We should go back inside." She curved one hand around my waist and the other found my breast, which her strong fingers teased.

"Sweet Jesus," I muttered. My knees buckled against hers but she caught me in time. "You should stop," I finally managed to whisper.

"Yes, I should." And somehow my blouse was open and her mouth was on my breast, and electricity shot through me as I arched against her. I should have stopped us right then, but at that point all reason fled, so I pulled her over behind the bushes and down into my arms, where we showed each other that one thing, at least, had *not* changed.

❖

I awoke the next morning in Elena's bed, happily ensnared in a tangle of warm, smooth limbs, unsure which were mine and not caring either way. When I shifted a hip, sore from making love in the garden at midnight, Elena stirred, and nuzzled against my neck. "I cannot believe you came back to me," she murmured.

Maybe we should have talked more before we gave in to our passions. I searched my mouth for a drop of saliva, but found only parched uncertainty. "We need to talk."

She groaned, then sat up, tossing off a wicked wink. "I'd forgotten how much you liked to talk." She reached for her trousers, so I searched the floor for my skirt.

"Elena, I have something to tell you that may be hard to believe."

She laced up her leather tunic over her shirt. "First, I prefer Luis. It has been eight years since anyone has called me by that other name. Second, you can travel between the present and the future. What could be harder to believe than that?"

I tugged on the edge of my own tunic, then could find no other solution but to just begin. "Years ago, you asked me if Rodrigo would ever drive the Moors from the peninsula, as you had once hoped."

She froze, as if gripped by a pain I couldn't see. "That is no longer important to me."

"In my history, Rodrigo Díaz, El Cid, rides into Valencia as its conqueror on June 15, 1094, eighteen days from now. Folklore credits him with starting the four hundred year drive to expel the Moors from this country."

"It takes four hundred years? That is pathetic."

"Well, that's another long story, but in my century, El Cid is a hero."

She tugged on her boots. "Rodrigo Díaz does not deserve to be a hero."

The sudden chill in her voice spiked my anxiety, but taking a deep breath, I plunged ahead, explaining about the change in the timeline, ending with Professor Kalleberg's proof that lives were being snuffed out as history readjusted itself from century to century. "Rodrigo must control Valencia, not Ibn Jehaf or al-Rashid." I stopped, suddenly unsure as the muscles along her jaw twitched. "Both my son and myself may disappear when the changes approach the twentieth century. We may cease to exist." I waited, arms heavy at my side.

Elena threw her traveling cloak over her shoulders, closed the clasp, then looked me in the eye. "Kate, you ceased to exist for me the day you disappeared right before my eyes in that cursed cave." My breath caught at the pain in her voice. "You were there, and then suddenly, you were gone, as if I had dreamed my time with you."

"I have not stopped thinking about you for eight years," I said softly.

She didn't smile. "I understand now why you have returned." Her eyes froze hard like a high mountain lake when she realized the truth. "You are worried about your future and that of your child." With my story, I drove away all the warmth we'd created between us.

Before I could tell her I also came back to save her, her stiff back and tight mouth told me it was too late for this information. She wouldn't believe me now. I ignored the twist in my heart. "Elen—Luis, Anna does something to alter history. She somehow sends Rodrigo away. He does not march into Valencia on June 15. The Moors, under al-Rashid, eventually consume the entire peninsula. It's the exact opposite of what's supposed to happen." I stopped, watching as she crossed her arms. "I need your help. I must find out what Anna does. I must keep Rodrigo here. I must make sure he takes Valencia."

"Rodrigo is a madman. He is no longer the leader I agreed to follow. He has changed more than you can imagine."

Confused, I waved a hand. "That doesn't matter," I sputtered. "It can't matter. He still must wear Valencia's crown."

"You have not come back to seek me out, to see if we might recapture what we once had. You have come back to play God with our lives."

"I wish you wouldn't put it that way."

"I can think of no other way to say it."

Now my jaw was set as firmly as hers. "Rodrigo is not the only one who has changed." This was not supposed to play out this way. I started to reach for her, then checked myself.

"Kate, do you have any idea what Rodrigo intends to do should he take Valencia?" I shivered, shaking my head. "He no longer tolerates prisoners and has no patience for slaves. He just wants the city. When the gates open to Rodrigo, he has a bloodthirsty general named Tahir, a man who answers not to me, but only to Rodrigo. Tahir and his men will spare no one. Do you understand? They have convinced Rodrigo the entire city must pay for locking us out. The city holds thousands too weak to defend themselves, and once the slaughter begins, it will be impossible to stop." She strapped on her sword, tucked her dagger into its sheath.

"You are dressing as if you leave us." When she didn't answer I swallowed a few times, furious I was the one stuck supporting Rodrigo the Asshole. "Look, you've all done things in times of war that you aren't proud of. I'm not saying that Rodrigo will be the best ruler of Valencia. I know, for a fact that he won't be. But he must be the next one."

"Is that right, my time-traveling pearl?" Her use of the old endearment cut me to the bone. "I used to follow Rodrigo in hopes he would rid my country of the Moors. Now I can see what you wanted me to see, all those years ago. Rodrigo is an animal, a cruel, heartless man, and I can no longer follow him blindly. Rodrigo used to be motivated by money. I understood that; we are mercenaries, for God's sake. But money no longer motivates him, only power and cruelty." She tucked her hands behind her back and strolled to the door. She stopped, spun on one heel, and considered me with a remote, cool air. "The *only* way Rodrigo Díaz will take possession of Valencia is over my dead body."

"What?" I whispered.

She smiled, almost amused. "Rodrigo does not know it yet, but he has come to the end of his power. When the moment is right, my men and I will destroy Tahir, capture Rodrigo, and put al-Rashid on the throne, or Ibn Jehaf. It makes no difference to us. But the Moors will rule the Moors, the Christians the Christians. We have no business here."

A vise clamped itself across my temples. Elena would not help me. Holy shit. She was *against* me. I traveled back in time. I found the one person who could help me ensure Rodrigo took Valencia, but she was on the wrong side. Thoughts collided in my head like bumper cars—violent, and not much fun. Elena plotted against Rodrigo. He would learn this, then attack and kill her. If she succeeded in stopping Rodrigo from taking Valencia, Arturo and I might cease to exist. If Rodrigo succeeded, Elena would be dead. Either way I lost. "Luis, it is wrong to alter what has already been laid down as the world's history. No one has the right, or the wisdom, to play God with the past."

"No one, including you, has the right to play God with my present." Her words turned my hands to ice. I had dreamed for years of seeing this woman again, and we now stood on either side of a huge chasm, just as impossible to cross as the centuries that had separated us for so long. She laughed softly, one of those chilling sounds empty of mirth, then shook her head. "Your talk of timelines means nothing to me. My future is my own to shape. I will not alter my path because you ordain it."

I clenched my fists so tightly my nails became needles piercing my palms. "But I…I need your help."

"I plan to betray Rodrigo. Nothing you can say will change that."

I crossed the room but didn't dare take her hand. "Please, don't go. We need to keep talking."

Elena shook her head and opened the door. "I return to Valencia."

"We will come with you. Maybe then—"

"Kate, I do not regret last night. But I cannot bear to let you back into my life knowing you will leave it once again. Return to your time, for there is nothing you can do here."

She strode down the hallway and out the front door, without even a goodbye kiss for her child.

❖

I was nearly frantic with fear. How could I do this myself? I gave Arturo the bad news, but he shook his head. "Don't be dumb, Mom. We can do this. Yeah, it would have been easier with Elena's help, but it's you and me. We can do anything."

His infectious smile and absolute confidence in his mom picked me up long enough that I could pack our gear and formulate a plan. We would follow Elena, catch up to her, and wear her down until she agreed to help.

Before Arturo and I left, Solana hugged me and planted a sloppy kiss on my cheek. "Pretty lady, my mama had to leave. But if you see her, tell her I don't want her to get hurted."

I smoothed back her wild, unruly curls. "Don't worry, Solana. Your mama's very strong and brave."

"I know." She clutched the Lion King hidden beneath her dress, then giggled when Arturo kissed her pudgy cheek.

Solana's nanny gave us directions for the nearest pass south through the mountains. From there we'd find the Río Jalón, follow that south to Calatayud where it joined the Río Jiloca, then head upstream along the Jiloca toward Valencia. "Go with God," Father Ruiz murmured.

"Bye, pretty lady! Bye, Turito!"

I waved to the little sweetie as I urged my horse forward, anxious to put miles on our horses. I knew two inexperienced riders had no chance of catching up with Elena, but that didn't matter since I knew where she was headed.

CHAPTER SIXTEEN

We rode hard all day, and that night we set up camp in a rocky enclave off the road. Arturo fed the fire while I filled our water bladders from a stream. Crickets chirped incessantly. People who thought the countryside was quiet had never spent much time there. When we started to eat, Arturo cleared his throat. "I'm sorry about Elena."

I handed him a chunk of bread smeared with herbed goat cheese, then shrugged. I'd known I wasn't staying here permanently, so why waste time being disappointed about my romantic life? Elena's refusal to help galled me, but I wasn't going to give up. There had to be some chink in her armor I could exploit, some reason why helping me would benefit her as well.

"Mom?" I looked up as I bit a date in half. "Not to change the subject, but how come one minute I feel like an adult, then like a kid, then like an adult?"

I chuckled. "Because you're both. Adolescence is a messy time." I finished my date and tossed one to Arturo.

"In this century fourteen-year-olds are considered men. Grimaldi called me a man. When I took out Rafael, I felt like one. When I ran from Anna and the horses, I felt like a little kid. All I wanted to do was... was find you." I blinked hard at his honesty. "Then when I pulled you and Solana from the stream I felt like a man again. When will I know I'm a man? Do I have to turn eighteen first?"

I struggled for an answer that made sense. Just because I'd lived through my own adolescence didn't mean I understood it, but it felt good to be talking this way again with Arturo. Maybe the best way to communicate with stubborn teens was to take them over nine centuries back in time. "Arturo, one of the joys of being a child is that you aren't held totally responsible for your actions. Maybe we become adults when we take responsibility for our actions."

Arturo chewed thoughtfully, shadows from the fire dancing across his chest. "So if I do something that affects another person, I'm a child if I say it wasn't my fault, and an adult if I admit I'm responsible?"

"Maybe. I'm not sure. I think being an adult has less to do with sexual maturity and everything to do with emotional maturity. I think responsibility is a huge part of that."

Arturo licked his lips, then held my gaze across the fire. "When you left Elena to come back and raise me, you were being responsible."

I shook my head, reaching down to stir the fire. "It was more than that, honey. I *wanted* to be your mom."

"I really, really like her," he said quietly.

"Me, too," I replied, letting a little sigh escape.

He accepted that with a nod, and we stared into the fire for awhile. "Mom?"

I lifted my gaze from the embers.

"You were right." A faint blush rose up Arturo's cheeks. "This whole time travel thing, while pretty exciting, has been harder than I thought it'd be."

"You miss our time?"

"I miss my friends. I miss Max, my MP3 player, movies, Mountain Dew."

"It's May 29, honey. A bit more than two weeks, then it'll be over." All I wanted to do that very moment was pack up and head us straight for the cave at Santillana, our ticket home.

He frowned, suddenly looking more vulnerable than since we'd come back in time. "It's more than just missing stuff. I was thinking about this last night as I was trying to fall asleep, and started to get how dangerous this whole thing really is." He stirred the fire with a stick. "Remember that TV show you used to make me watch with you, the one with the android?"

"*Star Trek…The Next Generation.*"

"Yeah, whatever. The coolest part of that show was the holodeck, where they could recreate any place or time and just go there. But whenever they were in danger or wanted to leave, all they had to do was say something, and this door would appear."

"I think they said, 'Exit program.'"

"Yeah. Well, yesterday, when Elena was galloping straight for me and I didn't know who she—or he was, and that kid was screaming like I was killing her or something, all I wanted to do was say 'Exit program' and have that door appear so I could get away."

I swallowed hard, feeling for my son's dawning realization that this was more than a really intense video game, and I doubled my resolve to get him home safely. "I'm afraid our 'exit program' door is well over a hundred miles away."

Arturo nodded, his face in shadow, appearing half determined, half frightened. "I know, and we're going to do this, Mom, so don't think I'm wimping out or anything."

"Never."

"It's just…I think I'll be ready to go home when it's time."

"You willing to put on some ruby slippers, click your heels three times, and say 'There's no place like home?'"

"Jeesh, Mom, no ruby slippers."

When the cool air settled above us, I fed the fire a few more twigs, then we each reached inside our saddlebags for a little bedtime reading. "Oh no, you don't," I said as I pulled Arturo's new dagger out of *my* saddlebag. "You're supposed to be carrying this."

"No weapons, Mom. Master Kim taught me that."

Disgusted, I stuffed the dagger into the bottom of my bag and pulled out the book I sought. I couldn't force him to arm himself.

"We shouldn't have brought back books, you know." I tried to sound severe, but took such great comfort holding this irrefutable evidence of my future, that I came off sounding as pleased as if I'd snuck contraband chocolate through customs.

Arturo had two books, one on Islam, the other a biography of al-Rashid. I had handwritten notes of the events as they should happen, as detailed by Professor Kalleberg. The books, of course, no longer told the history any of us had been taught, but spoke of the alternate history, the one working its way through the centuries toward Kalleberg and the entire twenty-first century.

Arturo read a section out loud that described how al-Rashid set up universities in every major European city and insisted that all children be educated. He spread the Moors' knowledge of medicine and science throughout the continent. "Hey, he's one of those who translated Aristotle and those other guys."

I finally held up my hand. "Enough. I know. There are many great parts to the Moorish culture, but we can't think about that."

"What's your book?" Arturo asked, pointing to the thin yellow book in my hands.

"A book of poems that Christian generations passed on to one another through word of mouth, sort of like an underground resistance. When I get too enamored of the Moors and their civilized culture, mostly from reading books like yours, these poems remind me life under Moorish rule wasn't a picnic for everyone."

"Meaning?"

I opened the book to a marked page. "Here's one example. It's a song about how the idea of harems swept across Europe and Africa, and even non-Muslim countries began adopting them until even the poorest city official soon had a harem. Women were packed ten to a house, beaten, treated as slaves."

Arturo had the good grace to wince, given his earlier excitement about harems.

"In 1109, only fifteen years from now, a young woman in a Zaragozan harem organized a rebellion. Six hundred women revolted and followed her into the streets. The song tells of S. Pidal's great courage and leadership, and how the Zaragozan army surrounded the unarmed women and slaughtered them."

"Jesus." Arturo passed a hand across his eyes. "Is history always going to be ugly, no matter who rules?"

"I'm afraid so. It's never—"

"Mom, don't move," Arturo breathed. I froze, still bent over the fire, as a sharp silence sent goose bumps crawling down my arms. "Jesus, Mom, do *not* move." Arturo's whisper was tight with terror. "Oh my god, oh my god," he chanted softly.

Painfully slowly, my hands exposed and held away from my body, I raised my face to Arturo's. Eyes dark with fear, he stared at something over my left shoulder, then over my right. I straightened my spine and understood. Red-caped warriors ringed the campsite on the rocks above with twenty arrows pointed directly at us.

"Oh, god," I whispered. Al-Saffah. No one moved. No one spoke. "Put your hands up," I whispered. As we both inched our hands over our heads, I prayed to all the gods and goddesses, Allah even, that raised hands was a sign of submission to the Almoravides, not aggression.

The tallest Almoravide, face barely visible under a red hood lined with white, snapped a command and all but two of the archers slid their arrows back into quivers strapped across their backs. The two remaining arrows remained pointed at Arturo and me. The men jumped or slid down the rocks and surrounded us, then two stepped forward and patted us down roughly, finding my dagger strapped to my calf. Chortling happily, the caped archer lifted his own loose pant leg and strapped the dagger Elena had given me onto his own shapely calf. *Very* shapely calf. I listened to the timbre of the voices now chattering softly around us. Wait a minute.

When the tallest warrior standing before me pulled back the hood to reveal a woman's face, the rest of them tossed off their hoods and laughed at my open mouth, at Arturo's wide eyes. Every one was a black woman, an Almoravide from northern Africa, and bald as a baby's butt except for a shock of hair on the very tops of their heads. The top knot of the fierce woman before me flopped back in a tangle of dreadlocks. Other women had swinging braids or thick ponytails, while others had shaved their top knots to short, black bristles.

"Wow," Arturo murmured, and as the shortest woman moved toward us, I understood why al-Saffah was here, now, in this place. Black eyes shining in the firelight, the young woman from the market who had been so enamored of my son strode forward and stopped in front of Arturo. Of course: reversible capes—white to be anonymous in town, red as al-Saffah warriors, incomparable archers who rained death on anyone who dared approach.

"Busaybah," the young woman murmured, touching Arturo's chest.

"Rabi'a." Arturo swallowed hard, apparently stupefied by her beauty, while I tried to figure out how he knew her name.

The older woman before me glared at Arturo, nodded, then spoke to me in broken Spanish. "I am Nugaymath. I lead al-Saffah. My daughter want your man."

"My son," I corrected as one of Nugaymath's pencil-thin eyebrows lifted. "He is but a boy. She may not have him." I pulled Arturo behind me.

The young Rabi'a snarled something at me, which in any Arabic dialect meant 'dried up old camel.' Nugaymath, black as pitch, clenched her wide jaw. "He is for my Rabi'a. He bed her, so now he is hers."

"He *bed* her?" I whirled to face my madly-blushing son. "What?"

"Mom, I'm sorry. I didn't know she was al-Saffah. But...I was back in this time, and...I..."

I could have shaken my son to death at that moment. "You came back here to get *laid?*"

"No! Of course not. Well, maybe. No. But Hazm helped me find her again. And I'm fourteen, Mom. Hazm lost...*his*, you know, when he was twelve. It's embarrassing."

I turned back to the woman, my arms rigid at my sides. "No."

"He is for Rabi'a."

"No."

I refused to flinch as Nugaymath reached casually over her shoulder for an arrow, notched it, and drew back the long bow, pointing the arrow at my heart. "He is for Rabi'a."

Arturo clutched at my arm. "Mom, don't do this. I—"

"Quiet," I snapped in English. Blood pounded in my ears as I glared back at her. "No." We locked eyes over the arrow, and even in the dim firelight I could see grudging admiration bloom on her face. She lowered the bow.

"You are the prisoners of al-Saffah. For tonight, I will let you live."

They kicked out our fire and dragged us to our horses. After a five minute ride, we crested a small hill to find dozens of small white tents and a handful of campfires. Arturo and I must have had over one hundred women following us all the way to Valvanera, and we'd had no clue. They'd waited patiently for us to leave the monastery before jumping us. They hadn't bothered Elena because they weren't interested in her. They wanted Arturo.

We were dumped at the first fire, guarded by four scowling women, then joined eventually by Nugaymath and Rabi'a. Nugaymath handed us each a mug of warm liquid, a spiced cider that chased the chill from my insides. As Arturo and I drank, Nugaymath stared into the fire. Rabi'a only had eyes for Arturo, and after a few guilty glances at me, he returned that look. Fear twisted my gut. There were so many more conversations he and I needed to have about being adults, like the one on the dangerous trap of lust at first sight, or the one on the practical aspects of abstinence.

"We have heard of al-Saffah," I said, breaking the silence. "You are greatly feared. But no one mentioned you were women."

Nugaymath snorted through flared nostrils. "We kill any man close enough to see our sex. Man scum of the earth, good only for penis. When we are through with them, may Allah dry up all the penis and cause them to drop like baobab pods."

I sensed a land mine around Nugaymath so resolved to tread carefully. "I had heard al-Saffah was three hundred strong."

"Main army at base camp."

"Where's that?"

She smiled. "Secret. Now, you answer questions. Why you flee Zaragoza? Where you go?"

"I sought someone...a friend." I struggled with what to say next. Where did this woman fall in the political mass of the peninsula? "And you? As Almoravides, why not fight at the side of Ibn Yusef of Valencia?"

"That ugly swollen camel? He moves his bowels at the first sign of trouble. He cries like baby in battle. Next time I see him I cut off shriveled balls and feed to my dogs."

No love lost there. So much for avoiding land mines. I reached out another tentacle. "You fight instead for al-Rashid of Valencia?"

"He is just another Moor. They all break the word of Muhammad. They drink alcohol. They over-tax the people. They consort with Christians. They shit through their mouths. Moors are scum. Pigs, all of them."

I tried to catch Arturo's eye, but he was too absorbed in something Rabi'a was saying, so I emptied my mug and Nugaymath refilled it. A giddy calm spread through me, and I wondered briefly what else was in this cider besides spices. "And the Christians?"

"Imbeciles, every one. Smell of armpit and toilet and rot. Tiny minds make tiny men." She spat into the fire, setting off a sizzle. Arturo and I each drank another mug of cider, and I sighed happily as my limbs began to float away from my body.

"So you hate the Almoravides, the Moors, and the Christians. What are you doing here?"

I don't know flashed through her eyes like a bolt of lightning, disappearing just as quickly. She straightened. "To spread the word of Muhammad. To return the Moors to the Prophet's path so they can once again honor Allah."

Arturo belched, then laughed, trying to apologize but not quite able to get the words out. When I started giggling, Nugaymath shook her gleaming head and stood. Rabi'a took Arturo's hand as if to lead him away, but I grabbed the other hand and yanked him to me. Both Rabi'a and Arturo protested. "Mom, I'm not a kid anymore."

Nugaymath held up a weathered, pale palm. "Enough. Mother and son sleep in here for the night." She pushed Arturo and me into the nearest tent, just big enough for two. "You sleep. We guard. Do not try escape."

Strangely limp, I laid out the rough woolen blanket, then covered us with the other. Rocks and lumps dug into our hips and shoulders, which brought more giggles from both of us.

"What a mess, huh, Mom?" Arturo's forehead touched mine in the dark. "I think I'm drunk."

"Two drunk superheroes," I chortled, which set us both off in a spasm of laughter I did not feel in my heart. "I think there was something in the cider."

"No kidding. I feel like I'm floating. Good thing I'm in a tent." He burped. "Maybe I should have kept it in my pants like you told me to." We both giggled wildly, but then he clutched at my hand as fear began to break through the drug. "I'm sorry I messed up, Mom. Do you suppose we'll ever set the timeline straight? We don't seem to be getting very far."

I tried not to snicker but had no control. "Don't worry. We'll do better. Remember, in the movies things always look really bleak just before they get better."

"This is the bleak part?"

"Yup. We're prisoners of a bloodthirsty band of pissed-off women who hate everyone, and we're no closer to saving Elena from Rodrigo, or making sure Rodrigo takes Valencia." We giggled uncontrollably now. "Can't get much bleaker than this."

Finally our hysteria calmed, and as we clasped hands under the blanket, a deep, black, suffocating sleep reached up and took us both.

❖

When I awoke in the dim morning light, I moaned softly as I shifted. Someone must have used my body as a punching bag overnight. Everything hurt, even my eyelids. Goddess, my head throbbed. What had been in that drink? The Almoravides were against alcohol, so it must have been something else.

I reached behind me for Arturo and felt nothing, so I rolled over. I was alone in the tent. I shot up, a big mistake, then gripped my head as the tent spun around me. "Arturo?" I whispered. He'd probably gone outside to pee, so slowly enough I wouldn't startle the guards and end up an arrow pincushion, I folded back the tent flap and crawled outside.

Only then did I hear it. Silence. Total silence. One hundred people could not be this silent. I stood, crying out as my nerves snapped to attention and my heart stopped beating. I was alone in the clearing. Every tent but mine was gone. Every horse but mine, grazing fifteen feet away, was gone. The only signs of al-Saffah were the charred fire circles. I spun around and around, refusing to believe the horrible truth. "Arturo!" I screamed. Not even an echo replied.

The horse raised its head to stare at me, grass dripping from its mouth, but that was the only change in the world around me.

I must have gone a little mad. I grabbed the reins, threw myself onto the horse, and galloped north. I searched for signs that many horses had passed—trampled grass, broken branches—but found nothing in the rough ground. I was not a tracker. I rode for an hour, then rode the hour back to the tent. I rode east up into the mountains, picking my way slowly through the rocks, but nothing. I returned to the tent and rode south, stopping to water the horse in a narrow creek. I even rode west, deeper into Christian territory, but found no sign of al-Saffah or my son.

Late morning I sat by the tent, the last place I'd touched Arturo, the last place I'd heard his voice, felt his breath on my hand. Hungry, thirsty, filthy, aching inside and out, I threw back my head, howling with grief. I pounded the ground with my fists, cursing all I could see, cursing the future, Anna, and myself. This was all my fault. I should have anticipated Arturo's actions and locked him up somewhere before I'd left home, because ever since he'd turned fourteen, he thought he knew best and that my IQ had suddenly dropped *way* under the radar.

But now my son was gone. I'd lost him—the little boy who wanted to be an adult but who wanted to go home so he could finish being a kid.

Screw the timeline. Screw the Christians, the Moors, and the Almoravides. I would push on to Valencia. Elena would help me find Arturo. She *had* to. Then I'd take Arturo home and never, ever return to this cruel time.

CHAPTER SEVENTEEN

Focusing on details was the only way to control my panic, the only way to avoid imagining Arturo lying broken and bleeding somewhere, or even worse. No, I would not think that.

Barring any problems, I calculated a grueling six-day ride to the coast and Valencia. Grimaldi had said al-Saffah was rumored to be based somewhere in the Sierra de Cuenca, the mountain range that cut straight west from Valencia, but I could wander those mountains and die an old woman before I ever found Arturo. I needed more information. Damn, and why did Elena have to be so fast on a horse and me so slow?

My saddlebags overflowed with Grimaldi's bread and oat cakes and sausage, so food would not be a problem, and Arturo's dagger rested in the sheath strapped beneath my skirt. Nugaymath and company must have decided to leave me a weapon in exchange for my son.

I'd studied maps of eastern Spain between Zaragoza and Valencia with Professor Kalleberg, so knew the terrain ahead was mountain ridges worn down by small rivers snaking their way north to the Ebro or east to the Mediterranean. As long as I stayed by the rivers I knew, or kept the early morning sun on my face for those stretches without river, I would be fine.

The mountains were so thick with spruce that from one high ridge they appeared as moss-covered stones stretching for miles. I suddenly felt as small as an ant facing the journey ahead. The road, nothing more than tracks worn in the grass, was easy to follow. Feather clouds dusted the highest ridges. God damn it. How *dare* it be such a perfect day? If my heart could influence life, furious thunderclouds would wrestle their way across the sky, lightning would blind al-Saffah, and rain would drown the wildflowers.

For years I'd worried about my ability to be a good parent and had watched poor Arturo so closely, terrified I'd do something wrong and mess up his life. Eventually Laura, and the parents I came to know, all convinced me I was doing a great job, and I became one of those proud and self-confident parents. Now, however, as I rode alone, all alone, I felt a sense of failure too deep to express. I had *lost* my son. I couldn't stop saying those awful words in my head.

I passed a few settlements where dusty children ran to the road and waved as I passed. By late afternoon I'd crossed the pass and begun my descent to the picturesque Río Jalón. Rabbits and deer skittered out of sight into the woods, and once I thought I heard a bear snort.

White sun baked every clearing, every rise in the road, as well as my back, neck, and head, throwing every dip, every small valley into blissfully cool shadows. By nightfall I neared Calatayud but chose to camp outside it in a grove of trees. My butt hurt and my thighs ached, but pain was unimportant.

I snuck into town, stole a man's shirt, pants, and tunic off a line, and abandoned my stupid skirt. In my loose pants, shirt and tunic, I either appeared as a noble down on his luck, or a peasant who'd done well. The tunic was a little tight across the chest, but I made no effort to disguise my breasts. Anyone having trouble with a short-haired woman wearing men's clothing could just stuff it.

For the next two days I followed the Río Jiloca to Albarracín, where late in the evening locals helped me find a fresh horse and the road to Teruel. The third day, as I joined the main road to Valencia, which snaked south along the Río Turia, I talked with anyone I met. A woman dragging a reluctant goat to market told me Ibn Jehaf had killed al-Rashid. Another gossip-monger, bent over his donkey's neck, said al-Rashid killed Ibn Jehaf. Whenever I asked about al-Saffah, people averted their eyes, searching the horizon for the red capes and drawn bows. The farther south I traveled, the more nervous people became, which lifted my spirits immensely. I was getting closer.

❖

Even though I'd chosen a mossy spot for my bed, the springy plant had quickly compressed under my weight, so I woke up grunting at the hard soil grinding against my hip. Lying on my back, woolen blanket around me, I watched the morning sky lighten in the east, a pale blue melting into indigo, but felt nothing. Ever since I'd lost Arturo, a coldness had spread through me. My body temperature remained the same, but my veins flowed with arctic water, my heart an iceberg adrift. Nothing mattered anymore, only Arturo. I would go through the motions to restore the timeline. and I would save Elena if I could, but I was an armored tank now. I would do whatever it took to get Arturo safely home. I would lie, cheat, steal, maim, or kill to have him once again roll his eyes at my bad jokes or protest with an impatient "Mom" when I called him "honey" in public. I struggled with my confusion over Elena. How could I pull this off with her working against me?

Camped in a small grove off the road, I heard the occasional creaking of wagon wheels or the subdued discussion of passing riders, so I rose and stretched, physically reluctant to climb back into the saddle. After eating and splashing off my face and arms in the pristine river, I pulled out Arturo's dagger to practice. In an odd way, it helped me think, Since nothing intruded, I focused on the tree and the dagger. After twenty minutes my right shoulder burned, but something had shifted since I'd come back in time. My aim was consistent, my throwing strength greater. I walked farther and farther from the target tree, grinning broadly when, at thirty feet, my throw snapped into the bark with a satisfying 'thunk.'

"Quite impressive, Señora Vicente."

I whirled around. The infernal Rafael Mahfouz stood behind me, shadowed by an ugly goon with a missing ear and a ragged, patchy beard. Both held drawn swords. I sprinted for my dagger, but Rafael grabbed the back of my tunic and yanked me off my feet. I struggled against him while the goon retrieved my dagger, then Rafael released me.

I pressed a palm to my forehead, amazed at how dead I felt inside. "Not you again."

Mahfouz grinned, but not as cockily as before, while he sheathed his sword. Malice tugged at the corners of his mouth and humiliation swam in his eyes. "I bring reinforcements. Where is your moron of a son?"

I exhaled loudly. "That 'moron' wiped your ass, Mahfouz, so watch it." I cut a quick glance through the trees to the road. No one passed. "*You're* the moron. How on earth did you find me?"

"Ask a question here, a question there. You were not hard to find for Caquito and myself, even in your ridiculous disguise. But where's your son? I want a piece of him."

I choked as I rolled up my blanket. "Arturo is not here. Al-Saffah took him."

At the happy gleam in Mahfouz's eyes, I wanted to squeeze his throat so hard his eyes would pop out.

Caquito growled at Rafael in disgust. "We both come all this way to capture one woman?"

Rafael shrugged. "Señora de Palma says it's vital that this woman be taken. We do what we must. Señorita, you will come with us."

"Go screw yourself," I snarled. "I'm not going with you." I stomped over to my horse and tied on my blanket.

Rafael chuckled as he came up behind me. "You may have the spunk of your son, but I doubt you—"

A squall line hit somewhere in my belly and spread through me. Although it had been a few years since my Tae Kwon Do days, my body still remembered its months of practice. Relieved I'd ditched the skirt, I calmly turned my back to Rafael. As he stepped toward me, I whirled and aimed a round house kick right for his solar plexus. A hair off balance, I missed, and slammed my heel into his groin. Mahfouz doubled over like a flower snapped off at the stem. "Oops. I missed."

"Hey, stop that," Caquito muttered as he lumbered toward me. Two sloppy jumping front snap kicks later, the smelly man rolled on the ground, clutching his jaw. The two Moors weren't the only ones in pain, since my thigh muscles screamed at the unfamiliar punishment. I found a rope in Rafael's saddlebag and tied their hands and ankles together around the nearest tree. I yanked my dagger out of Caquito's filthy boot. Rafael raised his groggy head as I mounted. "Kate Vincent, I *will* bring you in one day soon."

"Get used to disappointment, moron." I slapped the men's horses on their rumps to send them thundering down the road, then gathered up my own reins.

"I have no choice but to kill you the next time we meet. Señora de Palma will understand."

"Kiss my ass, Mahfouz," I snapped, and urged my horse up onto the road and toward Valencia.

❖

I'd been right. Six days' hard ride brought me to Liria, where the

Mediterranean sun softened the mountains into foothills, then melted everything into a vast, fertile plain stretching toward the ocean. Seagulls wheeled overhead, a sign I was almost there. During my journey I'd left May behind and slid three days into June, which meant time was leaping ahead, and I couldn't keep up.

A few irrigated fields exploded with life, but most had been trampled and destroyed. The devastation grew worse as I moved closer to Valencia. Whole villages were burned, with only charred stone foundations and a handful of old men left wandering in confusion. The road grew thick with merchants traveling to sell their meat, ale, and women to the men camped around Valencia. The smell of wet ash and rotting offal, left behind as the army butchered its meat along the way, became familiar as I moved from one outlying community to the next. Soon I passed knots of Christian soldiers sitting around overturned casks playing dice, downing huge mugs of wine. A few watched me, openly curious, but no one stopped me.

At a rise in the road, I reined in my exhausted horse and inhaled the scent of the sea. Half a mile ahead rose the rough wall enclosing the city of Valencia. Between my position and the walled city, stone and wood buildings formed a continuous forest that grew right up to the towering gray-brown wall. Valencia had obviously long outgrown its Roman walls, and what I'd call suburbs radiated in all directions. The city's white towers and massive arches seemed to float above the war-battered stone wall. Orange and blue tiles skipped across the roofs I could see.

Mosque peaks spiraled into the sky, gold and burgundy and white, but had there been a call to prayer, I certainly wouldn't have heard it over the din of men shouting and women clanking cooking pots and merchants advertising their wares. I don't know why I'd expected a siege to be quiet. Perhaps the noise stopped at the walls, where on the other side, in Valencia, people were starving, thanks to Rodrigo Díaz, the man I was supposed to ensure captured the throne.

I stopped a Christian foot soldier. "Rodrigo Díaz?"

The man spat a wad of phlegm about five feet, then jerked his head toward the east. After a few more grunted answers and jerky nods, I ended up at the edge of a neighborhood that Rodrigo had mostly spared. A few homes had been partially burned but still had walls and roofs. I saw only soldiers coming and going from the buildings, the residents having long since fled.

I headed toward the largest home, ignoring the stares of the bored men clustered in small groups. I was getting close to deciding this may not have been the smartest of plans when I caught sight of Elena up ahead, the faithful Fadri and Enzo at her side. They led their horses toward a massive whitewashed home.

I urged my horse forward. "Luis!"

Shaking her head at the sound of my voice, Elena turned, scowling, but waited for me to catch up to them.

Fadri took a minute to recognize me. "Bullocks! It's you!"

"Hey, Fadri, how's it hanging?" The guy blushed, since some things were offensive no matter the century or language.

"What do you want?" Elena snapped.

"Luis, Arturo is gone." I dismounted.

"I do not understand. He was with you—"

"Al-Saffah captured us as soon as we left Valvanera. They kidnapped Arturo."

"Sweet Mother of God," Elena muttered. "You do *not* want to become involved with al-Saffah." The look of horror on her face was gratifying. She wouldn't help me restore the timeline, but she had a child. She knew what it would be like to lose that child.

I pressed my lips together. "I have no choice. But I need your help. I can't find him alone."

We stared at each other, the recent fight over my other request still fresh in both our minds. Finally Elena rubbed the top of her head, sending her short hair up into spikes. "I will help you find Arturo, but you could not have come at a worse time." She stopped, perhaps measuring my ability to handle the truth. "The violence here escalates as Valencia continues to hold out. Rodrigo's barbarian Tahir stirs up the soldiers, and for every act of his band that I and my men prevent, he and the other renegades carry out three more. There is more wine than work here, a deadly imbalance for a soldier."

I patted my dagger. "I can take care of myself."

Elena snorted. "Not unless your aim has improved. Any woman in this area is either a prostitute or a slave, or both." Her eyes dropped to my chest and a warm flush started up my neck. "You do not hide your sex."

"No," I said, raising my chin. Imagine that, I shot back with my eyes. A woman in men's clothing who didn't hide her sex. I said nothing.

She jerked her head toward the house. "Ibn Jehaf comes out from the city to discuss surrender with Rodrigo. I must be there."

"And me?"

Her wry smile sent electricity flashing through my nerves. Only a few nights ago I'd fallen asleep in her arms. "Come, but draw your cloak across your chest. Stay in the background." I nodded, watching her stride ahead to the door.

Even though I'd found her, and she'd agreed to help, something made me jumpy, possibly the mood I'd sensed the closer I'd come to Valencia. People were starving inside the gates. Elena's world, the siege of Valencia, meant constantly breathing air thick with tension, keeping bored men out of trouble, controlling the violent Tahir and the others, and dealing with crowded living conditions, lack of food, and difficult political maneuverings.

I took a second to greet Elena's two faithful henchmen. Enzo grunted but looked pleased when I hugged him. His features were still blunt and unfinished, but age had sagged his cheeks and lower eyelids, softening his hard face. Fadri, taller and younger, had put on weight. He still grinned like a naughty teenager as I teased him about the extra inches around his waist. "Wife's too good a cook in the winter," the blond soldier said, patting his belly.

"Fadri, you—a wife?"

He held open the heavy wooden door. "Wife and five kids."

"The man is a rabbit," Elena growled.

"Ah, yes, but a happy rabbit," Fadri said with a chortle. "Don't pretend, Luis, that you aren't happy to see your own wife once again."

My heart hammered in my chest as Elena and I looked at each other out of the corners of our eyes. While worry for Arturo ate at me, there was no use denying the ache in my body. Impassive, resolute, neither Elena's face nor body gave me a single clue as to whether she felt the same.

CHAPTER EIGHTEEN

Rodrigo had taken over a huge section of Villanueva, one of the outer neighborhoods of Valencia, and he held the largest home, a sprawling stone structure with three inner courtyards that were once lush gardens. Now, Elena said, they were trampled mud where the men kept a few of their horses.

Elena led us into the main room, already packed with men who had not bathed in months. Rodrigo sat in a massive leather chair. Elena moved to his left side, and a glowering Moor stood on the other. As I tucked myself against the back wall, I decided the Moor must be Tahir. The man had more scars than skin, thin pale webs crisscrossing his mahogany face. Bulkier than most Moors, he hunched defensively, as if ready to tackle someone.

Behind Elena stood Nuño Súarez, and my heart soared to see Nuño looking so well. I tried to catch his eye, but he didn't take his gaze from the visiting emir standing before Rodrigo.

Ibn Jehaf was a short man in flowing blue robes and a turban trimmed with gold braid. He delicately pressed a perfumed cloth under his nose. I wished I could have done the same to ward off the stench of the unwashed in such close quarters. I tried to remember Professor Kalleberg's explanation of this whole mess. While Rodrigo and his army camped outside the city walls, within the walls a power struggle raged between Ibn Jehaf, the Moorish emir, and al-Rashid, a young man with enough financial and political clout to declare himself the new caliph, the spiritual leader of all the Moors. Clearly Ibn Jehaf and al-Rashid fought for the dubious honor of serving as Rodrigo's puppet if he entered the city.

"Al-Rashid is dead," Ibn Jehaf said, his voice surprisingly loud for his size. "My guards killed him this very morning. I can now negotiate peace on behalf of the entire city."

Rodrigo did not respond either way to the news. While I wondered if the young boy's death would make my job easier or harder, I couldn't take my eyes off the man, who, in the correct timeline, was known as El Cid. Rodrigo had aged poorly. Rough living and gravity had shifted all his features into a permanent frown, with deep lines along his mouth and furrows across his weathered brow. He looked from Jehaf to the emir's bodyguards, then back to Jehaf.

"Prove to me he is dead, then surrender," Rodrigo said, looking toward the edges of the crowd, then craning his neck to look through the forest of legs. Jehaf's hands fluttered as it became clear Rodrigo was looking for something, and the poor emir had no idea what.

Elena and Nuño scowled, while Tahir watched, mouth open in anticipation, hungry for blood. I shivered at the look in the man's eye. What was Rodrigo doing with a man such as this in his army?

"I have seen the boy's body myself." The poor man could only squeak out another sentence or two before losing his voice to fear.

Rodrigo folded thick fingers over his still-flat stomach. "Do you have anything to unload from your horses or camels?" Tahir now grinned openly. He needed to brush his teeth.

"No, no, my lord Rodrigo, we come with—"

"With nothing!" Rodrigo shot to his feet. "I am soon to be your ruler, the leader of Valencia, and you come empty-handed?"

Jehaf gasped as he realized his error. "Oh, no, my lord. It is just... the casks of gold are too heavy to—"

"Silence," spat the great Rodrigo Díaz, and my stomach lurched to think I was on this man's side. "You lie! Only a fool would come before me without an offering to show respect." He dropped back into his chair with a thud, then tugged on his beard, still braided at the ends. Rodrigo protected that beard as a woman would a child, tucking it into his mail before battle, then displaying it vainly as a sign of his manliness when it would be in no danger. "I think I will name my own gift," Rodrigo finally said. Tahir shifted, widening his stance in anticipation. Elena shot me a hooded glance, in which probably only I could detect a deep river of anger. "You have a son, no?"

"Yes, my lord."

"Age?"

"Fourteen."

Rodrigo slapped the arm of his chair and the entire emir party jumped, to a man. Jehaf's forehead darkened.

"Your son will be my gift. Bring him to me in three days' time and I will accept your surrender. We will ride back into Valencia together. The lives of your wealthy subjects will be spared as we assume possession of the city." He chuckled. "Their monies will be taken, of course."

My mind raced. Today was June 3. Rodrigo was supposed to enter Valencia on June 15. Damn, the professor and I had never discussed this. What would happen if he took the city on June 6?

"My son?" Jehaf now hid his hands beneath his robe, but terror curved his back and rolled his shoulders forward.

"He shall be my slave, to remind Valencians of my conquest." He leaned back and yawned, already acting the part of a sovereign ruler. "You may go now."

With deep, scraping bows, the soon-to-be-deposed emir backed from the room to the jeers and hoots of Tahir and the renegade Moors behind him. Obviously Tahir cared nothing that he helped a Christian conquer the Moorish city. He was a mercenary, just like Rodrigo. Just like Elena.

I followed the crowd, but waited outside the main door on a cobblestone walkway, grateful no one paid me any attention as the men trickled down to a few, leaving just Elena and Nuño.

I stepped before the large man. "Hey, big guy," I said, unable to suppress my grin, even though I wasn't sure he'd be glad to see me.

Nuño stared, unsure why this 'man' before him looked so familiar. I shrugged back my cape and Nuño's eyes widened, dropped to take in my clothes, then returned to my face. "Holy Saints," he breathed, then shot a protective glance at Elena.

"Do not worry," she said. "I met her earlier."

He swung his massive head toward me, shaking it now, throwing his arms wide. "Kate, you're always a surprise."

I squeezed him, wondering how women managed to hug men in chain mail without permanent scars on their cheeks. I stepped back, flicking his chin. "Speaking of surprise, where is all your facial hair?"

The beard had been trimmed to a thick moustache and narrower beard. Nuño smiled, revealing deep dimples in both cheeks, which until now had always been covered by beard.

"Oh!" I suddenly took another step back. Black curly hair. Deep dimples. Warm brown eyes. Shit, even the nose was the same. "Oh!" was all I could say. Maybe I was wrong. No, I could see her face and spirit in the gaze of the gentle man before me. Nuño Súarez had to be the father of little Solana Súarez.

"What is wrong?" Elena asked.

"Nothing," I sputtered, too stunned to sort any of this out.

❖

As I followed Elena and her men around all afternoon, they broke up fights, avoided Tahir's men, and generally kept the peace. I couldn't stop staring at Nuño. The resemblance only grew stronger as I did. Rumors flew around us, most of them having to do with al-Rashid, and whether the poor young man was actually dead. Elena and I had no time to ourselves, but as if magnetized, we rarely moved more than a few feet apart. Once, when I caught Elena watching me, I flushed with such a deep heat I was sure my clothes would ignite. I recovered and returned the look, struggling to mask my desire. That one night in the Valvanera gardens would never be enough, but it was all I dared take.

As night approached, her glances grew longer and more direct, and my own anticipation kept my heart pounding so loudly I was sure everyone could hear it and know my knees were weak and my mouth too dry to swallow.

At dusk the five of us sat cross-legged on the gritty tile floor of their quarters, Enzo thinking it would be safer if I didn't mingle with the men in the mess hall. The wise soldier, probably pushing fifty, chewed on a hunk of dried goat meat while Fadri tossed me the round loaf of bread. I tore off a hunk, wondering if Elena ever tired of the plain, bland fare of war.

"Al-Saffah camps near the Pelado pass," Nuño said before guzzling the last of his ale.

Elena shook her head. "No, I have heard they are farther south, by Utiel."

I sighed. "How far to either place?"

Nuño shrugged one broad shoulder. "Half a day's ride. The distance is not far, but the trail is steep and winding."

"When can we leave?"

All three men looked at Elena, then down at the floor, as if the answer were spelled out in the dirt swirled by our movements.

Elena ran a hand through her hair, and my hand would have followed hers if we'd been alone. "We are not able to leave now. Perhaps in two or three days."

I nearly spilled my water. "But Arturo was taken six days ago. I can't wait two or three days. We must go tomorrow."

"Impossible," Nuño rumbled, but he did not look at me.

"Look, nothing happens tomorrow," I said. "Just another day of siege."

They exchanged glances. "None of us can leave now," Elena said, her eyes dark in the faltering light.

What the hell was going on? The four of them seemed to be passing information between them without words, cutting me out altogether. Finally Elena leaned back against the wall, considering me through lowered lids. "I have already explained about Tahir and his men. They kill, maim, and torture for no other reason than sport." She exchanged a look with Nuño, likely remembering the Caballeros de Valvanera, Christians who roamed the countryside looking for Moors to kill. Elena, Nuño Súarez and Alvar Fáñez were the only three left. They had killed for revenge and for religion. Was that any more just than killing for sport?

"Rodrigo has always been a cruel man." I swallowed, feeling suddenly alone. "What is so new about that?"

Enzo snorted. "Tahir killed Alvar."

My hand flew to my mouth. "No!" Not the dashing one-eyed Alvar, who made everyone laugh, and Elena's closest friend, save Nuño.

Elena's face twisted in a pained anger I'd never seen. "He did it right in front of Rodrigo, to spite me."

"But Rodrigo loved Alvar, as he loves you." I blinked back tears. Not Alvar.

Nuño's jaw worked under the fine beard. "If we had not been breaking up a fight between Tahir's men and ours near the west gate..."

The tension in the room brought small beads of sweat to my forehead. "If you dislike Rodrigo so much, why are you still here?"

A woman screamed just a block away. "Not again," Elena muttered. They all leapt to their feet, drawing swords. She motioned me to the stairs. "Wait for me up there. Enzo, see she remains safe. Nuño, Fadri, with me."

"But—" The three Christians were gone, leaving a glowering Enzo, who motioned me toward the stairs. "What's going on?" I asked.

"Starving Valencians lower themselves down the walls at night, hoping to escape and find food. Tahir and his men like to wait for them. Sometimes they take them to the north edge of Villanueva, where slave traders have set up a shop and will buy everyone Tahir brings to them. Sometimes Tahir takes the people to Rodrigo, who the next day has them impaled on long stakes, then raised up so they can be seen from the Valencian walls."

"Christ." I headed for the stairs.

Enzo showed me Luis's pallet in the upper room. "As a mercenary soldier I have done many things of which I am not proud. But they all have made sense, at least to me. What Rodrigo does now, the torture, doesn't make sense to me." He patted me awkwardly on the shoulder. "You'll be safe here. Sleep well. I sleep downstairs by the door."

Before I lay down, I lit the candle on the floor by the bed, and pulled a blank notebook from my saddlebags, which Fadri had brought up earlier. In it I wrote, in Latin, one paragraph, then I copied it over once, over twice, and over again. Seeing it written on the page gave me hope. It must come true:

After a violent and lengthy siege, the great Rodrigo Díaz mounted his silver steed, Babieca, and on the warm, peaceful morning of June 15, 1094, rode up to the gates of Valencia, his brave and valiant army behind him. The gates opened, and the starving masses welcomed him as the new leader of Valencia."

My fingers cramped around the pencil stub, so I put the notebook back in my saddlebag. Still dressed, I lay down, pulling a blanket over me, stiff with sadness for Alvar, and worrying. Fear for Arturo left me shivering under my heavy wool.

❖

I am five and ice skating with my mother. Unable to start or stop myself, I cling to Mom's hand, my wooly mitten tucked into her nylon glove as we circle the huge outdoor rink. My favorite part is coming up, when I lock my knees and swing wide, free of Mom's shadow but still tethered to her. As we enter the turn, Mom trips. When my mitten comes off and goes down in her laughing pile of arms and legs, I am suddenly on my own. Screaming, arms wide, ankles wobbling, I fly straight toward the mountain of snow and ice lining the rink. I cannot stop. I cannot turn. Worse than getting hurt is the piercing knowledge I am on my own.

I woke up as the stairs below me creaked. I held my hand over a thumping heart, still able to smell the cold, hear the metallic swosh of skate blades, and feel the scream building in my chest. Mom always maintained I never hit the wall of snow, but that at the last minute, a young man grabbed my hand and swung me in a wide arc back to her. I have no memory of this. Just the panic of being on my own.

I flung off the blanket and struggled to my feet, suddenly embarrassed to be caught in Elena's bed, then realized it was actually morning. My pulse throbbed against my throat. What had been between Elena and Nuño? What might still be between them? An ugly green moth beat weakly against my heart.

"Rough night?" I said.

She splashed off her face with dirty water in a chipped yellow bowl, throwing me an odd look. "All my nights are rough."

"Is the woman okay?" Elena nodded, but offered no details. I waited until she had dried her hands on the edge of the shirt, then fluttered my own hand toward the wide pallet on the floor. "I'm sorry,... I didn't know where—"

"I slept downstairs." She reached for her sword and her chain mail. Eyes flashing, jaw grim, Elena stepped back. "I will help you find Arturo, but not today. I cannot let anything interfere with our plans. If he is still alive after all these days with al-Saffah, he will still be alive in a few more." She whistled, and within seconds Fadri came barreling up the stairs, looking uncomfortable. "Fadri, your only job for the next few days is keeping my wife in this room."

"I'm your prisoner?" I shouted.

"I prefer 'guest,'" she said. My jaw dropped. Anger burned up any words in my throat. She tugged at her chain mail, which clinked softly, and adjusted her tunic in the mail's armholes. "Fadri, I am serious. She stays here."

"I can't stay here! We need to find Arturo." Panic fought with fury, and fury was winning as I stomped toward the stairs.

Fadri grabbed me by the shoulders and pulled me back as I struggled in his grip.

Elena watched me, her face revealing nothing. "Kate, I have said I will help you find Arturo. I am not entirely heartless. As for you, Fadri, Kate knows we plot against Rodrigo. So tie her up, tie her down, knock her out. Do whatever you want. My wife and I no longer see eye to eye on...anything. Eight years is just too long." Without even looking at me, she shouldered her way past the stunned soldier and disappeared down the stairs.

CHAPTER NINETEEN

I sat on a stool by the window watching men and horses pass on the street below, then scanned the room for a means of escape. This building must have been a potter's shop judging by the broken potter's wheel slumped in one corner. Forgotten shards of orange clay pots had been swept to the edges of the floor. A lone cupboard along one wall contained a few dusty clay pots.

I blinked back tears of self-pity, but a few left a chilly trail down my cheek. What now? Damn.

Fadri sat on the floor, arms crossed, silent for the first time since I'd known him, so I turned back to the window. Moors and Christians passed each other with glares or insults. Tahir and his men might rip the army wide open before Rodrigo could take Valencia, or before Elena could implement whatever plans she had. The street filled with noise as horses clomped by, followed by wide-faced mules loaded down with bags of an armorist's selection of weapons. Rowdy laughter drifted up from groups of drinking soldiers.

I rested my elbow on the rough wooden windowsill. This was an absurd predicament, and one I had not foreseen. In all the scenarios Professor Kalleberg and I had discussed, none included Elena working *against* Rodrigo.

"Fadri, tell me more about Rodrigo and how he has changed."

The blond man shrugged. "He goes into rages, loses control, orders the torture of good men, forgives nothing. Then he will withdraw and not speak for days."

"How long has he been like this?"

"Six months, maybe more. We cannot talk or reason with him. Only an old Jew who comes with a vessel of ale can calm him. Luckily, the Jew started showing up months ago, as we began heading toward Valencia, and bears this ale that Rodrigo craves." Fadri ran a hand through his shaggy hair. "Rodrigo loses control. Nearly sliced off

Nuño's head one day. Shakes and trembles like a mad man. Only the Jew's ale calms him down."

An alcoholic? I suppose it made sense, since Rodrigo had always been a heavy drinker, but why had his personality changed now? Chewing the inside of my lip, I turned back to the window.

By the time I recognized him, Carlos was directly opposite my window, searching each face he passed. "Carlos," I hissed. As a wagon rolled over the cobblestones beneath me, I leaned out so Fadri would not hear. "Carlos!" I had almost forgotten my elderly spy, whom I'd sent on to Valencia to be my eyes. "Carlos!" He still didn't turn around, but I heard Fadri getting to his feet. Scrabbling along the floor, I found a chunk of pottery and flung it out the window at Carlos's back.

"Hey!" Fadri grabbed my arm and pulled me back inside. "What the hell do you think you're doing?"

I stared up into Fadri's concerned face and knew how I could escape. This was Fadri, after all. I didn't believe he would harm me, and I knew I couldn't use my only obvious weapon, my dagger, which neither Elena nor Fadri had considered dangerous enough to take from me. But I had another weapon.

I pushed Fadri away. "I'm throwing things. Haven't you ever seen an angry woman?"

"Luis only does what is best," Fadri said. "You should not be angry."

"Luis only does what is best for *him*." I touched the younger man lightly on the chest. "He thinks he can tell me what to do, but he can't." I ran a finger along his stubbly jaw. "Do you remember when we first met?"

Uncomfortable at my touch, Fadri took a half-step back. "Mirabueno. I was taking a piss with Enzo and that young Moor, and you appeared, wearing almost nothing."

I smiled shyly, not looking forward to what would come next, since Fadri had obviously taken the bait. I had been wearing shorts and a T-shirt, nearly naked for a woman in the eleventh century. "Do you remember you asked Luis if you could have me?" I wet my lips, letting my tongue graze the tips of my teeth. Oh, I was shameless.

"Ahh, yes." Fadri's gaze followed my hands as I unlaced my tunic.

"Even then Luis treated me as his property," I said. "But I'm not.

I can be with anyone I want."

Fadri took another step toward the wall. "Kate, I'm a married man."

"Are you faithful to your wife?"

"Now and then, but you and Luis—"

"Are over." My tunic dropped to the floor, and I reached for the laces on my shirt. I could feel my breasts moving freely under the thin linen.

Poor Fadri swallowed, but we were alone, and the growing bulge under his woven wool tunic told me I'd reached first base, or maybe second. I never understood that system. I dropped my shirt off my shoulders, letting Fadri's hungry gaze take me in. "Jesus," he breathed.

I backed him up toward the wall and reached for my waistband. Two more steps...almost there. With one hand I pulled Fadri's head down until we kissed, then when he clasped my breast with a rough-skinned hand, I fastened my other hand on the nearest pot from the cupboard.

Fadri moaned, kissing me deeply, tasting of ale, and I sent him a silent apology when I slammed my knee into his swollen groin. With a sharp gasp, he clutched at himself, and I stepped back, smashing the pot against Fadri's hopefully-thick head. I winced as the pot shattered and my jailer collapsed at my feet.

"Fadri, Fadri, I'm so sorry," I moaned as I dressed. "I'm afraid that when you wake up, you'll have traded your large erection for an even bigger headache." I grabbed my things and dashed down the rickety stairs. Carlos couldn't be that far away. A cooling mist fell as I entered the street, but I didn't care. I inhaled the freshness and ran in the direction Carlos had taken.

It didn't take me long to catch sight of the elderly tour guide from the future. "Carlos!"

He turned, then lifted his arms, worry creasing his well-lined face. "Kate," he murmured as we hugged. "I've been searching everywhere for you."

"Come, I must keep moving." I grabbed his elbow and hurried him along, telling him about Arturo and al-Saffah. He clucked with concern as I finished. "I need to know where al-Saffah camps. Do you know? Do you know anyone who might know?"

"There he is!" Behind us a wall of Moorish robes began to run straight toward us. Confused, I hesitated, then decided running seemed a good idea, since I was wearing men's clothing and could be the one they were after.

"They mean you?" Carlos squeaked as I dragged him into a run.

"I'm having a bad day. Where are you staying?"

"I know a man who can help. Meet us at dawn at the Roman ruins north of town. Go! I'm slowing you down."

He was right. "Tomorrow," I said, then sprinted ahead. Carlos stumbled back against the nearest building. Thank god the Moors paved their streets so my feet could find purchase in the rugged cobblestones. I ran for my life, taking the first side street, leaping over a game of dice in front of a blacksmith shop. I choked at the waves of heat until I cleared the shop and took another side street, where I skidded to a stop, flailing to avoid slamming into a ten-foot-high pile of rotting animal remains. Gagging, I stepped back, hand over my mouth, waving away the black flies suddenly thick around me. The army butcher obviously felt no need to transport the bones and skulls out of town, probably thinking what did it matter; it wasn't his town anyway.

Gasping for air, I stumbled, turned and ran right into a man's lowered shoulder barreling toward my stomach. "Oof!" The man stood, and I found myself draped over the shoulder of a human tree trunk.

"Let me down, you prick!" I beat on his broad back, but he just chuckled, then broke into such a rollicking jog my teeth and eyeballs nearly fell out. I gripped his robe to steady myself and soon my head was so filled with blood my ears rang.

"I got him!" the man crowed.

"Bring him along," a woman's voice answered. I twisted and turned but couldn't see behind me. The voice was familiar, but everything sounds funny after you've been upside down for awhile. My tree trunk walked, but I heard horses behind me, and when we turned a corner I was able to arch high enough to see a flash of blond hair, a woman's elaborate robe.

"Anna!" I yelled. "God damn it, tell Redwood here to put me down." I released a healthy string of curses in English.

"Tsk, tsk, my dear, your language has really deteriorated over the years."

I swung from the tree's shoulder, feeling like Fay Wray in Kong's paws, or Barbie in the hands of a sadistic kid. Fury pumped through me. Anna rode right next to me now.

"Anna, we have to talk. Put me down!"

"It's good to see you again. Although the only thing I see of you is your ass. It was always one of your best features."

Damn it. I clutched at the tree's robe and began bunching it up, pulling the back hem higher. Wonder what he wore underneath? Time for a little air conditioning. See how he liked having the world see *his* ass.

I exposed his hairy, stumpy legs, bringing delighted whoops from the riders with Anna. Filling my arms with fabric, I grabbed the last bit to really let some fresh air in, but he took three steps to the left, twisted sharply, and slammed me against a stone building.

I yelped, then dropped the robe to grab my head and stop the ringing.

"Relax, my love, we're almost there."

"I'm not your love," I snarled. I had intended to be cool and calm the first time I encountered Anna back in time, but the circumstances made that impossible.

"Oh, that's right. You love Luis, the *lovely* Luis."

Before I could respond, a horse clomped past me, manure-scented tail flicking in my face. Its rider stopped, and the whole procession creaked to a halt in front of a building. "My lord, Rodrigo Díaz!" the man called in a clear voice, using the odd mixture of Arabic and Spanish so prevalent in Moorish territory. "Under a white flag of truce comes Paloma de Palma, envoy and advisor to our great caliph al-Rashid, the one Allah smiles upon more than any other."

Hanging upside down, I could see nothing but my captor's robe, but I picked up the murmurs of Christians nearby. We must be outside Rodrigo's headquarters.

"We come to negotiate for the safe release of Valencia. We bring proof that we alone have the power to negotiate and avoid a battle for everyone involved."

More murmurs, then everyone dismounted, saddles creaking, and we all moved inside. My head still hurt so badly my eyes watered. I tried to raise up by arching my back and pressing my hands against

Redwood's hips, but the room was packed so tightly with men that I couldn't see a thing. Frustration rumbled in my throat as I gave up and hung there like a doll.

"I have spoken with Ibn Jehaf." Rodrigo's voice boomed from somewhere near the center of the room. Elena likely stood at his side. "Jehaf tells me al-Rashid is dead."

Anna's voice was strong, but shook. Anger? I listened closely. No, excitement. "Jehaf is a liar. The great al-Rashid is not dead. He will appear on the walls of Valencia tomorrow so you will know Ibn Jehaf lies."

Angry whispers ran through the Christian soldiers. "Silence," Rodrigo roared. "We shall see. But if he brings me his son as a gift, then he and I will negotiate."

"My lord," Anna said, "once again Ibn Jehaf lies. For he does not bring you his son. I do." A sharp clap of hands, then the crowd around me shifted. I heard the heavy lid to a chest being flung back. "Why would you negotiate with a weakling such as Ibn Jehaf?" Anna asked. "He cannot even protect his own son."

When gasps and sharp curses exploded in the room, I twisted around the tree trunk and for a second the man in front of me moved, just enough so that I saw someone holding, by the hair, the head of a young Moor. Just the head.

Shit. The gap closed and I swung back, breaking into a hot, steamy sweat. Dark-skinned. He wasn't Arturo, but he was so young. So many fourteen-year-old boys. Ibn Jehaf's son. Al-Rashid. Arturo. I moaned quietly with terror for my son.

The commotion died down and I struggled for breath all tangled up in Redwood's robe. "Very impressive," Rodrigo said. "Clearly al-Rashid does have some control in the city. I will consider negotiating with him. But..." I could just imagine his hard face contemplating Anna, one hand stroking his thick beard. "I do not negotiate with women."

When the men around him laughed, I searched the visible legs but couldn't tell if Elena was here. My heart sank. Of course she would be.

"That is very interesting, my lord Rodrigo, because I thought you enjoyed women in positions of power."

Rodrigo snorted and my heart pounded so loudly I could barely hear anything else. "There is only one position for women," he said, following up with a lewd grunt. Appreciative chuckles ran through the crowd.

"Then why, Rodrigo, do you allow women to dress as men in your army?"

Rodrigo's laugh was harsh. I tried to slow my racing heart with a palm pressed to my chest. "That is ridiculous," he boomed.

When my tree trunk moved forward through the crowd, I knew my day was about to get even worse. He stopped and set me down in the middle of the tile floor. My legs had turned to noodles so I collapsed on my hands and knees, deeply grateful to be upright again as my blood redistributed itself.

"Do you know this soldier?" Anna yanked my head back with a fistful of hair, forcing my face into Rodrigo's view.

He looked at me, then shrugged. "I have two thousand men. They all begin to look alike."

"Ah, but do they all feel alike?"

Shit, shit, shit. Someone pinned my arms back, two others grabbed my kicking legs and dragged me within Rodrigo's reach.

"Feel *this* man," Anna crooned. "See if he is manly enough for your army."

As Rodrigo leaned forward to cup my crotch in his filthy hand, I saw Elena behind him, face white as death. I winced as Rodrigo, now alarmed, poked and prodded. He drew back, hissing sharply. Then he looked, really looked, at my face. "You!" he spat, whirling to face Elena. "You told me the bitch left years ago. And now she's back. In men's clothing."

Elena said nothing, her thick brows tight together.

The men released me and my brain whirled. Keep the attention on me, it screamed.

"Do not expect Luis Navarro to be shocked by this woman's behavior," Anna said.

I stood, wiping my clammy hands on my pants. "Anna, don't do this," I said in English.

She smiled at me, almost radiant, also answering in English. "I have waited eight years for this moment. Why would I stop it?" She glanced at Elena, seeing, as I did, those eyes now dark with fear. Next to her, Nuño looked like a man about to be flattened by stampeding horses, powerless to get out of the way.

"My lord," Anna said smoothly, "Luis Navarro is *herself* a woman."

The absolute silence lasted the longest ten seconds of my life, then Rodrigo flung back his head and guffawed, the other Christians joining him. Elena's gaze never left Anna's. "Luis a woman?" Rodrigo had to stop and wipe his eyes on his sleeve. "It may be true he is too pretty for his own good, but Luis is no woman."

"My lord," Anna's voice shook, since she hated to be laughed at. "This is my gift to you. Not only are they both women, but because they have lived as man and wife, they are *unnatural* women. I know you don't like to be the butt of a woman's joke. Yet this *woman*, who calls herself 'Luis,' laughs behind your back every day. She laughs at *all* of you."

The room quieted as Rodrigo shook his head wearily. "You have an odd way of befriending me, Señora de Palma." He flicked a hand in Elena's direction. "Drop your pants, Navarro. It will amuse me to see the look on her face."

Elena snorted rudely. "Only if I can use what I reveal. Perhaps she would like to raise her skirts and spread her legs for me."

This set Rodrigo laughing again, and when he shook his head sadly at Anna, I could sense the shift. He would not press his best general any further. Elena's fear was replaced by a wary look, so my pulse slowed to a healthier rate.

Without turning her head, Anna flicked one finger toward me, and I was yanked off my feet, my head driven back by a thick arm. An ice cold dagger bit into my exposed throat. "Oh god," I muttered between clenched teeth, my feet dangling above the floor.

"Luis Navarro." Anna's voice dropped low. "Drop your pants before Rodrigo, or Kate Vincent is dead."

I bit back a moan as the dagger cut me and warmth trickled down my throat. By straining my eyes downward, I could only see the tops of heads. Above me loomed a wooden beamed ceiling. Dusty cobwebs. My last view of life? I shut my eyes. Arturo. I haven't found you yet. I can't die now. Unwanted tears slid into my ears.

The room was silent. I breathed through my mouth, shallow, short, carefully. I could hear Elena pulling up her tunic. Leave your sword belt on, I pleaded, then my eyes shot open. *This* would be why Rodrigo killed Elena. Not over treason, not over Valencia, but over a truth revealed.

"Holy Mother of God!" Rodrigo roared, and the dagger left my neck. Released, I stumbled, clutching my sticky throat.

Elena retied her pants, tugged down her tunic and chain mail. She had never looked more fierce, nor more beautiful.

"Christ, man! Did you take a knife to yourself?"

Elena rested one hand on the hilt of her sword. No part of her moved. "If I had been born with the genitalia you so value, I might have." A wry half-smile lifted her lips. "But no, I am as I was born."

I could scarcely breathe, frozen with fear, paralyzed with awe. She was a cat, calm, serene, ready to defend herself. "I am Elena Navarro. I buried my brother Luis when I was seventeen."

Rodrigo lurched to his feet, mouth twisting as he struggled to wrap his brain around the awful truth. "All these years? With me? As my soldier?"

Behind Elena, Nuño barely breathed, and every other man in the room had lost jaw control, mouths gaping as they, too, struggled to understand, every mouth save one. Enzo's grim countenance matched Nuño's. Ahhh, Enzo had already known.

My fear swelled as Elena's shoulders straightened even more. She'd spent years hiding her sex, denying it, leaving it behind. Except, of course, with me, and at least once with Nuño, long enough to create Solana. "I have always been a woman."

With a furious roar, Rodrigo drew his sword and lunged, but she was ready for him. The crowd drew back to avoid the heavy swords slashing the air, iron wings of death, and I winced as the swords clanged together overhead. I moved back with the crowd, looking for help. Only Nuño and Enzo might be counted on to help her, but they'd be cut to pieces by everyone else's angry swords, sure to be unsheathed if Nuño and Enzo drew theirs.

Brows fierce with concentration, Elena gripped her sword with both hands as Rodrigo battered at her, assault after assault. He knew enough to stay an arm's length away since any closer and El Picador would bury her dagger to the hilt in his belly.

Sweat beaded on Elena's face, and I knew she wasn't strong enough to defeat a furious Rodrigo without her dagger. I glanced at Nuño. He knew it, too.

I considered tackling Rodrigo, but Elena would then slice him across the throat, he'd die, and my future would be over. I could tackle

Elena, but then *she'd* die, and my life would be over.

Tension pulsed through the crowd as they reacted to every parry, every blow. No one but me seemed to notice Anna nod once to Tahir, who began, eyes fixed on Elena, to slowly work his way around the circle of men toward her. When he reached for his sword hilt, I read an almost sexual anticipation in his black eyes, his twisted smile, and I realized Tahir was going to stab Elena in the back.

Christ, there was no time. Rodrigo fought with his back to me, so I couldn't see Elena. Tahir sidled closer from the left, and I knew I'd lose my opportunity in seconds, so when Tahir drew his sword and raised it, I grabbed my dagger from my boot, aimed it at Tahir's chest, and threw it across the empty space between us.

Rodrigo suddenly screamed, clutching his left buttock, the high shriek of pain freezing us all. Both Tahir and Elena, swords suspended, gaped at their great leader as he writhed on the floor, ear-piercing howls filling the room.

Holy shit. I had just stabbed, in the ass, the only man who could keep my future from flying apart. Thank god Arturo hadn't been here to see this. I ran to the now-kneeling warrior and pulled out the dagger. Blood stained his fingers, which gripped his ass in agony.

"Kill the bitch," he was able to sputter through clenched teeth. "Kill them both!" Tahir turned toward me, but Nuño suddenly locked an arm around my ribcage, and once again my feet left the floor.

"No!" Nuño commanded. Elena disappeared out a side door. Tahir pointed his wickedly curved sword at my belly, but Nuño knocked it aside. "No. Luis fooled us all, so this woman is mine now. I will give her what she deserves." Before Tahir or Rodrigo could respond, Nuño pushed through the crowd, and within seconds we were outside, Enzo right behind us. Nuño let me down, and we ran.

"Where will she go?" I gasped, following Nuño around a corner. Enzo and I both slipped but grabbed each other in time.

"Stables," Nuño called over his shoulder, unbelievably fast for such a large man.

By the time we reached the stables, Elena had saddled and mounted her horse. "Luis!" Nuño called.

She reined in the stallion. "Nuño, nothing has changed. Understand? We go forward with our plans."

"But how—"

"You do your part. I will do mine. This changes nothing." White knuckles gripped the reins so tightly her horse fought for its head.

"Luis," I sputtered, "I—"

"As for you, this changes everything. Now the world knows I am a woman, I can do nothing to help you find Arturo. Your friend Anna has destroyed in thirty seconds the life it has taken me nearly twenty years to build." She urged the horse forward as horror choked off my words.

"What of Kate?" Nuño asked, now almost jogging beside Elena.

She threw me a glance over her shoulder that was worse than being knifed in the gut. "I do not care. Sell her as a slave to Ibn Jehaf or al-Rashid. Moors like white women."

Nuño slapped the horse's rump, and Elena galloped down the street, heading west.

"Where will she go?" I finally managed to croak around the lump in my throat.

Enzo and Nuño glared at me. "Damn you, Kate Vincent," the older soldier growled. "Because of you, everything has gone wrong."

I swallowed, touching my bloody throat, the pain of Elena's words squeezing the air from my chest.

"We can't sell her as a slave," Nuño muttered.

"Where is Fadri?" Enzo said.

I covered my eyes briefly with a filthy hand. "He has likely awoken with a very bad headache. I'm so sorry I had to hurt him."

"You can't stay here." Nuño clenched his fists. "I hear the others coming."

"The Roman ruins. I can hide there."

With a curt nod, Nuño saddled a horse with Enzo's help, then nearly threw me onto the saddle.

"My saddlebags. I dropped them about two blocks from your place, by the butcher's."

"Enzo will bring them to you when it is safe. Follow this street north, then turn east toward the ocean. The road goes straight past the ruins."

With another slap, Nuño's wide palm sent my horse leaping forward, and I fled for my life to the north. I had spent less than twenty-four hours in Valencia.

CHAPTER TWENTY

The road soon left the "suburbs" of Valencia behind and wound between trampled fields and a decimated olive grove. When it veered to the right and topped a rise, I reined in my horse. The Mediterranean Sea spread out before me, pulsing with white-blue energy. The scent of the sea was infinitely more pleasant than rotting manure and sweaty men. Seagulls and terns picked their way along the rocky beach as tiny ridges of whitecaps gently broke into quiet waves. I ached to be walking this beach with Arturo and Max. Planes would roar dully overhead. Someone's boom box would irritate me. Crushed Coke cans and empty McDonald's wrappers would disgust me. God, how I longed to be home.

I shook it off and urged my horse forward. Another fifteen minutes brought me to the ruins, half-walls and fallen columns, broken chunks of scrolls and arches. I tied my horse in the grass behind, out of sight from the road, then carefully explored the deserted set of buildings. Only two still had roofs, and one of those would have collapsed with one of my hearty sneezes, so I entered the other, aware that small rodents skittered out of sight as I moved from room to room.

A few campfire circles were the only sign I hadn't been the first to squat here. I found a room with a view of the road and sat down on the hard ground to wait. I rested my head against the rough-cut stone, and now that I was relatively safe, a few cold tears spilled onto my cheeks. She didn't mean what she'd said. She'd been hurt and angry and needed to lash out at someone. She couldn't have learned to hate me so quickly.

Every time a horse galloped by, I peeked out the window, but the rider kept going. Hunger began gnawing at me mid-afternoon, but that was nothing compared to the pointless pain of reliving that morning, every second of it, over and over again.

By the time Enzo rode up I was so low I could barely wave to him out my window. He climbed in and dropped my saddlebag next to me. "I put some fruit and meat in there, as well as a skin of water." He lowered himself against another wall.

I drank the water immediately, grateful for the warm moisture. "Where is Nuño?" I asked as I wiped my mouth.

"Struggling to maintain order. Pulling all the other generals together. Assuring everyone he's as shocked as they are."

I bit into the bruised, ripe pear. "But he isn't shocked. Neither are you."

Enzo looked at me through narrowed, heavy-lidded eyes. "Neither are you."

I blushed. "True. I have known since our...well, for a very long time. But how did you know?"

He shrugged. "I watch. I pay attention. In all these years, we never once pissed together."

"Ah, yet you remained loyal to her, as did Nuño."

The fading light dimmed and softened Enzo's rough edges. "Luis... inspires. There is something about him—about her."

Yes, there was. I tossed the pear core out the window. "How is Rodrigo?"

Enzo snorted. "Like a mad bull. I don't know which hurts worse—the truth about Luis, or the hole you made in his ass."

Probably both. "How is Fadri? Does he hate me?"

A smile finally cracked the solemn face. "Fadri the Fool wears a lump on his head the size of a goose egg. He would still be furious with you if the camp didn't buzz with the news about Luis."

"Fadri is confused."

"The randy bastard doesn't know if he wants to kill Luis, or fuck him."

We had a good chuckle, then when Enzo stood to leave, I scrambled to my own feet. "Enzo, what about me? When I have found Arturo, I need to return to Valencia. Will I be safe there?"

His level gaze steadied me. "You can remain with the three of us, as long as one of us..." He dropped his eyes for a second. "...as long as one of us claims you."

I patted his arm. "I would appreciate that. I will come straight to you when I return."

With a curt nod, the aging soldier climbed out the window and was soon a cloud of dust moving south toward Valencia.

Before the light totally disappeared, I pulled out my history book and skimmed through it. The history it told was false but would come true if I didn't foil Elena's plans and see that Rodrigo took Valencia. How on earth could I do that at the same time I searched for Arturo?

The sun had disappeared over the mountains to the west, deepening the sea to a slate black. I dug in my saddlebag for my blank book and pencil stub.

After a violent and lengthy siege, the great Rodrigo Díaz mounted his silver steed, Babieca, and on the warm, peaceful morning of June 15, 1094, he rode up to the gates of Valencia, his brave and valiant army behind him. The gates opened, and the starving masses welcomed him as the new leader of Valencia.

I could barely see, but couldn't sleep without adding more. For some reason, just seeing the words helped. Self-help books talked about writing down your goals and that somehow the act of doing that would help your subconscious in its quest to make the goal come true. Since my conscious mind wasn't doing a very good job, I figured I could use all the help I could get.

After Rodrigo saw that the people of Valencia were fed, he established a peaceful reign over the city. He allowed all the mosques to remain open so the Moors could continue to worship Allah. He abolished all the harems, however, and established women in numerous administrative positions. The highest post, that of mayor, he awarded to his longtime friend and general, Elena Navarro.

I stopped. I no longer wrote history. I wrote fantasy. I doodled in the margins, drawing Moorish arches, Christian swords, and a tiny Lion King keychain. Finally I put the book down, wrapped myself in the cloak Enzo had brought, and lay awake for hours in the starless night.

❖

When I did finally sleep, I slept so hard nothing woke me the next morning, apparently not even the sound of two horses approaching the ruins, nor the sound of two men clomping through the rooms. But when one of them entered the room where I slept, and he cursed in surprise, then I woke up. I wish I hadn't.

Rafael Mahfouz grinned down at me. "Ah, I love it when life goes according to a plan. You are right where you should be. Finally I can bring you to Señora de Palma."

I sat up, rubbing my face, refusing to be frightened by this nightmare of a man who wouldn't go away. "How did you know—"

"Paloma's spy told me. He tells us everything. It was his idea to bring you here." He smiled, almost wistfully, as he watched the truth dawn on my face even as the sun shot streaks of gold across the sea out the window. I rolled onto my hands and knees. Nuño, Enzo, and Fadri would never have told anyone, and the only other person who knew was the one who had sent me here in the first place. Carlos.

"Yes, I see you understand now. The good Carlos is a great friend of Señora de Palma's. They confer often. It was he who finally found you in Zaragoza."

"He was there looking for me?" God, I'd walked right into Anna's trap.

"Of course. His job was to tell me when you arrived in Zaragoza. My job was to bring you to Paloma." He scowled, I suppose thinking that while Carlos had succeeded in finding me several times, this goon couldn't seem to succeed in his mission. He wouldn't this time either. Mahfouz rested his hands on his sword hilt. "Carlos has been based here in Valencia for quite awhile. The old Jew really gets around."

The old Jew. That's how Fadri had referred to the man bringing the special ale to Rodrigo, who got the shakes without it. Like withdrawal. So that's what she'd done. She drugged Rodrigo. Got him hooked on whatever white shit she brought back. I shook my head to think the kind, gentle Carlos had cast his lot with her.

I'd gotten my period the day I arrived in Valencia and hated using the rags, and this jerk was just one problem too many, so I stomped toward him. "Look, asshole. This is getting *really* boring. Tedious. Repetitive even. Ridiculous. Three strikes and you're out, buddy. Give it up. Get a life." The cords of my neck pulsed with irritation. "If you were a movie, I'd have turned you off by now. If you were a book, I'd have thrown you away. Get a clue. I am *not* coming with you."

Mahfouz nodded, smirking with some secret pleasure. "I understand that now and do admire your courage and resolve."

"Then why the hell won't you leave me alone?" I yelled. Caquito came up beside us, using his sword to keep me at bay.

"Because, Allah willing, I have a job to do, and *this* time I shall succeed."

I hated smug people. "How? The instant your thug lowers his sword to do *anything*, I'll beat the crap out of him again."

Mahfouz nodded, irritatingly calm. "I know. But this time I remembered what Señora de Palma gave me before I left. It seemed silly at the time, so I put it in my saddlebag and forgot it." He began fumbling inside his studded leather tunic, his too-handsome face contorted in concentration, then removed his hand. "She said if I showed you this, you'd come along quietly."

My breath caught in my chest and I slowly, slowly, raised my hands, palms spread wide. It shone blue in this light, but there was no doubt that Mahfouz held a gun in his large hand. I licked my lips. "Be careful, Rafael. That thing is very dangerous." It was a small gun, one of those petite numbers nervous wealthy women carried in their purses or kept in their night stands. But it was still a gun. Jesus. Anna was crazier than I thought.

"Señora de Palma also said it was dangerous." He twisted his wrist to consider the gun from all angles. "But it is not sharp at all."

I took a step back, my heart racing so fast I was light-headed. "Rafael, put it down so we—"

"Let me see that," Caquito said, fascinated.

"No, only I am to hold it."

"You agreed to share everything with me." Sword still pointed at me, he moved next to Mahfouz.

"Guys, let's don't do this. We can—"

"This is Señora de Palma's, not mine, so I can't give it to you. Besides, I can't seem to get my finger out of this round loop. It's stuck."

"I'll get it out for you."

I clutched my head. "No, don't!"

The shot was louder than I had expected from such a small gun. My ears rang and my body jerked back, suddenly flaming with a white-hot heat. I stared at the dark stain spreading across my tunic, then back at Mahfouz. His mouth hung open, his eyes wide with alarm. "Why are you bleeding?" he whispered with almost touching horror.

I pressed a hand against the stain. It was so warm, such a beautiful red. Was this really my body bleeding? The world became splashes of blurred colors and high-pitched whines, my numb knees dissolved into vapor, and the Goddess or God or Allah opened the black, yawning earth and swallowed me whole.

CHAPTER TWENTY-ONE

*M*om," *Arturo said.*
I stood on an island. We were separated by water. By time.
By a woman.

"Mom, you must live," he whispered. How could I hear him when
he was so far away?

I had no boat.

"I'm here, Mom. I'll save you. Remember that."

"Arturo, come away before Paloma finds out you've been to see
your mother. She will be upset.

My island floated away. I finally lost sight of the boy on the
shore.

❖

Cool cloth on my forehead. Woman's face. "Elena," I croaked.
Why won't my lips work? So hot. So hot.

"No, Elena isn't here, honey. Besides, she's far too violent a
woman for you, Kate. Come, drink this. Swallow this pill. There. That's
good."

❖

Talking, talking. The woman always talked. So hot. I was melting.
Cold air froze to my skin. I was frozen in Spain. Frozen in time. Centuries
from now they would uncover me and study me. Why was she all alone?
they would ask. My son disappeared, I said. Elena made a baby.

❖

"Kate, I've never stopped loving you, but this is bigger than both
of us. Imagine—to change the world. To change history. Doesn't it just
make you wet *thinking about it?"*

I was a desert. My son was gone. Where was my oasis? My oasis left on a horse. My oasis hated me. She used to love me. "Water."

"Good girl, drink this. I've had it boiled to be safe. Swallow this pill. You're getting better, honey. It's the miracle of antibiotics. You're going to make it."

My world was patches of blurred colors, as if some mad impressionist had used my eyeballs as a canvas. A patch of brown covered me. A smear of green walked past me. A column of white stood still. Why were my eyelids so heavy? When I practiced blinking, the white column slowly became a Moor in a white robe and turban standing by a doorway, arms folded, face fierce.

When the green blur bent over me, I blinked furiously, squinting until Anna's face came into focus. "Welcome back," she said softly.

I couldn't move my lips, so she dabbed them with a damp cloth. I couldn't move anything. Other than a dull ache in my left shoulder, my whole body felt swollen and heavy, as if the earth's gravity had doubled. "What...happened?"

Anna clucked, such a loud, harsh sound. "Rafael shot you in the shoulder. I told him only to *point* the gun at you. I really didn't want you to get hurt. He's such a big fool."

With intense concentration, I managed to raise my right hand and clasp Anna's shoulder. Despite her protests, I pulled myself up until our noses nearly touched. "Not as big a fool," I rasped, "as the absolute moron who *gave* him the gun." The room spun around me, and I faded into my dreams.

"Lock those prisoners up in the holding hut. I don't want her to wake up and see them here. Not yet."

"I didn't mean to harm her."

"Go. She'll be fine, no thanks to you."

"I hate the thing that hurt her. I threw it far into the woods. Caquito wanted it, but I said that devil stick is for cowards, not soldiers."

❖

Warm soft fur rubbing against my neck. Purring into my ear. Smell of soil and wet animal and dead mice. Something kneading, kneading my thigh, my belly, my shoulder. Oh! Shooting pain! "Cassandra, no! Leave her alone."

❖

Sun woke me, creeping down my pillow and onto my face. When I stirred, a dark Moorish woman leapt to her feet and left the room. The white column still guarded the door, but Anna soon stood by my side. "Welcome to Valencia, the crown jewel of Moorish Spain."

I struggled to sit up, wincing as I used my shoulder, and Anna plumped the pillows up behind me. "How bad is it?" I asked. Valencia. Inside the walls. Without Arturo. Without Rodrigo.

She smiled brightly, as if being shot in the eleventh century was commonplace. "As gunshot wounds go, I'd say it's very good. The bullet passed all the way through you. You lost a lot of blood, of course, but you're recovering nicely."

"I feel like I've been drugged."

Laughing, she nodded toward a huge carafe of wine. "I've been keeping you full of wine and sleeping pills so you'd stay quiet and heal."

I stared at the tray of food. "Where did you get food? The siege has cut the city off."

She almost giggled. "One of the joys of knowing the future is you can prepare for it. I have stored enough food in this palace to feed al-Rashid and all our guards and servants for months."

"Anna?"

She leaned closer, blond hair brushing the shoulders of some elaborate lace number, far too classy for nursing duties. "Yes?"

"A gun. Are you insane? What else did you bring back?" My throat felt dry and scratchy from disuse.

"Oh, Kate, let's don't argue about that now. You need to get stronger."

Suddenly too sleepy to be coherent, I slid lower onto the bed and slept.

❖

A piece of bread was my first solid food after bowls of broth fed to me while I was semi-conscious. "Anna, you've brought back Viagra. You've brought back a gun. I suspect you've brought back drugs, which I know you're using on Rodrigo. You are being totally irresponsible."

She patted my knee affectionately. "Since I'm trying to do no less than change the entire course of history, you'll forgive me if I don't feel too contrite over a little gun." She sighed happily. "When I first knew you'd returned, I was furious. But then I realized what it meant. You came back because I *am* successful. I'm changing Spain's history, and you can't stand that." She stroked the thick fur of an orange tabby cat curled up on her lap. Another stalked across the bed, arching its back and leaping onto the wide windowsill.

"I will stop you." My head hurt and my arm was numb.

"Oh, cut the bravado, Kate. You're in no condition to stop a flea. You'll stay right here with me until, say, June 16th or so, the day *after* Rodrigo was to take Valencia."

I rubbed my temples, finally starting to notice more of my surroundings. "Where am I?"

"In al-Rashid's palace."

"Carlos. He set me up. He's been feeding drugs to Rodrigo, hasn't he?"

She snorted softly. "Can you blame him for joining me? You know how the Christians treated the Jews. With me, with the new history, he has the chance to erase all that. We have worked together from the start."

My stomach twisted as if she'd punched me. How much more could I take? And where the hell was my son?

I shifted, wincing at the sudden flare of pain in my shoulder. "How long have I been here?"

Anna pursed her lips, tipped her small head. "Rafael brought you to me immediately. I've kept you pretty much unconscious for..." She ticked off the fingers. "Five days."

"Five?" I squeaked. I closed my eyes and calculated the date. June 9. Instead of making a difference, all I'd done for the last five days was make a dent in this mattress. Six days left. And I lay here weak as a sick lamb with a hole in my shoulder. "Help me up. I want to walk around."

"No, it's too soon. Oh!" I threw my good arm around her neck so she had no choice but to help me. My stomach flipped as I stood, and my knees wobbled, but I didn't pass out. I had to get better, and quickly.

❖

That afternoon I was walking with the servant's help, whose name she shyly told me was Nabila as she shooed cats out of the way. "She loves animals," Nabila said apologetically, and I could smell cat urine coming from one corner of the room. Anna had never really been an animal person before, preferring the company of friends and students. When we passed the window, I could see much of a large square, bordered by two-story buildings, the mosque at one end. The Muslim call to prayer rang out five times a day, and the mountains rose far to the west like stern, blue-green guards.

I walked some every hour and asked for food just as often to help build back my strength. Nabila answered my questions but was too meek to offer much more. At one point I had her lift the loose bandage, and I inspected the small wound, now crusted with a scab. Thank god it had entered below my collarbone, but judging from the sharp pain when I moved the wrong way, my ribs must be bruised as well. Twice we both grimaced as one of Anna's cats walked into the room with a dead mouse and dropped it at the guard's feet. He kicked both cat and mouse out of the room.

While I walked, I forced myself to review the mess I called my life. Professor Kalleberg's voice lit up my head, and I wondered briefly how he fared, sitting in that abandoned cave waiting for a shift in history. Arturo was still missing. Carlos had betrayed me. Elena's true gender was revealed, and she hated me for it. Fadri hated me. I got shot. The al-Saffah leader Nugaymath had my dagger. Now that she'd captured me, Anna had Arturo's dagger as well. I had no weapon. And other than knifing Rodrigo in the ass and saving Elena, I had done nothing. I sighed. Professor Kalleberg should have come instead.

I leaned out the window, catching the cool breeze, and realized with a start that I was only on the second floor. Surely even I could escape from the second floor. The square, filled with trees and a small fountain, was lined with stone buildings with thick tile roofs. A Moor sat on a bench outside the building opposite me, only entering the small, windowless building now and then with a tray of food and a brown clay jug. Apparently I wasn't the only prisoner.

"Isn't the mosque stunning in this light?"

I turned slowly, wiping all thought of escape from my face. "It is. Do you spend much time there?" Anna nodded for the guard to step outside.

"I pray privately."

"Because Islam forbids women to pray in mosques."

She fingered one of her massive gold rings. "No, it doesn't. You just don't understand Islam, Kate. You don't understand what the Moors can do for women."

I snorted, dropping back onto my bed, partly to convince Anna I was still weak, and partly because I *was* still weak. "Enlighten me then."

Green eyes sparkled as she sat beside me. "Muhammad loved and respected women. He adored Khadija, his only wife for over twenty years. Many of Allah's revelations to Muhammad improved women's lives." For a second, time shifted, and we were back in our kitchen, and she'd just come home with news of a new research grant or a stimulating class discussion. "Modern Islam oppresses women because something went wrong along the way. The revelations meant to protect Muhammad's wives were misinterpreted, misapplied to all women. But in Muhammad's time women were involved in life. When Nusaybah and her husband joined the battle of Uhud, she saved Muhammad's life, refusing to leave his side even after the men fled. Muhammad's daughter Fatima led a victorious political struggle after his death."

I could feel my eyes beginning to droop, the predicable effect of Anna's lectures. She burrowed through a basket she'd brought. "While modern Islam has problems, the Moors got it right. The veil isn't strictly enforced. Women share in scientific advances. Girls are educated just as completely as boys." She pulled out a sheaf of thin parchment. "Here. I want you to read this. It's all in here."

I stared at the stack now on my lap. "You've written a thesis on this?"

Face flushed, Anna clasped her hands together, almost as if she sought my approval. "This is such a relief to talk about this with someone besides Carlos. When I learned about Mirabueno and realized I had a window back to the eleventh century, everything became clear, as if I, too, had received a revelation from Allah." I winced. "If I could increase the power and stature of the Moors, I could both increase Spain's importance in the world *and* help spread a more tolerant form of Islam."

I picked up the top sheet: "Thoughts on the Role of Women in a More Tolerant Islam."

"Please read it."

I didn't look at the papers in my hand. "Anna, why did you expose Luis?"

"Ahh, I wondered when you'd ask that. I'm very sorry I had to hurt her that way."

"How long had you known?"

"The more time I spent with her as she accompanied Rodrigo to meetings with Alfonso, the more I suspected it. She never joined the men in a communal pee, and I couldn't imagine you with a man."

"How did you know for sure?"

"Not until she dropped her pants. I took a risk."

Anna's games made me furious. "Why expose her at all? She was no threat to you."

Anna shrugged. "The more isolated Rodrigo is, the better."

I rubbed my temples. She had thought of everything.

"Kate, read this. It will take your mind off Arturo *and* Luis."

"And when I'm done?"

"Then I want to talk. Read this and you'll see why we need to work together, not against each other. I want you to join me. We made a great team once. We can do it again." She slid one warm hand over mine. "Think about it."

❖

I read every page. She profiled modern Muslim societies. Muslim women fight as soldiers in the United Arab Emirates. Iran votes women into Parliament and sends them abroad as diplomats. Turkey had a woman prime minister. In these countries women found valuable role models to follow from early Islam. Anna wanted to venerate these women—Khadija, Nusaybah, the prophet's daughters—and the Moors of Spain were the best suited for this.

I stopped to rub my eyes. As a feminist, I struggled with the thought that what Anna proposed actually made sense. Then I remembered. She'd have to manipulate history, impact billions of lives over the centuries, causing whole chunks of history, of culture, of people to cease to exist. Only a very sick person would believe she had the right, the ability, the *wisdom*, to alter the world.

I walked and walked, stretched my arm and shoulder, and pondered, just as Anna had asked me to. I thought of all the reasons Anna was crazy. I thought of all the reasons I had to find Arturo and get him home. I even thought of the one reason a small part of me was desperate to stay in this century.

Mid-list I stopped, really noticing for the first time that the bed had sheets, odd for this time period, but I suppose Anna had ordered them made. The bed, in fact, had two sheets, and Nabila had piled used sheets, likely drenched with my fever sweats, in the nearby corner. I shot a glance at the guard. Would it be that easy? Might *something* in this doomed operation go right? I looked out the window, gauging. Three sheets, maybe four, should do it. My spirits chugged to life, fueled by hope. Lose the guard, lose the servant, and I, too, could be gone.

CHAPTER TWENTY-TWO

That evening I watched for an opportunity but none came. While Nabila slept soundly on a grass mat along the wall, the guard stayed alert and wary, damn him, until he was relieved. I could hear two more guards talking down the hall, so Anna was clearly taking no chances. I had subdued Rafael and Caquito with Tae Kwon Do because they weren't expecting anything, but my sentry watched my every move with dark, suspicious eyes. Two swords hung from the leather belt wrapped around his robes. Before I could reason through my options, and exhausted by my day of recovery, sleep took me.

Anna returned the next morning after I'd finished my three eggs and a thick slice of bread smeared with sweet almond butter. She brought me a stunning white rose just beginning to open, the petals soft as the inside of Elena's thighs. I bent my head to the rose, inhaling deeply, eyes closed, remembering.

Anna sat on the bed beside me. "What do you think?"

I shook my head as I handed her back her thesis. "While you have been writing this, plotting your manipulations of history, you've missed so much."

"Like?"

"Like Arturo's first soccer game, or the day he finally stood up to Brent Jackson, or the Saturday he raided the neighbor's garden and picked every blossom just for me."

Anna dropped her gaze, stroking yet another cat on her lap. Her nails were bitten short, the cuticles red and inflamed. "You're right. I envy all those years you spent with Arturo, while I've spent them basically alone."

"You've had lovers. You have Carlos."

For a frightening second I thought Anna was going to cry. She rubbed her throat as if to dislodge something. "Not the same, Kate. You helped Arturo grow up. You've been a mother."

Regret? From Anna? I bit back words of sympathy, since she'd made her own choice.

The muezzin's thin call to prayer rang out in the square, and Anna sat on the edge of her chair, expectant, anticipating something. She squared her shoulders, then gave me a shy smile. "That's why I am so grateful I have the chance to make things up to Arturo, to help shape his journey into adulthood."

"What?"

She rose, motioning me to the window. "Come, I want you to see this. I hope you will share my pride."

Men moved toward the mosque, most of them slowly, exhausted with starvation, but a strong breeze billowed out every robe so the men appeared as colorful butterflies among the trees below, almost golden in the early morning light. They gathered around a high bench, on which stood a young Moor dressed in pure white robe and turban shot through with gold and silver thread.

When the young man raised his jeweled hands and turned in my direction, my lungs ceased to function. My mouth worked frantically but produced no sound. *Arturo.*

"Come, all you believers," Arturo began, his clear voice bringing tears of relief and confusion to my eyes. "As your caliph, Allah has spoken to *me*, and told me what we must do."

"Caliph?" I squeaked as he exhorted the men to remain strong during the siege. Wild-eyed, I whirled on Anna. "*Caliph?* Al-Rashid? Arturo is al-Rashid?"

"Calm down, Kate. You'll have a stroke." She gazed down at Arturo with such a loving smile a dagger of fear sliced through me. "We've been together over a week, and it's going splendidly."

"How? Why?" I sputtered.

"I needed a teenaged boy. That fool Jehaf murdered my original al-Rashid—"

"So you murdered his son."

"Precisely. My Rashid was a dear boy I'd spent two years training, and while it was a terrible loss so late in the game, I resolved to find myself *another* Rashid."

My nails dug half moons into the soft wooden sill. "But al-Saffah kidnapped Arturo."

"And then I offered them five thousand gold pieces. When I put out the word I sought a fourteen-year-old boy, Nugaymath delivered him herself."

Arturo, deeply tanned since I'd last seen him twelve days ago, had five guards around him, but he was so small, so vulnerable. "Anna, you stupid *bitch!* Ibn Jehaf murdered the first Rashid. He'll try to kill the second as well. You've put Arturo in great danger."

Her green eyes narrowed in agreement. "Yes, but it's a risk we're willing to take."

"We?"

Anna reached for my hand but I jerked it away. "Please don't be upset, honey. At first, Arturo resisted my plan and wanted nothing to do with me. But I gave him a white stallion and servants to wait on him. He has more money at his disposal than he could ever spend. He eats well, and drinks wine, in private of course. A caliph must appear to be devout to his followers."

Anna's words clanged in my head like a school fire drill, the kind that go off when you're standing right beneath them. Stallion. Servants. Money. Wine. Oh, my god. What had she done to my son?

"The secret to managing a teenager is giving him what he *thinks* he needs," Anna said, and my hands twitched to wrap themselves around her neck and squeeze her until she turned the color of ice. "The money helped, but I think it was getting his own harem that finally convinced him that life as al-Rashid was a great idea."

Stallion. Servants. Sex.

"You've brainwashed him."

"No, nothing that dramatic. Just given him the life he's always dreamed of." She leaned against the wall, arms folded. "I'm sure he still cares for you, though, since he asks about you often."

The crowd cheered wildly at the end of Arturo's speech, and he raised two triumphant fists, beaming with an excitement that burned my throat. When the guards helped him off the bench, everyone filed into the mosque behind him.

After Elena's refusal to help me and her harsh words before fleeing, I didn't think my life could sink any lower, but here I was, going down, down, down. I blinked furiously. I would not give Anna the satisfaction of seeing me break down. But, oh, Arturo. I trembled with horror, not just because Arturo had been swayed to work against Rodrigo, but at a deeper loss. "Leave me," I croaked.

Anna's face glowed with such sympathy I nearly punched her. "I need your answer. You could join us. You could be his parent alongside me."

She was offering, out of her generous spirit, to *let* me parent my own child? Blissful fury buried the pain burning inside me, and I struggled for control as Anna began pacing the wide room.

"Thanks to what you told Carlos, I know that my plans succeed. This only increases my resolve. You have failed, not something you're used to, and I understand that makes you bitter. But nothing you've done, or tried to do, has changed what *must* happen."

"If you change the timeline, you change your own history. Your ancestors may never be born, so you'll never exist. You could just pop out of existence. We *all* could."

"Rubbish. Al-Rashid will unite the Moors, conquer all of Spain, and the word of Allah will spread throughout Europe and North America. I'm not afraid of disappearing, and even if I did, my actions are more important than my life."

"North America? Europe won't discover it for another 400 years."

She smiled. "Why wait? I know where it is, so there's no reason to wait until 1492. Only this time we'll do it right. We won't enslave or murder or exploit the natives."

It was my turn to smile. "You don't really understand human beings, do you?"

She waved aside my comment, then paused, skin glistening with a thin sheen of perspiration. "This new history is inevitable, Kate. Join us."

I looked up at the slight break in her voice, which revealed her complete loneliness, then I took both her hands in mine. How isolated, how friendless she must have been these last eight years, which suddenly explained all the cats. She may have had affairs, but no one loved her but her pets. Tremors ran through her hands into mine, and when I gazed into that older, but oh-so-familiar face, something tripped in my heart. While I no longer actively loved her, I wondered if, after five years of entwining our lives and our hearts, perhaps a shadow love remained, nesting in a deep crevasse in my soul, a place that would always love her.

I brought her hands to my lips and kissed them, sighing softly. "You have really thought through all that you've done. You've approached this with the same devotion and concentration you applied to your teaching, despite how lonely you must be. You've even converted to Islam as a symbol of your commitment." Her breath quickened as her eyes filled with tears. "But to help you destroy what must be?" I suddenly bellowed. "To help you endanger and corrupt my son?" I stood, her hands trapped in my furious grip. "Not in a million fucking years. Do you hear me?" I said through clenched teeth. "Never. *Ever*. I am going to whip your ass and kick it all the way back to the twenty-first century."

She pulled free, her mouth open. "You refuse to join me?"

"What part of 'no' don't you understand?" I snarled.

Her face suddenly red, Anna squeezed her eyes shut for a second, shaking her head. "I don't believe this. You're too smart to refuse."

"Smart has nothing to do with it. I'm right, and you're just fucking wrong."

"You *can't* refuse. No one refuses me. I'm too powerful. I have shitloads of money. I even bought Tahir. Don't fight me."

"Tahir works for you?"

"Of course. I've thought of everything, anticipated every obstacle, looked at every angle. Tahir's a mercenary, just like your precious Luis. Tahir, Carlos, Rafael, the Valencian council, and hundreds others. They're all with me. Rodrigo's ancient history. He's done."

"Anna Lee, fuck you." She hated that word. So did I, but it was the only word that captured my fury.

"What?"

"Fuck you, baby. When I'm done, *you're* going to be ancient history."

Face now as white as the rose she'd given me, Anna grabbed her bangs with both fists. "Oh, god, don't make me do this. How could you *do* this to me?" She stormed around the room cussing me and every moment she'd known me, finally returning to her beginning rant. "Don't make me do this."

"Do what?" I expected there would be consequences to my refusal, but the terror on her face sent a tiny trickle of fear down my neck.

Anna turned toward me, her face streaked with tears. "I meant what I said earlier. Nothing is more important to me than this, not even you."

"So you're going to lock me up and throw away the key."

"No, my only choice is something more permanent."

I forced myself to laugh in her face, sounding much braver than I felt. "You don't want me dead, or you would have let me die from my wound."

"Then I still had hope you might see the truth, but that hope was obviously ill-founded. I can't run the risk of your interference."

"So you're going to kill me." She couldn't kill me anymore than I could kill her, but my fear grew.

"No, I'm not. The mullah of Valencia will do it for me." She glared at me, hands on her hips. "This morning I will deliver a letter, in Arabic, to the mullah. That letter will denounce Muhammad as a false prophet and question the word of Allah."

"Strange thing for a converted Muslim to do," I said tightly. I remembered Grimaldi's story of the Christian martyrs in which blasphemy was punished swiftly by beheading.

"The letter will be signed by Kate Vincent and others. The mullah will not waste any time because he must set an example. You will die tomorrow."

My jaw clenched. "Coward. Kill me yourself."

She shrugged, exhausted and suddenly distant. "No." Anna was petite, but now she seemed a wizened old woman, bones too brittle to support her flesh. "You did not choose wisely, my love. I tried to warn you." She rubbed her eyes. "Christ, now I have to deal with Arturo."

"Deal with?"

Distracted, she ran a hand over her head. "He can't know about this. I'll have to lock him in the tower and blame it on Ibn Jehaf or something." She glared at me. "May Allah forgive me for what I do, but it's your own fault. You have complicated everything." She snapped out an order in Arabic to watch me carefully, then left without a backward glance.

❖

I couldn't believe she'd go through with it. Maybe when I knelt by the chopping block with a sword suspended over my head, I might concede defeat, but not until that moment.

Outside, a group of servants constructed a platform, which held nothing but a rectangular chopping block with a shallow notch, clearly cut to hold the victim's neck steady. As a result, escape never left my mind for a second all day. When Nabila left the room to empty my chamber pot or go for food, I waited until my guard was distracted by a conversation down the hall, then I tied four sheets together and hid them under the bed.

I tried a coughing fit, but only Nabila came to my rescue. The guard stayed at his post. If I tried to overcome him in the doorway, the other guards would see.

At one point I even considered just taking my chances and leaping out the window, but too many people milled around the square. I wouldn't get far, and given my luck, I'd probably break both legs anyway. Now and then someone from the square would point up at my window, so word must have spread—Anna had wasted no time.

Think, Kate, think. At least the thought of escape kept my mind off Arturo. I absentmindedly stroked the black cat with eyes as blue as Elena's. At work I'd faced impossible deadlines, shortages, unruly employees, and indifferent bosses. I should be able to get myself out a two-story window. Several blocks away, rising above the Valencian rooftops, was a stone, windowless tower. That would be where Anna was keeping Arturo.

The sun set, a huge orange globe sliding behind the dark mountains, and torches had been lit in front of a few doorways where men gathered to talk. With dusk I had no choice but to try. I would have to surreptitiously tie the last sheet to the stubby wooden leg of the bed and climb out in full view of Nabila and the guard, hoping to at least get out the window before he could cross the room and grab me.

Just then Nabila let out a piercing scream as something dark raced across the floor. The cat launched itself from my lap, digging sharp claws in so deeply I yelled as I jumped to my feet. Cat and rat whizzed across the floor and Nabila, crazed with fear, practically climbed me. I yelled and she screamed and somehow, by the time all three guards reached the doorway, Nabila and I stood on the bed, clinging to one another. The cat chased the rat under the bed.

The men smiled condescending grins, and I found it totally humiliating when one guard waved to the other. "I think you can handle this." Chuckling, two guards left and returned to their posts.

"Kill it, kill it," Nabila moaned, bruising my arms with her desperate grip.

With a huge, macho sigh, the guard sauntered toward us, then knelt to look under the bed, where I'd stashed my getaway. With my good arm, I reached for the brown clay pitcher on the table beside the bed and grabbed it by the mouth. Nabila had time for only a squeak before I swung the pitcher in a wide arc and smashed it against the guard's head just as he began to stand.

Smashing men in the head with pots was becoming a habit.

Both the guard and the shards of pot ended up on the bed, so I grabbed his soaking robes and lowered him slowly enough there was no thump to attract the other guards.

Nabila still stood on the bed, hair wild, face pale as the bedsheets. She likely did not know who to fear more—me or the rat. I held my fingers to my lips, then ripped strips from the bed sheet. I gently tied her hands and ankles, then tied a gag around her mouth. Grateful eyes shone back at me because if she were tied up, Nabila might not be punished for my escape.

I pushed her down on the bed so I could use her weight when I went out the window. She still said nothing, even though the gag, more a Hollywood invention than a practical tool, did nothing to still her vocal cords. Apparently not everyone was as devoted to Señora de Palma as Rafael Mahfouz.

The cat and rat had disappeared by the time I retrieved my sheets. I quietly shifted the bed closer to the window, tied one end of the sheets to the bed, and threw the rest out the window.

A few torches burned around the square, but the wall below me was dark. Getting out the window with only one strong arm proved trickier than I'd expected, but I crouched on the sill, sheet gripped in my right arm, then let myself fall. The bed thudded against the wall but that was the last I heard as I half slid, half climbed down, the sheets clutched between knees and thighs. Wincing as I used both arms, I grunted when my feet touched the ground for the first time in days. I was free.

I untied the last sheet, wrapping it around myself. I knew any Moor I'd meet would see a person wrapped in a bed sheet, but I had to try anything to fade into the background. I ripped off a piece and tied it around my head. Heart pounding, shoulder burning, I skittered alongside the building and approached the street.

When two male voices approached near the corner ahead, I whirled around, a frantic spinning ghost with no place to hide, finally diving behind a rack of sheepskins curing outside a tanner's shop next to my former prison. The wooly hides hung over two wooden bars and offered camouflage rather than an actual hiding place.

"I hate my job," a deep voice grumbled.

"Haroun, you always say that before an execution. But look how easy your life goes. You do, what—three or four a year? For this the mullah sees you are well fed. Come. We check that everything is ready tonight, then tomorrow will go well. I envy your life, Haroun."

To my horror, the men stopped, leaning against the building only thirty feet from me, and when the skins around me moved silently in the cool breeze, I held my breath. I even tried Arturo's old trick of squeezing his eyes shut during hide and seek so no one could see him.

"I know, but the pressure is great. If I do not achieve a clean cut everyone suffers."

"No one blames you for last year's episode, Haroun. The woman moved at the last minute."

For Pete's sake, what morons. Couldn't they take their therapy session somewhere else?

A ragged sigh escaped what must have been a large man. "My axe goes dull after one, and tomorrow I have three. I will need at least two sharpened axes."

"I will help. Then when the mullah pays you, perhaps a little could trickle down my way."

My feet and calves began to fall asleep. Wool tickled my neck and I could smell lanolin and salt and bits of rank flesh.

"It's not just that. The woman and two men I execute tomorrow apparently all know each other. And friends tend to fall into each other's arms and wail and make me feel badly. It feels like I execute a family, not just blasphemers."

My bowels cramped, and I tensed every muscle. Oh my god. Who had Anna captured?

The other man grunted as he straightened. "No use putting it off. Let's go sharpen axes. Then after tomorrow, what do you think about taking up carpentry? When this siege is over, my cousin in Albarracín could use some help."

Now both men stretched and walked past me. "Oh, I'm terrible with wood. I tried a table once and hacked it up something awful." The woeful executioner and his friend faded into the next block.

When the men were gone, I ran. Sounds of laughter came from one street, so I ducked into another and stepped into a recessed doorway, so much adrenaline rushing to my head I couldn't think. The tower. Without being noticed, I made it two more blocks, hiding behind wagons, barrels of water, and a pile of putrefying garbage. Eyes watering from the garbage dump, I crept in the direction of the tower, but when I peered around the next corner, my heart sank. The tower, sized like a small, narrow lighthouse, had only one door, and that door was guarded by thirty soldiers. Shit. A howl of rage came from within the tower, and while I couldn't make out the words, Arturo was clearly cursing. He was angry. Good. Maybe that would break the spell Anna held over him.

I slumped onto the dusty street, twisted up in my sheet. The guards would soon discover I was gone. My heart thumped in my chest and my shoulder burned. I needed help. Two people I knew had been caught in Anna's web and would be executed tomorrow. Whoever Anna had captured, they were probably being held in the windowless building across from my own prison, the one with the constant guard out front. Could I escape twice from the same sticky web? I had no choice but to try, since I couldn't rescue Arturo alone.

CHAPTER TWENTY-THREE

Taking a deep breath to gather what little courage I had left, I leapt to my feet and ran, retracing my steps. I passed several groups of men, but in the dark my sheet did the trick. At the corner of the jail, I stopped. A handful of men walked the square, and amazingly, everyone was too involved in conversation to look up and notice the string of bed sheets fluttering softly out a second-story window, now snagged in the nearest tree. I nosed around a pile of junk behind the building in search of something heavy enough, then approached the front.

"Pssst!" I hissed. The guard, snoring softly against the wall, sat up suddenly. "Pssst! Come here." I lowered my voice as deeply as I could, poked my head around the corner, and spoke in simple Arabic. "I need help. She won't stop struggling. I have her clothes off. Come."

The randy guard stood, looked to make sure no one watched, then sauntered toward me. When he rounded the corner, I swung the iron bar hard against his temple. He staggered, and I hit again and again until the bloody man crumpled at my feet. After I dragged him down the side street, a quick search yielded no keys, so I yanked his turban off and wrapped it around my own head, wrinkling my nose at the acid sweat, and sauntered as best I could back the way he'd come. At the doorway, which had no lock, I pulled the torch off the wall and pushed the door open.

Rusty hinges squeaked when I stepped inside and closed the door behind me. The torch barely penetrated the oppressive blackness. Stuffy air, heavy with urine and feces, burned my lungs. I lifted the torch, peering through the iron grate before me. "Hello?"

Bodies stirred in the darkness and someone coughed. "Hello?" I repeated.

"Praise God," someone whispered.

"Kate?" Squinting against the torch, a man, filthy but recognizable, staggered toward the grate.

"Nuño!" A second limped into the light. "Grimaldi! Oh god, you're hurt." Someone shouted outside, so I flung off my sheet and grabbed the bars, yanking hard, but of course it was locked. "Key!"

"Don't know." Nuño's voice was flat. "They never open it." I began searching the walls and floor.

"On the guard?" Grimaldi offered.

"I checked already. Wait." I pulled a metal plate off the wall and found a shallow niche with keys. The shouts outside grew louder and enough horses galloped by to mount an army.

"Hurry, Kate." Grimaldi's voice was weak. He held the torch through the bars while I fumbled with the key. It clicked into place and the iron grate swung open.

"C'mon, not much time," Nuño said, supporting Grimaldi. But when I flung open the door into the square, my heart stopped.

"Shit!" I cursed in English. An entire army of Moorish soldiers filled the square and all faced the doorway where we stood. When we appeared, over one hundred swords left their scabbards, filling the moonless night with a terrible, silky smooth whoosh.

No one spoke, but a few horses snorted in the cool air.

"Not very good odds, I am afraid," Grimaldi murmured.

The army parted for Anna, her hair down, cape hastily thrown over her shoulders. We stared at each other. "What now?" I asked.

"To paraphrase the Wicked Witch of the West," she said, "the last to go will watch the first two go before her.'"

"You're sick."

"No, I'm right, so make peace with yourself and your god, Kate, because tomorrow it all ends." I had been wrong. No shadow love for Anna Lee remained in my heart, my soul, my body. I could not imagine *ever* having loved her.

A dozen guards advanced with swords drawn. For a second I felt my companions hesitate, and I understood. Would it be better to die in a hopeless escape attempt than to be tied up and beheaded in a public spectacle? As Nuño tensed, I decided I wasn't yet ready for suicide, so I stepped back into the jail. After a brief hesitation, Nuño and Grimaldi followed. The iron grate clanked into place behind us, the outer door creaked shut, and we were left in total darkness.

❖

Grimaldi explained politely that the right back corner was the toilet area, but the whole cell reeked so badly I had occasional gagging and coughing fits all night. As the three of us sat with our backs against the wall, I couldn't see three inches in front of my face, but my hearing grew sharp enough so that I could identify Nuño's boot scraping the dirt floor, or the rustle of Grimaldi's robe.

"Okay, explanation," I said softly.

Grimaldi chuckled. "Like why is an old guy like me chasing after a young chick like you?" I waited. "Before you and Arturo left Zaragoza, he told me..." I could sense Grimaldi looking toward Nuño. "Ah, hmm. Don't know as I should say this."

Nuño's disgust rumbled through his chest. "I don't want to know, right?" I'd used this line on poor Nuño a number of times as he was helping me rescue Elena from Gudesto Gonzalez eight years ago.

"Yes," I said.

"Forget I'm here, and say it."

"Kate, Arturo told me he'd read of your death. He knew the date. He knew how it was to happen. He begged me to do what I could to stop it."

"Date?"

"Tomorrow. The method of death is—"

"Beheading. Execution for blasphemy," I finished. So that's what Arturo had found in the footnotes of Kalleberg's book. "Why would my death have made the history books?"

"He said it had to do with you being the first foreigner beheaded, and the first in a long string of beheadings, all ordered by the mullah of Valencia."

I winced. Everything Arturo had read was about to come true. "Nuño?"

"I do not want to understand any of what you are saying, but I'm here for the same reason. Grimaldi came to us last week and told Enzo, Fadri and myself you were in danger, and if we did not find you by tomorrow's date, you would die." He sighed deeply, stirring the dust at his feet. "I do not understand how Grimaldi knew this, but I could not afford to take it lightly."

I swallowed, pushing against the emotion racing up my throat.

"You both came looking for me. To save me." Silence. "What of Enzo and Fadri?"

"In camp. We still have a job to do, and in case something went wrong inside the walls, I didn't want us all to be captured."

"And Elena? Any word from her?"

" I saw her once before Grimaldi arrived. I'm sure Enzo and Fadri have spoken to her since, but I don't know where she is."

"Nuño has told me what happened," Grimaldi said. "It must be hard on Luis...or rather, Elena, to have the truth revealed. I was startled myself at the news."

Talking of Elena suddenly became a way to lighten the oppressive heat a bit. Slowly, cautiously, we began sharing stories. Time passed and the darkness lifted as I told the story of the day at the grove outside Zaragoza when she dove naked into the pond at the sound of voices, and then emerged like a goddess rising from the sea to kill the two men who had attacked me. Grimaldi remembered when Luis came to his wedding in shining mail and red cloak, and had shown infinite patience with the throngs of children who'd wanted to ride Matamoros or hold Luis's sword.

We finished the last of the water in a mold-encrusted jug, and Nuño began talking about the years after I left, but stopped when he realized it might cause me pain. "Keep going," I murmured, so I heard about Luis and Rodrigo rejoining the Castilian army, still as mercenaries, following Rodrigo on raids to Aragon and Catalonia, about Elena's struggle to recover from losing me. "When she laughed again for the first time, six months after you left, I knew she would get better. I kept her mind off you with hard fighting, hard riding, and hard drinking."

Grimaldi laughed weakly from his corner, and I imagined his fingers laced across his wiry chest. "You weren't always such hard drinkers, Nuño. Elena told me of the time the monks harvested you and her from the trees like apples." Nuño protested but Grimaldi chuckled and continued. "When they were sixteen and still new to Valvanera, Elena and Nuño stole four bottles of wine from the cellar and climbed the wide oak tree near the stables, thinking they'd never be seen in the thick foliage."

"It was her idea."

"So they drank all the wine, and being unused to alcohol, became groggy and confused and fell *out* of their perches, landing on the lower branches."

"Ouch," I said.

"It was her idea," Nuño insisted.

"Father Ruiz came outside to check on this great crashing of branches and found them both draped over the lowest branch, legs, arms, and heads dangling, the four bottles on the ground beneath them."

Nuño chuckled now. "One minute I was straddling a high fork in the tree, then the next thing I knew, Father Ruiz was shining a torch into my face and my whole body ached."

It was subtle, but I noticed all of us referred to her with the female pronoun and used Elena rather than Luis. What if the world could accept her for the woman she really was? We talked into the night of families and children, of disappointments, of dreams. At one point Grimaldi and I switched into English to discuss life in two centuries.

Eventually, though, talking ceased, trickling down to an occasional murmur, then nothing. In our black tomb we had no way to gauge time. Had the sun crested the mountains to the east? Had Execution Day begun?

I had wrestled with a thought all night long, and finally decided. "Nuño?"

He murmured a reply, shaking himself awake. "Yes?"

I took a deep breath. Elena may hate me for this, but she hated me already. "You and Elena." Silence. "I know you and she...were together."

Air rushed in through his wide nostrils. "She told you. I am sor—"

"Nuño, it's okay. I'm glad you could comfort...that she has you..." I couldn't finish the sentence.

The large man sighed. "Well, it wasn't as you think. It was one night, and one night only." He shifted, feet scraping in the dark, and suddenly his story flowed from him like a bottle uncorked. "The fourth anniversary of the day you left, we went to Mirabueno, as we always did. I don't know why, but she always thought you might appear, just as she had found you the first time." Elena's pain must have been excruciating. All I'd had to do was step into that cave to return to her, but there was nothing she could do to get to me. "But once again, you weren't there. We drank ale, way too much ale. Elena cried. She said you were never coming back. Then she turned to me. She revealed her sex, which I already knew, of course. I...We..."

"You made a baby," I said softly.

The cell became so quiet my ears rang. "What?" he whispered.

Oh, Christ. He didn't even know. "You made a baby." I licked my lips. "It really isn't my place to tell you, but in case tomorrow really happens—"

"But—"

"It only takes one time. Did Elena go away for awhile after that?"

"No, we were part of the Elche campaign. That took three, four months. Then we...no, then *I* returned to Burgos. She..." His voice grew louder. "She wintered at Valvanera. My mother was ill, so I didn't pay much attention."

"You didn't see her for another five or six months."

"Yes! It was the longest we'd gone without seeing one another. Holy Christ!" Nuño leapt to his feet. "I have a child? Why did she not tell me?" I let him rant for a few minutes, venting to a woman who wasn't here. Eventually the anger subsided into wonder.

"Her name is Solana," I said. "She has black curly hair, and your eyes, and your dimples. She is stubborn and strong-willed. She loves adventure."

"Oh, my god." The wonder subsided into grief, and I could tell by his voice that he curled over his raised knees in pain. "I will never see her, will I?"

"I'm truly sorry, Nuño, but I thought you should know."

A ragged sigh came from his corner. "Yes, I am...glad to know." We joined Grimaldi in his silence.

I thought about Arturo, and imagined him home in his room with the race car wallpaper, with steady old Max by his side. This was the real Arturo, not the ruler Anna was creating. I thought about Elena, my brave, furious love, determined to do what was right. I thought about the professor. How long would he wait in that cave before he realized nothing would change? How would he live his last days, weeks, months before the disruptive history blinked him into oblivion?

Thanks to the letter Arturo had left for Laura, she'd know what happened to me, but would not likely believe it. She would lose her best friend for the second time. And then, when the wave moving through history extended its fingers into her past, she'd cease to exist as well.

The longer I sat there, sweat plastering my shirt and pants to my skin, eyes searching for some pinprick of light, the more I began to see this might be it. I would never hold Arturo again, never have a chance to reconcile with Elena, never figure out how I would fit into the world, how I'd make my life matter.

❖

When the door finally swung open, we were too blinded to resist. Soldiers jerked us to our feet and bound our hands loosely behind our backs, the rough jute chaffing my wrists. Eyes shut, I was led outside and the hot sun brought goose bumps to my arms. As I stumbled along, I was able to open my eyes wider and take in the scene. The square was filled with townspeople, Christian and Moor, and Moorish soldiers, all silent as they watched us enter the square, where a shaded viewing platform rose up from the crowd. No surprise, the platform held Anna, dressed in a somber black gown, but I choked to see Carlos sitting beside her.

The two were arguing, with Carlos nodding emphatically toward me. When he clutched at Anna's arm, it was clear he implored her to change her mind, so I wondered if Carlos now regretted his choices. Up until this moment, Anna's plotting had been political, almost academic, but as we neared June 15, she would let no one stop her, including me. She shrugged him off, shaking her head.

The guards paraded us past Anna's platform. Carlos wouldn't meet my eyes but instead studied his hands, his mouth working so furiously I knew he was on the verge of tears. Good. He *should* feel badly.

Arturo was absent, so Anna must still have him locked in the tower. Even though Arturo had been swept up into Anna's world, I knew he loved me. He had to know what day it was and was powerless to help. I, in turn, could do nothing to help him.

Anna and I exchanged steely glares, and one corner of her mouth lifted, a sort of "sorry about this, old chap" smile. She raised a hand, halting the procession, then walked smoothly toward us. She stood in front of me, then touched my neck.

"What—one last look before it's chopped off?" I said, struggling to sound more defiant than I felt.

"No, my dear." She reached around my neck and unclasped my pearl necklace. "It would be a shame to harm such a lovely jewel. I will keep it safe and give it to Arturo as a keepsake of his *first* mother."

I stunned us both when I spat in her face. I didn't even wait to see her wipe if off, but whirled and continued my march. Damn, that felt good.

We clomped up the wobbly steps onto a platform of heavy beams and deep brown planks. Next to a cube of granite towered the angst-ridden executioner I'd overheard last night. Face impassive, eyes focused over our heads, Haroun was hardened clay compared to last night's pile of sand.

As the guards lined us up facing the crowd, then stepped back behind us, I became acutely aware of the world. Silver acacia leaves fluttered in the breeze. A woman's brilliant saffron robe made my heart ache. Browns seemed richer, blues more intense, and grays were such a deep velvet I could almost feel the softness against my fingertips.

Grimaldi caught my eye and smiled bravely. Time did not slow down as I expected it would, but rushed on with such helpless inevitability I knew things were really, truly, out of my control. Last winter, when I'd hit a patch of ice on the drive to work and spun around like a top, I'd cranked the wheel to the right, then to the left, trying to control the skidding, but nothing worked. As the world whirled around me outside the car window, I gripped the wheel and moaned at the knowledge that I was going to crash.

That same helplessness filled me now, and I felt again the car jump the curve, slam into the stop sign, and plow into the snow pile. A ragged sigh escaped. This landing would not be as soft.

The mullah, a fierce bald man with thick eyebrows and sallow skin, read the charges against us. I tuned him out even though he spoke slowly enough to understand. Instead I gazed up at the walls of Valencia, imagining Enzo, Fadri, and the others going about their lives on the other side. Elena was goddess-knows where. Rodrigo was an addict. Christ, what a mess.

My heart pounded like a piston when I realized the mullah had fallen silent. He had finished his part and turned to the executioner, who nodded to the guards. It took three of them to drag Nuño to the granite block and force him to his knees. No. Not Nuño!

"My child," he moaned. "I would have liked to see my child."

Oh, god, why had I told him about Solana? My heart ripped open as I searched the crowd for a friendly face because, in all the movies, this was where the good guys in the crowd would fling off their disguises and save the day. But I saw no help, no spark of sympathy, no hope, so I whirled toward Anna. "Anna Lee, you stop this right now!" I roared in English.

She shook her head stiffly, as if her spine had fused with indifference.

Nuño's head hung off the front of the block and his powerful body trembled, but he had stopped struggling. His eyes were open and sweat glistened in his curls. He whispered, "Solana, Solana," over and over again. Haroun the executioner hefted his gleaming axe and moved into position.

Christ. Oh my god. I swayed against Grimaldi. This couldn't happen. Why didn't someone stop it? How could these people just stand there and watch a man be murdered? He'd done nothing, nothing at all but care. He would never see Solana. He would die with that deep sadness.

The executioner raised the axe over his head, and I moved without thought across the platform. "No! Stop!" I rushed the executioner. "You can't kill my brother. Or my uncle. We're family." I pushed my tear-streaked face against the surprised man's chest, the axe still overhead. "We're all my mother has left. If you kill us she'll be alone in the world. We're family. How can you wipe out an entire family?"

Haroun stepped back, lowering the axe to his side, eyes wide with horror, disbelief creasing his face. "No, Allah, no. Not another family," he moaned. Conflicting emotions churned within the man's chest, contorting his features, cramping his fingers into claws. Finally he threw back his head and let loose a mournful howl, an animal betrayed by the world.

The crowd murmured in confusion as the howl bounced off the buildings, an echo of misery, then he flung down the axe. "I cannot do this any longer. Allah knows I have tried, but I am not strong enough. The money be *damned*," he roared, stomping down the stairs and pushing his way through the crowd.

"Come back!" cried the mullah, but the man disappeared down the nearest street.

Confusion erupted at this unheard-of event, but the guards quickly closed around us to prevent our escape. Nuño sat back on his heels, forehead resting on the warm stone, and I dropped to my knees beside him. "Nuño, are you okay?"

He raised his head, and I watched him struggle back from wherever he'd gone to prepare himself for death. "What happened?"

"I bought us a little time." He slumped back against the stone, and my heart nearly broke, since without a rescue, Nuño would have to go through this a second time. It might have been kinder to let the axe fall.

Grimaldi drew closer to us as a ring of twenty guards towered over us. There was no hope of escape. Shouts and arguments swirled through the crowd as the mullah struggled to enlist a replacement. Thirty minutes later, the guards stepped back, and the executioner's friend, so hungry for money, stepped forward, glowing with the thought of the extra coin in his pocket. I tried to hate him, but his robes were frayed and didn't hide his gaunt frame.

Once again we were lined up facing the crowd, the guards behind us, with Nuño kneeling before the stone. I choked on my own breath as the guards forced Nuño's head down onto the block. The new executioner licked his lips, wiped sweaty palms on his robe, then took a few practice swings with the axe, giggling when the heavy blade swung him around. God damn it, this would *not* be good. Nuño turned his head and looked straight at me.

Finally the man raised the trembling axe over his head. Blinking furiously, I refused to look away from Nuño's pained brown eyes, sending all the love and courage I could through my own.

Thwap! Instead of lowering the axe, the executioner gave a surprised "Ho!" When an arrow pierced his chest, the man fell over backward and I whirled to face the crowd. Fifteen red-capped al-Saffah archers knelt on the roof directly across from us. "Drop!" I shouted, and Grimaldi and I joined Nuño on the planks. Arrows whizzed over our heads and into the guards behind us. Hope surged through me. "Untie me!" I yelled over the screams and the shouted orders erupting around us. Back to back, we fumbled with each other's ropes, and the three of us were soon free.

Nuño leapt to his feet, knocking over the two guards nearest us. "This may turn out to be a good day after all!"

Female war cries sent my pulse racing even faster as mounted al-

Saffah warriors poured into the square from every side street. Swords began to sing their shrill song. "Run," Nuño shouted, grabbing my hand. We jumped off the platform into chaos, townspeople swirling like a cyclone as they ran from swords, flying horse hooves, and al-Saffah arrows. A wave of terrified people swept us apart.

"Nuño! Nuño!" I called. He'd yanked away someone's sword and was slashing his way through a phalanx of soldiers, roaring with triumph. "Nuño!" Finally I gave up and turned to run with the crowd to avoid death by trampling. The crowd surged around acacia trees, over bodies, past al-Saffah women and Moors locked in hand-to-hand combat. I stumbled but recovered as I turned down a side street with the others, seeing out of the corner of my eye that a mounted al-Saffah barreled toward us on a snorting black stallion. Screaming, those nearest clawed their way past me, but still I ran. I would not go from Moor prisoner to al-Saffah prisoner, no matter how grateful I was.

The hooves thundered closer but I ignored the stitch in my side and almost reached the corner. "Stop!" rang out a familiar voice. "I cannot rescue you if you flee."

I whirled around, hand to my throat. The woman pulled her horse up just short of me, flinging back her red hood as she did. Elena, lips tight with aggravation, her eyes ice blue even in the heat of this battle. She reached down, I raised my good arm, then with a hefty grunt she pulled me onto the saddle behind her.

An al-Saffah yell sent the red capes for their horses, and the ones bringing up the rear fought off the Moors as they retreated. While I clung to Elena, Nuño and Grimaldi rode double with al-Saffah women. We raced through the narrow streets, ducking under the lower balconies, then approached a narrow gate in the wall, open, guarded by al-Saffah guards and a pile of dead Valencian guards. We thundered through the gate, then flew north toward the "suburbs," the sea glistening to our right. As we passed Villanueva, the twenty horses slowed.

"Stick with the plan," Elena shouted to Nuño and Grimaldi as they slid off their rescuers' horses near Rodrigo's camp.

"What about me?" I shouted into the wind as we picked up speed, the horse's gait rattling my bones.

"You come with us," she said as her cape whipped my face and stung my cheeks. Her words didn't cheer me since her voice was as steel-edged as her sword.

CHAPTER TWENTY-FOUR

I held myself stiffly in the saddle for two hours, not wanting to touch Elena any more than she wanted to touch me. We climbed up the sides of blue-green mountains reaching toward clouds so white they looked painted onto a false sky. While the horses wove their way through scattered basalt boulders and snags of gooseberry bushes, I left mental bread crumbs along the way. We turned left at a rock shaped like a howling wolf. We turned right by the three live oaks alone in a meadow.

Somehow, in the week I'd been recuperating, summer had blown in and the air was fifteen degrees warmer. Fields of orange poppies stretched between rocky outcroppings, turning the mountainsides sweet and pungent. As we climbed, yellow sedum crept over the rocky ground on either side of the trail. The sun was so warm that at one point I closed my eyes and nearly let my head fall forward to rest on Elena, but I snapped up just in time.

Often I found my hand at my neck, searching for a pearl that wasn't there, which was just as well, since it was an outdated symbol of an outdated love. Old news. The woman sharing her saddle with me had changed too much. Besides, there was absolutely no point in rekindling the romance, even had Elena been interested. When I accomplished what I'd set out to do in this accursed century, I'd drag Arturo kicking and screaming from his precious jewels and sex-on-demand harem, remind him of all he'd left behind, and then we'd return to our own time through the cave at Santillana del Mar. Back in Chicago, Arturo would be grounded for ten years, and I would serve him nothing but vegetables. Canned vegetables. And maybe week-old bread without any butter or jam. The only computer games he'd be allowed to play would be Pong, the antique from the 1970s. The only DVDs he could rent would be Disney movies. I was feeling better already.

Nugaymath stopped us to water the horses in a wide mountain stream where fish flashed in the shadows of overhanging elms, then we began climbing a narrow rocky path single file. Elena and I rode last.

I cleared my throat. The worst she could do would be throw me off the horse. "I need your help, Luis. I know you hate Rodrigo even more now, but he must take Valencia."

"No."

"Over time, Rodrigo has been given a substance in his ale. It's affected his thoughts and his actions. That's why he has changed."

"I am not interested."

"One of Paloma de Palma's spies, an older Jewish man, brought Rodrigo ale spiked with this substance. His body has grown to need it, so the changes you see in him aren't his fault."

"I do not believe any substance has that strength."

"What happens to Fadri when he drinks too much wine or ale?"

"Too much wine makes him morose and too much ale makes him obnoxious, but nothing could so drastically alter Rodrigo. Now stop talking."

"Remember how violence ripped open the fabric of your family?" Man, could I stoop much lower? "If Rodrigo does not take Valencia, the fabric of history will rip. Thousands, no, millions of people will cease to exist."

"No."

I clenched my teeth. The timeline mess was too distant, too esoteric, since of course Elena didn't care about faceless millions. But the only faces I could put on the impending disaster were mine and Arturo's, and she didn't care about either of us.

"I will pay you. I buried thousands of gold pieces near Mirabueno. Marta and the others need some, but you can have the rest if you and your men—"

"They are no longer my men, thanks to you." She twisted in her saddle until our eyes met. I shivered. "No is the same in your native language as it is in mine. Have you gone light in the head these last eight years?"

My glare sent her facing forward again, and I said nothing more. I was relieved and grateful, of course, that she had rescued me, but I was no freer than if I'd still been trapped in Anna's palace, since every step this damn horse took was a step in the wrong direction—away from

Arturo, away from El Cid, away from Valencia.

The path narrowed ridiculously. When the horses lunged up between more boulders, I leaned forward to stay in the saddle, then when the path took a nose dive, Elena's hips slammed back against mine. As the riders ahead splashed across a slender stream, my anxiety increased, knowing I would be a prisoner again. Elena would not let me go until she'd destroyed Rodrigo. Damn it. I was tired of her distance, tired of her anger, and tired of my own failures.

"You've changed," I suddenly snapped. She said nothing as we waited in line to cross the stream. "You stink."

"I *what?*"

"You stink. You smell. You used to care about being clean, but no more. You've lived too long as a Christian." I could feel her anger stir. She gripped the reins and moved us into the stream. "I stink too. I haven't had a bath in days. This century is cruel, it's ugly, and it stinks." My fresh fury flamed the fire.

"You want a bath? Fine, take one," Elena muttered, and with a sudden yank on my bad arm, she dumped me off the horse and into the stream.

Ice cold water and sharp needles of pain shooting through my left arm stole my breath. I sputtered, spitting out water as I struggled to sit up, water running into my eyes and ears. "God damn you," I finally managed to spit out.

She finished crossing the stream and waited while some of the al-Saffah women laughed. I stood, my legs already numb from the cold. I sloshed up onto the bank we'd just left, then scrambled up the trail.

"Hey," Elena shouted. "Come back. Do not be ridiculous. You cannot get away from me."

I knew she was right, but I'd be damned if I'd make it easy for her. Inhaling sharply at the pain in my shoulder, I crashed into the brush and climbed, noting fresh blood on my sleeve. The wound had re-opened.

Vivid cursing followed me, as did snapping branches and more cursing. My flight was futile, but it felt good to be doing something, and as I crested a hill, hope surged through me. Another hundred feet and I could get lost in the rocks ahead, so I winced at my shoulder pain and the brambles cutting my palms, but pushed on.

"Oof!" Elena tackled me around the waist. We both went down and I cried out as I landed on my injured shoulder. With my good hand,

I reached for a stick, a rock, anything, but she pinned me to the ground. I squirmed in fury, but soon her weight and my shoulder made movement impossible. Besides, with her entire body pressed against mine, those parts of my body that could throb insistently began to do so.

"Get off me."

"Why must you be so damned difficult?"

I couldn't move my legs. "Rape may be your fantasy, but it's not mine. Get off me."

"I do not want to rape you," Elena growled, voice heavy with disgust. Her face hovered inches above mine, a tanned face I used to stroke and kiss and gaze upon with such love she'd blush.

"Then get the hell off me." My defiance had begun to drain as the pain grew, and much of my sleeve was now sticky with blood. A thousand daggers stabbed my arm, my shoulder, my chest as the pain spread.

Elena rolled off me with a snort and yanked me to my feet. "Why are you bleeding?"

My head spun to be standing so suddenly. "What do you care? If you must know, Rafael Mahfouz wounded me." Whoa. White dots flickered across the trees, across Elena, across the ground. Whoa.

She grabbed my belt and my right arm, and half-dragged, half-carried me back down the hill. Why did everything sound so far away? I stumbled crossing the stream but Elena jerked me up by my belt. Nugaymath waited for us.

"Navarro, I understand lying with a woman now and then. Many of us do. But could you not choose a more cooperative one?"

My feet and calves turned to ice. My shoulder burned to ashes, and the world broke up into white dots. Damn it. Passing out yet again. The world twisted faster and faster into more white dots, then disappeared altogether.

❖

She stroked my face, nuzzling me gently with her warm lips. Her hands roamed my neck, loosening my tunic, my shirt. She sucked on my throat, hungry now, needing more, lowering her head to take into her mouth what her insistent fingers had already hardened. I rose to meet her, but when I shifted my shoulder, a flash of pain cut through me, and I moaned. "Saints' blood, I am sorry," she whispered.

I opened my eyes and looked around. A twig snapped nearby. "Luis?" Moonlight filtered through thin canvas onto the ground next to me. A tent. A dream. I was alone. The pain had not been imagined, however. Wincing as I shifted onto my back, I sighed at my ridiculous fantasy but then cursed and sat up. A heavy iron shackle was locked around my right wrist. A chain dragged across my waist. Grimacing in pain, I felt along the thick links and found a stake buried deep in the rock hard soil. Confusion pushed through the pain. I was chained to the ground? Like an animal?

Moving slowly to save my shoulder, I touched my clothes, finding my shirt stiff with dried blood and the leather tunic shrunk tight against my ribs from my tumble in the stream. I looked down. Even in this weak light I saw the leather no longer hid my breasts, but defined them. Great, just great.

I touched my tender shoulder. Someone had wrapped a bandage around it, probably miles away from being sterile, but at least the bleeding had stopped. My joints had begun to ache, and not just my shoulder. I flexed my fingers and gasped. I was too young for arthritis, but now that I thought about it, my aches had begun even before I'd been shot.

Refusing to think more about this, I stood up, relieved my head seemed to have returned from la-la land. Dragging the chain behind me, I stepped outside into the moonlight, where dozens of tents filled a flat meadow surrounded by pines. Al-Saffah camp. I could see sentries, their red cloaks nearly black in this light, as they moved around the edges of camp. Still-smoldering campfires reminded me of camping with Arturo, Laura, and Deb. Snoring came from many tents, the sounds of love from one nearby. I flushed in the dark, remembering my dream.

My chain allowed me to move about eight feet from the tent opening. Beside the tent, someone had hacked a crude hole in the ground and piled up leaves beside it. How thoughtful. My own toilet. I used it, awkwardly pulling up my pants with a sore left arm and a right one dragging about twenty pounds of iron.

I moved to the end of my chain and considered my options. I couldn't get away, but damn it, I could make their lives as miserable as mine.

The silence shattered with my yell. "Let me go!"

Yelps and grunts and heads popped out of tents, a few with swords.

"What? Who?"

"Let me go," I yelled, satisfied when my voice echoed off the trees. Arabic curses joined the echo, then tent flaps closed.

"Let me go!"

"Navarro!" I recognized Nugaymath's gravely voice from one of the tents.

"What?" Her voice came from the woods.

"Shut her up."

"Let me go!" More Arabic curses, and I actually smiled, coming as close to having fun as I could under the circumstances.

Elena had shed her red cape and chain mail and now wore simple trousers and a loose shirt. She marched up to me, hands jammed on her narrow hips. "Let me go!" I shouted.

"For the love of saints, woman, shut up."

"Don't call me 'woman.' You know I hate that."

"Get in the tent, *woman*."

"Let me go!"

She grabbed my shirt front and shook me. "Damn it, Kate, these women risked their lives to rescue you. Three women did not even make it back. Are you that ungrateful?"

I swallowed. "No, but—"

"Get in the tent."

I opened my mouth to speak, but her nostrils flared, so I got into the tent.

She followed me inside but squatted by the door. "I know you dislike being held here, but until Rodrigo is out of the way, I cannot let you return to Valencia." I couldn't see her face, and her voice gave nothing away.

"Why did you rescue me then? Why not let Anna finish me off?"

"Arturo was once an orphan, right? I did not want him to lose yet another mother."

"How touching," I said, not wanting her to know I really meant it. "Please come sit down. Can't we just talk for a few minutes? I know you're angry with me."

"Very perceptive of you." Elena crawled into the tent, folded her arms, and tucked her legs beneath her. I didn't need a translator to read her body language, but I pressed on.

"How did you know I needed rescuing?"

"After Nuño disappeared last week, Enzo told me about Grimaldi's odd prophecy of your death. I knew it was likely news from your time and not merely a seer's rantings."

"How did you convince Nugaymath to help? She kidnapped Arturo and sold him to Anna. Nugaymath's daughter Rabi'a hates me." Enough light from campfires outside filtered through the tent so that I could see Elena's proud profile, and some of my anger melted.

Her soft chuckle thawed the rest. "Rabi'a is too busy hating her mother for selling Arturo to feel much for you. Besides, she thinks she loves Arturo."

I snorted. "Everyone loves a Romeo and Juliet story until it's your son playing Romeo."

"Romeo and Juliet?"

"Forget it. You didn't answer my question."

"Nugaymath cannot be convinced to do anything, but her services can be purchased."

My childish behavior outside had apparently loosened Elena's tongue. If only her tongue...I tightened my jaw, so confused about what I wanted from this woman. "When you left Valencia, you joined al-Saffah?"

She nodded. "I had always suspected they were women. Besides, what else am I to do? My future is over." Heavy silence hung between us. "It must please you I can no longer be a soldier. I can no longer fight."

How was I supposed to respond to that? It was true I'd always worried about her safety, but to be exposed as she'd been? "Elena, I never wanted this. Never."

She hugged her knees to her chest and laughed harshly. "Do you realize what has happened?" Her voice dropped to a whisper. "Luis Navarro is now truly dead. I can no longer keep my brother alive, in even a small way, by living his life."

I struggled to speak around the lump in my throat. "Perhaps Rodrigo will forgive you. He—"

"—has been knifed in the buttocks by you and humiliated by me. He will not soon forget either. No, my life as El Cid's favorite is over."

Maybe the darkness helped, or perhaps Elena's loneliness trumped her anger, but we began to talk, little by little, as we used to. I avoided mentioning Solana or Nuño or Arturo or Anna or Rodrigo and my purpose for coming back in time, since all those topics would lead us down painful paths. We talked of Duañez and the community's struggle to survive. As we talked, a soft voice whispered in my head, *Stay. Stay in this century.* I shot bolt upright.

"What?" Elena asked.

"Nothing." Impossible. I wouldn't do that to Arturo. He'd been ready to return to our own time after only a few days. I wouldn't be so selfish as to condemn him to this life. "Nothing. I'm fine."

After ten more minutes, it was as if all our conflicts, and all those years, had fallen away, and for a short time, we were simply two women talking. However, my heart struggled to be consistent as we sat in the warm, dark tent. It wasn't fair, but I wanted all of her while I was in this century. In fact, a crazy idea occurred to me. What if, after Arturo and I returned to the future, I came back to visit now and then? What if, while other families took vacations to the Grand Canyon, we took one to eleventh century Spain? Would that be possible?

No. As I watched Elena talking, I realized how arrogant I was to even imagine I could hold Elena in my life with just two weeks a year. Despite this, a tiny spark caught fire in my heart, and I so desperately wanted this woman in my life that at one point I forgot myself, reached out, and touched her thigh.

Elena froze up quicker than a Canadian lake and rolled to her feet. "I am tired. If you think you can refrain from waking everyone up again, I would like to return to my tent."

Stay here, stay here, my head screamed. "Please unchain me."

"No."

"When do you expect to release me?"

Elena opened the tent flap, firelight flickering across her boots, the cool air brushing across my skin. "Sooner than anticipated." I waited. "Rodrigo is not well. The old Jew stopped bringing him the ale after Anna exposed me. Rodrigo shakes and shudders and rants, I am told. He sleeps but grows ever wearier. You might have been right about that substance in the ale, but no matter now, Rodrigo has lost the will to fight, some say the will to live." Her voice should have rung with triumph, but all I heard was a deep sadness. "Because the army has already begun to break up, I will not have to do anything to stop

Rodrigo from taking Valencia. He will fail all on his own." She stepped outside. "It is over. In just a few days a sick Rodrigo will slink away, leaving Valencia to Ibn Jehaf and al-Rashid to fight each other for the city until one is dead. Goodnight, Kate." The flap slapped shut.

No, no, no. That would not be what happened. Because my young, inexperienced son did not stand a chance against Ibn Jehaf, even if Anna thought she could protect him, I refused to cave in to the heavy sadness that hit once Elena left. This wasn't over yet. Until June 15, four days from now, I was still in the game. I wouldn't give up.

CHAPTER TWENTY-FIVE

A l-Saffah's camp filled the small clearing, but through a break in the twisted cork trees, I could see the blue foothills of the Sierra de Cuenca shimmering in the sun's haze. Myrtle bushes formed a protective snarl around us, the buds just breaking.

Breakfast was a mug of white milky liquid apparently fermented from a vegetable root. Both the archer who brought it and I lacked the language skills to communicate such details, but its thick sweetness was welcome. Despite my bravado last night, my body continued to fight the effects of being shot, and all I seemed able to do was sit around or nap. This was fortunate because the chain prohibited anything else.

My guard changed every hour, since apparently the duty was too boring to be sustained beyond this. Each woman sat nearby, probably less to stand guard than to make sure I didn't start shooting off my mouth again.

The fifth guard was Rabi'a, who wore a long woven blue shift and wide loose trousers with patched knees and frayed hems that dragged on the ground. She handed me a bowl of something warm, then sat cross-legged under a nearby tree. She seemed smaller, and more pinched than I remembered.

I blew on my spoon to cool the soup. "Rabi'a, you and I didn't begin well that day in the Zaragozan market. I'm sorry if I was rude."

She looked at me, blinking those warm brown eyes framed with impossibly long lashes. Her wide cheekbones and broad nose were perfectly balanced with voluptuous lips. No wonder Arturo had been captivated. Mouth compressed, she didn't speak.

"I'm very angry with your mother for selling Arturo...your Busaybah." Little Kiss. The young woman's long strong fingers tightened their grip on her knees. "Rabi'a, how old are you?"

"Seventeen." Her low voice was smooth as honey.

"Do you miss Arturo?" I was rewarded for my patience with a

nod barely perceptible to the naked eye. "You are seventeen, yet your mother still treats you like a child." Look at me. I should talk.

She blinked rapidly for a minute until her lashes became wet triangles, then she rose without effort and disappeared into the woods. While another woman soon replaced her, at least I had planted the seed. Now if only Rabi'a would water it with her own tears.

Mid-afternoon the need to escape, to do *something* gripped me around the throat, so when Nugaymath passed between two nearby tents, I called her over. Surprisingly, she came. When she was close enough, I swung my foot out in my own version of a half spin kick and connected with the side of her head. With a yell, she dropped and rolled out of my reach. "That was for selling my son!" I shouted.

Curses flowed freely from both of us as we faced each other. "You ugly, camel-faced whore," she sputtered.

"Takes one to know one," I shouted. Her eyes widened when she sorted through my primitive speech, and nearby women began to murmur in alarm.

"Sell me," I commanded before she could release another colorful string of names for me. "Sell me to Paloma de Palma as you did my son. She will pay you twice what she paid for Arturo." Not true, of course.

The woman's fierce dreadlocks bristled. "Good idea. But I am done with Valencia. We will ambush travelers instead. Besides, Navarro say you stay here, so you stay here."

Frustrated, I pulled on the chain, ignoring the sharp dig into my wrist, and Nugaymath took a step back. "How could you sell a *boy?*" I snapped. "Have you no sense of what is wrong with that? Do you have no human feelings at all? Are you an animal?"

Wrong thing to say. Nugaymath drew her sword and crouched, no doubt trying to figure out how to both avoid my kicks and kill me. I stepped back to loosen the chain's tension and raised my hands in the fighting stance.

Elena appeared out of nowhere and stepped between us. "Enough."

Nugaymath's sword trembled in anger, and for a second I feared she would slash right through Elena to get to me. "My warriors are starving. The Christians have stolen or bought all the food in the area." She lowered her sword a fraction. "Have you not seen Rabi'a? She is nothing but bones." I swallowed at the fear seeping into Nugaymath's voice. "I sold your child to save my own." When she stepped back and sheathed her sword, my breath escaped in a low, shuddering sigh. "You are a mother. You must do what you can to save your child, and so must I. With the money from Paloma, I sent riders to Zaragoza for food. I'll buy fabric for new clothes. We have broken swords to repair, more bows to make."

I held up a hand, weary with the weight of the chain, and I suddenly saw history as a long string of mothers, and fathers, doing what they thought they must for their children. Nugaymath whirled on her heel, leaving Elena and me alone, save for the guard now sitting safely out of range of my foot. Speaking of starvation, had Father Ruiz delivered my message? Did Marta, José, and the others have food to eat? "She is right, you know," I said. I didn't want Elena to leave. "We must all do for our children."

"Kate, I do not know why I spoke so freely last night. You continue to bewitch even as you infuriate." She looked me squarely in the eye. "Nothing we have said, or done, changes anything."

"But Elena, you have a child. Her future will be different, will be *wrong*, if the Moors take over this land."

"The Moors cannot conquer all of Iberia. They are too disorganized, and King Alfonso, King Sancho, and the others are too strong."

"But the Moors do conquer the peninsula, and then much of the world. I have seen the history books, Elena. I've read what happens."

"Your history said I would die at Rodrigo's hand. I did not. Who is to say that everything else will not change?"

"First, Rodrigo did not kill you *this* time. And second, your role in history, and please do not take this as an insult, will not likely alter what is inevitable." Elena squinted toward the horizon. "Please, sit with me again. I'm going mad with boredom and worry for Arturo. The least you can do is help the time pass."

She smirked. "Women who get too close to you can find themselves kicked in the head. You have acquired new skills these last years."

"I will not kick you."

She considered me with the wariness of a former lover, all trust destroyed, but did sit down, stretching out her long legs, her boot leather worn to nearly white across the toes and heel.

"Elena, what will you do now? You cannot ride with Nugaymath forever. Al-Saffah are bandits. They exist only to spread terror."

She stared past me. "Once I help Nuño and the others save Valencia from Rodrigo and Tahir, perhaps I will give it some thought."

I was ready for her this morning, after lying awake all night, aching for how Elena's life had been turned upside down. "You are a warrior. You are a leader of men."

She smiled without a hint of humor, and I suddenly remembered how impossible it was to rattle her, to tap into the insecurities all normal women carried around and nursed. "You forget, Kate Vincent. Luis Navarro is gone forever. As Elena Navarro, I can lead nothing but a horse to water."

"Bullshit." Once again, eight years melted away, and we were sitting by the hearth at Duañez, sipping spiced ale and sparring gently.

"You do not understand the conventions of this time. I—"

"I know of many stories of women in history who led, perhaps not with a sword in her hand, but a leader nonetheless."

"I have a child. Perhaps I will settle down and raise more."

A sharp dagger through the ribs would have hurt less than her words. "But what will you *do*?"

"I will be a mother. That is enough."

No, it's not, I wanted to scream. But then the fight drained out of me, like blood from a wound too massive to close. I shrugged. "You're right. Perhaps you should settle down. Return to Duañez . Be a farmer. Raise sheep with José."

She laughed, *really* laughed, sending the most amazing rush to my head. Shaking her head, she stood, and I with her. "You are amazing, Kate. Chained to a stake, and still..." She gazed at me, inscrutable. "I had forgotten that about you."

"Unchain me."

"No, I cannot. You will help Rodrigo." She turned sharply on one heel and left me alone again.

At least the guard was gone, since the women had finally relaxed, realizing I could not get away. Rabi'a brought my supper, so I tried again. "Rabi'a, Arturo is in grave danger." Head bowed, she played with the tip of her black braid, which curled around her neck. "There are many people who want him dead. If I do not get back to Valencia, he might die."

She bit her lower lip. "My mother...I cannot..."

"Rabi'a, Arturo will die if you don't let me go."

"I cannot," she whispered and left.

Damn it.

I used the handle of my wooden soup spoon and chipped away about an inch of soil around the stake. The handle broke, so I dug with the shattered edge. After an hour my frantic claw marks surrounded the stake, but did nothing to loosen it.

❖

I spent most of the night staring at the water-stained ceiling of my tent. I was almost out of time and Elena wouldn't listen. The one night we'd spent together hadn't meant very much, obviously. I clenched my fists, unable to bear the idea that I might not accomplish my goal. I'd told Kalleberg it was nearly an impossible task, but now that I was here, and could sense how wrong everything had gone, I knew the wave of change crashing through time was real, and I was desperate to stop it. If Elena didn't relent, that wave would hit me, Arturo, Grimaldi, and even Carlos and Anna. I believed we'd cease to exist. Anger replaced my earlier resignation.

The next morning my joints burned as hot as my anger. Willing the pain away, I was finally able to drag myself outside and bellow for Elena until the other women, complaining loudly, yelled for her themselves. She stood outside the invisible line around my tent, stiff as a board. I glared at her, voice shaking after a night of little sleep. "You've *got* to let me go. I insist."

"Insist?" Now both thick brows arched smoothly.

"Look, I'm not some goddamn property you can chain to the ground. Does it excite you to know I'm shackled, unable to flee from you?"

Now two roses bloomed on her cheeks. "How dare you. Clearly I was wrong to let you seduce me back at Valvanera. I—"

"I seduced *you*?" I practically screamed.

We glared at each other, and a tiny piece of me died inside. It really was over. "You have no feelings, do you?" She raised another eyebrow. "I feel so sorry for little Solana. She'll be raised by a mother without emotion. Then when she's an adult, poor Solana Súarez, daughter of Nuño Súarez, will have no idea how to relate to others." I now dug as frantically around her heart as I'd dug with the wooden spoon around the stake.

Elena stepped back as if slapped. "How did you know?"

"I figured it out and Nuño admitted it."

She closed her eyes briefly. "I was weak with missing you." Her eyes flew open, flashing in the light. "I am better now."

"You are heartless and care about no one but yourself. You don't care about either Súarez in your life, Solana or Nuño."

"I did not give Solana her father's name, nor mine. Life is hard enough without being the daughter of two Caballeros de Valvanera, one of them a woman who lives as a man. I gave her the name of my mother's family. It is a good, strong name, and I am not worried about her emotions. Solana Pidal will grow up to be safe and strong."

Solana Pidal? S. Pidal? Christ. I dove into my tent and dumped out my saddlebag. I grabbed the book and dashed back outside, searching for the dog-eared page with trembling fingers. There. I held up the book. "Do you know what this is?"

She snorted. "It is a book. A very small book."

"Come closer. I won't kick you." I opened the page and thrust it into Elena's face. "It's in English, but—"

"Holy Bullocks! How could someone write that small? And so perfectly?"

"No, this wasn't written by a person's hand. Just forget that for now. Look here, on this line. You cannot read English, but a person's name is the same no matter the language, correct? What name do you see here?"

Elena moved closer, tipping the book for more light. Her face paled. "S. Pidal."

"Now look at this date in the next sentence."

"1109."

"Fifteen years from now. You'll have to take the rest of this story on faith, and to do that, search your memory. Have I ever lied to you?"

She paused, looking into the trees, then shifted her gaze to me. "Not that I know of."

"I'm not lying to you now. Here's what this paragraph says:

After eight years as a slave in a minor official's harem, S. Pidal was able to organize a rebellion among the harem women of Zaragoza. Using secret messages passed by servants, the women arranged a time when they all fled their harems, killing guards as they did so. But before the women could escape the city, Zaragozan soldiers surrounded them. All six hundred women were killed that afternoon, their bodies carted to the edge of the city and left in a pile as carrion.

I slammed the book shut. Elena's eyes had gone black with shock. "That is not my Solana. The 'S' could be one of many names."

"The years work out. She will be eighteen in 1109. This is the world's history, Elena. What if S. Pidal is Solana?"

"I will protect her."

"How? What if Rodrigo kills you? What if someone else kills you? What if you get sick? How can you protect your daughter against something that will happen fifteen years from now? How can you be certain you'll be able to prevent this?"

"That book lies. It is evil—"

"Why is it that whenever Christians come up against something they don't understand or do not want to think about, it's suddenly evil? The book isn't evil. It's fact. It was written in 1986, about events that will happen in fifteen years."

"But you read of my death. That did not happen. So this awful rebellion may not happen."

My jaw twitched with tension. "Are you willing to count on that? Are you willing to bet your daughter's life on that? As long as the real timeline is not restored, you'll never know."

"Solana may die in what you call the real timeline." Elena's voice faded to almost nothing.

"Raid party!" called Nugaymath. The camp suddenly sprang to life. Excited women ran for their horses. "Navarro! Come!"

I grabbed her hand. "Under the real timeline, the Moors will control very little of the peninsula in 1109. She won't be in a harem. She'll be a free woman."

Elena touched her forehead briefly, and my heart pounded. But then she raised her head, and shook it, like a woman shaking off a bad dream. "No, this is too preposterous."

"A supply wagon comes down the river from Zaragoza," Nugaymath yelled. "We can use whatever they have."

Elena looked over her shoulder. "I must go."

"What about Solana? You're her mother. You must do whatever it takes to keep her safe." Elena shook her head again and ran across the clearing to her horse.

"You are still upset with her?" Rabi'a came up beside me, tying on her cloak, red side out.

"Yes." Desperation helped me focus. "Rabi'a, why did your mother leave your father?"

Rabi'a frowned, tucking her quiver under her cloak. "There is no time for that now."

"Why?"

She shrugged. "My father wanted more than one wife. Nugaymath want to be only wife. We do not like to share."

"You share Arturo." She stopped. "Arturo is living in Valencia as al-Rashid." Her coffee eyes widened. "He has been given horses, jewels, and a harem."

"A *harem*?" the young girl bellowed.

"Yes, full of young, beautiful women. He can have them whenever he wants."

Her nostrils flared across her cheeks. "After what he said to me? I was his first, and his last, he said. I will kill him."

"Help me get free, Rabi'a. I'll stop him." Rabi'a watched the others gather their gear. I touched her arm. "He's probably with one of those harem women right now."

"Get in the tent." She pushed me in. "Allah as my witness, I will kill him for this. Stay here."

In minutes she returned with a chisel and a mallet. Oh, the fury of a woman scorned, and all that.

"Where is the key?" I asked.

"Navarro has it. They are still preparing to leave, so will not hear this." She stretched the chain across a flat rock she'd dragged into the tent, lined up the chisel, then with a sure, strong hand, shattered a link with one blow. I sat back, still wearing the manacle and five links, but my arm felt pounds lighter. She tossed the chisel aside.

"Rabi'a, my dagger. Your mother took it when you stole Arturo from me. Do you—"

"Wait here." She returned in minutes with my dagger and sheath, which I strapped to my thigh, relieved to be armed once again. Rabi'a squatted by the tent's opening. "We stay here until they leave. They won't notice I'm missing. Then while those left behind to guard the camp are busy elsewhere, we shall sneak away." Her jaw tightened. "I will kill him."

Within the hour we were able to sneak along behind the tents, saddle two horses, and make our way down the rocky trail. Rabi'a knew exactly where she was going, which saved my ass. Nothing looked the same as it had on our approach. The howling wolf rock looked like a turtle from this direction. Without Rabi'a, I would have been hopelessly lost. She said nothing during the three-hour ride down the mountains toward Valencia. At dusk we reached the Roman ruins, where we camped for the night. I curled up in a tight ball while Rabi'a tossed restlessly under her blanket and worried a thumbnail.

I counted the days in my head. I'd been back in this century for twenty-five days. I only had two left. I didn't know what I'd find when we rode into Valencia, but I'd do whatever I had to do, and I'd do it without Elena.

CHAPTER TWENTY-SIX

When dawn broke, Rabi'a and I mounted and headed down the dusty road toward Valencia. Not only did my heart ache over Elena, but hot flames licked at my hip joints, my elbows, my knees, my wrists. Until I spoke with Grimaldi or Arturo, I couldn't confirm my theory, but I suspected no pain reliever in the world would touch the source of this pain. That wave was rolling through history, decimating my ancestors, and breaking down my body. I only hoped that Carlos and Anna suffered the same agony. The short chain on my wrist clinked as we rode.

Groups of disgruntled Christian soldiers passed us, the horses loaded with tents and bedrolls and the supply wagons driven by exhausted camp women. Rodrigo's mercenary army was breaking apart. Was I too late?

In fact, we didn't even reach the outskirts of the devastated suburbs before we ran smack into over one thousand Christian soldiers spilling out from the main tent camp, all gathered around a large, rocky rise. The men and horses created such a din we were able to ride close to the edge of the crowd unmolested. But still we couldn't see, so Rabi'a pointed to a live oak nearby, and we soon stood on its sturdy lower branches, our horses tied below. I forced the pain into a dark corner of my mind.

Tahir and a handful of his goons stood on the flattest rock, a gray-haired Christian soldier crumpled at his feet. "This man is *weak*! He is *sick*. He has lied to all of us." Tahir kicked the man in the belly, rolling him over. Rodrigo Díaz, the only link to saving my future. "He promised us great wealth, and we have been given only hunger." The Christians stood silently as Tahir motioned to a short, squat renegade Moor, who drew his sword.

"No," I whispered. "We must stop him."

In one smooth, silent arc, Rabi'a slid an arrow from her quiver and drew back her bow. "Dead or wounded?"

I gulped. "Dead." We were too far away. I knew the al-Saffah women were good, but there was no way she was going to hit her target. On the rock ledge the angry Moor standing over Rodrigo raised his sword high over his head. Rabi'a released the bowstring, and with a soft twang, sent the arrow arching across one hundred yards into the belly of the short Moor. He toppled over backward, sword clattering on the rocks. Holy shit.

A thousand heads turned in our direction, but before we could even think about dropping down onto our horses and fleeing, four riders plunged into the far side of the crowd. Men shouted and flung themselves out of the way.

"Stop!" the first rider yelled. I squinted. Elena. She barreled through the crowd, followed by Nuño, Enzo, and Fadri, only stopping once she reached the rocks. "Let him go, Tahir." She *had* listened to me. She'd heard me. Hope for Solana's future, and my own, surged through me like a drug.

The ugly man threw back his head and laughed. "Look, a *woman* comes to save the great Rodrigo Díaz. You are as weak as this donkey dung at my feet."

Elena stood in her stirrups, surveying the army she once led. "Rodrigo has made wealthy men of all of you. When he takes Valencia, your wealth will double, yet you stand here and watch this?"

"Be gone, you worthless bitch," Tahir shouted. "I do not waste my time with weaklings. You—"

"Your best warrior!" Elena roared. "Now!" She leapt off her horse, drew her sword, and scrambled up the rock.

A green-turbaned Moor had already drawn his sword. When he approached, she attacked with a fury that stunned me as well as the Moor. Every man watched the battle, and even the camp women and children at the far tents stood silent. In less than two minutes, Elena raised a bloody sword in triumph. Tahir began bellowing a command but stopped when he felt Nuño's sword at his throat.

Elena faced the men. "We have a job to do. Tonight the people of Valencia will know terror because tomorrow the great Rodrigo Díaz and his fearsome army will attack Valencia and batter down its gates if the city does not surrender." She scanned the crowd. "Diego, Sanchez, and Menendez! You and your men—"

A rude guffaw from the crowd cut her off. "We do not take orders from a cunt like you."

Elena hopped off the rocks and slashed through the crowd to the outspoken soldier. I could see little but the tips of swords flashing in the sun, but heard the clashing, the grate of metal on metal, then silence. The men parted and Elena climbed back onto the rock, her dagger now as bloody as her sword. Awe and revulsion collided in my belly.

And then it happened. While it was true Luis Navarro, El Picador to his men, was dead, someone else was rising in his place.

"La Picadora," a few of the men murmured. "La Picadora," the chant grew. Elena stood there, letting the sound build as her cape snapped back in the breeze, revealing the heart of a leader and the body of a woman. I wiped away the tears streaming down my face and was so proud of her courage, all I could do was hug a surprised Rabi'a. Finally Elena held up a gloved hand.

"You are mercenary soldiers," Elena roared over the dying chant. "Do you want wealth?"

"Yes!" came the cry.

"Do you want power?"

"Yes!"

"Then we stay together. We take Valencia as planned. Menendez, take your men and begin harassing the walls of Valencia. Diego, prepare for an assault of those walls tomorrow at noon. Everyone else clean your gear, bed your women and say your prayers. Jorge, where are you?"

"Here, Navarro!" A hand waved from mid-way back in the crowd.

"When a house has vermin, what do you do?"

"Drive the vermin *out*, Navarro."

Elena swept her sword toward Tahir. "These vermin have crapped among us long enough." Energy pulsed through the crowd and faces glowed with relief to have something to do. An army needed a leader, and now they had one. I was so moved I nearly leapt onto my horse to join her men.

"What if they do not leave?" Jorge called.

"Will you let a few hundred rats stand between you and Valencia?"

"No!" roared the men, and many had already drawn swords and surrounded the nervous Moors.

Elena whistled for attention. "When we take Valencia tomorrow, we take their wealth, not their lives. There has been enough killing. Any man who kills needlessly tomorrow will die by my hand."

"La Picadora," someone cried.

"Tomorrow we conquer. Today we prepare. Now go!"

"La Picadora!" chanted the men as the pumped soldiers began running to do Elena's bidding. I lost sight of her and Rodrigo as her men milled about them or pursued the scattered bands of Tahir's men.

"Come," I said to Rabi'a, and we climbed down and made our way slowly through the men, horses, and wagons. It took us an hour to reach Villanueva. Luckily we encountered nothing but a few stares and harsh questions and no one stopped us. Soldiers milled through the streets, shouting orders, running. After a week with an ill, unavailable leader, the men were willing to follow Elena's orders, even if she lacked a penis. My god, she was going to be okay. I could leave this century without having totally ruined her life.

I shouldered my way into Rodrigo's villa, going from room to room until I discovered Elena and about twenty men standing outside Rodrigo's bedroom. She looked up, neither surprised nor pleased to see me. Grimaldi turned and gave me a weak hug.

"You're safe," I whispered, aware of Rabi'a at my shoulder.

"Yes, but I grow old," he murmured as the others talked among themselves. "My bones ache like an eighty-year-old's."

"Like you haven't moved them for years? Hot pain every time you move?"

His shaggy brows fluttered high into his forehead. "You as well?"

I nodded, then exhaled. There could be no doubt. I pulled Grimaldi closer. "Our future is unraveling, so we are, too."

He rubbed his eyes. "May Allah give us strength to face the end."

"The end isn't here *yet*," I replied, then stepped toward Elena. "How is he?" I asked her.

Elena shook her head and turned away, so I raised my voice to call her back. "He needs a substance Paloma de Palma has been slipping him in the ale sold him by the old man."

"I knew letting that old Jew in was a rotten idea," Fadri muttered.

"She likely increased the dose over these last weeks until Rodrigo's body needed more and more," I said. "He's been cut off, so his body's suffering. It's not his fault."

"What is this substance?" one of Elena's generals asked.

"I don't know. Paloma will have it with her in the palace."

The men moved as one toward the door. "No!" I turned to Elena. "Arturo is in the palace. Because she will use him as a shield to stop any attack, it should be a small party."

Elena nodded. "Chavez, spread the word to the others along the north, west, and south walls. At the next call to prayer, create a diversion with arrows, curses, whatever. I and a small party will slip over the east wall."

"Yes, sir." The men filed out, glowering to be denied a chance to storm the gates and the palace.

"I know the area of the palace where Paloma lives," I said.

Elena said nothing, but considered my filthy clothes, my dagger tucked into my boot, and my determination. "You may go, but Rabi'a—"

Rabi'a stepped forward, chin out. "I shoot arrows. Plus, I must kill Turo."

Elena's eyebrow arched at me. "He has a harem," I said. "She's offended."

"Ah."

"Let Rabi'a accompany you," Nuño said. "She's the only one of the three of you who will blend in."

We all stared at the young girl in her billowing trousers, long flowing tunic, and headdress that could be swept across her shoulder into a veil. I chuckled, then looked at Elena. "I have an idea."

"No," Elena said.

"Fadri, can you borrow two more outfits like Rabi'a's from the camp women?"

"No," Elena said.

"I can," Fadri crowed happily, having obviously forgiven me for smashing a pot against his head. "Be right back."

"No," Elena said.

"Yes."

"Who is in charge here?"

I grabbed a stick of charcoal from a nearby hearth and headed for the nearest white wall. "This is what I know of the palace layout." Apparently, at least for a few minutes, I was in charge.

❖

When the call to prayer came, shouts and taunts rose up all around the city, so Rabi'a and I were able to follow Elena to the nearest rope on the east wall, the rope some poor starving Valencian had used to escape the city. Rabi'a climbed up, hand over hand, then slid silently over the wall, making it look so easy.

"You next." Elena held the rope for me, and I tightened my aching hands around the rough hemp. Physical Education had not been my favorite high school class, and twenty years had done nothing to change that. Nor had the effects of a disintegrating timeline. I looked up at the twisting rope. At least the manacle around my wrist was gone, thanks to Enzo's help.

"Keep the rope tight between your feet." I jumped up, trying to do just that, and somehow found myself five feet off the ground, moaning softly. "Do not look down," Elena whispered.

That only left up. Halfway up my arms trembled, my shoulder flamed, and I could no longer feel my feet. Oh why couldn't I climb like the Zamboni twins? The two redheaded girls in my tenth grade gym class climbed like monkeys. Sheri Zamboni later confessed to me after too much beer that she and her sister were built in such a way they each had at least three orgasms on the climb up. I had no such experience to distract me as I pulled myself higher with trembling arms.

And then I was over the wall and crouching on the walkway. Elena climbed over the wall right behind me. We found a short stairway, ended up on an empty street, and headed for the palace.

After all the disasters I'd had, I couldn't believe we reached the palace without a problem. My heart thumped in my ears as I nodded to Elena, only her eyes visible above the veil. I certainly felt as ridiculous as she looked. She moved like a boy wearing his sister's clothes, totally weirded out by the feel of the unfamiliar cloth against his skin. "We split up," I said. "Rabi'a, you go with Elena. The powder will be in a small box or chest in or near her quarters. She should be in prayer for a while."

"And you?" Rabi'a whispered.

"I seek something more important."

"When you find him, I kill him. He is Rabi'a's man, not a harem man."

"Of course, dear." Head down, taking meek but quick steps, I found the stairs. Arturo's quarters would be near Anna's but probably not as grand or extensive. I passed a vase of dying flowers and snatched it up. The first guard I met set my pulse hammering through my veins, and I stopped. "For my lord, al-Rashid." The guard nodded, unconcerned, and stepped aside.

At the only door with two guards, I stopped and repeated my act. It was as easy as that. They stepped aside, unlocked the door, and let me in.

Arturo, wearing silky trousers and long shirt, sat on the edge of his bed, bare head in his hands. My breath caught in my throat when I realized he struggled to regain his composure. He had been crying. "Go away," he muttered. "I can't discuss politics or my next speech today."

Even though he'd chosen Anna and the life she could give him, I had to believe he would be happy I hadn't died. "Arturo, it's me."

He straightened as if yanked up by an invisible cord. Disbelief rounded his eyes and mouth. He shook his head, blinking rapidly, then when he rose to his feet, I dropped my veil. "Mom?"

"Yup, and my head is still attached to my body."

"*Mom!*" In three steps he closed the distance between us and crushed me to his chest. Sobs wracked his body as I held him. My own eyes were none too dry by the time he let me go, sniffling. "I thought you were dead," he whispered.

"Because of what you read in Kalleberg's book."

"Yes, and because of this." He reached under his wide braided belt and pulled out my pearl necklace. "Anna gave it to me. She said she'd tried to intervene with the mullah on your behalf." He clenched my necklace in a tan fist. "I was trapped in a tower, kidnapped by Ibn Jehaf. I could do nothing. I had planned all along to save you, but I couldn't."

He latched the pearl back onto my neck, then I took his face between my hands. "Oh, but you did. You told Grimaldi, who told Nuño, who told Enzo and Fadri, who told Elena."

His wide grin brought a deep shuddering sigh up from my chest. "Elena saved you," he said. I nodded. "She still cares for you."

I shook my head. "No, but that's not important now. Arturo, I know you're enchanted with your new life. You have money, horses, and even a harem, I hear." He had the grace to blush. "But you aren't safe. As al-Rashid, your life is in danger. Anna will protect you only as long as you serve her. I want you to consider—"

He held up his hand, then shook his shaggy head. "You think I've joined Anna."

"You're pretending to be al-Rashid. Willingly. I heard your speech outside the mosque last week."

He grinned. "That was one of my best. But Mom, I can't *believe* you. You think I'd give up on what we set out to do just for life as al-Rashid? What about the wave heading for the future?" He spread his hands in agitation, frowning at my apparent stupidity. "I'm *acting*, Mom. This is the role of a lifetime. I pretend to like this life. Anna trusts me. I stay close to the action. Then come June 15, maybe I can do something."

Now it was my turn to look astonished. "Acting?"

"Jeez, Mom, I can't believe you'd think I'd be such a jerk."

Now we both grinned at my stupidity, and a huge boulder rolled off my chest. Suddenly I could breathe again. "My mistake," I said. "One I won't make again. But now that I've found you, I know we'll make it back to the future. Hang on just—"

"Go back? Mom, until I thought you'd died, I was having a blast!"

"But that night before al-Saffah, you were really unhappy. You couldn't wait to get back."

"Yeah, well, I hadn't found my groove yet. But you're okay. And I got my groove now, and I'm kicking ass, Mom. I love this time period."

I shook my head. He was still so young and had no clue what a bad idea it would be to stay, so I'd have to be the adult for both of us. "We'll discuss that later. First we have to figure out how to get you out of here. There are two guards—"

"Yes, but—" When Arturo grabbed my hands, he noticed my wince. "What's wrong?"

"Our future is unraveling. It's affecting both me and Grimaldi. Every joint aches."

Arturo nodded. "That would explain my knees. I felt thirty when I got up this morning."

I let the ageist comment pass. "You're younger, so you probably aren't feeling the effects as strongly as we are. A few more days and I may not be able to move."

He cupped my hands gently. "All we need is one more day, Mom. That's why I can't come with you."

"What?"

"I am al-Rashid. The guards are outside my door to keep Ibn Jehaf and his men out, not to keep me in. I can leave whenever I want. I need to play this out until the end."

"But you're in danger. Ibn Jehaf—"

"I can't leave now, Mom. Tomorrow's the day."

"Rodrigo's men have sent an ultimatum. Open the gates tomorrow, or they'll swarm the walls. It's too—"

"I have to, Mom. When I thought you were dead, it took me days to accept that restoring the timeline was now my responsibility alone. I can't just let go of that."

My mouth dropped open. My fourteen-year-old son driven by responsibility? Sticking to something he started? When two thumps and a groan outside turned us toward the door, Elena and Rabi'a entered, dragging the unconscious guards behind them. Oh oh. "Arturo, I should tell you that Rabi'a—"

"Rabi'a!"

"Busaybah!" She flung her arms around Arturo's neck and was suddenly more intent on kissing him than on killing him. I had not missed the look of pure joy on his face when he recognized her.

Elena crossed her arms while we waited. "I thought she wanted to kill him."

"Me too."

Shaking her head, Elena shifted her silky tunic, revealing her sword belt and a plastic bag of white powder. "I found it."

Finally I tapped Arturo's shoulder. "No time for this, Turito."

Somehow we disentangled Rabi'a, then I explained that Arturo would remain. Even though Rabi'a burst into tears, Arturo assured her he would be fine. He shooed us all out the door.

"I'll deal with the guards," he said. "Go."

I don't know which of us, Rabi'a or I, was more upset to leave Arturo in that palace, but somehow Elena got us both back to the wall. The rope burned my weakened hands and I lost control the last ten feet, sliding onto the hard cobblestones. If anything happened to Arturo in the next twenty-four hours, it would rest on my shoulders since I had left my son in the clutches of a power-hungry mad woman.

❖

Rodrigo was too far gone to recognize either Elena or me. We fed him a weak dose at first, which he drank, then an hour later I increased the dose to half a spoonful. He drank that as well, then fell into a fitful sleep.

Elena and I didn't speak as we took turns sleeping and watching Rodrigo. Two lanterns warmed the dark room, and I slept on a mat in the corner. At one point I woke up to Elena's voice.

"Drink it all, Rodrigo. Your body needs what is in this ale."

Rodrigo coughed, then the blankets rustled as he sat up. I didn't move. "Navarro. What the hell are you doing here?" The drug was working. "Are you trying to poison me, bitch?"

"Not today, Rodrigo. Some day, perhaps, but now I need you strong and healthy."

"I am dying. Go away."

She chuckled softly. "You are not dying, and I do not give a damn what you want. Tomorrow, against all that I believe, I am going to make you a hero, may the saints forgive me. So shut that hole in your face, old man, and listen as I tell you what you must do."

I closed my eyes. In a few more hours, it would be over. History would either reshift itself, sending a new wave through time, restoring what must be. Or nothing would change, which meant everything would.

CHAPTER TWENTY-SEVEN

I woke the morning of June 15 to a high-pitched whine that no one else seemed to hear. Even when I pressed my trembling palms over my ears, I failed to muffle the insistent sound of time coming apart. My stomach churned so violently I could take nothing for breakfast but a small hunk of bread Enzo offered me. Water tasted so metallic it grated against my teeth.

I ran my grimy, aching fingers through my hair. The instant this day was resolved, I was heading for the nearest Valencian bath house. I would soak so long even my fingernails and toenails would wrinkle. I wouldn't drag myself from that tiled heaven until every grain of dirt, every molecule of scent from this century had dissolved in the bath salts.

Enzo and I fastened each other's mail, then he found me an extra pair of metal gauntlets to strap onto my wrists and forearms. Neither of us expected a battle, but it felt better to look prepared. Enzo tugged on his polished helmet, the nose-piece jutting down into his stony face. He tied on his black cape, transferring himself from middle-aged man to fierce warrior. "Ready?" he asked. The others had already left.

"No, but I have no choice." I tucked my dagger into the sheath. "Let's go." The rain had slowed to a mist, but heavy clouds lumbered across the sky, bringing with them the smell of salt water.

Valencia's closed main gate was constructed of towering timbers that stretched nearly to the top of the wall itself. To use the term "city wall" was misleading because half of the city now stood outside the protective Roman walls, yet it was still a wall separating me from my son.

Outside the wall was a plaza of sorts, where half a dozen side streets emptied themselves in a spoke around the gate. Christian soldiers, armed to the eyeballs with swords, daggers, mace, and hatchets, stood ten deep in the plaza behind me, stretching as far as I could see. Ahead, Elena and her generals waited by the closed gate, their saddled horses kept down a side street by a few young boys. When Enzo and I joined the circle, Elena was too deep in a discussion with Jorge to look up. Grimaldi held one palm over an ear, and we exchanged grimaces as I did the same. The whine dulled a bit, but continued, so I was pretty sure we didn't have much time left.

Enzo muttered an Arabic curse under his breath and pointed up the wall, where fifty Valencian archers appeared, bows drawn, arrows nocked and pointing down directly at us.

A few Christians then turned and pointed to the buildings behind us ringing the plaza where Nugaymath, Rabi'a, and dozens of al-Saffah lined the roof tops, their bows pointed at the men on the wall. The Valencian archers raised their own bows until the two groups aimed at each other.

"This could get ugly," Fadri said cheerfully. Just then the great wooden gate swung open, creaking and groaning like an old man who has remained in one position too long. Anna, dressed in a brilliant blue tunic and trousers with a heavily embroidered cape, rode out from the city with an armed escort. Where was Arturo? Carlos and Rafael Mahfouz rode beside Anna, and I watched Carlos carefully. He winced as he shifted in the saddle, and he repeatedly stuck a finger into one ear. Good. I felt no obligation to tell him why he hurt.

Anna's gray mare, mane braided with silver cord, pranced in place before Elena. "You?" Anna said in surprise. "I thought we were rid of you days ago."

"I'm like a bad dream. It's hard to get rid of me."

Anna waved a slender hand. "No matter. Your supposed leader, Rodrigo Díaz, had the audacity to demand our surrender, yet I know Rodrigo is no longer here."

As Anna spoke, I became aware of Rafael's concerned stare at me, and at my shoulder, as he searched for signs of a wound. I surprised myself by letting a smile escape. He nodded, and his chest rose as he inhaled deeply, relief relaxing his brow. I was oddly touched by his concern. He'd shot me, but was still rattled that the metal stick had done such damage to human flesh.

Anna's speech was well-rehearsed, and Carlos didn't even seem to be listening as he stared straight ahead. Anna then motioned to the

Christian soldiers surrounding the walls. "Rodrigo has tucked his tired tail between his legs and fled. So the rest of you might as well leave. There will be no surrender. We have enough food to last for months. Can you say the same?" She gazed over the crowd, smiling when she saw me. "All of you, go home to where you belong. Leave us in peace. Without Rodrigo, you aren't an army. We'll only negotiate with Rodrigo."

"So be it!" boomed Rodrigo's voice from a side street. The crowd parted like grass in a breeze, and Arturo himself could not have wished for a more dramatic entrance. Pale, gaunt, but upright for the first time in days, Rodrigo took his time approaching our tense circle. I knew he was too wobbly to walk any faster, but he gave the impression of a man in control, unhurried, heightening the tension unbearably. He looked as fierce as Enzo, only twice as large. His beard had been cleaned, re-braided, and spread across his chest like a badge of courage.

This was it. Anna's mouth dropped open, but by the time Rodrigo reached us, she had recovered. When she dismounted, a brief second of pain flashed across her face, so she, too, felt the effects of the unraveling timeline. The rest of her party also dismounted. "Rodrigo, you look well. The rumors, then, were false."

Rodrigo stopped, tucking his thumbs into his sword belt, which hung lower without his ample belly. "Never felt better. So let us discuss surrender. But as I believe I mentioned earlier, I do not negotiate with women. Where is al-Rashid?"

"He cannot be bothered with trifles such as you. He—"

"—would not miss this for the world." The shout came from inside the gate, where Arturo appeared on a pure white stallion, both of them so loaded with gold and embroidered cloth it was a wonder either could move. He rode into the circle, head high, but I was his mother and recognized the shadow of worry and fear in those brown eyes. He was likely tormented by the same incessant ringing.

He turned and faced the archers on the wall. "Lower your bows!" he cried.

"No," Anna snapped. "Do not—"

"Silence, woman! Lower your bows." The men did so. "Arrows in quivers." They complied. Then Arturo turned toward Elena, waiting until she issued the same command to Nugaymath. The al-Saffah women grumbled, but obeyed, and a collective sigh of relief issued from every chest. No matter what went wrong down here, at least death would not rain down on us immediately.

"My lord Rashid." Anna moved toward him, frowning. "Remember what we discussed last week?"

Arturo dismounted with a flare, handing off his reins to a guard. "We discussed resistance. We discussed refusing to yield to Rodrigo Díaz."

Rodrigo stepped forward, wobbling slightly. "Surrender now, al-Rashid, or lose everything."

"He is but a child," Anna said. "He—"

"Silence! I am the caliph al-Rashid, the spiritual leader of Valencia and all of al-Andaluz. The great Allah speaks through me, and Allah sees the wisdom of this Christian's request. I have prayed every hour for Allah's guidance, and I have received his word." Murmuring Valencians inside the gate pressed closer at his ringing shout.

"Rodrigo Díaz of Vivar, leader of the most powerful army in all of Iberia, if I surrender will you spare my people?"

"I will, my lord."

Anna shook her head so violently her hair came undone. "No, you—"

"Will you feed them?"

"Until they can hold no more, my lord." I caught Elena's eye. Whatever she'd told Rodrigo, it was working.

"Will you spare my most precious jewel, the sparkling city of Valencia?"

A split second pause, then El Cid's reply came. "As if it were my own home, as God is my witness."

When Arturo strode around the circle, stopping when he reached me, Anna could not miss his message. He had chosen me, and her precious creation was about to bite her in the butt. My son then raised his arms and spoke in the firm, clear voice that his drama coach had helped him develop these last two years. "Then I, as the caliph of Valencia, and as Allah's messenger here on earth, do hereby surrender Valencia to Rodrigo Díaz of Vivar, the one who from this day forward shall always be called 'al-Sayyid.'"

Great cheers arose from both sides of the wall and laughter bubbled up inside me. Nice touch, Arturo. Over the years language changes would convert al-Sayyid to al-Cidi, to al-Cid to El Cid. History would have its El Cid.

But then something prickled up my neck, and I looked at Anna. Her eyes held resignation, not panic, and a cramp of fear gripped me. She'd expected this. She had something else planned. Only I seemed to notice when she reached inside her wide belt and pulled out, unbelievably, the gun Rafael had thrown away into the woods. Caquito. He must have retrieved it for Anna, since Rafael hated it too much to touch it again.

Anna raised the gun toward Rodrigo, and I read the future in her eyes. First Rodrigo, then Arturo, then Elena, then me. Four bullets was all she needed to bury the original timeline forever.

I opened my mouth but no sound came out. Elena saw my face but did not understand. Luckily, Arturo, Carlos and Rafael did.

Carlos, standing off to Anna's side, flung himself in front of Rodrigo as Anna pulled the trigger. The shot was nearly silent in the celebration around us. Carlos dropped to the street, blood already blooming across his arm. Rodrigo gaped at the bleeding man at his feet.

Time does slow down in a crisis. That had to be why Arturo began, in slow motion, to cross the circle toward Anna. Tae Kwon Do versus a gun? Elena's sword flashed at my side, but neither Arturo nor Elena would ever reach her in time. Anna gave me a languid, triumphant glance, then pointed the gun at Rodrigo's chest. Furious, Rafael saw me, saw he stood in the way. He took one side step and my path was clear.

Pain forgotten, I drew my dagger out. Without thought, without fear, I sent it spinning, slicing through the morning air. The only thing that stopped its endless, flashing flight was Anna's heart. She straightened, and looked at me, her eyes wide with surprise. She swayed, staggered a step, then collapsed.

Only the inner circle of men knew what had happened. They tightened around us protectively as the celebration continued. I scraped my knees against cobblestone as I reached Anna's side. I cradled her head in my lap, crying as blood pumped from the wound, the dagger still buried to its hilt. "Anna, Anna. Oh my god. Oh my god." Arturo knelt beside me, pried the gun from her hand and tucked it into his boot.

Blood gurgled up from her throat and began running out her nose.

Christ, I must have hit an artery. What were the chances?

"Anna, oh my god." I rocked her, half-relieved, half-horrified at what I'd done. This was happening too fast. "A doctor," I managed to croak hoarsely. "We need a doctor."

Elena, Rodrigo, and the others encircled me, a forest of steel and strength. Elena shook her head. "No, Kate. She bleeds out. There is nothing anyone can do to save her, not even a Moor surgeon."

Everything around me blurred as I held her, Arturo's warm hand on my shoulder, his head pressed against mine, the three of us together for the first time, the family that never was. There were no last minute regrets or apologies or forgiveness in Anna's eyes, only surprise, then something calmer. Peace? Oh please, let it be peace. Her startled frown relaxed as my clothes grew wet and heavy with her bright blood. "I'm here," I whispered. She blinked twice, then left. One second I held a living woman in my arms. The next second, I held a body.

I bent my head, pressing my lips against her hair. "Anna," I whispered into a deaf ear. "I had to. I had to."

"Mom?" I looked up at Arturo, his face pinched at my pain. "I'm sorry, but we're not done. There's one more act left to this play, so I need to leave you here for awhile." I nodded, wiping my tears with a bloody hand.

Arturo stood. "Al-Sayyid, allow me and my men to escort you into the city."

Rodrigo nodded and motioned for the horses. Elena opened her mouth, but I shook my head. I couldn't bear whatever she had to say.

I lowered Anna's body gently, stood, then watched everyone mount and line up. Arturo and Rodrigo rode side by side, followed by Elena and Rafael, then Nuño and Enzo. Fadri still crouched on the stones near me, aiding Carlos, who lay on his side, conscious but in pain.

The sun had come out, shining on the procession of helmets and mail heading through the gate. Wet cobblestones glistened like jewels scattered across the ground.

Arturo swept his arm wide as they moved through the gate and up the hill, calling to the people of Valencia to rejoice. The siege was over.

It was June 15, 1094. Rodrigo Díaz of Vivar, El Cid, future hero of Spain, the man whose legend would become the repository for all the traits Spaniards most admired, rode into Valencia as its new ruler. He was led to his throne by my son, an eighth grader from Chicago, who would never, ever again consider history a boring subject.

Nearly faint with pride, I turned. Fadri was helping Carlos sit up, but still pressed a corner of his cape against Carlos's right arm. "I couldn't do it," Carlos said weakly. "At the last minute, when I saw that gun and realized the world would change forever, I could not let it happen."

"What the hell weapon did this?" Fadri asked, but I only shook my head.

"How are you?" I whispered to Carlos. Neither of us spoke of the price the world's Jews would have to pay for his valor.

"It's just my arm," Carlos said, face drawn with pain. "I'll heal." He grimaced as he tried to stand but failed. "Ironically, I feel better than I have in days."

I listened closely to my own body and realized every soldier's shout, every coo of the pigeons on the roofs, every scrape of a horse hoof was clear. The ringing was gone. I flexed my fingers and cried out in relief. No flames of pain. The wave of change racing toward the twenty-first century had smoothed out into nothing.

Fadri and I helped Carlos stand. "Kate Vincent," Fadri said. "Why do men always find themselves in pain around you?"

I tried out a small grin on my tense face, and did not shatter, so I kissed him on his hairy cheek. "You're a gem, Fadri Colón, and I promise never to hit you again."

He shrugged. "Not to worry. The vision you provided before smashing my head was worth it."

I shook my head. "You're terrible. Take Carlos into the city. Find a doctor to help him. Keep the wound clean." I touched Carlos on the uninjured arm. "Thank you."

The man nodded wearily. "I do not enjoy learning such important lessons so late in one's life. It exhausts me."

"What have you learned?"

A twinkle crept into his eyes. "That I am but a flea on the wide rump of time. I can do naught but ride along."

I let myself chuckle despite the body and blood at my feet. People had begun streaming out the city gates.

Fadri moved Carlos toward the gate, then turned. "You do not come? There is nothing more you can do here." Valencian men, women, and children now ran freely in the streets to reclaim the city's suburbs, and many of the soldiers had followed the procession, eager to see the city they had lived outside all these weeks.

"No, I must stay here, with her. Send a wagon when you have seen to Carlos." With a nod, Fadri helped Carlos into Valencia.

I stood alone in the street. As the Valencians fell silent and skirted around me, I stared down at Anna's face, at her vacant eyes, then closed them.

Sighing, I wiped my hands on my cape, which had grown weighty from Anna's blood. I could bring her body back with Arturo and me, and bury her in her own time. But what *was* her time? Despite her loneliness, despite her misguided plans to change things, she had loved this century. No, I would have Enzo and Fadri help me dig a deep, deep grave here, somewhere in the countryside near Valencia. I would place her there, in her most elaborate gown, then surround her with everything she brought back from the future. The only exception would be the white powder, which Elena would use to slowly reduce Rodrigo's addiction. I didn't know how long it would take, but I expected Rodrigo would be his old, obnoxious self within a few weeks. By then I would be sitting in Laura and Deb's living room, trying to describe a vacation too unreal to believe.

I moved outside the pool of blood, then sat on the street, pulling my legs up against my chest, resting my forehead on my knees, and thought about time. Time had laid down a train track for history to follow, but when Anna violated that by keeping Rodrigo from Valencia, she forced history to jump its tracks. The further history moved from its destiny, the more our bodies felt the pain of our future breaking apart. History was now back on the right track and would progress as it should. Even if Carlos decided to stay in this century, he now knew enough not to mess with it. All of us would stay out of history's way, especially Arturo and me. Our job here was done.

CHAPTER TWENTY-EIGHT

That afternoon Arturo officially resigned as al-Rashid. He did so before a large crowd of Valencians and soldiers gathered outside the mosque, and my sigh of relief nearly stripped nearby trees of their leaves. He was no longer a target for assassination. He told the crowd he was too young to be caliph at this point, and that he wanted to take some time to learn more about life, and to spend more time with his mother, which choked up every woman in the square.

The next task was one I knew I couldn't do alone, and I was relieved when Nugaymath and Rabi'a both agreed to help me prepare Anna's body. The dried blood had turned her clothes to cardboard, so we had to cut them off. After I broke down several times, Nugaymath cursed softly and sent me from the room. "Go pick out a dress for the body. You are no good here."

Anna had turned one whole room into her closet, so I picked out the most elegant gown I could find, a green wool trimmed in ermine. Very expensive. Very Anna.

I pawed through every box, every chest, every pile, searching for twenty-first century items, since every trace of the future must be buried with her. I found three copper chests of gold coins, and decided I could keep them. No use throwing good money away.

The only chest I couldn't open was plain, made of heavy wood, locked tight. I returned to Nugaymath and Rabi'a, but stopped outside the hall, hovering out of sight. "Umm, did you find any keys on her?"

Rabi'a handed me a small chain with keys, and I gave her the green wool dress. "I appreciate your help," was all I could say. She nodded, then folded the bulky dress over her arm.

The chest held some coins, a few packs of gum, and Anna's wallet, with her driver's license, about $200 in cash, and her VISA card. These must have been her insurance in case she wanted to return to the future.

I dug deeper and unwrapped a small flat package, gasping when the black velvet fell away from a framed photo of Anna and me, taken years ago on our trip to the Grand Canyon. Tucked into the corner of the frame was the photo of five-year old Arturo I'd lost eight years ago. She must have taken it from me, knowing I wouldn't need it, since I'd have the real thing.

I searched the rest of her quarters, and other than some history books and empty prescription bottles, I found nothing more. Heavy with a sadness I couldn't shake, I locked everything up in the chest.

❖

The next day it took Enzo, Fadri, Arturo, and me over three hours to dig the grave. I chose a site up in the foothills, hoping the slopes wouldn't be developed for centuries, at least until time had reduced the coffin and its contents to dust.

"Deeper?" Enzo asked from the hole, his dusty head even with the ground.

"Deeper." Good thing Fadri had thought to throw a ladder onto the wagon.

I insisted on taking my turn and found the cool, crumbling soil more comforting than I'd expected. Finally, the four of us used two ropes to lower the coffin. I had shed all my tears the day before and felt nothing but an unbearable thickness in my limbs, as if my bones had calcified. Arturo and I each tossed down a handful of wildflowers we'd picked on the way.

No one spoke as Enzo took up the shovel, but I jumped when the clods of dirt knocked hollow against the coffin. Anna loved Spain. Now she would be here forever.

"Mom?" Arturo asked as we rode back to Valencia. "Are you all right?"

The sun was setting behind us, flaming the hills ahead of us as orange as a monarch butterfly's wing. "No, but I will be."

❖

The day after we buried Anna, I sat alone in my room, wallowing in the knowledge I'd killed her. Someone knocked on my door. I jumped, and my heart began its frantic drumbeat.

But it was Grimaldi, pale forehead creased with concern, so I waved him in and he lowered himself onto the opposite bench. "How are you?" he asked.

I shrugged. "Tired. Relieved. Horrified."

He nodded. "You accomplished your goal, Kate."

"I don't know for sure, so I must ride to the Mirabueno cave to see if Professor Kalleberg has sent back a note telling me what happened. I should have gone already, but with Anna's burial…"

"Understandable. Still, you should be proud of what you've done."

No, pride didn't describe the hollow ache in my chest, the dull emptiness that I couldn't banish. I stared at Grimaldi's cloak, his bags. "You're leaving."

He laced his long bony fingers together. "I miss my family." He met my eyes. "Kate, I'm sorry I couldn't help more, but—"

"Grimaldi," I interrupted. "You saved my life. If you hadn't traveled to Valencia, Elena never would have known to rescue me." He hesitated. "What else is bothering you?"

"The future. What happens now, Kate? I'm a Christian converted to Islam. My wife and children are Moor. How do I keep them safe?"

I patted his knee. "The good news is the Moors' fall is fairly gradual over the next seventy-five years or so. King Alfonso will eventually take Zaragoza, but I think he allows the Moors some degree of religious freedom."

"You once said the last Moorish city to fall will be Granada."

"In 1492, when Ferdinand and Isabel kick out Boabdil."

"Maybe we'll move to Granada," he said. "That will buy my family a few years."

"Wherever you go, Grimaldi, keep a low profile."

He smiled, rose, and pulled me into a bear hug. "Always, my dear Kate. Always. And if you ever decide to return to this century again…" He leaned close to my ear. "Bring more M&Ms."

❖

I finally tracked down Nuño, and he agreed to take me to Mirabueno the next day. I took yet another bath at the palace, torn between worry and hope that I'd run into Elena. But she never appeared and seemed to be going out of her way to avoid me. I knew she was busy because Ibn Jehaf had come out of hiding after al-Rashid "resigned," and everyone was working to put together a city government and defense that made sense.

My room looked out over a section of the wall, and now and then I saw Elena and Nuño walking there together, heads bent in deep conversation, shoulders bumping companionably. I also witnessed the amazing sight of the kind-hearted warrior Nuño and the fierce Nugaymath walking together occasionally, which brought a wry smile to my lips. How did he handle her constant insults of men? And why was she still here? I thought she'd be back out terrorizing the countryside by now, but once when I saw them talking, their heads bent close together, I suspected Nugaymath would not be leaving Valencia without Nuño.

I saw little of Arturo, since Rodrigo wanted him there during the discussions. Ibn Jehaf was more comfortable when he saw how little al-Rashid cared about the proceedings. When the now-retired al-Rashid wasn't with Rodrigo, Elena, and the others, he spent all his time with Rabi'a. In a few days I would have to burst his romantic bubble. It was time we returned to our own century.

I sat on the narrow iron balcony outside my room, unable to believe it had only been four days since I'd killed Anna. Call to prayer ended, and the clear ringing song seemed to hang in the air, a sound you could feel more than hear. I watched a Christian soldier and a young woman hurry along the wall's walkway toward the nearest guard tower. Not another one. It'd taken me a few days to catch on, but couples repeatedly disappeared into the tower, the man hanging his sword belt on a hook near the narrow wooden door. When a couple approached the tower with a sword belt already there, they'd turn around and seek another tower. Hotel Valencia, high on the thick Roman walls.

I watched the traffic passing below. Having spent four days practically alone, thinking about me, about Arturo, about our lives, I was tired of thinking, tired of the nagging feeling that there was something I must do.

Then a triumphant shout below brought me to my feet to peer over the balcony.

"Thanks be to all the saints in heaven! We're here. The big, fancy palace." A man with a limp climbed down from the wagon and walked in a circle to loosen his hips. "My cousin Lopez says this here city is the best, but I don't see anything that special."

"José!" I cried. The man craned back his neck, as did the woman still on the wagon. Marta! My friends from Duañez.

"Señora Navarro? That you? The very person we've come to see?" He slapped his thighs. "What are the chances? I was just telling Marta here we'd likely spend days tracking you down."

Marta threw me such a desperate look I laughed out loud. "I'll be right down."

"We got someone here in the wagon." Musicians began playing in the square, drowning out my old friend.

"Stay there," I called. "I'm coming down."

I fairly skipped down the two stone staircases and raced through the central courtyard and out into the street. "Marta!" I clung to her with a fierceness that surprised us both. "It's so good to see you."

"And you, too." She dropped her voice. "Another day with José, and I'd have been forced to cut my own throat, no matter how near to Valencia we were."

José moved to the back of the wagon and flung back a blanket. "Move careful now, poor devil. No use scraping things and making 'em worse." José helped a man inch his way toward the back of the wagon.

"Kalleberg?" I nearly screamed as the professor twisted toward me. The professor. "Holy shit."

"Kate, oh, thank god." Kalleberg spoke in English as José helped him from the wagon.

"Go gentle now, man." José winked at me. "We brung him on a horse, but after two days of that, his soft bottom nearly burst with blisters. Poor sot screamed in pain so we had no choice but to switch to this here wagon."

"Oh, Kate, you can't imagine what I've been through. These kind people—"

"Marta made up a salve, one of those really smelly ones that make you want to toss your supper, and she spread it on the poor man's backside." José leaned against his cane, settling in for a long story. "She made me help, a cruel, cruel thing. I saw more of that man's ass than any man should see. Close my eyes and still get the nightmares. Lordy, I ain't ever seen such a hairy—"

"José! Please! Where did you find him?"

Kalleberg now draped himself against the wagon wheel, grimacing so woefully I had to bite back a chuckle.

"That cave you done sent us to." Thank god my trust in Father Ruiz had not been misplaced.

"We reached the cave," Marta said, "and found him sitting outside, looking a bit like a lost puppy."

"So he did," José said. "Like a cat who finds himself stuck up a tree and don't know what to do."

"He doesn't speak Castillan or Hebrew or Arabic, or Galician, so we haven't understood a word he's said." Marta shook her dark head. "Of course these last few days all he's done is moan."

"We could understand that, all right. And your name. When we found him, he kept saying your name, that he did. What are his chances two people who knew you would come along?"

Marta touched my arm. "The only thing we could think to do was bring him to you."

"I'm glad you did." I smiled at Kalleberg. "You're a big surprise, professor."

He laughed softly, then winced. "Even thinking hurts, but I had to come see you. You won't believe—"

"Señora Navarro, that ain't all we brung." José pulled me to the back of the wagon and dropped his voice to a stage whisper. "We dug up the bags of money like you said."

"There was more than enough to buy flour and meat in Burgos, so we can feed everyone in Duañez."

José flung back the tarp. "But we found more and thought we best bring it to you. Marta and me had a spat over whether you said to dig to the left or to the right, so we done both." Ten small chests lay in the wagon, identical to the chest I had buried with Anna. "They be full of gold, that they do."

Anna must have buried her own stash of gold in the cave as well. I knew just what to do with it. Rebuild the homes and fields and gardens and orchards of Valencia. Repair the damage done by Rodrigo's siege.

"José, do you remember Nuño Súarez ?"

"Big bear of a man. I nearly crapped in my boots the first time he towered over me."

"He's here, perhaps in the palace, or nearby. Find him, and he'll show you a safe place for these chests. Marta, could you run into the palace and ask for Salaam? He is the court physician."

Kalleberg and I were suddenly alone in the busy street. "I cannot believe what riding a horse does to human flesh." Kalleberg moaned.

"Man, it's good to see you. All these weeks I kept thinking about you in the cave."

"Not to worry. I got tired of camping out, so took a room in a little hotel a few blocks away. I checked the books constantly, but nothing changed. Then on June 15, everything in the books changed back to the original history, as if the altered timeline had never happened. I knew you'd done it."

I hugged him carefully. "June 15 was one hell of a day. But why did you come back?"

He rubbed his chin ruefully. "When I realized I wouldn't be blinked out of existence by that altered timeline, it was like being cured of cancer. As I stared at that ledge after you left, I realized what an opportunity I was giving up, both as a scholar and as a man, and I suddenly knew what I wanted to do with my life. So I just sat on the ledge, and the rest José has told you."

I hugged him again, then he suddenly pulled back. "Kate, Arturo slipped past me while I slept. I woke up just as he disappeared. I've been worried sick—"

"He caught up to me in the cave, Professor, and other than being kidnapped by a band of bloodthirsty archers and sold to a madwoman and trained to serve as the religious leader of all the Moors, he's been with me the entire time."

Kalleberg winced. "You feared your young son would come to harm in this century."

I smiled. "He's fine and is here in Valencia. I think you'll find him changed, almost grown-up, in fact."

"Excellent," the professor said as he looked around. "I still can't believe I'm here."

"Perhaps when we get you something for the pain, you'll start enjoying yourself. But what did you mean about proof?"

"That's the other reason I came back, and the most exciting. I wanted to tell you that you will write the most astounding—"

I held up my hand, heart pounding. "No, please. I'm done knowing my future." I waited, listening to the pulse of my body. I didn't want to know what I *should* do, for that would box me in as tightly as if I were back in Anna's prison cell. No. I was done doing what was expected of me, by friends, by Arturo, by time. My future stretched out before me, blissfully blank. "Professor, no hints, no clues. Nothing."

"But you're going—"

"No."

Flushed and frustrated, Kalleberg shut his mouth, then nodded. "You've gained much wisdom these last four weeks."

Salaam flowed from the palace in search of a new patient, a new challenge. When I told Kalleberg that Salaam spoke flawless Latin, the professor brightened considerably. "Go with the doctor. I will find you later."

❖

Suddenly restless, I saddled my horse, fairly competently, if I must say so myself, and rode east toward the sea. At the edge of the grassland leading to the beach, I tied the mare to a piece of driftwood, then pushed through the tall grass, drawn by the sound of crashing waves. I'd been so caught up in my mission that I'd forgotten how healing the sound of water could be. I pulled off my boots and let the warm sand heat up my feet and ankles, then walked and walked along the shore, marveling that I was still alive.

Thanks to Kalleberg, I now knew I had a future I could return to. My future. Sudden turmoil stopped me in my tracks as the foam from the most recent wave slid up the hard-packed sand and licked my toes. A future without Elena.

How could I leave her again? She was still angry with me and protecting herself, but who could blame her? I started walking again, relishing the cool water lapping at my ankles.

Being a parent meant sacrifice; I'd done that eight years ago, and it was absolutely the right thing to do, but Arturo had been frightfully on target when he'd said he'd never seen me smile like I smiled when Elena was around. I'd felt that myself, but refused to admit I was unhappy. Parents don't have the time, or the right, to feel unhappy, right? But what kind of parent would I be if I was miserable all over again?

A flock of skinny-legged terns pecked at the sand ahead of me, then skittered out of the way as I passed, peeping in alarm. From the very first moment I'd seen Elena at Valvanera—so furious and protective of her child—I'd known there could never be another woman in my life. When I returned to the future, I did so knowing I'd leave my heart behind.

No, that was melodramatic. My heart would return with me, but it would crack open and its contents leak out, never to be shared with anyone. Would there even be enough left for Arturo?

Was my stubbornness about doing the right thing for Arturo blinding me? And what *was* the right thing? Arturo had been right weeks ago when he'd listed all the dangers of the modern world. There would be no way I could protect him from a car accident or a random shooting or getting cancer or any of the other dangers of the time.

I looked around at the ocean, the walls of Valencia rising in the distance, and felt a deep ache at the beauty and solitude. Was this really such a bad place to raise a child? As a Moorish city, Valencia was filled with scholars. Arturo could receive the highest quality education in art, mathematics, music, classical literature, and history.

My pulse raced as I began pacing a short stretch of beach, back and forth, startling a seagull who'd been following me. I tasted salt water on my lips as I thought this through. Maybe Arturo could train to be a historian. What better qualifications than to actually live it? When he turned eighteen he could return to the future; I'd go back with him to help him get established. That was only four years from now. Valencia would be a calm, peaceful city for five years until the Muslims once again took control. Perhaps I could return to the future long enough to get a stash of antibiotics and other medical supplies. If Arturo ever got sick we'd head back to the future faster than a lamb runs for its mama.

I stopped pacing, tears stinging my eyes. To be a good parent for Arturo meant I needed to take care of myself as well. All I needed was Elena. I had to believe that beneath her cool treatment, she still loved me. A warm sudden flush shot through me; our night at Valvanera proved she still desired me. With Solana, the four of us could form a family, with Nuño too, if he wanted.

I turned into the bracing wind blowing in off the ocean and laughed out loud, suddenly as light as the sea foam dancing at my feet.

Surely Arturo could live a few more years without a Mountain Dew or Spiderman movie.

❖

I searched the palace, then headed for the nearest outside staircase up to the wall. Jogging along the narrow walkway, I circled half the city before I found her, one leg up on the wall, staring out at the horizon. My breath caught in my throat. How could I make her understand how much I loved her? How could I convince her I was staying, that she didn't have to push me away any more. "There you are," I finally said.

Elena whirled around. "There *you* are. Where have you been?"

I crossed my arms and frowned. Man, this woman could push my buttons. "What do you mean where have *I* been? You've been avoiding me for days."

"You are right. I no longer want to avoid you." Then she smiled at me, and my heart skipped a beat. She kept smiling and my heart skipped a few more beats.

She took three strides and stopped in front me, her face alarmingly open. "I have given it a great deal of thought these last few days, and I have decided I will not let you leave."

Now my heart skipped rope. "How will you stop me? Chain me again?"

A woman of action more than words, Elena took my face in her hands and kissed me, long and hard and with such need my head spun. I clung to her to avoid falling over.

I don't know how long we kissed, but when I finally pulled away, my cheeks were wet, and her hands trembled as they held my own. I inhaled deeply. "Okay, that might slow me down a bit, but I still might leave."

She looked around to make sure we were alone, then pulled me even closer, slid one hand up my blouse, found my breast, and whispered something highly suggestive in my ear.

"No fair," I whispered back, my body on fire.

She kissed me again, then smiled, her eyes warm as turquoise. "I do not regret letting you go the first time because Arturo is a delight, and it is right you should be his mother. And I would not have Solana if you had not left. But if I let you go again, I will not recover."

I touched the black brows, the scarred nose, the tan forehead. "I'm not leaving, Elena. Not again."

I could feel a shudder of relief pass through her. "Saint's blood, say it again."

"I'm not leaving. Even if Arturo is upset, I've decided that for the next four years he must do what I decide."

She dropped her gaze. "When I realized you had come back to change history, not to be with me, I swore I would feel nothing, so when you left again I would still feel nothing."

"I'm sorry," I whispered. "If it helps at all, I learned in the future that Rodrigo would murder you. I came back to stop that."

She played with my hand, lacing our fingers together. "I suppose I should thank you. Knifing Rodrigo in the ass was very effective." She gazed into my eyes again. "I tried to feel nothing, but every time I looked at you," she stopped, swallowing hard, "and every time you smiled or laughed or tipped your head the way you do, I—"

"I love you, Elena Navarro." Once again, I covered her mouth with my own.

After a long, deep kiss that fueled my hunger rather than cooled it, I pulled back, one unsaid thing hanging between us. "I'm so sorry Anna revealed the truth about you."

Elena jammed her hands under her belt, stepped back, and began scuffing at the rough stone with her boot. "I was devastated. I thought my life was over. But since then, many men have come to me in private, expressing both anger that I had fooled them, and a wish that I not abandon them."

"You're a great leader, Elena, and they know it. They're just trying to adjust." I wanted to erase her confusion, but I recognized that figuring out what came next was something we all struggled with, regardless of the century.

"I do not know what I will do now. I am a soldier without an army. I am a mother without a husband." She looked at me through her lashes. "And I am nothing without you."

"Elena Navarro! You're flirting with me." Her wicked grin sent me back into her arms for more kissing. God, I was going to love life in this century.

A few minutes later someone coughed awkwardly behind us. "Excuse me, Mom." I jumped back.

Arturo and Rabi'a stood on the wall, hand in hand, faces glowing. Arturo gazed at Elena. "Did you tell Mom?"

Elena shook her head, a funny smile on her lips.

Arturo looked decidedly nervous. "I thought you were going to tell her."

"I decided it was your place to tell her," Elena said, "not mine."

"What's going on?" I said. "Tell me what?"

"Mom, ah, we have some news." Arturo took a deep breath as Rabi'a pressed her face shyly into his shoulder. "We're getting married."

I stared, unsure if my ears worked. "What?" I finally said, calm as a turtle.

"Married. Me and Rabi'a."

"You're fourteen, Arturo."

"I know." He gulped, then took a deep breath. "But we thought it would be best for the baby."

Fire alarms clanged in my brain. "I'm sorry. I didn't hear that correctly."

"The baby, Mom."

I threw up my hands. "Don't be ridiculous. How could she possibly know this early?"

"She's very regular. After that night in Zaragoza, well..." He shrugged. "She's pretty sure." I was gratified to see he looked a bit stunned himself. "I'm going to be a father."

I slapped my forehead.

"So I won't be going back to...you know where. I can't."

"Just wait one minute, young man. How do you know she's pregnant? How do you know it's yours?" I couldn't believe the words coming from my mouth. This was a feminist talking?

Arturo smiled at Rabi'a, one of those intimate smiles that exclude the mother. "Even if she's not pregnant, I still want to stay. We're in love."

I threw up my hands again and felt like a sit-com mom, but I couldn't help it. "Love? You don't know love, Arturo. Do you have any idea what you face? The responsibility, the time a child requires? You'll have to sacrifice too much. I can't—"

"Mom, *listen*. Eight years ago you sacrificed everything for me, your child." His eyes flickered to Elena. "Would you have me do any less for my child?"

"Well, I don't think they're the same—"

"Mom, I'm not asking your permission." His chin raised with resolve. "I'm telling you. This is what I'm doing. I hope you'll support us. I hope you'll stay here."

With a firm nod, he and Rabi'a left the wall.

"Christ," I exploded. "Can you believe that?" Even in my fury I noticed Elena was laughing. She took my hand and led me in the opposite direction.

"A *baby*? He's still a child himself." That Elena seemed unable, or unwilling, to stop laughing didn't help. "This isn't funny, Elena. I told him to keep it in his pants, but did he? No! Christ, take a fourteen-year-old boy out of the twenty-first century and you know what you have?" Elena stopped at a guard tower. "You have trouble, that's what." She unbuckled her sword belt and hung it on a nail by the open door, then ushered me in and closed the wooden door behind us.

I stood in the narrow window and pounded a fist on the sill. The sea beat against the shore, roaring waves of sound audible even up here. "And I didn't get to tell him *I'd* decided we were staying. That's a huge thing, and he just went ahead and decided on his own."

She unbuckled my belt and let it drop with a clatter to the floor. "You know what I think?" Elena asked, her voice unusually husky.

"What? That I'm a controlling mother? You just wait until Solana turns fourteen."

She shook her head as she unlaced my tunic with strong, firm hands. "No. I think you are upset you will be a grandmother."

I groaned. "I'm thirty-seven. Don't you—"

"Thirty-eight."

"Okay, thirty-eight. Don't you think that's a ridiculous age to be a grandmother?"

"I think it might be fun." She tugged at my waistband. "Besides, Solana is at the age where she would love to fuss over a baby."

I stepped back, hands on my hips. "Well, there's one thing I don't understand." Amusement flashed through her eyes.

"Yes?"

"How did we end up in this guard tower and why am I half naked?"

Elena's slow smile sent my blood pulsing everywhere, and she began unlacing her own tunic. "Your sword belt is hanging outside, isn't it?"

Her tunic fell to the floor, and I seemed to have developed a breathing problem. Then the look in Elena's eyes affected my pulse. One corner of her mouth rose. She pulled off her shirt, and my breathing problem only got worse. She no longer bound her chest with a strip of linen.

She reached for my shirt and I raised my arms over my head, then she pressed me against the stone. "Since you have returned, I have been plagued with fantasies every night."

Our entire bodies touched from knees to shoulders, and I licked my lips. "Shouldn't we go slower? It's such a cliché to profess great love and then hop into bed."

She kissed my neck and I shivered. "There is no bed here."

"I've noticed." The scent of vanilla and lemon drifted between us. "You've bathed," I whispered.

"So have you...finally."

My heart clicked back on track, just as history found its right path again. Elena's hands found *their* path as well. I cleared my throat. "It occurs to me it might be dangerous here with you, alone, naked."

She murmured into my ear as my body began to tingle. "Do not worry, my pearl. You are safe here with me."

She was right.

EPILOGUE

The Iberian Scholar
Fall, 2007 issue, published by the University of Wisconsin.

"The Gender Question: Who Was 'The Pearl'?" By Sheila House, Ph.D.

Debate continues to rage over the authorship of *The Chronicles of El Cid*, the stunning, yet controversial, illuminated manuscript unearthed last year in an archeological excavation of old Zaragoza. When city officials tore down a run-down tenement building to build its first Wal-Mart, they allowed a six-month dig on the site of a minor Moorish palace. The dig revealed a thick manuscript wrapped in an astonishingly well-preserved leather pouch.

The manuscript, which reads like a modern day journal, was written by the anonymous "Spanish Pearl." It contains the earliest known chronicle of El Cid's life, including a remarkable detailed description of his 1094 victory over Valencia, his five year reign, and his death in 1099. It also chronicles the life and death of his trusted first lieutenant, Alvar Fáñez, who died before the Valencian victory. This manuscript was referred to in many songs and other documents written throughout the centuries, but this was the first copy to come to light. Carbon dating places the manuscript in the early twelfth century, perhaps 1125. But critics who have studied the Latin document maintain the language is too modern for the twelfth century and insist it was not written until at least the fifteenth century.

The document has broken historians into three camps: the classical, the feminist, and the lesbian feminist, but all agree the "Spanish Pearl" chronicles a long life spent with Elena Navarro, "La Picadora," the woman warrior still celebrated today in Spanish folk songs. Together they raised a daughter, Solana Pidal, which classical scholars, led by the Harvard historians, say proves "Spanish Pearl" was a man.

Feminist historians counter that the writing turns increasingly irrate and impatient about once a month, leading Dr. Sarah Connelly of George Washington University to declare "Spanish Pearl" to be a woman subject to monthly hormonal changes. Researchers at the International Lesbian Archives in Paris maintain *The Chronicles of El Cid* presents the earliest documented evidence of a long term, sexual relationship between two women. The classical historians, led by Dr. Mark Eerdman, accuse the lesbian feminists of concocting pure fiction "in a desperate attempt to justify their lifestyle."

The feminists have suggested "Pearl" was female because the manuscript contains a thorough accounting of everyday life, something other scribes of those medieval centuries neglected. The lesbian feminists suggest the use of the name "Pearl" may hint at a common, though modern, euphemism for part of the female anatomy.

The classical historians refute both theories. Dr. Kyle Peterman writes that the pearl was a symbol of great wealth in those times, and not necessarily associated with females. The "Spanish Pearl" was likely a wealthy lord with an interest in daily details. "You do not have to be a woman to care about the difficulties of making bread, or how to protect your children from wild bobcats, or how to assist pregnant servants," writes Dr. Peterman. And as for the genitalia theory, Dr. Wilbert Pinkey has retorted that the lesbian feminists will turn even the most innocent of words into sexual innuendo "in their desperate attempt to justify their lifestyle."

The family structure of this "Pearl" is further complicated by a Nuño Súarez, who lived either with or near them and helped raise Solana. The traditional historians have suggested the titillating prospect of a ménage à trois, but the existence of Súarez 's wife, the war-like Almoravide Nugaymath, makes this unlikely. Nugaymath would likely have killed Súarez for marital infidelity.

Elena Navarro only had the one child, but both she and the "Spanish Pearl" played some role in rearing the five children of Arturo al-Rashid, a Zaragozan artist, poet, and actor of unknown origin.

The Chronicles provide an unflinching portrait of Rodrigo Díaz, his weaknesses, his greed, but reveals a grudging respect for the man as he worked to improve the lives of all Valencians—Christian, Moor, and Jew alike— aided by his Jewish administrator, Carlos Sanchez.

Despite the work's title, *The Chronicles of El Cid*, the manuscript continues for many years beyond El Cid's death. The entries begin to shorten and falter in 1130 or so, when the "Pearl" is believed to be between sixty and seventy, an amazing age for that century. The journal therefore presents over thirty years of life beyond the time of El Cid. While the gender of the author of *The Chronicles of El Cid* may never be known, this mystery does not detract from the manuscript's invaluable contribution to Spanish history.

Author's Note

Whenever I read historical fiction, I always wonder which characters actually existed in history. Of course, Kate and Elena are more real to me than any of the 'real' characters, but that said, here's the scoop on the real-life characters from *The Spanish Pearl* and *The Crown of Valencia*:

King Alfonso VI actually did rule Castile (and León and Asturias) from 1072 to 1109. Rodrigo Díaz of Vivar, "El Cid," was a mercenary soldier whose relationship with King Alfonso was complex, to say the least. Alfonso sent Rodrigo into exile at least twice because Rodrigo had offended or enraged Alfonso in some way. They didn't have the most mature of relationships.

When Rodrigo was exiled from Castile from 1081 to 1086, he spent much of that time in Zaragoza, where he worked as a mercenary soldier for al-Mu'tamin. Rodrigo brought with him one of his most trusted men, Alvar Fáñez. Rodrigo did take control of Valencia in 1094 and held it until his death in 1099.

When al-Mu'tamin died in 1085, he was succeeded by his son, al-Musta'in. There is no record of a daughter, but another Walladah did exist in the eleventh century. She was Walladah al-Mustakfi, daughter of the caliph of Cordoba and an Ethiopian slave. She was a fiery poet, designed her own clothes, and refused to wear a veil. On one jacket she embroidered the words: *I feel free to give my kisses to whomever asks for them.* She took both men and women lovers, falling especially hard for another Moorish woman poet, Ibn Zaydun. As Vicki Leon reported, "...whole camel-loads of their correspondence in verse still survive."

A band of Almoravide women archers also fought during this time, but there exists very little information on them.

What I love most about writing historical fiction is that I don't have to struggle to make up characters totally from scratch. All I need do is look over my shoulder—all the characters we could ever ask for have already come before us.

About the Author

Catherine Friend is the author of six children's books, including *The Perfect Nest*, illustrated by John Manders, and was awarded the 2007 Loft/McKnight Artist Fellowship in Children's Literature. Her memoir, *Hit by a Farm: How I Learned to Stop Worrying and Love the Barn,* won a 2007 Golden Crown Award and was a finalist for both a 2007 Lambda Literary Award and the Judy Grahn Award. Her nonfiction book, *The Compassionate Carnivore*, will be released by Da Capo in May, 2008.

After more than fifteen years of writing, not publishing much, and not making any money, she's delighted to find herself in a new phase of her life: writing and publishing more. She's still not making any money, but that's not why she writes.

Friend is working on her next novel for Bold Strokes Books, *A Pirate's Heart*, and raises sheep in southeastern Minnesota with her partner of twenty-four years.

Learn more about her books and her Farm Tales blog at: www.catherinefriend.com

Books Available From Bold Strokes Books

Queens of Tristaine by Cate Culpepper. When a deadly plague stalks the Amazons of Tristaine, two warrior lovers must return to the place of their nightmares to find a cure. (978-1-933110-97-4)

The Crown of Valencia by Catherine Friend. Ex-lovers can really mess up your life...even, as Kate discovers, if they've traveled back to the 11th century! (978-1-933110-96-7)

Mine by Georgia Beers. What happens when you've already given your heart and love finds you again? Courtney McAllister is about to find out. (978-1-933110-95-0)

House of Clouds by KI Thompson. A sweeping saga of an impassioned romance between a Northern spy and a Southern sympathizer, set amidst the upheaval of a nation under siege. (978-1-933110-94-3)

Winds of Fortune by Radclyffe. Provincetown local Deo Camara agrees to rehab Dr. Nita Burgoyne's historic home, but she never said anything about mending her heart. (978-1-933110-93-6)

Focus of Desire by Kim Baldwin. Isabel Sterling is surprised when she wins a photography contest, but no more than photographer Natasha Kashnikova. Their promo tour becomes a ticket to romance. (978-1-933110-92-9)

Blind Leap by Diane and Jacob Anderson-Minshall. A Golden Gate Bridge suicide becomes suspect when a filmmaker's camera shows a different story. Yoshi Yakamota and the Blind Eye Detective Agency uncover evidence that could be worth killing for. (978-1-933110-91-2)

Wall of Silence, 2nd ed. by Gabrielle Goldsby. Life takes a dangerous turn when jaded police detective Foster Everett meets Riley Medeiros, a woman who isn't afraid to discover the truth no matter the cost. (978-1-933110-90-5)

Mistress of the Runes by Andrews & Austin. Passion ignites between two women with ties to ancient secrets, contemporary mysteries, and a shared quest for the meaning of life. (978-1-933110-89-9)

Sheridan's Fate by Gun Brooke. A dynamic, erotic romance between physical therapist Lark Mitchell and businesswoman Sheridan Ward set in the scorching hot days and humid, steamy nights of San Antonio. (978-1-933110-88-2)

Vulture's Kiss by Justine Saracen. Archeologist Valerie Foret, heir to a terrifying task, returns in a powerful desert adventure set in Egypt and Jerusalem. (978-1-933110-87-5)

Rising Storm by JLee Meyer. The sequel to *First Instinct* takes our heroines on a dangerous journey instead of the honeymoon they'd planned. (978-1-933110-86-8)

Not Single Enough by Grace Lennox. A funny, sexy modern romance about two lonely women who bond over the unexpected and fall in love along the way. (978-1-933110-85-1)

Such a Pretty Face by Gabrielle Goldsby. A sexy, sometimes humorous, sometimes biting contemporary romance that gently exposes the damage to heart and soul when we fail to look beneath the surface for what truly matters. (978-1-933110-84-4)

Second Season by Ali Vali. A romance set in New Orleans amidst betrayal, Hurricane Katrina, and the new beginnings hardship and heartbreak sometimes make possible. (978-1-933110-83-7)

Hearts Aflame by Ronica Black. A poignant, erotic romance between a hard-driving businesswoman and a solitary vet. Packed with adventure and set in the harsh beauty of the Arizona countryside. (978-1-933110-82-0)

Red Light by JD Glass. Tori forges her path as an EMT in the New York City 911 system while discovering what matters most to herself and the woman she loves. (978-1-933110-81-3)

Honor Under Siege by Radclyffe. Secret Service agent Cameron Roberts struggles to protect her lover while searching for a traitor who just may be another woman with a claim on her heart. (978-1-933110-80-6)

Dark Valentine by Jennifer Fulton. Danger and desire fuel a high stakes cat-and-mouse game when an attorney and an endangered witness team up to thwart a killer. (978-1-933110-79-0)

Sequestered Hearts by Erin Dutton. A popular artist suddenly goes into seclusion; a reluctant reporter wants to know why; and a heart locked away yearns to be set free. (978-1-933110-78-3)

Erotic Interludes 5: *Road Games* eds. Radclyffe and Stacia Seaman. Adventure, "sport," and sex on the road—hot stories of travel adventures and games of seduction. (978-1-933110-77-6)

The Spanish Pearl by Catherine Friend. On a trip to Spain, Kate Vincent is accidentally transported back in time...an epic saga spiced with humor, lust, and danger. (978-1-933110-76-9)

Lady Knight by L-J Baker. Loyalty and honour clash with love and ambition in a medieval world of magic when female knight Riannon meets Lady Eleanor. (978-1-933110-75-2)

Dark Dreamer by Jennifer Fulton. Best-selling horror author, Rowe Devlin falls under the spell of psychic Phoebe Temple. A Dark Vista romance. (978-1-933110-74-5)

Come and Get Me by Julie Cannon. Elliott Foster isn't used to pursuing women, but alluring attorney Lauren Collier makes her change her mind. (978-1-933110-73-8)

Blind Curves by Diane and Jacob Anderson-Minshall. Private eye Yoshi Yakamota comes to the aid of her ex-lover Velvet Erickson in the first Blind Eye mystery. (978-1-933110-72-1)

Dynasty of Rogues by Jane Fletcher. It's hate at first sight for Ranger Riki Sadiq and her new patrol corporal, Tanya Coppelli—except for their undeniable attraction. (978-1-933110-71-4)

Running With the Wind by Nell Stark. Sailing instructor Corrie Marsten has signed off on love until she meets Quinn Davies—one woman she can't ignore. (978-1-933110-70-7)

More than Paradise by Jennifer Fulton. Two women battle danger, risk all, and find in one another an unexpected ally and an unforgettable love. (978-1-933110-69-1)

Flight Risk by Kim Baldwin. For Blayne Keller, being in the wrong place at the wrong time just might turn out to be the best thing that ever happened to her. (978-1-933110-68-4)

Rebel's Quest, Supreme Constellations Book Two by Gun Brooke. On a world torn by war, two women discover a love that defies all boundaries. (978-1-933110-67-7)

Punk and Zen by JD Glass. Angst, sex, love, rock. Trace, Candace, Francesca...Samantha. Losing control—and finding the truth within. BSB Victory Editions. (1-933110-66-X)

Stellium in Scorpio by Andrews & Austin. The passionate reuniting of two powerful women on the glitzy Las Vegas Strip where everything is an illusion and love is a gamble. (1-933110-65-1)

When Dreams Tremble by Radclyffe. Two women whose lives turned out far differently than they'd once imagined discover that sometimes the shape of the future can only be found in the past. (1-933110-64-3)

The Devil Unleashed by Ali Vali. As the heat of violence rises, so does the passion. A Casey Family crime saga. (1-933110-61-9)

Burning Dreams by Susan Smith. The chronicle of the challenges faced by a young drag king and an older woman who share a love "outside the bounds." (1-933110-62-7)

Fresh Tracks by Georgia Beers. Seven women, seven days. A lot can happen when old friends, lovers, and a new girl in town get together in the mountains. (1-933110-63-5)

The Empress and the Acolyte by Jane Fletcher. Jemeryl and Tevi fight to protect the very fabric of their world: time. Lyremouth Chronicles Book Three. (1-933110-60-0)

First Instinct by JLee Meyer. When high-stakes security fraud leads to murder, one woman flees for her life while another risks her heart to protect her. (1-933110-59-7)

Erotic Interludes 4: *Extreme Passions* ed. by Radclyffe and Stacia Seaman. Thirty of today's hottest erotica writers set the pages aflame with love, lust, and steamy liaisons. (1-933110-58-9)

Storms of Change by Radclyffe. In the continuing saga of the Provincetown Tales, duty and love are at odds as Reese and Tory face their greatest challenge. (1-933110-57-0)

Unexpected Ties by Gina L. Dartt. With death before dessert, Kate Shannon and Nikki Harris are swept up in another tale of danger and romance. (1-933110-56-2)

Sleep of Reason by Rose Beecham. While Detective Jude Devine searches for a lost boy, her rocky relationship with Dr. Mercy Westmoreland gets a lot harder. (1-933110-53-8)

Passion's Bright Fury by Radclyffe. Passion strikes without warning when a trauma surgeon and a filmmaker become reluctant allies. (1-933110-54-6)

Broken Wings by L-J Baker. When Rye Woods meets beautiful dryad Flora Withe, her libido, as hidden as her wings, reawakens along with her heart. (1-933110-55-4)

Combust the Sun by Andrews & Austin. A Richfield and Rivers mystery set in L.A. Murder among the stars. (1-933110-52-X)

Of Drag Kings and the Wheel of Fate by Susan Smith. A blind date in a drag club leads to an unlikely romance. (1-933110-51-1)

Tristaine Rises by Cate Culpepper. Brenna, Jesstin, and the Amazons of Tristaine face their greatest challenge for survival. (1-933110-50-3)

Too Close to Touch by Georgia Beers. Kylie O'Brien believes in true love and is willing to wait for it, even though Gretchen, her new boss, is off-limits. (1-933110-47-3)

100th Generation by Justine Saracen. Ancient curses, modern-day villains, and an intriguing woman lead archeologist Valerie Foret on the adventure of her life. (1-933110-48-1)

Battle for Tristaine by Cate Culpepper. While Brenna struggles to find her place in the clan, Tristaine is threatened with destruction. Second in the Tristaine series. (1-933110-49-X)

The Traitor and the Chalice by Jane Fletcher. Tevi and Jemeryl risk all in the race to uncover a traitor. The Lyremouth Chronicles Book Two. (1-933110-43-0)

Promising Hearts by Radclyffe. Dr. Vance Phelps arrives in New Hope, Montana, with no hope of happiness—until she meets Mae. (1-933110-44-9)

Carly's Sound by Ali Vali. Poppy Valente and Julia Johnson form a bond of friendship that becomes something far more. A poignant romance about love and renewal. (1-933110-45-7)

Unexpected Sparks by Gina L. Dartt. Kate Shannon's attraction to much younger Nikki Harris is complication enough without a fatal fire that Kate can't ignore. (1-933110-46-5)

Whitewater Rendezvous by Kim Baldwin. Two women on a wilderness kayak adventure discover that true love may be nothing at all like they imagined. (1-933110-38-4)

Erotic Interludes 3: *Lessons in Love* ed. by Radclyffe and Stacia Seaman. Sign on for a class in love…the best lesbian erotica writers take us to "school." (1-9331100-39-2)

Punk Like Me by JD Glass. Twenty-one-year-old Nina has a way with the girls, and she doesn't always play by the rules. (1-933110-40-6)

Coffee Sonata by Gun Brooke. Four women whose lives unexpectedly intersect in a small town by the sea share one thing in common—they all have secrets. (1-933110-41-4)

The Clinic: Tristaine Book One by Cate Culpepper. Brenna, a prison medic, finds herself drawn to Jesstin, a warrior reputed to be descended from ancient Amazons. (1-933110-42-2)

Forever Found by JLee Meyer. Can time, tragedy, and shattered trust destroy a love that seemed destined? Chance reunites childhood friends separated by tragedy. (1-933110-37-6)

Sword of the Guardian by Merry Shannon. Princess Shasta's bold new bodyguard has a secret that could change both of their lives. *He* is actually a *she*. (1-933110-36-8)

Wild Abandon by Ronica Black. Dr. Chandler Brogan and Officer Sarah Monroe are drawn together by their common obsessions—sex, speed, and danger. (1-933110-35-X)

Turn Back Time by Radclyffe. Pearce Rifkin and Wynter Thompson have nothing in common but a shared passion for surgery—and unexpected attraction. (1-933110-34-1)

Chance by Grace Lennox. A sexy, funny, touching story of two women who, in finding themselves, also find one another. (1-933110-31-7)

The Exile and the Sorcerer by Jane Fletcher. First in the Lyremouth Chronicles. Tevi and a shy young sorcerer face monsters, magic, and the challenge of loving. (1-933110-32-5)

A Matter of Trust by Radclyffe. When what should be just business turns into much more, two women struggle to trust the unexpected. (1-933110-33-3)

Sweet Creek by Lee Lynch. A celebration of the enduring nature of love, friendship, and community in the heart-warming lesbian community of Waterfall Falls. (1-933110-29-5)

The Devil Inside by Ali Vali. The head of a New Orleans crime organization falls for a woman who turns her world upside down. (1-933110-30-9)

Grave Silence by Rose Beecham. Detective Jude Devine's investigation of ritual murders is complicated by her torrid affair with pathologist Dr. Mercy Westmoreland. (1-933110-25-2)

Honor Reclaimed by Radclyffe. Secret Service Agent Cameron Roberts and Blair Powell close ranks to find the would-be assassins who nearly claimed Blair's life. (1-933110-18-X)

Honor Bound by Radclyffe. Secret Service Agent Cameron Roberts and Blair Powell face political intrigue, a clandestine threat to Blair's safety, and the seemingly irreconcilable differences that force them ever farther apart. (1-933110-20-1)

Innocent Hearts by Radclyffe. In a wild and unforgiving land, two women learn about love, passion, and the wonders of the heart. (1-933110-21-X)

The Temple at Landfall by Jane Fletcher. An imprinter, one of Celaeno's most revered servants of the Goddess, is also a prisoner to the faith—until a Ranger frees her by claiming her heart. The Celaeno series. (1-933110-27-9)

Protector of the Realm, Supreme Constellations Book One by Gun Brooke. A space adventure filled with suspense and a daring intergalactic romance. (1-933110-26-0)

Force of Nature by Kim Baldwin. From tornados to forest fires, the forces of nature conspire to bring Gable McCoy and Erin Richards close to danger, and closer to each other. (1-933110-23-6)

In Too Deep by Ronica Black. Undercover homicide cop Erin McKenzie tracks a femme fatale who just might be a real killer…with love and danger hot on her heels. (1-933110-17-1)

Erotic Interludes 2: *Stolen Moments* ed. by Radclyffe and Stacia Seaman. Love on the run, in the office, in the shadows…Fast, furious, and almost too hot to handle. (1-933110-16-3)

Course of Action by Gun Brooke. Actress Carolyn Black desperately wants the starring role in an upcoming film produced by Annelie Peterson. Just how far will she go for the dream part of a lifetime? (1-933110-22-8)

Rangers at Roadsend by Jane Fletcher. Sergeant Chip Coppelli has learned to spot trouble coming, and that is exactly what she sees in her new recruit, Katryn Nagata. The Celaeno series. (1-933110-28-7)

Justice Served by Radclyffe. Lieutenant Rebecca Frye and her lover, Dr. Catherine Rawlings, embark on a deadly game of hide-and-seek with an underworld kingpin who traffics in human souls. (1-933110-15-5)

Distant Shores, Silent Thunder by Radclyffe. Dr. Tory King—along with the women who love her—is forced to examine the boundaries of love, friendship, and the ties that transcend time. (1-933110-08-2)

Hunter's Pursuit by Kim Baldwin. A raging blizzard, a mountain hideaway, and a killer-for-hire set a scene for disaster—or desire—when Katarzyna Demetrious rescues a beautiful stranger. (1-933110-09-0)

The Walls of Westernfort by Jane Fletcher. All Temple Guard Natasha Ionadis wants is to serve the Goddess—until she falls in love with one of the rebels she is sworn to destroy. The Celaeno series. (1-933110-24-4)

Erotic Interludes: *Change Of Pace* by Radclyffe. Twenty-five hot-wired encounters guaranteed to spark more than just your imagination. Erotica as you've always dreamed of it. (1-933110-07-4)

Honor Guards by Radclyffe. In a wild flight for their lives, the president's daughter and those who are sworn to protect her wage a desperate struggle for survival. (1-933110-01-5)

Fated Love by Radclyffe. Amidst the chaos and drama of a busy emergency room, two women must contend not only with the fragile nature of life, but also with the irresistible forces of fate. (1-933110-05-8)

Justice in the Shadows by Radclyffe. In a shadow world of secrets and lies, Detective Sergeant Rebecca Frye and her lover, Dr. Catherine Rawlings, join forces in the elusive search for justice. (1-933110-03-1)